TWO BOYS FROM ADEN COLLEGE

TWO BOYS FROM ADEN COLLEGE

Qais Ghanem MD

iUniverse, Inc.
Bloomington

Two Boys from Aden College

iUniverse books may be ordered through booksellers or by contacting:

iUniverse
1663 Liberty Drive
Bloomington, IN 47403
www.iuniverse.com
1-800-Authors (1-800-288-4677)

ISBN: 978-1-4697-9626-0 (sc)
ISBN: 978-1-4697-9628-4 (hc)
ISBN: 978-1-4697-9627-7 (e)

Printed in the United States of America

iUniverse rev. date: 03/14/2012

To those millions of Muslim women—decent, delicate, and dedicated—who suffer lives of oppression, repression, and depression, I dedicate this fictional tale.

CONTENTS

PREFACE

I was encouraged by the positive response to my first novel, *Final Flight from Sanaa,* which predicted some important changes in Yemen as seen at the below sites.

- http://www.waterstones.com/waterstonesweb/products/ dr+qais+ghanem/final+flight+from+sanaa/8683975/
- http://www.chapters.indigo.ca/books/FINAL-FLIGHT-FROM-SANAA-Qais-Ghanem-MD/9781926945125-AllReviews.html
- http://www.dialoguewithdiversity.com/

This new novel was an easier task, because I had retired from the practice of medicine and had more spare time. Consequently, this novel is nearly twice the length of the first one, but I wrote it in half the time. That is not to say that it is twice as good! That will be left to the judgment of the reader. However, the novel spans a period of about fifteen years in the lives of the two main characters—a doctor and a lawyer—and therefore involves interactions with many more individuals in several countries. Not surprisingly, the events of the novel occur in about the same areas of the world, for they must, perforce, reflect the real experiences or observations of the author if they are to be credible. Much in this story is taken from anonymous secrets shared with me by very close and trusting friends whom I cannot thank by name, but they know who they are.

The emphasis this time too is on the poor human rights accorded Muslim and Arab women. Once again I have told it like it is and did not shy away from what some may consider taboo subjects, such as sexuality (including homosexuality, pornography, and prostitution), hypocrisy, racism, fundamentalism, class struggle, dictatorship, nepotism, and corruption in high places.

Hopefully, we will soon see the reaction of the public to such an approach, but I tend to agree with Kingsley Amis, who said, "If you can't annoy somebody, there's little point in writing!"

Q. G.

CHAPTER 1

~

LEAVING HOME

It was the last day of August 1967. The two old classmates from Aden College, the highest institute of learning in South Yemen, were preparing to leave for the United Kingdom. Hasan Alawi Al-Qirshi and Ahmad Shawqi Saleh were virtually all packed and looking forward to their flight to England to study law and medicine, respectively. They had scoured all the major stores for the biggest suitcases they could buy in that sparsely stocked market, but it was not easy to find one. They blamed it on the violence associated with the guerilla war of liberation in the south. In North Yemen, the civil war had been raging since 1962 between the monarchists, supported by Saudi Arabia, and the republicans, backed by Egypt.

Ahmad had a bit more money to spend, being the son of the minister of trade, a drug sales representative by training. He was a proud citizen of Aden who had been born in the small town of Crater, so named because it was nestled in an extinct crater apparently thousands of years old. The highest seat of learning was Aden College where all the brightest boys went, including these two. No girls were allowed; they had their own girls' college, where Ahmad's fifteen-year-old sister, Salma, was receiving her secondary education. She was destined to graduate from high school

1

over the next few years and hopefully get married. No girl had ever been to university, for she would have to leave the country and live in a foreign land, away from close supervision. That would simply not be permitted.

Hasan, like Ahmad, was twenty. He too had passed his general certificate of education exams in nine subjects, at the ordinary level, and then two subjects at the advanced level. He was very competitive and dearly wanted to know by how many marks he had beaten his friend and archrival Ahmad. He was endowed with a superior memory, compared with Ahmad, and thus did very well in history and botany. He was also a proverbial bookworm. Ahmad, on the other hand, found remembering the different names of the digestive system of the frog and the earthworm quite onerous, if not boring. But give him a mathematical problem to solve, and he would do it ahead of everyone else, without pencil or paper. He so looked forward to the geometry classes given by his Pakistani teacher with the typical accent and the limp he suffered from polio in early childhood. Ahmad always knew when that teacher was approaching the classroom, from his asymmetrical steps accompanied by a shuffling sound as he dragged his withered leg along the floor. Ahmad just knew he would shine in the geometry class and needed to reassure himself that he was, from time to time, cleverer than Hasan. He also enjoyed sports like badminton and volleyball, whereas Hasan would spend his time swatting instead. It was a strange rivalry; both boys knew their strengths and weaknesses.

They were both rather skinny. Hasan was five feet, ten inches in height, unusually tall for a Yemeni, with light brown skin, black hair, and black eyes like nearly all Yemenis in the south. He was not handsome, but at that age he had the attractiveness of youth stamped all over his face. Ahmad was only five feet, eight inches, with wavy black hair and brown skin. He too was not handsome by any stretch of the imagination, but he exuded a pleasant and friendly nature and radiated an almost constant smile.

Hasan's father and mother were known to have moved to Aden about twenty years earlier from the small Yemeni town of Turbah. No one seemed to know where Hasan was born, but he did have a birth certificate issued by the British colonial system indicating that his place of birth was Aden. With that came certain privileges, including attending government schools, receiving government bursaries, and acquiring jobs. Given that the available resources were limited, the fear was that the relatively huge population in North Yemen might overwhelm the South. North Yemen was a poor and very backward country with ten times the population of its counterpart. It was ruled by a long dynasty of absolute kings known for their macabre dungeons from which very few prisoners ever left to tell the tale. Many young boys were kept there as hostages to ensure the loyalty of their parents. Word leaked that many of them were routinely physically and sexually abused by the wardens and the older prisoners.

That night Ahmad and Hasan spent some quality time with their parents and siblings and received members of their large extended families who traveled from nearby towns and villages. A few tears were shed over many hugs and kisses before the boys went to their beds and spent most of the night wondering what awaited them over the next few days.

Both families took their young and promising sons to the airport, with luggage bulging out of the car trunks, the trunk doors being tied down with some yellow string. The cars were so small and the large families had to fit in, or at least as many members as possible. Each of the boys was the eldest in the sib ship. For their younger siblings, it was going to be a great adventure seeing an airplane for the first time at such close range. Some even imagined that they might be allowed inside to take a look, but they were later disappointed. Hasan's mother did not go to the airport, however, for his father was a conservative Muslim who did not allow his wife outside the home. He looked after her well, but her place was in the home. She had to say her tearful good-byes at home as Hasan got into the car heading for the airport.

Both cars took the pretty seaside Abyan Road from the town of Crater to the airport. Shawqi Saleh, Ahmad's father, being a minister, had a driver assigned to him by the government, and his car had an official government number plate; thus he did not have to rush. Alawi Al-Qirshi's car came up to the checkpoint behind the Queen Elizabeth Hospital and slowed down to the orders of the sweating British corporal standing by the barrier in his classic khaki uniform, holding a menacing rifle in his right hand. As he lifted it, the underarm sweating was extensive and hideous.

The corporal came up to the left side window and started asking questions. "Where did you just come from?"

Hasan, who spoke much better English than his father, said, "From Crater of course."

"Why *of course*? You could have come from anywhere, for all I know!"

Hasan sensed anger in the soldier and explained, "As you know, Abyan Road goes along the beach and has to end up in Crater from here."

"Really! And where are you off to?"

"Excuse me?" asked Hasan, who had learned school English but had never come across the term *off to* before. "You mean where are we going? Oh, to the airport. We are already late, and I have to catch a flight to London; I am going to your country to study law. I will be a lawyer," Hasan added boastfully.

"What do you have in the trunk? Why is it tied up with all that rope?"

"I just told you that I am flying to London, and that is my luggage; the suitcase is too big for the trunk."

"Open it up!"

"Excuse me, I am in a hurry. Please let us through," Hasan said angrily.

"I said open the trunk!" was the equally angry reply.

"Please, please, let me speak to your officer there in the tent. I am sure he will be cooperative."

The corporal paused for several seconds, trying to contain his frustration at the defiant student, and then walked the twenty paces back to the tent. He emerged with the sergeant who looked at the car from the tent for a few seconds and then gestured with his hand the unmistakable order to search the car. Hasan, now seething with rage, had to get out of the car and start undoing the tight knots in the yellow rope holding down the lid of the trunk.

The soldier watched him. "Take that suitcase out!"

"What for?"

"I said take it out!"

Hasan struggled to lift it out and demonstrated that the trunk was otherwise empty. The soldier gestured to him to put the suitcase back in. As Hasan walked back to the passenger door of the car, the soldier ordered him to stand still and lift his arms straight up in the air. Still holding his rifle in his right hand, the soldier proceeded to frisk him with the left.

"What are you looking for?" Hasan asked. "I told you I am a student traveling to London."

"Shut up, and keep your arms up!"

At this point, Shawqi Saleh's chauffeur-driven car approached the scene with Shawqi in the passenger seat. He told his driver to stop behind the other car. The corporal looked up and saw Shawqi, and recognized the official number plate.

Shawqi said, "Good morning, officer. What seems to be the trouble? This young man is Hasan. He is a friend of the family; he is like a son to me. In fact, my son and he are traveling today to study in Britain."

Now the sergeant came out of his tent, having noticed the events outside. He walked over and gave the corporal a subtle signal to let the boy go.

~

Alawi started the engine again, under the contemptuous gaze of the triumphant corporal, and resumed driving toward the airport. During those few minutes, Hasan promised himself that he would get his degree in law as fast as he could and would use that knowledge on his return to Aden to evict the British colonizers.

"*Ibn al-kalb* [son of a dog] will make me late for my flight!" Hasan said.

"You will have to learn to control your temper, son."

"Me, control my temper? Why are you defending this dog? Do you like to be humiliated, Father?"

"Of course not! This soldier is obeying orders; he cannot think for himself. He is not educated like you, otherwise he would not be a corporal. He would be a teacher or a lawyer, or at least an officer. What he has going for him is his six-foot frame and those huge muscles with which he carries his rifle all day."

"I think he did that to show us he is boss."

"That too, probably."

"Well, I am not going to stand for that. I am an Adeni, and this is my country!"

"Son, I have a secret to tell you, which your mother and I had decided to keep from you. However, now that you are going away for many years, and who knows what will happen to us in the meantime, I have to tell you the truth."

Hasan, looking alarmed, said, "Tell me quickly. We are almost at the airport."

"You are not an Adeni really. You are a Yemeni, born in North Yemen in the town of Turbah."

"But I have my Colony of Aden birth certificate and my British passport; they are right here in my hand luggage."

"That is your brother's ..."

"What brother?" interrupted Hasan.

"Look, my son! One year before you were born in Turbah, your mother gave birth to a premature baby here in Aden, in the same house where we are living now. He only weighed four pounds. I still remember how his ribs stuck up under his skin, because he was so scrawny. He developed some infection in his lungs, and fever, and had great difficulty breast-feeding because he was so weak. When he breathed, his chest wall would sink in between his tiny little ribs; he could not keep milk down in his small stomach and was vomiting a lot. Your mother had no experience with babies. He was her first, and she did not know how to look after him. We took him to the doctor, of course, but he just gave him some antibiotic syrup, which the baby kept vomiting. I even remember the name tetra ... tetra something. Anyway, he died before he reached the age of one month."

"So?"

"We got a birth certificate for him here in Aden; then we forgot about it. But then your mother got pregnant again; we were very young at the time, and she was very keen on having a son. But this time, she decided to go to Turbah to deliver, where she had the help and guidance of her mother, your *gidda* [grandmother] Fattoom. You were born at the right time, and you weighed just above seven pounds. There, in the north, there is no birth registration. So we all came back to Aden, and since we already had a British Colony birth certificate, we decided to just give you his name: Hasan. Your mother felt as if Allah had given her back her firstborn. Anyway, it would be a great advantage for you, because you would have a right to free schooling all the way to the end of secondary school, and now also to a scholarship to England."

"I still don't see it. So, you gave me his name, Hasan? I wish you did not."

"What's wrong with Hasan? You know it is the name of the grandson of Prophet Muhammad, peace be upon him; it is a wonderful name."

"But that means that I am actually one year younger than my supposed age?"

"Yes, but you are smarter than those who are one year older than you. You always have been, and I can see a wonderful future awaiting you."

"Okay, Father, we have arrived at the airport, and I am going to London under false pretenses!"

Excitement was in the air at the airport, and Ahmad's was intermixed with anxiety about the future, especially as his father addressed him. His father said, "Now don't forget to write every week. It is very important for us, and your mother here will be very upset if you don't. She is already depressed."

Ahmad's mother nodded her head in agreement as tears welled in her eyes. After all, this was her firstborn leaving home for the first time ever. Arab families have a special place for the *bekr* [firstborn] if he is male. He is the one who has the responsibility of looking after the family and making all the important decisions in the absence of his father, or after his death. *What if he does not return home because he might find a foreign wife over there? Or he simply decides to stay in England?* she wondered.

"No, no, don't worry. I will write, *inshaallah*," Ahmad said.

"You must write, Ahmad! Don't worry about the postage; I will send you a monthly allowance, in addition to the bursary from the government, to cover the cost of the stamps."

"Yes, Father!"

The whole family now came round to hug and kiss Ahmad. Salma, fifteen years old, knew what was happening. She was close to her brother. But the younger daughter, Zahra, only nine at the time, was much closer to him; Ahmad really loved her and pampered her. One more kiss from his mother, and Ahmad was on his way to the departure lounge, waving all the while to the family, but not before he also said a warm good-bye to Hasan's father, addressing him as *Uncle* as custom dictated. Hasan had already preceded him to the departure lounge.

Suddenly, a man in civilian clothing recognized the minister of trade and rushed toward him, offering to allow him through the gate leading to the departure lounge to be with his son a few more minutes. He identified himself as a member of the *amn* [security]. Shawqi thanked him for the offer but excused himself by saying that he was with *al-usrah* [literally *the family* but used to mean the wife] and he would rather stay with her.

Twenty minutes later, the Dakota took off for Cairo, where the two young men would make a connection with a British Airways flight to London.

CHAPTER 2

~

ENGLAND

The change of climate was the first thing that hit the two young men as they landed at Heathrow. There was no sun; the sky was gray and raining lightly. The size of the airport, and the time it took the airplane to taxi to its gate, took them by surprise. They had heard and read about the great city of London, but now it was up close and personal.

Passport control was simple since both carried British passports. They picked up their suitcases and went through the nothing-to-declare green door into a throng of people awaiting the arriving passengers. Despite the huge number of travelers around them, the process seemed smooth and rapid. It was the two young men's first international journey, and they could compare it only with the confusion they had witnessed at the Aden Airport whenever they met incoming passengers.

"What! No customs check?" asked Hasan.

"Does not seem like it. We are already in the reception area; I wonder who is meeting us. They told us someone would; they are mostly Indians here!" Ahmad replied, impressed with the ethnic makeup of the crowd.

The two Yemenis inched forward, pushing their heavy carts toward the crowd, scanning the cards held up by people, distracted by the multitude of shapes and colors and ages, and above all by the large number of beautiful women in the crowd. Suddenly there was one such young woman holding a big card with their two names written in blue, correctly spelled.

They headed toward her as she gave them a big smile. "Welcome to London!"

"Thank you," they said in unison.

"I am Isobel from the British Council. I'll drive you to your temporary accommodation in London. I hope you had a good flight? Which of you is Ahmad?"

"Yes, it is me. How do you do?" Ahmad blurted out what he had been told was the typical British greeting.

She looked at his friend. "And so you must be Hasan?"

"Yes, I am. How do you do?"

Isobel smiled. "So, let us go up one flight to the garage, where I parked my car."

~

Hasan got the privilege of sitting in the passenger seat next to Isobel, while Ahmad sat in the back. They were soon on the fast motorway toward London. By then it was considerably brighter, as the sun rose a bit higher. It was all very exciting, especially seeing so much grass and so many trees, and everything seemed green and cool and fresh. What a contrast that was with Aden at the end of August with temperatures near forty in the shade.

Isobel was wearing a yellow skirt, which tightly hugged her anatomy, and a brown blouse, which showed an ample cleavage. But from where he was sitting, pretending to look straight ahead through the windshield, Hasan was watching Isobel's full thighs and smooth and shapely legs exposed all the way to slightly above the knee. At first he scolded himself for ogling her legs, and for letting his imagination run wild. He would never do that to a Yemeni woman at home, not only because the opportunity would never arise but also out of good manners and *hishmah* [respect].

Ahmad had to content himself with looking through the side window and making small talk with Isobel for the half hour drive to Kensington Road.

~

The small bed-and-breakfast had room for four student guests, each with their own little room but only one shared bathroom with a bath but no shower. They would be allowed one bath per week, with gas-heated water, which would only fill half the bathtub. And since homes were not air-conditioned, taking a bath was the art of washing as much of one's skin as possible in the shortest possible time, and ensuring that the towel was as close as possible at the end of it.

The landlady gave them her routine pep talk about the rules and regulations within her house and pointed out that each student was responsible for cleaning the bath after himself. They also had to be home by ten in the evening, otherwise they would find the front door locked in their faces. No alcohol was allowed in the premises either, and the final rule, which she repeated twice, was that girls were not allowed either. The two boys wondered why she had emphasized that when they had never even considered indulging in either of those two sins.

There were two other young men of about their age. One was from Uganda. They met him over breakfast the next day. He told them that there was a *"sik* man" in the fourth room, but he had gone away for the day and would return the next day.

"What is wrong with him?" Ahmad asked the Ugandan.

"Who?"

"I thought you said there was a sick man in the other room?"

"He is okay. There is nothing wrong with him."

"Oh, so he is not sick anymore? I am glad; otherwise he might infect us."

"No, no, he is not sick. He is *Sikh, Sikh.* You know, with a turban on the head!"

The two Yemeni boys looked at each other, suppressing their laughter. The next day they did meet Nirmal Singh and found him to be more than okay!

~

During a week in London, all four students went through a course of orientation to British society and its very different customs. But that education started in the small bed-and-breakfast hotel bathroom, at least for Hasan, who had made daily prayers part of his routine. While traveling from Aden, he did not manage to pray, but that was within the rules of Islam as he knew them. Now he wanted to return to that daily routine and indeed make up for all the missed prayers, as a true observant Muslim is supposed to do. And for that he had to perform his ablutions, which required washing his face and arms, and feet too. But the plastic cup which he kept in the bathroom at home, to help him wash his backside after going to the toilet and to wash his feet for prayers, was nowhere to be found. Thus, Hasan struggled to lift his feet, one at a time, into the washbasin and managed to mix the water flowing from the separate hot and cold taps to arrive at a tepid mix. He then washed his feet before performing a long session of prayer to catch up with all the ones he had missed on that long journey. He liked the velvety feel of his ornate prayer mat with a picture of the Kaaba, that big square structure draped in a huge sheet of black silk, around which Muslims would circle seven times during the annual *hajj* [pilgrimage].

Ahmad, by contrast, did not bother with all that stuff, even when he was back home, except for the occasional attendance at a mosque on a Friday when his father embarrassed him into attending, or on very special occasions.

~

The next morning, the four students came down to breakfast prepared for them by the landlady. There was a large jug of milk, the likes of which the boys had never seen, and cereal in a tall cardboard box, but none of them knew what to do with it. The Ugandan student eventually stuck his spoon in the box and brought it out full of crispy cereal flakes, which he put in his mouth. He enjoyed the crunchy sound they made between his teeth.

The other three famished students followed suit, and even that bit of food made them feel better. They poured themselves some tea, for which they knew the British were world famous.

"This tea is very weak, isn't it?" said the Sikh boy.

"And there is no cardamom or anything else in it," responded Hasan.

On a large plate was half a loaf of sliced, square, white bread, to which the hungry boys helped themselves. Each also noticed a boiled egg in an eggcup on each of their individual plates. Ahmad felt the egg; it was still warm. He picked the egg out of its cup and started cracking it on the breakfast table. He must have hit it hard in his anxiety to get at the contents because the soft white of the egg burst open and some of the yolk splattered over the tablecloth. Ahmad looked at his three friends, quite embarrassed. As he tried to clean the yolk off the table cloth before the landlady would see the mess, he also knocked his teacup over and screamed in frustration.

That was enough to bring Mrs. Grimond from the kitchen into the breakfast room. Mrs. Grimond was a stern-looking widow of around sixty-five, on the heavy side, with thin lips, ruddy cheeks, and quite a few wrinkles. She had sad gray eyes. She also had a light moustache with hairs quite a bit darker than the gray hair tied at the back of her head in a bun. She could see that her four new student lodgers were not used to the classic English breakfast.

"Now, now," she said. "I can see that we should have a wee chat about breakfast, and especially how to eat an egg in Britain!"

"I am very sorry, Mrs. Grimond. I made a mess on my first day," said Ahmad.

As she was mopping up the spilled tea, Mrs. Grimond gave the boys their first lesson on survival in Britain.

"In this country, we eat our boiled eggs in their cups. What one does is to hit the blunt end of the egg several times with a teaspoon, until the shell breaks into numerous little pieces. Then one lifts them off with the tip of the special egg spoon, and one finds the white of the egg underneath. One then uses that special egg spoon to scoop out that delicious white and yolk of the egg, which one eats with a piece of toast or bread. However, if the egg is soft boiled, one could slice off the shell with a knife and then proceed to scoop out the egg. One could also sprinkle a wee bit of salt and pepper on the egg. Is that clear?"

The boys shook their heads, suppressing their urgent desire to burst into laughter at Mrs. Grimond's lesson and the schoolmistress manner in which it was delivered.

∼

One hour after breakfast, Isobel came over to the small hotel for an orientation session in which she taught them how to conduct themselves in public. She was used to receiving and orienting new students from the Middle East and other parts of the world, especially former British colonies. So she went over a list of dos and don'ts that she knew by heart. Most important was advice not to ask British people personal questions unless they were close friends. In fact, she pointed out that strangers did not converse unless they were first introduced. She emphasized that men did not kiss in Britain, unlike in Aden and Africa. But she also said that it was perfectly fine to shake hands with women once they were introduced. The boys looked amazed when she added that a man may kiss a lady too, if he knew her well enough, "on the cheek, that is."

Isobel spoke about transportation and how to use buses and the underground trains. She thought they should all invest in umbrellas and joked about British weather. She gave each student his travel plans and railway tickets to be used at the end of the week. Hasan was to study law in the city of London, whereas Ahmad was going to Edinburgh at the end of the week to study medicine. He was given the address where he would stay and was told that someone would meet him at Waverly Railway Station.

Over the next couple of days, the two Adeni boys explored the long, wide streets of London in great wonderment at the beauty of the city: its huge crowds walking up and down Oxford and Regent streets, the very organized traffic with those typical red double-decker buses, all the wonderful exhibits in the shop windows, and above all those lovely women who had such different hairstyles and all shades of hair colors. Back home they had only seen straight black hair made shiny with applied oil, except for the occasional elderly woman with henna-dyed red hair. And the legs! They had never seen any in their lives, not even in their mothers or sisters who always kept everything covered in their long dresses. Those legs in London seemed so shapely and smooth, and even shiny. It took them a few days of furtive, lustful observation to realize that the smooth and even shiny legs were due to the stockings covering them!

The boys also explored Hyde Park and St. James' Park and were amazed at all that green grass punctuated by hundreds and thousands of trees and bushes and adorned by flowers of all kinds. Coming from arid Aden, they hardly saw any greenery unless they ventured to the village of Lahej or to some of the privately owned small gardens in the village of Sheikh Uthman, which would require a long car ride.

"What a wonderful city this is!" said Ahmad.

"Absolutely!" exclaimed Hasan. "Look how these people live—not us! All we do is wake up, go to school, and then back home to do homework. We are lucky if we go out one evening a week with friends to eat beans or *meshwi* lamb, and always with boys! Look at this man here in front of us, walking with his arm round the waist of the woman in the red and white dress, and all the others holding hands. Wow! Can you imagine if you were able to do that?"

"Don't stare now, but you see that couple just in front of the restaurant? They are kissing in broad daylight. They don't seem to care about other people looking at them. Wow! This is the life to live; we are really lucky to get this scholarship."

"We worked hard for it; we deserve it. I have been dreaming about this for the past two years, and I am going to make the most of it," Hasan replied, almost as a threat.

"Including kissing women in the street?"

"If they allow me, sure!"

"What if a girl lets you do more … you know, go all the way? Apparently girls do that here."

"Of course I will, but I have never done it. What if I don't do it properly and then she laughs at me? Have you?"

Ahmad, also a virgin, avoided answering the question but continued to tease his friend. "But you are supposed to be a good Muslim. You pray five times a day and you fast the month of Ramadan. You know it is forbidden, *haram*. I can do it because I don't pray or fast or anything."

"Listen, my friend! In life there is a balance sheet with debit and credit. My prayers are the credit, and girls and other sins are the debit. And the two will cancel each other. Allah is forgiving and merciful."

CHAPTER 3

~

THE MINISTERS HOME

Isobel had arranged for Hasan to live in what students called "digs," where he would be a paying guest with a British family in the Bayswater district of London. The idea was that the student would improve his spoken English, learn about British customs, and at the same time have a sort of surrogate family which would guide him and take him under its wing.

While looking for such digs, she came across the home of the Reverend James McCartney, a minister of the Church of England, who long ago had spent a couple of years in India with his wife Elizabeth. He always had a lingering interest in foreign students who reminded him of those happy days. There, he had mingled with Hindus, Sikhs, and occasional Muslims and had developed a great interest in the similarities and contrasts among different religions. He grew to respect the other religions of India, while he was tending to his own Christian congregation.

Weeks before, his son Albert left home to study genetics in the United States; he therefore had an extra bedroom to rent out, for that extra cash would always come in handy. He still had a daughter, Biddy, seventeen, and a son Stephen, eleven, each with her and his own bedroom. Stephen's was on the top floor, between his parents' bedroom and the minister's little office, while Biddy's was on the ground floor and next to Albert's, with whom she shared a full bathroom. The only time anyone else used it was when the McCartneys entertained, which occurred very rarely; the minister had such a busy social life within his church, that he hardly ever entertained at home. Isobel negotiated a weekly deal for room and board, for a very reasonable monthly rate of twenty-two pounds and ten shillings. That left Hasan with the balance of the thirty pounds which his bursary allowed him. In expensive London, he would have to be very careful with his money.

~

That Saturday afternoon, Hasan took a cab to the McCartneys' home in Bayswater, which cost him a few precious shillings. As he stood facing the front door, suitcase on the ground, he rang the bell. Stephen opened the door and looked vacantly at the stranger, for he was not told about him by the family.

"Dad! There's a brown man at the door!" he shouted.

Hasan was taken aback, for until then no one had called him that before; and although he knew that he was indeed brown, he now felt so self-conscious and did not want the fact announced so blatantly.

Mr. McCartney, with Elizabeth a couple of paces behind him, was rapidly walking toward the door. "That would be Hasan, the student from Aden," he said.

Soon he was extending his hand to Hasan and welcoming him into his home. He shook his hand warmly and introduced him to his wife, a good-looking yet somewhat overweight middle-aged woman with gray hair, blue eyes, and a few wrinkles extending from the outer canthus toward her temples.

As she smiled at the young man, she said, "Come away, come away. It's a wee bit chilly outside this afternoon. Bring your luggage in."

As they all sat down in the family room, Elizabeth McCartney asked Hasan if he would like a cup of tea and a biscuit. Hasan, who was desperate for one, felt that he had to say no, for that would be his standard and expected answer back home.

"Are you sure, now?" asked Elizabeth.

"Of course he'd like a cup of tea, Bettie. He's just being polite. Don't you remember how people in India answered that question? We had to ask them three or four times before they would say yes. That's what their culture tells them to say. Right, Hasan?"

Hasan did not know what to say; he just smiled sheepishly at Elizabeth. Suddenly, a beautiful girl in her teens entered the family room. She had a tall, five-foot, seven-inch, stunning figure with shapely and smooth legs showing up to her mid thigh under her short purple skirt. Her blouse was beige. She had long blonde hair and beautiful clear-blue eyes that looked straight at the stranger for a couple of seconds before her face broke into a big and warm smile, which emphasized her full pink lips.

"And this is our Biddy. Come and meet Hasan, Biddy," Mr. McCartney said.

The two shook hands. For Hasan, that was an experience of a lifetime. He had never shaken hands with a grown-up female before, apart from Isobel earlier at Heathrow Airport—certainly no one so beautiful. He stared into her eyes in utter wonderment but then suddenly looked away toward her father to gauge his reaction. He was sure in his own mind that the father would be upset at him for staring at his daughter. However, the arrival of a large tray with several cups and a pot of tea, its spout proudly poking from an ornate knitted wool tea cozy, interrupted the awkward situation, to Hasan's relief.

Over the next few minutes, the conversation turned to finding out about each other, but most of the questions were for Hasan, who told the family a lot about his hometown, his family, and his flight from Aden, selecting the interesting parts and minimizing the negative and awkward bits.

∼

A half hour later, Hasan was shown to his bedroom by Mrs. McCartney. It was a small room, seven feet by ten, with a small window overlooking the side of the house next door. A single bed was pushed against the wall. At the head of that bed was a very small bedside table with a bedside lamp covered with an aging, pinkish lampshade with a clean glass already sitting on it. An old maple-wood wardrobe was against the other wall. A comfortable easy chair with old leather upholstery cracked in places sat near the foot of the bed. The floor was covered wall to wall with a somewhat bald carpet of an ugly green color. There were two hooks behind the door, which Hasan appreciated, for he hated to neatly fold his trousers or put them on pant hangers before getting into bed. Back in Aden he would hang all his trousers, all three of them, on such hooks. He never needed a wardrobe there, only a small chest of drawers which he shared with his brother. There was no fireplace or other source of heat in the room.

～

Hasan spent the next two hours unpacking rather slowly, deciding where everything would be placed in order to use the available space to maximal advantage. After all, he was planning on staying in this room at least for his first year at university.

At six o'clock, he emerged from his room to join the family for their evening meal. Mrs. McCartney had gone out of her way to make that a very special meal of roast lamb with Yorkshire pudding, roast potatoes, and peas. She wanted to impress their new paying guest, and what could be more British than roast lamb?

The atmosphere during the meal was pleasant and relaxed, and even jovial, especially when Stephen would tease his older sister by telling stories about those whom he called her boyfriends at school, both real and imagined. He let slip that one of the older boys at school told him that he was his sister's boyfriend, and that she was "his." Stephen felt mad and ashamed, he said, especially because that boy was known as the school bully who had threatened Stephen that if his sister did not do what he wanted, he would beat him up. She in turn would tell Stephen to mind his own business. The two went to the same school, but he was six grades behind her. She was in the final stages before university, although she still was not sure what she wanted to be. She would talk about studying psychology, because she had a yearning to help people who were depressed or anxious, and for whom she felt deeply sorry. For his part, Hasan was surprised by the lack of angry reaction on the part of Mr. McCartney when he heard that story of Biddy's boyfriend from Stephen, and the way he changed the subject of conversation. Mrs. McCartney too did not seem too concerned. She simply told Stephen to be quiet.

Although Hasan was physically exhausted that night, he was emotionally charged and found it difficult to fall asleep. The new unaccustomed bed and surroundings only aggravated his sleep onset insomnia. He could not stop or even slow down the hundreds of thoughts that crossed his mind as he surveyed the many new experiences he had gone through since leaving home. He came to the conclusion that a new and exciting chapter in his life had just begun, and he decided that night that he would live life to the full, no matter what and no matter who got in his way.

As he rolled over on his side, facing the wall, he started thinking about Biddy and how utterly beautiful she was. However, even that could not stop him from drifting into deep slumber.

CHAPTER 4

~

SCOTLAND

Getting on the Flying Scotsman at Euston Railway Station was a brand-new experience for Ahmad; he had never seen a train except in movies. The noise and smell at the railway station were quite distinctive; the long carriages with dozens of people all assigned seats and the overhead luggage racks were fascinating. Some people were rushing to catch the train, others were struggling with huge suitcases, while many women were preoccupied with small children in their arms or walking and clinging to their skirts. But his attention was particularly drawn to the many couples who were tightly held in each other's arms, some in full lip-to-lip kisses, something he had not seen before, except for that couple on Oxford Street when he was taking a walk with Hasan.

~

The journey was about seven hours long, but Ahmad managed to doze off for several minutes and had the opportunity to buy a sandwich and a cup of tea from the snack cart that came by. But for the lovely scenes of the very green countryside, it was a lonely experience. He did exchange a brief "good morning" with the man facing him, but not much else because the man was hidden from him behind the *Daily Express* for most of the journey. On his left, in the window seat, a very elderly man wearing a hearing aid was mostly sleeping with his head leaning against the window. Ahmad wondered how he could sleep with his head bouncing against the glass pane of the window, with the train shuddering over the steel tracks, even when the driver would sound the deafening whistle of the train every now and then. The only time the old man spoke was when they stood up to leave the train in Edinburgh. He said, "We're here at last; thank goodness!"

~

Mr. Donald Robertson was waiting for Ahmad on the railway platform, screening all the passengers as they descended from the train. He was in his fifties, only five feet, eight inches in height, and somewhat balding with round cheeks and a large belly. He was dressed in gray baggy pants and a Harris Tweed brown jacket. He almost had given up, when a young, slim, brown-skinned young man, panting under the weight of an enormous suitcase, appeared. He was unmistakable. The vast majority of passengers were white, but there were a few black African faces, two turbaned Sikh men, and Ahmad.

"Ahmad, I presume?"

"Yes."

"I am Donald Robertson. Welcome to Edinburgh. I hope you had a nice trip?"

"Yes, thank you."

"Fortunately, it's a nice day, today; it was raining a lot yesterday."

"It never rains in Aden," said Ahmad with a chuckle.

"Do you need any help with the suitcase? It looks awfully big."

"No, thank you."

"Well, let's go this way to the right, where I've parked my wee car; I hope the suitcase will fit in. We live in Bruntsfield; it shouldn't take more than fifteen minutes to get there. You are aware that you will have a room at our house for six months? Then we will find you another place because

Mary and I are going abroad, to Dubai, to teach. I am an English teacher, or maybe I should say a Scottish teacher, given my accent!"

The joke was lost on Ahmad, but at that moment he was just too distracted by all the new sights he was enjoying, especially that of Sir Walter Scott Monument, on beautiful Princes Street, next door to Waverly Station.

~

The Robertsons' home was a relatively modest middle-class bungalow with three bedrooms, two bathrooms, a family room with a small fireplace, and a large kitchen with sufficient space for a dining table that could seat six at a pinch.

A small well-groomed garden, mostly of roses and other flowers, provided a pleasant view from the family room bow window. The wrought-iron gate was painted white. Mrs. Mary Robertson opened the door to the two men and welcomed Ahmad warmly with a firm handshake.

"You must be thirsty. Would you like a cup of tea?"Mrs. Robertson asked.

Ahmad felt he had to say no, for that was how he was brought up, unless the host insisted. Mrs. Robertson did insist, to Ahmad's relief, and soon he was seated in a comfortable easy chair and sipping a hot cup of weak but delicious tea. He had to go through the routine of adding milk and a spoonful of sugar, but it was worth it. Back in Aden, his mother would make what they all called Adeni tea, which was strong and boiled for ages with the milk and sugar already in the pot, and with a pinch of that inevitable concoction of crushed cardamom and nutmeg.

~

The Robertsons had no children. They had taken in paying student guests before and enjoyed the company, as well as the extra income. There were three bedrooms, one of which Mr. Robertson used as a study, with a typewriter sitting on his large rosewood desk. Ahmad's bedroom was only six feet wide, but the length was close to ten feet, and it had a small window overlooking the house behind. Next door, there was a half bathroom without bathtub or shower but with a hand washbasin and toilet with a wooden seat and cover. Ahmad was happy to see that hot water was available. He managed to wash his hands and face before he started to unpack. The old wooden wardrobe was big enough for Ahmad's clothes and other items; there was a shelf at the top above the long wooden bar on which he would hang his shirts and the one jacket which he brought with him. He was pleased to find that shelf for the many books which he brought with him from Aden, and for the many he would need for his studies.

~

The Robertsons had their dinner early, as close to six as possible, and that day was no exception. Mrs. Robertson was not sure about Ahmad's eating likes and dislikes. She was determined to find out later, but she guessed that he would not touch pork. After all, the couple was going for a teaching contract to Dubai and they had educated themselves about Arab and Muslim culture. She also correctly assumed that Ahmad would not take any alcohol. However, that did not stop Donald from having his beer before and during supper. He did politely ask Ahmad if it would bother him if he was to have a drink, but to his relief Ahmad had no objection at all. The main dish was a chicken and mushroom pie with green peas. For dessert they had spotted dick with thick custard. Ahmad found the food different but surprisingly tasty and filling, despite the absence of bread and rice served with every meal back in Aden. He told himself that he would need to adapt to his new home, which he was starting to like. The Robertsons had so many questions about Ahmad's family, his home, his old school, his journey to Edinburgh, and his plans for the next day.

~

All the new students were to meet in the huge main hall of the University of Edinburgh in the Old Quadrangle, usually shortened to Old Quad.

Ahmad had to register there and was given many little pamphlets about the university and its surroundings. The student debating society, the chess club, and the volleyball team all competed for his interest and participation. He was pleasantly surprised to know that there was a volleyball team which would allow him to continue with his favorite sport. He had always associated the British with cricket, which he found boring, and he could never figure out its scoring system. In that big hall with hundreds of young men and women, everyone seemed to be talking at the same time, and the crowd seemed so vibrant and enthusiastic. He had never seen so many young women in his life and was struck by their fresh faces and beautiful figures.

As he walked home across the Meadows Park to the Bruntsfield area of the city, he knew that he was going to fall in love with Edinburgh and its people. That night, as he lay in his bed while looking at the white ceiling above him, he had great difficulty falling asleep. This was not because of any jetlag, for he had changed time zones a whole week before, but because he started reviewing those numerous new experiences he had gone through in just one week since leaving home.

CHAPTER 5

~

THE FACULTY OF LAW

In London, Hasan went through the same student induction process, which he too found so exciting and different from anything else he had experienced. He was not surprised to find a clear male predominance among his fellow students. After all, law was a man's profession, and all the famous names in the profession were male ones. What did surprise him was the relatively high proportion of older students in their thirties and forties. As he chatted with some of them, he found out that this was a second career for them, for they would be graduates in history, the classics, education, or from the London School of Economics. Many former graduates of the LSE were foreign students, especially from Africa or the Far East. Hasan too was approached by student recruiters for the debating society, the chess club, the cricket club, and several others.

~

Back in his digs, Hasan began to settle down and got on well with his hosts, especially with Mrs. McCartney, who seemed to care for him. He felt warmth toward her, her demeanor reminding him of his own mother. With Mr. McCartney, there was a somewhat cold but genuine mutual respect. He found Stephen to be somewhat aloof but sometimes quite amusing, while Stephen looked at him with a measure of suspicion. But Biddy, to his eyes, was a stunning and rare beauty who often engaged him in conversation and sometimes long discussions about serious issues of human rights, social justice, women's rights, international affairs, race, and religion. Although her knowledge about these matters was superficial, certainly compared to his, she nevertheless would raise them whenever the opportunity arose. As she got to know him better, she would debate him about religious issues, and whenever she had the opportunity would tease him about his religiosity and beliefs. He was often uncomfortable talking about that, but since it came from Biddy's beautiful, pouty, bee-stung lips, he would listen adoringly.

It was during one of those discussions when she asked him, "How can you find the time to stop for prayers five times a day?"

"How do you know I do that?"

"I assume you do, don't you? And I often see you going to the washroom at certain times of the day, coming out with a wet face and hands and often with water splashed on your shirt. After all, we share the same bathroom, and sometimes you seem to spill water on the tiled floor."

"Well, I try to pray whenever I can, but sometimes I am unable to do so at the appointed time; so I postpone it until I come home. This happens a lot with the noon and afternoon prayers, while I am at my class. That is allowed in Islam."

"And why do all Muslims have to face south?"

"I face south east because Mecca is southeast of London. But those who pray in my country would face north, because Mecca is north of Aden."

"But why should you all face Mecca? God does not sit in Mecca! The churches don't all face in one direction."

"That is because the first mosque in the world was there, so it became a rule."

"Are you sure there is a god?"

"Of course; how can you ask such a question?"

"Because I don't think there is. At least, I am not as sure as you seem to be. And you call your god Allah. That is not the same as ours, and obviously not the same god as that of the Hindus or the Jews. So, there must be so many gods?"

"Maybe there is only one. We believe there is only one, and we call that god Allah. And our Prophet is Muhammad, the last and final messenger from Allah. We also believe in Jesus, but only as a prophet."

"And another thing: I noticed last week, when my mother's friend and neighbor came for a cup of tea, do you remember? ..."

"Oh, the one who brought her black dog with her?"

"Yes, that's the one. You seemed to be terrified of the dog; and you kept saying '*sig*' to him. Is that Arabic? What does it mean?"

"No, it is not really Arabic, but that's what we say when we want to chase dogs away."

"But he was a lovely and friendly dog. We pat our dogs and pamper them."

"I noticed! Dogs are not clean, in our religion."

"They are very clean here. And we have vets for them when they are sick."

"So I hear. I am not allowed to let a dog lick me, because then I am no longer considered clean and I cannot pray before washing seven times."

"Seven times! You have to have seven baths?"

"No, no. I wash the licked area seven times."

"How bizarre!"

"I suppose, for you. Look, why don't we talk about something more exciting? About your boyfriends, for example? The ones your brother mentioned."

Biddy, blushing, said, "Oh, he is an idiot. I don't have any. They just like to tease me at school because the older boys are always asking me out and following me."

"I am not surprised; you are beautiful."

"Do you really think so?"

"Of course!"

"So, how come you don't ask me out?"

"Well, um, um, what will your parents say?"

"Don't you want to know what *I* would say?" asked Biddy.

"Well, naturally. But your parents will be upset with me, I am sure."

"They don't have to know. It will be our secret. But I am not sure I want to anyway. Did you leave your girlfriend back home? Do you miss her?"

Hasan giggled.

"Why are you laughing, Hasan?"

"In Aden, we do not have girlfriends or boyfriends."

"Why not?"

"Boys and girls live separate lives there and they never socialize together."

"Why not?"

"They can only be together if they are married."

"Why?"

"I don't know. It is not allowed in our religion. If a girl is found alone with a boy, her reputation would be ruined. So, she would never allow that to happen."

"And what about the boy's reputation?"

"Oh, that's different."

"Why should it be different?"

"Look, I don't make the rules. We have to follow tradition back there."

"So what happens when… say two or three families go out together to a party or wedding or the fair or the beach?"

"First of all, they don't. But if they did, then the men of the three families would socialize together, and the females would do the same."

"So, all these years you have never touched a girl?"

"Never even spoke to one, unless she was with my sister at the time, let alone touched her!"

"So how do you shake hands? I understand that Arabs are forever shaking hands."

"Never with girls."

"Needless to say, you have never kissed a girl?"

"Well … I tried … but she did not like it," said Hasan, making up a story.

"Maybe you should get some lessons while you are here?" said Biddy with a mischievous smile.

~

The Bar Professional Training Course was quite demanding, requiring a lot of reading, which Hasan did not mind, and was used to. He found the course on the history of law fascinating. But even Hasan, the well-known bookworm with the phenomenal memory, found the demand for reading, rereading, and research difficult to cope with at times. He spoke English fluently and did surprisingly well for a very young freshman from Aden. But he also listened carefully to the British students and admired those who could speak with that enviable Queen's English accent that seemed to bestow on them an aura of superiority and class. He would go home and try to practice that accent, which he desperately wanted to acquire. Being in the huge city of London, he did not know or run into any Adenis, something which caused him to communicate in English all the time. He liked to attend the student debating society sessions, and several months later he managed to participate in a debate where, to his own surprise, he did quite well.

~

It was Christmas season already. *How time flies,* Hasan thought. It seemed as though he just arrived in London, but so much in his life had changed. The bright lights of Oxford Street were on; huge crowds were milling around Regent Street and Piccadilly Circus, some loud and clearly inebriated, which was so unusual for the British, or so he thought. The whole country seemed to be in party mood.

The McCartneys too were going out much more than usual. Biddy was invited to a big party to be attended by most of her schoolmates in the senior grades. A hall had been rented, and a band was hired for the dinner dance. The girls were busy shopping for dresses and shoes to wear on that night. Biddy bought a beautiful, deep-purple, body hugger of a short dress with a scoop neck and matching shoes with elegant high heels. As she stood in front of the mirror at the Bates Department Store, she congratulated herself on her own looks. She was confident that she would turn many heads at the party. Several of the boys at school had asked her to be their date for that night, but she turned them all down and decided to join a group of girls who would go without partners and take their chances. She also had another motive. She thought she might persuade Hasan to go to the party too. After all, he looked a few years more mature than the many acne-pocked and unsophisticated, if not crude classmates, she had. He was also tall, dark, and reasonably handsome, in her eyes at least. She was sure the other girls would be envious if Hasan did agree to go with her.

Hasan agonized over the invitation for quite a while before succumbing to the irresistible Biddy. His primary worry was the humiliation he might feel if he had to get up on the dance floor, where he would make an utter fool of himself. The only dancing he ever had done in his life was the crude samba-like dance known in Yemen as *raklah*. During it, one or more men would rhythmically sway left and right to a monotonous beat while the audience would egg them on with rhythmic clapping. No women were ever involved, and there was certainly no touching of any kind. He had seen the waltz and the quick step in movies and was therefore mortified at the thought of making all those precisely timed steps—all synchronized with Biddy's.

"You know, Biddy, you should go with someone who can dance. I have never danced in my life," Hasan blurted out.

"Don't worry; it is quite simple."

"Not what I have seen in the cinema!"

"No, that is professional dancing. At school, all they do is rock and roll, and they just twist their bodies with the music. I will show you. You just follow me and follow the beat of the music. None of the other boys know how to dance either. So, you are not the only one."

"Are you sure? I do not want to embarrass you in front of your classmates."

"Don't be silly. We will have a good time. Trust me!"

~

The Saturday of the party, over lunch Biddy dared Hasan to attend the party with her, and he eventually accepted. Stephen responded with a loud whistle. Her father was surprised but did not say anything. Mrs. McCartney, on the other hand, looked quite amused but pleased, and when Hasan expressed his trepidations she was full of encouragement.

Hasan had managed to buy a new blazer which he wore to university every day. It still looked fairly new, and quite smart in combination with light gray pants, and his black leather shoes which he did shine for the occasion. He bought a blue and yellow patterned tie that he wore over his white shirt. As they left the house to take the underground train to their party, the couple looked great and felt really excited. For Hasan, that was his first date ever.

~

There were hundreds of male and female students, in approximately equal numbers, already filling the hall and the passages into it. The thickest congregation of bodies was around the bar. The three barmen seemed unable to cope with the orders for drinks, mostly large pints of beer, handed by the barmen over the shoulders of the students to arms reaching out to grab them, and almost missing at times. Hasan became aware of the strange new smell of alcohol permeating the air. He had never drunk alcohol and he was not about to break that rule. Biddy was still a few months shy of eighteen, but the barman did not challenge her. The usual sign above the bar asked "R U 18?" but it seemed that no one was paying any attention that night. Hasan felt that as a man, he had to buy the drinks, but he had never gone up to a bar before. He also had learned that it was against Islam to even carry alcohol, and yet he ordered the gin and tonic Biddy wanted, and for himself he ordered a cola.

The couple moved over toward the dance floor but had difficulty entering because of the crowds. They decided to go up on the balcony which overlooked the dance floor, with a three-piece band playing fast dance music, rock-and-roll type, punctuated by the occasional waltz or foxtrot. From there, they had a panorama of hundreds of beautiful young bodies dancing to the rhythm, while the whole mass rotated clockwise round the dance floor. The two of them sipped their drinks, and intermittently looked into each other's eyes. They smiled broadly.

"You see that tall black boy there?" Biddy asked. "Watch how he dances. He knows what he is doing, and he has perfect rhythm; that's what you need to do. He must have been doing this for a very long time, but you get the idea."

"The music is great, but how do you know which foot to move, and when?"

"There is just one rhythm you need to remember for the fast dances— slow, slow, quick, quick, slow, slow, quick, quick. That's it."

"And for the slow ones?"

"Oh, that is too easy. You just shuffle one foot then the other. Are you ready?"

"I suppose!"

~

The two made their way down the spiral stairs from the balcony, and after much pushing and shoving made their way to the dance floor as the band started a slow waltz to the lyrics of that famous black crooner, Ray Charles, singing, "Set me free." Now Hasan became very self-conscious and imagined that all eyes were on him, just waiting to witness the moment when he would step on Biddy's new shoes or would fall to the floor so they would all laugh. Biddy took command of the situation and linked her right hand to his left, then to his horror grabbed his right hand with her left and placed it on her soft left hip. She rested her left hand on his right shoulder. All that was done in two seconds, and Hasan found himself for the first time in his life not only holding hands with a woman, but also feeling her waist and hip.

Biddy smiled reassuringly, and the two drifted slowly with the rotating mass of youth to the music of Ray Charles. It was such an overwhelming experience for Hasan. There was nothing to compare it with. Here he was holding this beautiful, soft, tender creature round the waist and getting these tingling feelings in his left hand, which was holding her soft and warm right hand. *Was he dreaming or what?* Suddenly he woke up from his thoughts as he mistimed his shuffles and kicked Biddy's left foot with his right and almost stumbled. Biddy corrected the problem very quickly and smiled, yet again.

The slow dance came to an end with the applause of the crowd, and the two made their way back to the bar for another drink. As they stood there awaiting their turn to order, two of Biddy's female classmates came up behind Biddy and asked who the new boyfriend was. Reluctantly, Biddy had to introduce Hasan to Margaret and Jill, who then tried to find as much as possible about Hasan before they left giggling. Biddy was reluctant to share any details about Hasan with them, and had previously competed with Jill over boyfriends, and in fact won two such competitions, to Jill's chagrin. Hasan, on the other hand, was quite flattered by the attention of the girls. He found Jill, although no match for Biddy, to be especially attractive and friendly.

~

After finishing their second drinks, the couple went back to the dance floor, this time holding hands; the taboo had been broken for Hasan, who kept congratulating himself for dating such a beautiful girl. If only the boys in his class could see him with her!

Hasan now had some clue how to do a sort of twist to the music, egged on by the admiring Biddy. It was so warm and comfortable in that hall, even though it was near zero degrees outside. Hasan unbuttoned his jacket and continued to dance with the jacket swinging to left and right with the beat of the drums. The orchestra switched to a slow waltz to the lyrics of "Save the Last Dance for Me" sung by that famous British singer, Engelbert Humperdinck. It was beautifully rendered, and Hasan could not believe his luck when Biddy moved toward him, putting her right cheek against his, her arms behind his neck, and her pelvis firmly against his.

Hasan wanted to break loose in order to camouflage the stirring stiffness that began to poke at Biddy, but he was unable to do so because of her arms round his neck. Slowly their lips slid toward each other, and they went into a deep, wet kiss, Hasan's first ever.

～

Although it was cold outside, the young couple decided to walk part of the way before getting the underground train. On the way there, they stopped numerous times to warm themselves against each other and to repeat that memorable kiss. When they got home, the lights were out but they could see the light peeking under the door to the parents' bedroom. Biddy knew her mother would be worried about her. As if to prove it, her mother opened her door a crack and asked, "Is that you, love? Did you have a good time?"

Hasan could not sleep for ages that night, not until he masturbated and felt thoroughly drained.

～

Although Biddy was open about her new feelings for Hasan, and was used to dealing and flirting with boys and even kissing one or two that she especially liked, Hasan wanted the new relationship to be kept secret. He still imagined what an irate father in Aden would do to him if he messed around with his daughter. Biddy agreed with that arrangement, and would try to suppress her feelings at home, but they would meet after school and sometimes skip school to meet at a coffee bar or a park for heavy kissing and fondling. They almost got caught by Stephen one evening when he came downstairs and found them in an embrace in the hallway.

～

A few weeks later, Mr. McCartney's sister in Carlisle died unexpectedly. He and his wife had to drive there, taking Stephen with them. His family up north hardly knew Stephen, and it was an opportunity for them to get to know him. Biddy had exams that week and could not go. Not that she would want to be away from Hasan. In fact, she could see great opportunities for some privacy for the two of them. Her mother did pull her aside just before they left for Carlisle and warned her to keep her bedroom locked at all times while she was sleeping. She emphasized that, while she did not think ill of her lodger, she did want to protect her own daughter against a hot-blooded young man who might attempt to take advantage of her. Biddy thanked her for her concern, and promised to keep her door locked as instructed. After that conversation between mother and daughter, Mrs. McCartney was able to reassure her husband, who had asked his wife to "have a word" with Biddy.

The McCartneys, with Stephen in tow, left early one morning in the hope of arriving in Carlisle before sunset, after a seven-hour drive on the A6 motorway. Mrs. McCartney had left some prepared meals in the freezer but encouraged Biddy to cook if she had the time. After all, Hasan was paying a weekly five pounds for his board and lodging.

~

That day there was excitement in the air for the two young people. They came home as soon as their respective classes finished, arriving around five in the evening. Biddy came home ahead of Hasan and decided to have a bath and change into some comfortable and attractive blouse and skirt and sandals. She began chopping some onions and tomatoes, which she would later use to make an omelet for the two of them. Hasan had told her how much he liked onions in his food, and she was going to surprise him. What she had not anticipated was that her eyes would sting and water so much. After she dealt with that, she decided to help herself to a drink of gin and tonic from her father's stock. After all, she persuaded herself, she was going to turn eighteen later that year. It felt so good, especially with two ice cubes, and within minutes she felt a lot calmer.

She had just poured her second drink when the front door key turned and Hasan entered. He hung his coat on the rack, put his briefcase on the floor, and turned toward the kitchen. Biddy was behind the counter giving him a huge smile. He paced quickly toward her and kissed her on those full and now very familiar lips, pulling her head toward him with his left hand and her waist with his right. It seemed like ages before they broke loose to look at each other.

"Are you alone in house?" Hasan teased.

"No, I am not; there is a horny intruder here."

"And this horny intruder is going to intrude where he has never done before," Hasan retorted as he slid his right hand under Biddy's blouse and ran his fingers over her back as she whimpered with pleasure. He noted that she was not wearing a bra; her firm and shapely breasts had no need for that. He kissed her on her neck just below her jaw, and noted how much pleasure she got from that. They had done those things before on their secret dates, but there never was the opportunity to go any further. Now they had all the privacy they could ever hope for and all the time in the world.

Biddy did not want to lose control, but Hasan did not give her time to stop him and quickly proceeded to undo the three buttons on the front of her blouse, exposing what he thought was the most perfect pair he had seen, even in paintings. Only these were so soft and warm. As he placed his right hand under her left breast, lifting it gently, he stroked her nipple with his palm, to her heavy breathing, which made him feel even more aroused.

Biddy made no further effort to stop him. She had her left hand on his right shoulder, stroking it in rhythm with his own strokes. Several strokes later Hasan, pushed the two parts of the front of her blouse to the side, stepped back momentarily to take in that incredible view, then buried his face between the two mounds while Biddy held him behind his neck, pulling his face into her chest for even closer contact, all the time breathing noisily in supreme pleasure.

Hasan started to unzip her skirt.

"No, no, not in the kitchen. What if someone comes in?" Biddy stopped him.

"Who would do that? They are in Carlisle."

"You never know. Let's go to the room, to my room."

At that stage, Hasan would have followed her to the moon.

It was the first time Hasan had seen Biddy's bedroom. It was lovely; it looked so tidy and feminine, and the air had a touch of perfume. Life-sized pictures of the Beatles decorated one wall. The bed was queen size, as opposed to his single bed, and it was made, something Biddy always did before leaving for school.

Biddy removed her skirt and draped it neatly over the back of her chair. But she would not remove her black underwear. She looked gorgeous in it. Then she slid under the bed covers, waiting for Hasan to do the same, which he tried to do in such haste that he almost stumbled. He too would not remove his underpants, but his erection was clearly visible to Biddy who knew about those things from fooling around with some of the boys at school. But she had never actually made love to anyone.

Under the covers, the two lay on the side facing each other, chest to breasts and groin to groin. Hasan put his right hand behind Biddy's left buttock and pulled her toward his erection. He had never gone that far with anyone until that moment, but he recognized bliss when he felt it. He had read and heard about virginity and hymens and blood on the sheets, but he did not know what to do at that point. Biddy seemed to come to the rescue. Her hands went down to her hips, and she slid her underpants off without saying anything. She thought that the signal was clear enough. As she did that, she touched his erection, lingering momentarily on it. Hasan could not believe how pleasurable that was.

"Where is your condom?" she asked when she noted the absence of one.

"What condom?"

"You can't do it without a condom; you will get me pregnant."

"I have never used one, or seen one," he admitted, totally embarrassed.

"I want to give myself to you. You make me so happy. I want to make you happy."

"And I think I am in love with you."

"Are you really?"

"Yes, you are gorgeous. I think about you all the time."

"I love you too. I knew that from the start."

"I am so lucky, and I don't deserve it."

"I am lucky too. You are so gentle with me, and I know you will be gentle when you do it."

"I am also very clumsy with … this … sex … It is so new to me."

"Look, let us just lie together and just hold each other, without doing … you know …"

Hasan now finished slipping his underpants off and lay against Biddy. His erection nestled between her upper inner thighs and her fine pubic hair matted with her very slippery secretions. Their pelvises soon rocked and ground against each other in a steady but accelerating rhythm to a consuming crescendo. As Hasan spilled his seed, he uttered a loud cry of passion that stunned Biddy, who was not able to reach her climax.

"Biddy, I love you. I want you to be mine … always. I am crazy about you. I want to make love to you every day … *properly,* I mean. I must get those condoms tomorrow. Where does one buy them? In special sex shops?"

"Oh, no. They are sold in all pharmacies like Medical Mart and Koots. I will show you tomorrow, but you will have to go in and ask for them. I can't. Now you had better go back to your room, just in case they come back from Carlisle unexpectedly early."

Despite the excitement Hasan had gone through, he fell asleep fairly quickly, following that sexual release, and slept solidly until seven in the morning. It was one of the very few times when he skipped his evening prayers.

After a late breakfast, the couple walked down to the nearest Koots store. Biddy decided to stay outside but urged Hasan to go in. He entered hesitantly and then looked around at many shelves, he but could not see what he was looking for. He had nothing to go by, since he had never seen them in or out of the packet. He was sure in his own mind that all the sales assistants and customers knew what he was looking for, and he felt very embarrassed. He decided to escape into the street when a female sales assistant asked him, "Can I help you, sir?"

"Oh … yes … yes … ah … do you have any toothpaste?"

"What kind? There are three brands."

"Oh, Whiteshine, please."

"Here you are, sir," said the young woman handing him a tube of Whiteshine, of which he already had two in his bathroom.

"That's it, thank you," said Hasan, who continued to look around looking puzzled.

"Is there anything else, sir?"

"Um, um, yes, do you sell, um ... um ... condoms here?"

"Which kind would you like, sir?"

"Um ... um ... the big ones," blurted Hasan, for want of some answer.

An involuntary smile appeared on the girl's face, which had turned red as she tried hard to suppress her laughter.

"I meant, with or without lubrication."

"Oh, I see ... um ... um ..."

"Perhaps I should show you where they are, sir, and then you can choose at your leisure."

"Yes, yes, thank you," said Hasan, by this time sweating profusely with anxiety and embarrassment.

As he emerged from the store, he saw Biddy standing under the lamppost and gave her a triumphant wink. Biddy left on her own, heading for the stationery store three blocks away. She was busy preparing for her exams later in the week. The two were to meet back at home late in the afternoon for dinner, and to try out the new purchase from Koots.

$\sim$

Hasan came home earlier. The first thing he did was to open the packet of three condoms. He tore the plastic wrapper, and what looked like a ring of beige rubber popped out. The ring felt quite oily and slippery, and there was a flat diaphragm filling the hole in the ring, but with a round, blind-ended, finger tip sized balloon. He was very curious how it would be worn. He pulled on the diaphragm, but nothing happened. He then pulled on it in the other direction, and the ring did unfurl into a long tube with a diaphanous wall of rubber. So, that's how they were packaged! Now he knew.

~

By the time Biddy came home, after her visit to the stationery shop and the library, Hasan was more than ready to try his new toy, and so was Biddy. She poured herself a large gin and tonic and hesitantly offered one to Hasan, who turned it down. She sat in the sofa, enjoying sips of her drink, while Hasan sat on her right and started running his fingers through her long, fine, blonde hair and massaging the back of her neck while she purred with pleasure. As she put her empty glass down on the coffee table, she turned right, faced Hasan, and slowly brought her full lips to his in a long, sensuous kiss, which urged them toward the unfinished business they were determined to complete.

Hasan started undressing her by removing her T-shirt, which fully exposed the beautiful breasts that he had seen for the first time only the previous night. He paid a lot of attention to them, while Biddy placed her right hand on his left thigh, and made slow strokes toward the midline to check his level of readiness. That was the signal Hasan needed to stand up, gently pulling her by her right hand to her bedroom.

As she stood by her bed, Biddy wriggled out of her jeans, leaving only the pink knickers for Hasan to pull down her legs to the floor, at which point she stepped out of them. There was still some daylight coming in through the window, enough for Hasan to appreciate that stunning figure of a totally naked and shapely young woman, something he had never ever seen before, not even the previous day when Biddy quickly had slid under the bed covers. He stood right against her, still in his pants, kissing her again, then slowly dropping his right hand to her pubic hair, stroking it with his fingers. It felt so good, and as he reached lower he became aware of the copious slippery juices of an aroused young woman.

Biddy was uttering loud moans of pleasure, which got Hasan even more excited. After he took off his clothes, he laid on top of the bed. As he stood by the bed, the prostrate Biddy turned her head toward him and saw his full erection at eye level. She reached over and held it. She had done that with one or two boys from her class, partly because they more or less forced her to do so and partly out of curiosity about this renowned organ about which boys never stop bragging. But she never went further than that. She always warded off the boys by telling them that she was under eighteen, but now she was only a few weeks away from that magical age, and with the boy whom she loved. She would let him do anything to her.

Hasan fished a new condom out of his pants pocket and proceeded to unfurl it over his hard, youthful erection for the first time. It looked comical to him, especially with that small bubble at the tip for collecting the fluid which he was soon to release.

"Do you love me, Hasan?"

"Of course I do. I will love you forever."

"Are you sure? Will you?"

"Yes, darling."

"This is the first time you called me darling."

"But you know that I love you. I don't know all the right words in English."

"You will be gentle with me?"

"Yes."

"Will it hurt?"

"I suppose so. I don't know. It is my first time too. I will do it very gently, slowly."

"I am glad it is you who will take me."

"I am so lucky."

"Do it! Do it!"

For the two new lovers, it was a very memorable night of lust.

⌒

The parents returned at the end of five days in Carlisle, during which time they renewed their ties with the family there, and even Stephen enjoyed his time there, once the funeral was over. He found some cousins and more distant relatives of his own age in the setting of a small town with lots of empty spaces, compared to the hustle and bustle of the crowded city of London.

Biddy and Hasan had to be careful to avoid touching, something they had gotten so used to in the previous few days, and acted as though nothing unusual had happened. They had to meet outside the home as before, but there was no opportunity for real intimacy, even in the secluded parks they had to frequent, partly because of the heavy clothing they had to wear in the cold weather.

Mrs. McCartney, however, detected a subtle difference in the body language between her daughter and the lodger, as only a woman would. She wanted to ask Biddy about it, but then she decided that it was simply because the two had more time to get to talk to each other in the absence of the rest of the family in Carlisle. Or maybe she did not want to hear the answer. And yet she liked Hasan and thought highly of him. She would not have minded if her daughter found a promising young lawyer like him for a husband, one day.

CHAPTER 6

~

EDINBURGH

The famous faculty of medicine of the University of Edinburgh was a dream come true for Ahmad. He knew he was lucky to be accepted as a first-year medical student at the age of twenty, and he would be there for six years, provided of course he passed all his exams. But Ahmad had some real difficulties with his studies in those early months at the faculty of medicine, and he had no one to guide him. He found it difficult to cope with the subjects of biology and chemistry because that involved committing so many names and details to memory. He wished he knew Latin to help him with all the anatomical terms he had to learn by heart. He had much less difficulty with physics because it required much more reasoning and mathematics rather than pure memory work. Many times he wished he had been endowed with that superior memory of his old classmate and rival, Hasan.

He also discovered, to his dismay, that he was not at all the brightest in the class, like he was back in Aden. Now he was competing with the seventy students who had come to the same class in Edinburgh from all over Scotland and beyond. He even had classmates from Sweden, Nigeria, Iran, Trinidad, and Uganda, and they were the brightest in their respective classes back home. He made friends with a young man from the Shetlands, but this one was rather quiet and studious. Thus, Ahmad did not have a friend to go out with in the evening for months; until early in January of the following year, that is. The chaplain at the university told him about The International Club, which met in the Mound area of Edinburgh. It had been started by a Maltese professor in the faculty of divinity.

When Ahmad got there, to his utter amazement he met an older man of about forty-five who was also from Aden. Although they had never met back home, the man recognized his family name, which was not surprising given that his father was a government minister. He was a teacher who came to Edinburgh for a six-month refresher course in education at Moray College. He had arrived in September too and was planning on returning home in March. Humaid invited Ahmad to Sunday lunch at his apartment on Craig Road, which he shared with a Sudanese student at the faculty of agriculture and a Somali student also studying education. Ahmad could not wait to join them that Sunday.

~

When Ahmad rang the bell at noon, a Sudanese man called Sharif opened the door. He had a cigarette in his mouth, was wearing a white Sudanese *jallabiyah* [robe], which clearly needed ironing, and on his head he wore a turban made up of his large orange bath towel. It was a bizarre combination, for Ahmad.

"*Salamat.*" Then reverting to English Sharif continued, "You must be Ahmad. Welcome, welcome! Humaid told us about you. He has not yet emerged from his bedroom, but I heard him go to the bathroom, so he must be awake." He led Ahmad to the small living room, and offered him black tea in a very small cup made of glass, with lots of sugar but no milk.

"How many of you are there in this flat?" Ahmad asked.

"Three. There is also a Somali student, Moosa. You will like him. He is great fun, especially when he speaks broken Arabic!"

"And how long have you been living here?"

"It is different for each one of us. I have been here the longest, two years. Moosa, I believe, for one year. But Humaid joined us only in late

September, and he is leaving in March. Whenever any one of us finishes his studies, another student replaces him. If you would like to join us, you can take over the rent from Humaid."

"Well, as it happens, my landlord is leaving for the Middle East just about that time, and I will need to find new digs somewhere."

"What can you cook?"

"Cook? Nothing!" Ahmad was clearly not prepared for the question.

"That's no good. We take turns to cook and wash up, and clean, although you wouldn't think anyone cleaned this place, looking at the mess in here!"

"I never had to cook before, or wash up or clean for that matter."

"Well, my friend, there are no mothers or sisters here. You have to learn, and learn fast. At a minimum, you have to be able to make tea, create an omelet, and most importantly boil rice, and make a stew. Stew on rice is the staple food in this place. There is nothing to it. You just need a sharp knife to chop the onions and cut the stewing beef quite small to make it last longer. Then add salt and cumin and chili powder, and empty a whole can of tomato paste. Let it simmer for two hours. And don't forget the okra, especially to make the Sudanese happy."

"Is that what you are having today?"

"Yes, of course. This is Sunday."

"So, is the stew made?"

"Oh, no. It's Humaid's turn to cook."

"But if it takes two hours, then we'll be eating this afternoon!"

"Don't worry, my friend. Lunch will be fast-tracked, especially for you!"

"At least this way I will be learning how to make a stew, to qualify for a room in the flat!" Ahmad said with a smile.

~

Humaid emerged from his bedroom, with a young woman of about thirty-five, both being nicely groomed and dressed. He came into the living room to greet his guest.

"Good morning, *ahlan wa sahlan, marhaba* [welcome].This is Linda. Linda, this is Ahmad, the medical student from Aden."

Ahmad stood up to shake hands with Linda, a nice-looking woman with red hair, red freckles on her face, green eyes, and ample breasts. She was somewhat overweight with large buttocks but nice legs. She stood a couple of inches shorter than Ahmad, wearing flat shoes at that point. She had red nail varnish on fingernails and toenails. A sweet smile on her face revealed a set of perfectly aligned teeth.

"Pleased to meet you, Ahmad. Humaid told me about you. So, you are the guinea pig for the local stew this week, are you?"

"So I understand. Why? Is there a choice?"

"Not in this place, my friend. It's the SOS system here: stew or starve! But you are lucky today, because I am here to help big chef Humaid, and I will speed things up so that it is lunch and not supper!"

"Thank God for that. My landlady insists on early breakfast at seven, even on Sunday, because she has to go church well before the service to help out. That's what happens when you get old; you want to go to bed by nine and wake up by four in the morning."

Linda went into the tiny kitchen, which had a gas stove with only two rings: small and large. She quickly chopped up some onions and started frying them in a huge but cheap aluminum pot. The delicious smell of fried onions soon filled the flat. It must have sufficiently tickled the olfactory nerve of the third student to cause him to emerge from his room, with his girlfriend Sheila, a chubby, dark-haired woman in her twenties. She had brown eyes and a mild squint. She wore a white blouse with jeans and black sandals. She looked at Ahmad, said good-morning, but then sat quietly in an easy chair in the living room and busied herself with the Sunday papers. Moosa, on the other hand, was very sociable and beamed a big smile at Ahmad.

"I have to warn you that Humaid's stew is not at all of good quality, and it is not for lack of good-quality meat!" Moosa said.

"You are all getting me worried about this so-called stew. But I am somewhat reassured by the fact that Linda is supervising," Ahmad said, looking in the direction of Linda.

"No, don't worry! We have survived many pots of Humaid's stew, as you can see. But you are from Yemen. The stomachs of Yemenis have special lining inside. It must be from all the *qat* that they chew," Moosa added with a chuckle.

"Well, that is the one thing we have in common with you in Somalia, also with Ethiopia. What a dubious shared honor! What a loss of resources, not to mention the negative impact on health."

"Oh, yes, you are going to be a doctor, so Humaid tells me. Do you know of something to control sex drive?" Moosa asked with howls of laughter while eying Sheila, who turned crimson.

By two that afternoon, all six of them sat around the table with their own plates and cutlery. Humaid tried to carry the heavy pot of stew to the table. The handle was held to the pot by a single pin, the second pin being broken. The pot wobbled on the single pin. Humaid tried to balance it but tripped on the rubber thongs he wore on his big feet and the pot lurched to the side, spilling half its contents on the floor before Humaid could regain his balance.

"Now we have neither quality nor quantity," said Moosa, laughing as they all busied themselves with cleaning the mess.

"No problem," said Humaid as he topped up the pot of stew with boiling water.

With the watered-down pot of stew, and a smaller pot of rice in the middle, the group had a great time dishing out from the one or the other, adding salt and lime pickle as required, and seemed to have a hearty meal.

Ahmad became a regular guest at those stew parties, and he enjoyed them immensely, especially because they reminded him of home and allowed him to speak Arabic on the weekend. As Sharif did not have a regular girlfriend, Ahmad developed a relatively closer friendship with him, and from time to time the two would go out together. But whereas Ahmad never touched alcohol, and never smoked, Sharif was heavy on both, which presented a significant problem when going out together. All that changed one day, at a bar.

"Why don't you have a beer, Ahmad? You know, Edinburgh is famous for its beer. The McEwen and Usher breweries make great bitter. I think you might like it."

"Bitter? Why would I drink something bitter?"

"No, no. It is called bitter, but it is not. Not really."

"I don't want to be drunk. Besides, it is forbidden in Islam."

"Listen, so much is forbidden in Islam, but everyone does it."

"Don't tell me you eat pork too?"

"That is something I have not tried or ever wanted to. And why would I want to, when I have Humaid's beef stew?" Sharif added, giggling.

"When did you start drinking?"

"Ever since I came here."

"What does it do for you?"

"It makes you feel relaxed, uninhibited, and puts a big smile on your face. Just taste it before you condemn it." He went up to the bar and ordered a half pint for Ahmad.

"It's not all that bitter," Ahmad noted, with beer froth lining his upper lip.

"I told you; it is the national pastime here, apart from football and sex," Sharif retorted with a laugh. "And it is not as hard on the stomach as whiskey or gin or vodka or rum."

"Wow! Have you tried all these?"

"Yes, but now I only drink bitter, I mean beer. There is also a lighter beer called lager. You should try that next time."

"And how many pints would make you drunk?"

"I never have more than three, occasionally four, so I never get to that stage."

By the time the boys decided to call it a night, Gray Friars Bobby was packed with young bodies, all seemingly chatting at the same time. As Ahmad and Sharif emerged from the door of the bar, that unmistakable smell of beer lingered in their nostrils for a while.

$\sim$

Humaid's departure date came sooner than they all thought. He was due to fly that afternoon, from Glasgow Airport down to Heathrow and then to Aden. The send-off party was going to be over lunch, and for that special occasion Sharif, with help from Linda, was going to organize skewers of *shish kebab* with lots of beer, and a bottle of wine mainly for Linda and Sheila. Ahmad had alerted the Robertsons of when he would be leaving their home, which was in fact one week before they themselves were supposed to leave for Dubai. They were happy that he found a new home to his liking and felt content that they had contributed to helping him integrate into Scottish society.

~

That morning, Ahmad brought his still meager belongings by taxi to the flat. Humaid had removed all his belongings from the bedroom, and his suitcase, and cabin luggage sat near the door. Ahmad was able to move in very smoothly. As Ahmad was hanging his clothes in the small wardrobe, placing items on his desk, he felt excitement at the onset of a new chapter in his life, and the freedom it would offer. He looked down at the street below his bow window, and noted, with satisfaction, that there was a busy bus stop facing his new flat.

All six friends were there, and there was a lot of laughter during lunch, when Sharif and Moosa consumed a lot of beer while the two women finished a bottle of wine. By then, Ahmad was a fully converted beer drinker, thanks to Sharif's influence. Humaid never took alcohol, and his six months in Scotland did not change that.

As the hour of departure approached, Linda began to shed a few silent tears. She knew that this was good-bye and that Humaid was going back home to his wife and family. They all said good-bye to Humaid, but Linda went downstairs with him for that final kiss and hug.

Linda came back upstairs to pick up her handbag and some personal items she had kept in Humaid's room, including a toothbrush in the bathroom. She found the group in the living room, in a rather reflective if not pensive mood, wondering what life in that flat would be like without Humaid. They all felt sorry for Linda and invited her to come and see them any time she was free. They also promised her the best stew ever the following Sunday, which Linda said she would not miss. However, she had to pick up her personal items from Humaid's room, which now belonged to Ahmad. When the two went back to the room, it was understandably in a mess.

"I feel guilty leaving a young man like you with all this mess to tidy up."

"Oh, don't worry, I can manage."

"No, no, let me help you at least make the bed and put on fresh sheets and pillowcases. It usually takes two people to make a bed of this size."

"To tell you the truth, I have seen my landlady changing my bed, and it looked quite intimidating. So I don't mind you showing me how."

"Humaid never did that. He always expected me to do it. I suppose, back home he was used to being pampered by his wife."

"But, but … you mean you knew that he was married?"

"Yes. He was upfront with me from the start."

"But, why … I hope you don't mind me asking, but why did you agree, when you knew that?"

"We met at a party six months ago. I had just gone through the trauma and depression of a nasty divorce. I suppose I was lonely, and he was pleasant and funny, and I liked him. It's not fun being alone. Do you like being alone? I'll bet you don't."

"It is terrible being alone. Until six months ago, I was surrounded by people back home."

"I don't suppose you have a wife at your age?"

"Of course not. I am only twenty."

"But Humaid was married in Aden in his early twenties. He has a teenage son and three younger daughters."

"Maybe, but this is changing now. Young people are getting educated and need to go to university, which means that they have to leave the country, since there are no universities at all in Aden."

"But your girls are still getting married very young, aren't they? I read somewhere that about a third of them are under fifteen—here fifteen is considered a child."

"Yes, because they usually finish their education at around sixteen; I mean those who are allowed to study, at secondary school level, and none of them are sent abroad for higher education."

"Why is that?"

"Their families want to keep them safe at home and marry them off as soon as possible."

"Safe? Safe from what?"

"Safe from men who might lead them astray."

"So you admit that it is you, men, who lead us astray?" Linda said with a naughty smile.

"What is that saying in English? It takes two to tango?"

"So, who are *you* tangoing with these days?"

"Nobody! First I have to learn the steps. I hear they are quite complex," Ahmad said with a mischievous smile.

"Oh, the steps come quite naturally. You pick them up in one dance. For a man it is even easier. All he has to do is to be very firm and move forward and backward until it comes to a crescendo!"

"It sounds as if you know lots about it."

"I started about your age, so I have fifteen years of experience."

"I guess you would make a good teacher then?"

"I don't come cheap, you know." Linda feigned a big frown.

It took Ahmad some courage, but then he said, "Why don't I invite you to dinner at the Fratelli Restaurant, where you will find the best Italian food, much better than Humaid's stew at least, and no doubt excellent white wine. Would that do for a down payment?"

"It would do just fine."

"All right, I'll book a table for Friday at six. I heard that one needs to reserve a table there."

"Right, well, now that you have a nicely made up bed with fresh smelling sheets and clean pillowcases, I shall say good-night. See you Friday."

~

Friday could not come soon enough for Ahmad, who spent the next five days fantasizing about Linda and all the things she was going to teach him. In fact, he was so distracted from his university work that he did very little reading, even though he had a lot of material to cover for the exams coming up in one month. But that Friday, Ahmad was at his table in one corner of the restaurant by ten to six. He had heard that the British prided themselves on being very punctual, and he was determined to make an impression on Linda.

The restaurant was practically full, and the clientele appeared to be well dressed and upper class. But there was a lot of chitchat too and much noise from a large round table at which six Italian-speaking people talked, laughed, and gesticulated. Ahmad looked somewhat odd in that background, not only because he was alone but also because he was the only person with dark skin. He felt very self-conscious as he was scanned by so many eyes around him. There were no smiles, except for one from a young woman at the Italian table, which reassured him immensely. But at that very moment, Linda was shown to the table by the headwaiter, and as Ahmad rose to greet her she put her cheek to his before he had time to put his hand out for a handshake.

"Great to see you," Linda said as she took the initiative while some customers were observing the couple.

"You look lovely. I like your new hairstyle."

"Thank you. I am amazed that you noticed. Most men don't bother."

"Well, I am training to be a doctor, and the first thing we learn before touching the patient is to inspect him or her."

"Are you saying that the touching part will come later?" Linda teased him.

"It all depends on the professor."

A male waiter arrived.

"*Buona sera*! Can I gette you somethingge to drinkke to starte?"

"I will have a beer, a pint of bitter," Ahmad said, "and the lady will have white wine. What do you have?"

"The wine menu hazza dozens, but by the glasse there arre the three at the toppa."

Linda chose the Mantato pinot grigio from Sicily.

"Does it come in half bottles?"

"Si. Would you like that, Signiora?"

Linda nodded her head, and started looking at the menu.

The waiter returned with the drinks, and took the orders for lasagna and veal.

"That tastes delicious," Linda said after two sips of wine. "You should try it."

"I've just been converted to beer drinking and am beginning to enjoy it, and now you want me to take up wine?"

"But wine is much nicer, and it does not make you burp either. Here, have a sip!" She handed him her glass. Lipstick was clearly imprinted on one side. Ahmad rotated the glass and sipped. He very much liked the taste.

~

It was coming up to eight thirty and the restaurant was already gradually emptying. The lively Italian group had just left. Linda offered to pay half the bill, but macho Ahmad would not hear it. To him, a deal was a deal. As they left the restaurant, the air was cool and fresh in the month of April and they decided to walk the fifteen minutes to Ahmad's new home for coffee. While walking, Ahmad had his hands in his side pockets, just like most men. Linda put her right arm on the inside of Ahmad's left arm, and the two maintained their paces in perfect synchrony as Ahmad shortened his pace slightly. Eventually, Ahmad took his left hand out of his pocket, and took Linda's hand.

It was the first time in his life that he held a woman's soft and gentle hand, and it was truly an enormous pleasure and a unique experience for him. He just could not believe how strong, sensual feelings could be transmitted through the hands between a man and a woman. He still remembered when his mother would put the palm of her hand on his forehead to feel the degree of his fever when he was sick with tonsillitis, a frequent occurrence back in his childhood, and how comforting that was. But this was quite different, and so powerful.

As he gently squeezed her hand, the couple turned their heads toward each other and smiled broadly. They continued walking with their fingers clasped into each other's, all the way to the apartment block. It was very quiet in the apartment, and the two assumed that Moosa and Sharif were out for the evening. *How convenient,* Ahmad thought.

~

As they entered Ahmad's room, the moon was shining brilliantly through the bow window and Linda, who had just consumed half a bottle of wine, took the initiative. She turned around and faced Ahmad, putting her hands on his back and pulling him toward her. She held him to her ample breasts while she placed her cheek against his. She could feel Ahmad's racing heartbeats, even through those big breasts. Silently she broke cheek contact, and brought her lips to his. It was evident that Ahmad had never kissed a girl in his life, but Linda took her time and slowly went into a very sensuous and wet kiss with him, as he began to reciprocate.

As they broke loose, they smiled at each other, and this time it was Ahmad who came back for more. But then, as though instinctively, he started planting kisses all over her face: on the cheeks and the forehead and then back to her lips. When he got down to her neck, Linda went crazy with passion. He had discovered her erogenous zone, he thought. Little did he know, at that point, that there was a lot more to come.

She unbuttoned his shirt and gently rubbed his nipples with slow, circular strokes as he breathed noisily with eyes closed. Within a minute his trousers were pulled down, and as he stepped out of them his erection was clearly attempting to break through his underpants. Linda looked down at it and reminded herself that middle-aged Humaid never could do that at such speed. In fact, he needed a helping hand—literally. For her, it was so exciting seducing such a young virgin with all the passion and performance she had fantasized about.

She lost no time in removing her clothes in the moonlight streaming through the bow window. As she stood totally naked, she could see Ahmad's eyes almost popping out of his head. She now pulled his underpants down.

She led Ahmad by the hand to the bed, where she had enjoyed so much sex before, and lay on her back, pulling Ahmad on top of her. Ahmad knew nothing about foreplay. It was just a matter of forceful entry for him. The sensation was so overwhelming for him that he came within seconds, just as Linda was starting to get into the rhythm. The heavy panting came to an abrupt end to the deep embarrassment of Ahmad, who turned his face away from Linda as he still lay on top of her, not knowing what to say. Although Linda was clearly disappointed with her aborted pleasure, she reminded herself of her first sexual encounter and how clumsy and ignorant she was.

"Did you like that?" Linda asked to break the silence.

"I am sorry. I finished too quickly. I could not stop myself."

"That just means that it was very exciting for you."

"But it was not exciting for you. I am sorry."

"You know what? Next time, it will be."

"Next time?"

"Sure! In a little while, you will be ready again."

"How do you know? I feel that I … emptied everything."

"I started fifteen years ahead of you; I know these things. Trust me."

～

Ahmad slid off Linda, and lay on his left side, facing her, putting his right hand on her left breast. She shuffled toward him and put her lips to his, to which he hungrily reciprocated. She slid her left hand slowly down to his limp organ, to his sudden moan of pleasure. She started that rhythmic movement which Ahmad had used hundreds of times on himself. She was absolutely right of course, for Ahmad was ready for the encore within ten minutes. But that time, Linda reversed positions, and rode her new young lover to an earth-moving climax.

Over the next year, Ahmad and Linda settled into a very happy relationship, and Linda continued to sleep in the apartment most nights of the week, because Ahmad's sexual stamina seemed endless. But his studies were getting more complex every month, mainly because he had to cover more ground in anatomy, physiology, biochemistry, and later pharmacology. They were all subjects which required memory and learning by heart. He struggled with biochemistry and had to dedicate more and more time to studying it; until he met Ann, that is.

Ann had done a bachelor of science degree, with honors in biochemistry, before joining the medical school. She knew the subject backward. When Ahmad met her by chance at the university cafeteria, he thought that she was very smart, and pretty as well. She was interested in his stories about Aden and in the different culture of people in that country. When she was a child, her parents lived in Kuwait, where her father was employed as a petroleum engineer. When it was time for her to go to school, she was sent back to Scotland, but she would go back during her long summer breaks, flights paid by the Kuwaiti company. But she still remembered a few Arabic words and recognized Arabic music when heard it on the radio by chance. It was only natural that Ahmad would admit to her his difficulties with biochemistry, which somewhat surprised her, for the subject was so interesting and easy for her.

A few weeks after that casual meeting, Ahmad took what was designated the professional examination, but he failed the biochemistry section. He was devastated, and depressed, and he considered quitting the study of medicine. He wrote a letter to his father telling him the bad news and warning him that he might leave the faculty of medicine and that medicine was not for him. There was enormous concern in the family. They could not figure out how their brilliant son, who was consistently top of the class back home, would fail any exam. He had aced all exams at Aden College. His father wrote that he would come over to Edinburgh to help and support him. At that point, Ahmad needed to stop his parents from coming over to babysit him and embarrass him before his friends. He asked Ann if she would give him private tuition, if he would pay her. Ann readily agreed but suggested that, instead of payment, Ahmad would teach her everything about Yemen and that part of the world. He was therefore able to write back to his father that he had the biochemistry problem under control.

~

Ann's intervention began to show results. Ahmad was pleasantly surprised, for he had convinced himself that he was becoming stupid, and that he would have to quit his medical studies because he would never cross that hurdle of biochemistry. The exam re-sits, as they were called, were to occur three months later. His nearly weekly meetings with Ann gradually came to be events to look forward to. Ahmad tried to deny this to himself. After all, she was only there to teach him and was probably not interested in him as a man. What's more, he already had a regular girlfriend who was very attached to him, and whom he cherished for his physical, if not emotional, needs. When he went into the examination room to tackle his biochemistry paper, Ahmad was much more relaxed than at the initial exam, and almost brimming with confidence. When he found out two weeks later that he did indeed pass the exam, Ann was the first to know, and they decided that they would go out to celebrate.

"It's a nice restaurant you've chosen," Ann said.

"It wasn't difficult. There are only two: the Ganges and the Bombay. And someone told me the Ganges was better. So, here we are."

"There is a strong smell of spices though."

"Yes, you will find that in all Indian restaurants. They use curry to make their food. Are you going to be adventurous and try some?"

"Of course I am an adventurous person," she said with a smile. "But is this anything like the food you have back in Aden?"

"Ours is similar, only less spicy than in India. But rice is very much a common ingredient in both. In Aden, which is a port city, there is a lot of fish in our food."

"I love fish."

"You mean Scottish fish and chips?"

"That too. You must like it, don't you?"

"Only if served traditionally: on newspaper!"

Almost two hours later, the couple walked out of the restaurant into the dark cool night, around eight thirty, feeling satiated, and somewhat inebriated after sharing a whole bottle of fruity Gewurztraminer. Ahmad took Ann's hand and held it lightly, prepared to let go if Ann pulled it away. She did not, but squeezed back. They turned their heads toward each other and smiled.

"My head is spinning," said Ann, "I should have ordered coffee after the meal."

"I know just the place where you can get a strong cup of coffee."

They turned and smiled at each other as they walked nonchalantly toward his apartment, where they made passionate love.

As they came back down to earth from that lofty peak of pleasure, Ann looked at him demurely and said, "I don't usually do it on a first date, you know."

"I am glad you did though. Why did you break the rule?"

"Because you are so special; you are very special to me."

"And you are gorgeous, and so hot."

"Do you think so?"

"Of course I do. You have a beautiful body and an intelligent mind. How many people can say that? But this was not our first date, in any case. We have been meeting almost every week for three months now."

"Oh, yes, I forgot about our biochemical romance! It's that wonderful *chemistry* between us!"

～

As they lay on their backs, they heard the door handle being turned, at first tentatively and then much more firmly and repeatedly as Linda tried to open the door. When the door did not open, Linda started calling Ahmad's name repeatedly, but she heard no response. Ahmad pretended that he was not there, putting his index finger on his lips, for he did not want to have a confrontation with Linda in the presence of his new girlfriend. Ann looked puzzled but played along, and made no sound. Later, Ahmad had to reassure her that he had broken off with the other woman.

Later in the week Ahmad leveled with Linda. She found it difficult to be dumped by Ahmad, even though she knew from the start that, being fifteen years older, she could never hope for a long-term relationship. He did run into her at the pub several weeks later and was happy to see her with a Scottish man of her own age. He always felt a certain degree of gratitude to her for taking his virginity.

Over the next two years, Ahmad's performance at university was much more satisfactory, and he began to look forward to clinical training at the Royal Infirmary once he finished his theoretical studies of pathology, forensic medicine, and public health. Ann, who was equally busy with her own studies, was very supportive of him, and was there for him, whenever he needed her.

CHAPTER 7

~

BACK IN LONDON

Things became more complex and difficult for Biddy and Hasan once they became lovers. On the one hand they wanted to keep the relationship secret, and yet they were subjected to temptation every day and night, because they lived under the same roof. They even slept in adjacent rooms, and shared a bathroom, while the parents and Stephen slept upstairs. They would occasionally resort to what they called "a quick one" in the bathroom which they shared. Although the McCartneys considered the possibility of a relationship developing between the two, they would quickly dismiss it.

"What was that sound?" Mr. McCartney asked his wife.

"I don't know. I thought I heard something, like a muffled cry from downstairs."

"I wonder what those two are up to. I am really worried."

"Oh, I don't think Biddy would get into anything with Hasan. I am not even sure that she likes him that much."

"I don't know. I have seen how she looks at him, especially since we went to Carlisle. We should have never left them here by themselves. This guy comes from a very conservative Muslim background, but he is young and human, and his hormones are very active at this age."

"You mean like yours were when you seduced me?"

"Are you sure it was not the other way round?" asked Mr. McCartney with a smile.

"I was a completely innocent twenty-year-old busy working away and had no interest in men at the time."

"You soon made up for it, didn't you?"

"I fell for your charm, I suppose. You were at university then, just after the war, and there was a shortage of men."

"But that was fine, because we are the same … I mean we were both British, and were born here, and went to the same church. This boy is Arab and Muslim, and he is here only to study and will go home as soon as he finishes his law degree."

"He would make a good catch for Biddy … if only he was, as you say, British. Anyway, why are we worrying about this? I am sure Biddy will not allow anything to happen; I did have a word with her."

"Really, and what did she say?"

"She just told me not to worry."

"Maybe you are right; maybe I am worrying unnecessarily. Only I would never forgive myself if he was taking advantage of her. You know he is three years older, and she might look up to him."

"Go to sleep, dear. I will have a word with Biddy again tomorrow."

〜

The legal exams at the end of first year meant a very busy period for Hasan, who had to do a lot more intensive reading than usual, but his phenomenal memory helped him pass the exams with flying colors. The afternoon he got the news, he wanted Biddy to be the first to know. He rushed home two hours ahead of his usual time. Biddy was home, as was Stephen, but the parents were out at a late afternoon reception held at the church for flood victims in the Philippines. He found Stephen looking at comic books in the family room. He asked and was told that Biddy was in her room. Hasan produced two half crowns, worth five shillings, and asked Stephen to go down to the store three blocks down the road to buy chocolate bars for everyone to celebrate his passing his exams. Stephen, who had never handled that much money before, immediately went on his errand.

Ahmad entered Biddy's room, virtually shouting out his good news. Biddy ran into his arms, and they were locked in a long passionate kiss. Realizing that they were alone at last, and in the privacy of Biddy's room, the couple half undressed quickly and proceeded to make hurried and passionate love for ten minutes, all the time knowing that Stephen would be back in about fifteen minutes. During those stolen moments of passion, after a forced abstention of nearly one week, the two came together with a big bang. As they disengaged, Biddy looked down at Hasan's organ.

"Where is the condom? How did you take it off so fast?"

"I didn't use any. I am sorry. I could not stop in my room to get one, because I wanted to see you so desperately to tell you about my results. I don't even know if there is one in my secret hiding place. Why didn't you remind me?"

"Me, remind you? You are supposed to know what to do."

"Don't worry. Nothing will happen. It may be your safe period. When did you have your period?"

"Two weeks ago; this is the worst time to do it."

"Look, get into the bathroom and wash out my stuff, and it should be all right."

"Are you sure? What if ..."

"Oh, I am sure everything will be all right. You can't get pregnant from one ..."

"Why not?"

"That's what I read, somewhere."

"You'd better be right. I'll be ruined if ..."

"No, don't worry, my love. Nothing will happen."

They heard the door close and quickly got dressed. Biddy came out first, after attempting to wash out Hasan's ejaculate, to see Stephen with all the chocolate he managed to buy for five shillings. Hasan joined them for a chocolate party.

~

Hasan had a three-week holiday after his exams. He decided to visit his old classmate in Edinburgh, something he had planned by mail with Ahmad. When the two got together over many hours during the visit, they both noted big changes in each other. Their interests had diverged, their attitudes were different, and their close friendship had cooled considerably. Hasan was allowed to sleep on the sofa in the boys' flat, and Moosa as well as Sharif got to know him fairly well. During that short time they managed to teach him how to play Sudanese whist, but all attempts to introduce him to alcohol failed. What the boys found most annoying was his insistence on praying five times a day, preceded by the obligatory ablutions, which made access to the bathroom difficult at times and produced puddles of water on the bathroom floor, which he did not bother to mop up. By the time he left, all three boys were relieved and decided never to be so hospitable in the future. Ahmad realized then how little he and his long-time friend still had in common. Their friendship had changed forever.

~

Hasan's train arrived at Eusten Station at four in the afternoon, but it was almost five when he arrived at the McCartney residence. Stephen was in his room, but Mrs. McCartney was downstairs and was excited to see him. She asked many questions about Edinburgh while she offered him a cup of tea with biscuits. However, she herself had nothing new to report, except that Biddy looked somewhat depressed during the time he was away. As she said that, Mrs. McCartney studied his face for any reaction, but she detected none. A few minutes later Biddy arrived. As she entered the family room, she saw Hasan sitting on the sofa, cup in hand, and almost ran toward him, but then she stopped in her tracks as her mother emerged from the kitchen next door.

"Hello! You're back. How was it?" she asked.

"Oh, it was fun, and different. I caught up with the news of my old classmate Ahmad Shawqi and met a few of his friends."

"Did you see any men in kilts?"

"Yes, but not too many."

"And did you get to speak to them?"

"Not really. I wouldn't have understood what they were saying anyway. They do have a peculiar accent, don't they? But how have you been?"

Biddy glanced at her mother and then said, "Fine. I did want to ask your advice about a book I saw in the shop window just three blocks from here, near Koots. Do you have time to go there with me before the stores close at six?"

"Why would I be able to advise you on what to read? I am only a law student."

"It is because you are! The title is *The History of the Legal Status of Women*. I have a school assignment about that very subject. I actually have to do an essay about women's human rights, and I think this book should be very helpful."

"All right, let's go!"

The two left hurriedly, leaving Mrs. McCartney to tidy up the coffee table.

As they turned the corner from the house, they stopped on the footpath facing each other and hugged for a long time.

"Hasan, that story about the book, it's only a story. I had to see you alone. I have been sick with worry. My period is two weeks late; it has never happened before. What are we going to do?"

It all came out in a rapid torrent. Hasan was taken aback; he felt a sinking feeling in his belly, mixed with nausea.

"Are you sure?"

"Of course I am sure; it never happened before."

"Maybe there is some other explanation. Have you seen the doctor?"

"No. I wanted you to be the first to know. I wanted to share this catastrophe with someone I love and trust, and who would understand."

"Does your mother know?"

"No, of course not. She would kill me," Biddy replied with anger in her voice.

"Do you know any friends in your class who have been through this?" Hasan asked.

"No! Girls don't go around advertising that they are pregnant when they are not married."

"No, I meant ..."

"I know what you meant. What on earth am I going to do now? My life is finished. How many times have I told you about always using a condom?"

"I always did. It was only once, when we both got carried away ..."

"Yes, and it had to be just that once to get me pregnant. I am ruined; my parents will kill me; I will have to leave school; I can't go to university now. What am I going to do? What are *you* going to do about it?"

"Me? What can I do? I don't know anyone in this country. You know that I am a student here for four years to get a degree."

"Well, now you will also get a baby!"

"Why are you blaming me for this? You were a full partner in it."

"But it was *you* who was supposed to wear the condom."

"You could have stopped me, or reminded me. You know, that night when ..."

"I have to assume that you are wearing one every time. How can a girl know if the condom is on, if she does not see it or feel it with her hand? During the ... thing ... she only feels the fullness ... the stiffness, that's all."

"Listen, Biddy, maybe we are jumping to conclusions. Maybe it is a false alarm. The period can be delayed by factors other than pregnancy. In fact, in our lecture series we had a full lecture on pregnancy and the development of the fetus. It was fascinating to see pictures of the fetus at three months and four months ... and six months. We need to know these things as lawyers."

"Well, I don't need any lecture to tell me that I am pregnant. What are you going to do about it?"

"What would you expect from me?"

"That you will be with me on this, that you will do the right thing, that you will still love me, as you told me so many times."

"Of course I love you. But I am only a student. How can we possibly live on my meager allowance?"

"Don't expect any help from my dad. He will disown me and throw me out of the house."

"I think your mother will support you; she is a woman, after all. If it is confirmed, and you don't have a period next month, you will need to tell her. She will find out sooner or later. It is better to go to her and throw yourself at her mercy."

~

That evening at supper, Biddy was clearly distraught and quiet. Hasan was trying to make polite conversation, but his mind was distracted. Mrs. McCartney wondered what was wrong, but Biddy explained that her school performance deteriorated lately and she was therefore concerned. Mr. McCartney talked about the ongoing activities in his church and about the upcoming christenings on Sunday, to which he was looking forward, pointing out that of all his duties as the parish priest, christening babies was the most joyful and fulfilling. Stephen was the only one who tried to introduce some humor into the conversation around the table, without much success.

~

Over the next few weeks, Biddy's health deteriorated. Her appetite dropped, and she began to feel nauseated. Her sleep pattern became highly fragmented, and she began to be morose, avoiding conversation and spending more time secluded in her bedroom. However, she carefully camouflaged all these symptoms from the rest of the family. It was in fact her science teacher, Mrs. Wakefield, who detected a problem. She had always been very kind to Biddy, as she was to all the students in the class. But she was especially caring about the girls. She knew that at that age they were far more fragile than the boys. She had gone through emotional upheavals of her own when she was a teenager, and she still remembered.

One afternoon, she asked Biddy to stay behind at the end of the science class, ostensibly to discuss her poor test results.

"So, how is it going, Biddy?"

"Fine, Miss."

"Are you sure now?"

"Yes. Why do you ask?"

"Well, you know that your test results were not as good as usual, so I was wondering if I could help perhaps."

"Oh, I have not been feeling well. It will be all right, I am sure."

"Did you see your family doctor?"

"No, it's not that kind of problem."

"What kind of problem is it then?"

"Just some trouble with sleep, and worries."

"Yes, Biddy, the two often go together. What are you worried about?

"Oh, exams and all that."

"But until these last few weeks you were doing very well, and you always aced your exams."

"In that case, I am sure it will pass; I just have to study more."

Mrs. Wakefield came to the point. "Any problem with boys? I did not think you had a boyfriend at the school here. When I was your age, I had a lot of boyfriend trouble, believe me."

Biddy was silent for a long time.

"You know, Biddy, if there is a problem, it won't just go away if you don't talk about it and seek help. Who is he?"

"He is not at school; he is a university student," Biddy said with some pride.

"I see. So he is a bit older than you? You just turned eighteen a few days ago?"

"How did you know that?"

"I know because I care, and I make it my business to know."

"You have always been kind to me, and I appreciate it."

"Sometimes it is easier to talk to someone outside your own family; so talk to me … please."

"He is twenty-one, and he is a foreign student studying to be a lawyer."

"All right. That sounds nice. Go on!"

"He is a lodger at our house, staying in the room vacated by my brother who went to study in America."

"So, you have fallen for the foreign student. What else? Did you break up? Did he drop you for another girl? Boys are like that, you know. They like new toys. You've heard the saying, 'Toys for boys'?"

"I wish!"

"I am still listening, Biddy. You need to unload all this enormous weight of worry."

"Mrs. Wakefield, I … I … I think … I think I am pregnant, and I am frightened."

Biddy went into a long paroxysm of sobbing as Mrs. Wakefield tried unsuccessfully to console her. As she lifted her eyes to look into those of Mrs. Wakefield, what she saw was a warm, sympathetic smile rather than the look of disgust and horror she had expected.

"You mean you are not shocked, Miss?"

"Of course not! You are not the first teenage girl, or the last one, to go through this, Biddy."

"I don't care about any other girls just now. Why did it have to happen to me? My dad is a pastor of the church; he will be devastated."

"Would it help you, Biddy, if I told you that I went through it when I was your age? And that was in the forties, when society was much more puritanical than now."

A look of utter surprise came over Biddy's face as she asked "Really? I cannot believe that. Are you just saying that to make me feel better?"

"Why is it so difficult to believe?"

"Because … because … you are so wise and would not let that happen to you, not like stupid me."

"I might seem wise to you today, but … I too was a teenager; a long time ago it would seem now. That's the time when we all make our mistakes. That's the age when you are expected to control your passion and your lust, but your lust controls you instead. You go from one orgasm to another, and all you want is for the man to love you more. No wonder in some cultures in the Horn of Africa they make sure girls are secluded from boys, and some routinely circumcise little girls."

"But that's barbaric."

"Of course it is, but that is how they justify it. They hardly ever hear of pregnancy outside wedlock."

"So what happened to you, Miss?"

"That was just after the war. There was so much turmoil in our lives; there was anxiety and fear everywhere. So many men were lost, and even more were badly wounded or psychologically scarred. There was a shortage of men and an abundance of women trying to find love and attention. To cut a long story short, I got pregnant. In those days we did not even have the basic condoms of today. Some women might get hold of the diaphragm, or it was simply the so-called safe period. Well, mine was not so safe." The teacher paused and stared at the wall.

"What did you do?"

"I hate to talk about it, but I went through a backstreet, barbaric abortion, and the man abandoned me."

"I should do the same then?"

"It's not that simple. That backstreet abortionist did not warn me about all the complications, and I was so desperate to get rid of my shame. I remember how painful it was when she introduced the plastic tube into my uterus and injected some irritant liquid, some acid I think she said, to make it contract and expel the fetus. It was irritant all right; I can still remember. But it was not sterile, so when I tried to get pregnant years later I kept having recurrent miscarriages; and the obstetrician told me it must have been due to chronic irritation and scarring inside the uterus. You know what these doctors are like. They spend five minutes with you, then pronounce some sort of diagnosis, but do not tell you what to do about it. For them reaching that diagnosis is an end in itself."

"I know, you are absolutely right. So what happened?"

"Nothing! My husband and I were unable to raise a family; we resigned ourselves to that."

"I have to do the same. I don't care about the complications. I hope I die in the process. That should solve the problem for me and my parents."

"No, don't talk like that, Biddy. You are so young and beautiful and intelligent, and you have the whole of your future ahead of you. Please don't try anything stupid like that. Let me speak to your mom. I know her; she came to school a few times. She seemed like a kind woman."

"My dad will kill me. I just know that. He is a minister at his church. The scandal will be too much for him."

"I know he is, although I haven't met him. But he will come around to accepting it."

$\sim$

Mrs. Wakefield made an appointment to see Mrs. McCartney at home, pretending that she wanted to discuss Biddy's school performance. She had asked Biddy to be at home that morning, because she wanted her to be there when she broke the bad news to her mother. She reckoned that Mrs. McCartney's reaction would be modified by her own presence there to protect Biddy.

Over a cup of tea, Mrs. Wakefield began, "I am sure you have noticed how depressed Biddy has been lately."

"Yes, of course. There is something bothering her, but she refuses to talk about it. How is her school work? I suppose you are here because of that?"

"Well, the two are very much linked, as you can imagine. She is very worried, and I want to talk about her depression, if you don't mind. So, I'll get to the point, Mrs. McCartney. It's not the first time and it won't be the last time that a young impressionable girl gets pregnant ..."

The look on Mrs. McCartney's face suddenly changed, and her pink cheeks turned pale, as she put her tea cup down in the saucer, spilling some tea into it.

"Oh my god! I was so afraid of that. I thought about it, and then I dismissed it. I just said to myself it could not happen to our daughter. You always say to yourself these things happen to other people, but not to you. What are we going to do? What can I do? Her father will be devastated. He kept wondering what was happening downstairs, when we heard sounds from there. How do you know that, Mrs. Wakefield? Did she confide in you, but not in her own mother? Oh my god! We have let her down. We should never have allowed that reckless boy into our house, and I was the one who liked him and was so kind to him."

"Mrs. McCartney, Elizabeth, sometimes it is easier to confide in a friend rather than in family. The risk in hurting someone you love is a lot lower that way. She knew you would not take it well. I had the same problem when I was about her age, and I could not bring myself to tell my mother either."

"You? You got pregnant too?"

"Yes, I did. We just don't hear about them, but there must be thousands of girls getting pregnant every year."

"I suppose you are right. But why did our Biddy have to be one of them? Why?"

"Because she is young and passionate, and human, and easily led by a man, like you and I were when we were her age; at least I was."

"No, you are right. We all were, one way or another. But what to do now?"

"Well, if you don't mind, allow me to call her in here so that we can all talk about it. You are her mother, and her best friend, maybe the only friend just now. You need to talk about all this, after I leave, but allow me to start the conversation."

~

It was a very traumatic meeting for Biddy, and the saddest experience in years for the mother, who was extremely concerned about her husband's reaction to the news. She knew him well enough to realize that he would not take it very well. Indeed she thought it might give him a heart attack. He was a god-fearing man with self-imposed strict moral standards, which were getting even stricter as he got older. She, therefore, decided to postpone announcing the bombshell to him, until Hasan left the house, with the pretext that he was going to join an old school friend from Aden. Biddy was therefore to ask Hasan to find other accommodation within days, and she was to warn him that her father may otherwise do him physical harm. Although Hasan was aware that he was living in England, not in Aden, he still could imagine the type of retribution that would be meted to him by a girl's father and her brothers in such circumstances in Aden. Biddy, on the other hand, did not wish to see Hasan leave their home and thus lose touch with him. She was still deeply in love and needed his support more than ever before. However, she did manage to persuade him to find a bed-sitter to rent within walking distance from home.

~

Over dinner later that week, Biddy was not at the table.

"Where is Biddy this evening?" Mr. McCartney asked his wife.

"She is out with Stephen to the cinema, to see that James Bond film."

"So, we have the house to ourselves then?" Mr. McCartney said with a wink, which couldn't have come at a worse time.

"Biddy is not well, James."

"I thought she looked quiet, even depressed, lately. What's wrong with her? Has she seen the doctor?"

"It's not that kind of problem."

"Oh? What kind then? Is she in love?"

"Funny that you mention that; she is indeed … I might as well spell it out; she's pregnant!"

Mr. McCartney's knife fell out of his right hand into his lap.

"Jesus Christ! Pregnant? What do you mean? How can she be?"

"James, are you blind or what? It's Hasan, our lodger. They fancied each other, it would seem. Young people do that, or have you forgotten?"

"You mean that bastard whom we sheltered in our home? He took advantage of a young girl five years his junior …"

"Three!"

"Three, four, five, what difference does it make? He still took advantage of a younger gullible girl. She was not yet eighteen; that's against the law. And under our own roof! What an idiot I must be in his eyes when he can fornicate with my daughter downstairs while I am sleeping upstairs. No wonder he made a run for it before I could break his bloody Arab neck."

"I too have been blind. I thought it was the exams and her deteriorating school performance causing her to worry; it was the other way round."

"You are the one that is supposed to watch your daughter. I have to go to work all day, and on the weekend, and some evenings too. I cannot be expected to monitor that bastard."

"So, it's my fault now. It was you who was keen on renting Albert's vacant room for extra cash."

"You agreed that we needed the extra cash. We did advertise for a girl lodger, but there was none. So we decided *together* to take him rather than keep the room empty. And then we were dumb enough to keep their rooms next to each other, downstairs, while we slept upstairs. We should have put Stephen next to his sister …"

Mrs. McCartney interrupted her husband's tirade. "And bring Hasan upstairs, in Stephen's tiny room, so that he can be witness to all our conversation, and to your snoring? You also said you did not want to share the bathroom with him. Remember? You said he would spend too long in the bathroom shaving and doing his ablutions before his five prayers a day, whereas Stephen would not. So don't try to put the blame on me now."

"Look, Bettie, whenever there is a catastrophe within a family, like a suicide, or death or pregnancy, I mean *unwanted* pregnancy, parents tend to trade accusations and blame, and often split up. As a minister of the church, I know that, and I counsel my parishioners accordingly. Let's not argue; we need to support each other; we need to find a way out. If this ever gets out to my parishioners, I will be ruined. I won't be able to look them in the eye; I'd have to resign."

"What shall we do then? Maybe he will marry her."

"There's another problem for you. Even if he did, they cannot be married in church; he's Muslim. I can just imagine the headlines in the *Global News*. Where is he now, that despicable bastard?"

"He moved to an apartment with another young man from his country. Are you thinking of talking to him?"

"What I want is to kill him, but I will have to swallow my pride and ask him to do the honorable thing."

"You had better be prepared to go to his place and talk to him nicely. I have a feeling he won't come to this house; he would be scared. I'll ask Biddy to make the arrangements, shall I?"

"Imagine! I give this young foreigner a roof over his head, I try to help him integrate, and what does he do? He seduces my daughter and gets her pregnant, and then runs away from his responsibility like a coward and expects me to go to him, cap in hand, begging him to marry her. And she'll probably end up in some dusty Yemeni town as one of his four wives and three goats."

"Poor Biddy! We have failed this poor innocent girl by exposing her to temptation, and him too. He too is a hot-blooded young man; he did what other young horny men would do."

"So, you are finding excuses for him now. Whose side are you on, his or your own daughter's?"

"How dare you say that? Of course I care about my daughter more than anyone in the world. And may I remind you that I am a woman who had three pregnancies, and each one was an ordeal. But isn't his behavior typical of anyone at that age? Isn't it you men who seduce as many women as you can and brag about it too? You're never happy until you stick your … thing into some gullible, impressionable woman. And when you were at that age, did you ever remind yourself that you were seducing the daughter of some unsuspecting teacher, or coalminer, or maybe even a priest? Of course not! She was fair game, if she fell for your charm. Well, it's your turn now. Maybe his people are right, after all, when they keep boys and girls apart. Not even seeing each other, never mind dating, and we dare to criticize them."

"All right, you've made your point. I said I would go see him."

~

At the appointed time, Mr. McCartney rang the bell of Hasan's flat. Hasan had rented it through an advert in a local paper for three months only, because the Polish landlord was planning on selling it after doing a few renovations.

The men did not greet each other. Their faces were very serious, without smile but also without visible animosity. They both knew that they had to get it over with, and both hoped that there would be no shouting, or worse.

Hasan had boiled the kettle and made a pot of tea. "I made some tea," he said as he pushed a cup toward Mr. McCartney.

"Thank you." He took a sip and put the cup back in the saucer.

"How's Mrs. McCartney?"

"Fine! Not really. She is very upset about Biddy, as you can imagine. So am I."

"I am sorry; I am also upset. It was an accident because we did not take precautions that one single time. Ask her, if you don't believe me."

"What's the use of asking? It's too late now," he replied angrily. "The important thing now is what are *you* going to do about it, as an honorable soon-to-be lawyer?"

"What should I ... what can I do about it?"

"Let me get to the point. Have you two talked about marriage?"

"Not really. I am not even sure that she wants to do that. She is in shock at present ... more in depression."

"But you got her into that situation. You have to take the initiative and do the honorable thing, don't you think?"

"I don't know where to start. I am only a first-year student with no money or house or degree."

"Well, the degree will come in another two years. You have a bursary, and you are renting a flat. Her mother and I can help. She will help Biddy with the baby later. Together we can make this happen."

"The flat is only a rental one for the next three months. I need the peace of mind that we have our own flat, so that the monthly bursary can cover our electricity and other bills, as well as food."

"And how do you propose to do that?"

"I was thinking that you would buy this flat, as our wedding present perhaps? The owner wants four thousand, six hundred pounds. Maybe he will come down a bit. And the flat should be in my name."

"What! What on earth for?"

"Because in my culture, the husband is responsible for his wife and children. I will undertake to look after them, always. I also will pay you back half the cost of the flat by the time I graduate. Think of it as a short-term, interest-free loan to me, and a gift of the other half to your daughter."

"You must be joking. That is my annual salary."

"Well, I cannot see me coming back to your home, and I suspect that you would not want that either."

"You got that right!"

"In that case, mine is the only reasonable suggestion."

Mr. McCartney was seething with anger and considered walking out of the flat. He remained silent for a few moments, reminding himself of Biddy's growing fetus. "What about the wedding expenses?"

"In my country the fathers pay for that, and since my father is far away, and is a poor man, you will need to cover those too. In fact, if my father knew that I was to marry a Christian woman, he would disown me, before having a heart attack."

"A heart attack! Why? Is it a crime?"

"Not a crime, but he would want me to marry a Muslim like me. But we are allowed to marry Christian or Jewish women, but not Hindus or others."

"Why only those two religions? Are they better than the others?"

"They share what we call 'the book,' meaning that the Quran shares much with the Torah and the Bible."

"What if you fell in love with a Hindu or got her pregnant?"

"She would have to convert first."

"And what if your sister wanted to marry a Christian or a Jew?"

"Oh, no, that's not allowed. He would have to convert to Islam. Many do."

"So why is it different for you and your sister? That's what I found out when I was working in India."

"I don't make the rules. We believe that in our patriarchal society the children of the marriage have to follow the father's religion, so even if a

Muslim man married a Christian woman, his children would be brought up Muslim. For example, Biddy's son …"

"Or daughter," Mr. McCartney interrupted.

"Yes … or daughter … would be Muslim."

Mr. McCartney had become aware of those rules during the time he spent in India, but now it was up close and personal. He said, "So, the wedding will be in the registrar's office. Obviously you cannot be married in church."

"Yes, that's right, but when we go back to Aden, my family will not accept Biddy unless she goes through an Islamic wedding conducted by a proper imam."

"How do you know she would want to go there? Have you asked her?"

"Of course not! She will have to follow her husband. I think she will, and might even like it there. I know several such mixed marriages there."

"Who do you want to invite from your side to the wedding ceremony?"

"Nobody! I don't know anyone here. But even if I did, I want to keep this secret. My father would disown me if he knew, and I might lose my bursary."

"Aren't you going to tell your parents about the baby?"

"That won't happen for another six months. I will decide then."

Mr. McCartney left the flat quite dejected. He had prepared himself for most of Hasan's answers but did not realize that he would have to buy him an apartment worth nearly the whole of his annual income. Back home, he discussed the meeting in detail with his wife. Although she too thought that they were being blackmailed by Hasan, she also saw the positive side of the arrangement. At least Biddy would return to normality, or so she hoped.

～

She busied herself with finding a suitable wedding dress for her daughter. She wanted it to be a happy and memorable occasion, for it only occurs once in a lifetime, at least for the majority of people. She had always fantasized about being the mother of the bride ever since Biddy reached adolescence. Now she was determined to play that role fully, even though her original fantasy included a church wedding with all her friends and family, many coming down from Carlisle.

At the time of the wedding, Biddy's abdomen still appeared normal. In her wedding dress, she looked absolutely stunning. A handful of her trusted girlfriends were invited, including Jill and Margaret, which added to her joy, especially since Hasan had no one on his side. As the guests came in, they all headed for the left side of the wedding hall, the bride's side, while the right pews remained nearly empty for the longest time, until Mrs. McCartney realized how asymmetrical it looked and persuaded some to sit on the right. Among these were Jill and Margaret who got themselves quite tipsy during the reception that followed, Jill flirting with a couple of the younger men there. That night the couple stayed at one of the four-star London hotels, also paid for by the McCartneys, for their first night of uninhibited and now legitimate lovemaking.

~

Over the next few days, Biddy gradually moved her belongings to her new home and returned to her school routine, now as a very young and pregnant but married woman. Her classmates fussed over her, and congratulated her. She was happy to have that much attention, although only a few days before she did not want anyone to know her secret. However, Jill made sure that as many students as possible knew. A couple of the boys who had claimed her as their girlfriend would tease her and would ask her to go to bed with them now that she was no longer a virgin. Biddy learned how to rebuff them, and soon they stopped badgering her. Whenever she had any worries, she would talk to her new friend and confidante, Mrs. Wakefield. At the end of the school year, she did well at her general certificate of education exams, but her application to study psychology in university did not secure her a place. She was advised to apply again the following year, not that she was all that keen on attending university given that she was only a few weeks away from delivery.

~

Her mother visited regularly and was very supportive. She would come over and cook wholesome meals for her and Hasan, especially since Biddy had acquired very little experience in cooking. Her father, on the other hand, stayed away most of the time, citing his work as the reason. But everyone knew that he did not want to see his son-in-law who had blackmailed him and extracted all that money from him during his hour of weakness, and impregnated his unwed teenage daughter. He did send messages of love to Biddy through his wife, which Biddy appreciated, although she tried to stay out of that dispute given her mixed loyalties to her husband and father.

In the final few weeks of her pregnancy, tension began to appear between the newlyweds, for Hasan was always demanding to have sex with his wife, despite her late pregnancy. She had gained a disproportionate amount of weight, without developing any signs of eclampsia of pregnancy, and she found it physically awkward to accommodate her husband, much as she wanted to, for she always suspected that he would not hesitate to cheat on her if given half a chance. One night as he was trying to be intimate with his reluctant wife, he reminded her that if he was back home, he would take another wife as his religion would permit him to do. When she asked him what he would do with his second wife when his first wife was again available for his sexual desires, he replied with little hesitation that he would just divorce her. It was after that exchange that Biddy lost respect for Hasan, who was not willing to abstain for a few weeks in consideration of her physical status. The warnings of her father about how cultural differences of couples mattered came rushing back at her.

CHAPTER 8

∼

JASMINE

Biddy delivered around three in the morning. Because that was her first pregnancy, it was a difficult and slow vaginal delivery, which as the baby's large head was pushing against her perineum required a quick episiotomy to avoid a disastrous perineal tear. And with that, Biddy heard her little daughter's lusty cry as she took in the first breath of her life. Suddenly, all the pain and suffering was forgotten as she looked down between her legs. But all she could see was a thick mop of black hair contrasting with her own golden blonde one. But the nurse wrapped the baby in a warm towel and handed it over to Biddy, whose look of happiness could not possibly be put into words.

∼

When he arrived at the hospital, Hasan was quite anxious about what he was going to see in the baby. For some reason, he assumed it would be a boy. At least, if it was a boy, the chances were much higher that his parents would be less upset than if it was a girl. As he entered the screened area where Biddy was holding her lovely little daughter, he beamed a smile toward Biddy and then her mother and bent down to kiss his wife on her forehead. His mother-in-law got out of her chair and offered it to him, then left the room to give them some privacy.

"It's a girl, Hasan, our beautiful girl. She is almost eight pounds."

"Oh ... yes, she looks lovely, with lots of hair already. Are you okay?"

"I am now. It was not easy because of her size. I had to have an episiotomy."

"What's that? Anesthetic?"

"No, it is a cut down there to make it easier for the head to come out."

"Does it hurt?"

"Not so much now, but it was awful at the time."

"What's that on her back, that big dark mark on her lower back? Looks like a large ink blot"

"I don't know. Mother did not know either. I'll ask the nurse when she comes in."

Hasan could not wait. He called a nurse.

"Oh, that's a Mongolian blue spot. It's nothing," the nurse explained.

"Mongolian? You mean she will be a Mongol? There is no Mongolian blood in our family."

"No, no, she's fine. But if one of the parents is ... you know ... colored, or from the Mediterranean area, then the baby might have it. It goes away by itself after a few weeks."

"Thank God for that."

"What shall we call her?" Biddy asked.

"I don't know yet. I was going over some names for a boy on my way here in the bus."

"Are you disappointed then?"

"This is Allah's choice."

"Well, she's here now. I was thinking of calling her Barbara, after my grandmother."

"Barbara? Are you serious? She will be the laughing stock of everyone in Aden. Did you know that it is the name of a port in Somalia from which sheep are exported to Aden? The school kids will nickname her 'Somali Sheep.'"

"How would I know that?"

"We will call her Jasmine … Yes, Jasmine … because it is good in both languages, and jasmine is white and has a nice smell."

Biddy knew that Hasan was not asking her opinion but rather telling her his final decision. She liked the name, as it happened, and shook her head in agreement.

He continued. "Congratulations, my dear, at least it is over. I have to go to a debate this afternoon so I'll catch a bus, and I'll be back either this evening or tomorrow. When do you come home?"

"I believe routine deliveries are discharged after four days, but it may be a week or longer because of the episiotomy."

~

Hasan was clearly dejected when he walked alone out of the hospital and toward the bus stop. At that point, the realization that his life was forever changed hit him, for there was a new human being linked to him in every kind of way, wherever he lived and whatever he did for the rest of his life. And he was only in his early twenties. His sad thoughts stayed with him all the way to the crowded bus stop.

"Hello, stranger," came a feminine voice behind him as a finger touched his shoulder. As he turned around, Jill was only a few inches in front of him.

"Gosh, Jill, what are you doing here? Do you live in this area?"

"Oh, no, I couldn't afford it. I came to the department store because of a sale on dresses, and I need to buy a new dress to attend an engagement party tonight. I always leave things to the last minute. But I believe you know Margaret? She was at your wedding, remember?"

"Of course I do. And she was with you at the school dance too."

"That's right. She must have left an impression on you. I am jealous."

"No, not really; she was a nice girl."

"And do you prefer nice girls or naughty girls?" Jill asked with a wink.

"I like all girls."

"I understand that you dooo! I can believe it too. But you chose Biddy. Or maybe she chose you? Anyway, how is dear Biddy?"

"She just delivered a baby in the early hours of the morning. I just came from there."

"How exciting for you both! Was it a boy or a girl?"

"A girl."

"But you don't sound very excited."

"Just tired and occupied with my university work; I am almost halfway through my degree now."

"Wow! Half a lawyer already! So are you a *law* or a *yer?*"

"You are funny. I like witty girls. And when they are pretty as well, I just fall for them."

"Thank you for noticing. So you have done half the battle?"

"The second half, I am told, is much worse."

"Sounds to me that you might need some distraction from all this boring legal stuff? Tell you what. Why don't I invite you to Margaret's engagement party tonight?"

"No, no, I am not really in the mood, and besides I cannot gate crash. Another time, perhaps."

"Margaret will be thrilled to see you, and you obviously fancied her, and there is no gate crashing involved. You will come as my *date* so to speak; not a real date, just for tonight. At least you should return the compliment to Margaret. After all, she attended your wedding so you owe her one."

"But why are you not going with your boyfriend?"

"Don't have one."

"How is that possible? A pretty girl like you, as I said before, so full of life."

"I'll have you know I am very choosey. I am waiting to meet a lawyer," Jill added with a smile.

"You always have the last word. You should study to be a lawyer yourself."

"Tell you what. This evening you will give me my first tutorial on how to become a lawyer."

Jill wrote the address quickly on a corner which she tore off the *Evening Times* that she was carrying and shouted, "Seven o'clock!" as Hasan quickly climbed onto the bus.

~

Hasan arrived twenty minutes late, after agonizing long over whether to go back to the hospital or to have fun with jolly Jill. As a strict nondrinker, it never crossed his mind to buy a bottle of something for the party. He need not have worried at all.

CHAPTER 9

JILL

Jill was standing a short distance outside the door of Margaret's building to be able to survey whoever was walking toward it. She wanted to join the party but wanted to make a grand entrance with Hasan, just to let the girls there know that he was her date, exclusively. She was pretty, but not as beautiful as Biddy. She had a great figure, however, that was so tightly hugged by her newly bought black silk dress, with a plunging neckline, that her nipples easily poked through the thin bra and dress, crowning her size thirty-six breasts. The lordosis of her lower back cascaded into very shapely and bulging buttocks that few men could ignore. She had natural wavy red hair and a few red freckles randomly distributed over her face and forearms. A beautiful gold-plated watch adorned her delicate left wrist, and a short gold necklace dangling from her neck and ending in a small golden heart pointing straight down, drawing even more attention to her deep cleavage.

When she saw Hasan walking toward the door, she did the same from the other direction, carrying a large shoulder bag on the left. As they met, with broad smiles, she took the initiative of closely hugging and kissing him on the cheek. To Hasan, she looked even more stunning than she had at the students' dance a few months before.

"You look ravishing."

"I'd rather be ravished!"

"There you go again with those words."

"Let's go in," Jill said as she pulled him gently by his left hand.

~

The room was already full of young women and men, with slightly more women, it seemed. They were all talking at the same time, and nearly everyone was standing with a glass of something, mostly beer for the men and wine, gin and tonic, or vodka and lime for the women. Margaret was deep inside the large living room of the flat and Jill again led Hasan by the hand and introduced him to Margaret and her fiancé. Margaret surprised him with a very warm and close hug. She seemed very happy and welcoming, which eliminated Hasan's lingering worries about gate crashing. Out of her shoulder bag, Jill brought a nicely wrapped gift box containing a special red wine and handing it to her friend said, "This is a special wine, guaranteed to keep a man up all night, if you see what I mean." She winked at the fiancé, who pinched Margaret on her bottom.

Jill and Hasan circulated in the crowded room, she with a gin and tonic and he with a cola. At one point, he had to convince one of the friendly but loud men that he was drinking his favorite rum and Coke just to stop the man from offering him beer. Finger foods were laid out on the long dining table, and people helped themselves. Jill was always by his side, and she smelled of what he remembered as a rose.

As the evening proceeded, the conversation became wilder and the laughter louder. Margaret and her fiancé delivered their short speeches, punctuated by frequent and progressively longer kisses to the applause of the crowd. Eventually, wild music was put on, and nearly everyone took to the limited floor to do some form or other of the rock-n-roll. Some of the men took their jackets off and loosened their ties.

Margaret dimmed the lights just before nine. She put on some slow, romantic songs by the big names of the time. And with that, the tempo slowed down into what might be called the shuffle: two bodies in full frontal body contact, moving to and fro in very short steps, trying not to bump into the other dancers. Jill and Hasan, who had tried a couple of fast dances, came together in that classic hold, and soon had their cheeks against each other's.

"Do you like dancing, Hasan?"

"I like *this* kind of dancing. I am no good at the fast ones."

"I'll bet you would be good at it, if you learned it earlier in your life."

"You know, I never danced before I came to London."

"In that case, you've done very well."

The words of the crooner Matt Munro were getting even more romantic toward the end of the song, and the two moved even more closely together. Jill became aware of Hasan's developing hardness. She said, "I read somewhere that dancing is a vertical expression of a horizontal desire. Do you agree?"

"That's a clever saying, which I never heard before. We don't have such expressions in Arabic."

"Are you glad you came?"

"I am so lucky."

"And I am so lucky to have met you at the bus stop today. I am having a real good time. Are you?"

"Yes, of course. I nearly didn't come ... because ... because ..."

"Because of guilt?"

"Yes. I mean Biddy ..."

"Biddy is busy, and happily so, with her baby. Nothing makes a woman happier."

"How would you know? Have you had a baby?"

"No, but I have many women friends who have, and all they endlessly talk about is their children and how wonderful, and beautiful and clever, they are. And besides, I am a woman too. Or have you not noticed?"

"How could anyone *not* notice!"

"I am aware of you being a real man from something happening down there," she said as she lowered her eyes, "and a man needs to have relief—even a married man. It must be some days for you, right?"

"More like weeks."

"Poor you! Maybe something will have to be done about it. I am worried that you might just explode … like a volcano erupting or something."

Hasan laughed aloud, looked into her eyes, and then brought his lips to hers in a very long and wet kiss, their first that evening.

~

Out on the street after the party, which was enjoyed by all, the two held hands and walked silently toward the bus stop. It was after eleven and there were few buses running at that time, judging by the near absence of people at the bus stop, apart from two drunk young men who had vomited in front of where they sat on the ground. Hasan and Jill decided to get a taxi instead. They would drop off Hasan first, as he lived closer than Jill.

Having given the driver the address, the two got into some heavy touching and petting, their hands wandering all over in the last few moments before they would part. When the taxi pulled over at Hasan's address, he handed over the fare and, without any words, the two got out, hand in hand.

As the apartment door closed behind them, they turned to each other and locked in a passionate embrace followed by numerous kisses. Jill seemed to be in a frenzy of passion as Hasan probed all her sensitive zones, almost tearing her beautiful silk dress, which was so well fitting that it almost got stuck around her hips. Within seconds they were standing against each other totally naked. Hasan started his rhythmic movement against her while panting aloud, ignoring the cold temperature in the room.

"No, not here. Let's go to the bedroom," said Jill.

"It's in a big mess, and I haven't made the bed or changed the sheets in days. I'll get a blanket and spread it on the floor here."

"No, it doesn't matter about the sheets. They just smell of you."

On the bed, Jill was soon on her back, with Hasan firmly inside her.

"Now, I want you to make love to me all night, in Biddy's bed, but that will be our secret."

That was enough, after so much deprivation, for Hasan to erupt like the volcano Jill had been talking about earlier, and Jill was not far behind.

Hasan rolled off Jill and lay on his back with his face turned toward her.

"You are so hot, you know? I want to do this every day. But why did you say that about Biddy? I was under the impression you were friends. After all, you were at our wedding."

"Let's just say that was a woman's revenge."

"Revenge? What do you mean?"

"Ever since we blossomed into teenagers and started fancying boys, Biddy has always been the beautiful one in the class. She stole my boyfriends, not once but twice. It was payback time. I know it is mean, but I just had to do it."

"So, you did it not because you liked me but out of revenge?"

"Both, I suppose."

"And now that you have done it?"

"It's up to you. If you want to be faithful to your wife, I can understand."

"Now that I know what hot stuff you are made of, how can I stop?"

"It's called self-control, my dear," Jill teased.

"I can control myself. It's him I can't control," he said as he looked downward. "He's ready to go again."

Jill slid her hand under the blanket.

"Wow! You'd better not keep him waiting."

At the end of the second session, Hasan was worn out and felt very sticky with Jill's and his own fluids. He got out of bed, carefully washed those sticky areas, did his prescribed ablutions, and performed his evening prayers.

∽

The lovemaking sessions occurred every night during Biddy's week in hospital, except for the final night when the bed sheets and covers and pillowcases were changed. That night Hasan slept over at Jill's even smaller apartment. They both decided to cool it for a while but promised to see each other as soon as circumstances allowed.

Biddy looked happy to come home, clutching her beautiful baby in her arms, while Hasan carried a fairly big hamper of baby clothing and other items. She had shed some of the weight she had gained, but her legs still appeared swollen. She looked paler and a few years older than she had been only days before that. Once home, however, she discovered that Hasan remained distant from her and made no effort to help her whenever Jasmine woke up hungry and screaming in the middle of the night. He constantly reminded Biddy that it was her duty to look after the baby that she brought to this world, for that was how it was in his own family back home. He also reminded her that he needed his rest and sleep in order to attend his lectures and debates and pass exams, something she no longer had to do.

The lack of warmth and absence of intimacy was bewildering for her, and very hard to take, for only a few months earlier they were in love and seized every opportunity to make illicit love. Not only did he never say that he loved her anymore, but his contact with Jasmine was also brief and seemed detached. She did consider, albeit briefly, if he had found another woman, but then she dismissed the thought. He would come home later than usual once or twice a week, which he accounted for by claiming that he had more reading to do at the university library rather than at home in the midst of the noise from the baby. Biddy would not ask him directly, for fear that he might just confirm it, something she would find totally devastating. She, therefore, started to blame herself—her fatigue, her weight gain, her deteriorating looks, and even her episiotomy scar—to account for it. Biddy's mother did visit once a week for the whole morning, and Biddy eagerly looked forward to her support and sympathy, but her father never came along.

Months later, it was Jasmine's first birthday, and Biddy felt it would be a golden opportunity to invite her father over to enjoy his granddaughter in her own surroundings, and perhaps resume contact with Hasan.

"I don't want to ever see his face again," Mr. McCartney said to his wife, who delivered the invitation. "He is a parasite and a blackmailer. He is no good for Biddy; she got herself into this situation, and she has to live with him, but I don't."

"I agree with you, James, but we have to think not only of Biddy's happiness but also of Jasmine's future. Whether we like it or not, our only granddaughter is half-Arab. Who knows what will happen in a year or two when he finishes his studies, becomes a prosperous lawyer, and decides to take his family back to Aden? It would break my heart if I never saw Jasmine again."

"I worry about that a lot. I think Biddy should refuse to go there. You know what will happen there, don't you?"

"What?"

"It is a Muslim country, and a backward one at that. It would not surprise me if Biddy was put in *hijab* or even in *niqab*, completely covering her face, and if Jasmine was brought up as a Muslim girl and married off to some wealthy old man at the age of thirteen or something."

"But that's the more reason why we need to maintain a good relationship with him, at least respectful if not warm. He is a crafty devil, that one."

"You can say *that* again. All right, I will come. Have you bought a wee birthday present for the baby?"

"Leave that to me."

~

Jasmine looked adorable in her white dress with pink little flowers and with her dark wavy hair nicely groomed by her mother. She resembled her mother a lot, but her dark eyes and thick eyebrows reminded one of her father. She was taking steady steps by then. She would utter single syllable words. She related to her "gran" but not to Mr. McCartney. Nevertheless, he very much enjoyed seeing her that day, put her on his knee and played with her, and went through all the baby talk that he could muster. He even helped her blow her single candle when the time came for the birthday cake ritual. Hasan looked on with little interest or warmth, but he let the grandparents have their afternoon with Jasmine and avoided any personal questions and answers with them. An hour later, the McCartneys left, after showering Jasmine with kisses, but there were no handshakes between the men.

~

Over the next year, Hasan's third and final year at the school of law, nothing dramatic happened. Infrequent dates with Jill continued, but he had made very few new friends. This was partly because he was a loner who spent a lot of time studying, but also because of his religiosity, which made him a strict teetotaler and caused him to stick to the daily rituals of praying five times a day and fasting during the month of Ramadan. Other young men of his age would go out to the pub or to a restaurant where they would order beer or wine and socialize. During his few years in London, he came across just a few other students from Aden, but he never mixed with them mainly because they enthusiastically adopted the local custom of socializing over a pint of beer in the local pub. Consequently, none of the Adeni students knew anything about his marriage to Biddy, and none of them attended his hurriedly arranged wedding. He therefore found it easy to keep it a secret and never told his parents about his marriage or about his daughter. He just kept postponing the decision to confront them with it, fearing a backlash of denunciation. His relationship with Biddy continued at its accustomed routine. She busied herself with bringing up their rapidly developing daughter, for whom she started knitting pretty little cardigans, and spending a lot more time reading library books, especially romantic novels.

~

Hasan's studies during the final year were even harder and required more reading, but his phenomenal memory helped him tremendously. His late afternoon or early evening sex with Jill continued once or twice a month on average, but the novelty was beginning to wear off. Jill found a receptionist job at a big law firm in London and found herself in demand by some of the horny middle-aged, married lawyers in that firm. Having fulfilled her revenge against Biddy, her interest in Hasan was greatly diminished, which depressed him greatly. He had somehow assumed that because Jill chose to partner with him, despite the fact that he was married, she must have found him very handsome or desirable, and he chose to forget that it was mainly an act of revenge against Biddy.

The final examinations took place at the end of July, and Hasan passed them with little difficulty. Now he only had to article at a law firm for several months to complete his training before he would head back to Aden. In the meantime, Aden won its independence from British rule to become the People's Democratic Republic of Yemen, and it was headed by the leaders of the Southern Liberation Alliance, the leftwing revolutionary group which had liberated the country. Hasan was following the news with great interest, if not excitement, and letters and expensive telephone calls between him and his family and contacts in Aden became more frequent.

CHAPTER 10

~

THE BIRTHDAY PARTY

Ever since her wedding, Biddy had never gotten to meet any other men and remained dedicated to Hasan, initially due to blind love and admiration and later, as things cooled off, through a sense of loyalty to the integrity of her small family of three. Deep in her heart she did fantasize about a wonderful young man who would bring joy and love to her life once again, but the opportunity never presented itself.

That changed one day when Jasmine was invited to join the third birthday of the daughter of a young woman whom Biddy knew from her father's church. Jasmine was only a few months younger than the birthday girl but hardly ever had the opportunity to develop friends, and Biddy thought it would be a great idea.

Jasmine, like any toddler, showed great interest in dogs, babies, and the little children whom she saw in the neighborhood park whenever her mother would take her there for a walk and a romp. On the afternoon of the birthday party, Biddy took Jasmine there by bus. There were six invited children, four girls and two boys, all of the same age, most with their mothers who had to be there with their children, except for one child who was dropped off to be picked up later. The birthday girl's uncle, David, was also there to help with organizing the barbeque of sausages, the lighting of the three candles, and playing all the roles traditionally relegated to men. The birthday girl's own father was at the annual convention of drug salesmen held in Cardiff that day, and as he was the vice president of the association, he was unable to avoid attending.

David was a tall, masculine thirty-year-old with wavy blondish hair, gray-blue eyes, and big hands. He had worked for the police, now as sergeant, at the local police station since he was twenty-four. He stuck out as the only man at the party, and he did apologize for that, but his sister came to his rescue by explaining that she did ask him to help, especially because she dreaded lighting the gas barbeque. David was affable and exuded confidence, and everyone attributed that to his daily contact with strangers, part of his police work, not to mention his rugged masculine looks in the midst of a bevy of seven young women. He was born in Ireland but moved with his parents to England as a teen. He paid a lot of attention to his niece, as well as the other children and their mothers, repeatedly lamenting that he did not have a wife or child. In a way, he was the life and soul of the party, or so it seemed to the guests, including the children.

∼

As the successful party was beginning to wind down, the children and mothers were picked up, one after the other, by their fathers, between five and six in the evening, on their way back from work. Biddy was getting Jasmine ready for the bus ride home, after thanking her hostess.

"And where are *you* going, Jasmine?" David asked the child.

"Home."

"And where do you live?"

Jasmine looked puzzled but repeated, "I live at home."

"Your daddy is late, isn't he?"

"No, we're taking the bus. We came on the number 26. It's not far," Biddy interjected.

"Oh, I can give you a lift. Where do you live?"

"No, no, I wouldn't want to take you out of your way."

"I'm just going home myself. It's no problem, really."

"No, thank you. I refuse to take you out of your way."

"You just told me it's not far. Really, I would be delighted to drive Jasmine home. If you want to take the bus, go right ahead, but I'm taking *Jasmine* home!"

Biddy couldn't help laughing.

"Now I know what they mean when they say that you people have the gift of the gab."

"It's the only thing that works, believe me," David said with an infectious smile.

It was a relatively short distance by London standards, but because of the rush-hour traffic, it took thirty minutes, during which David extracted a detailed personal profile of Biddy, helped no doubt by his police training. And just as Biddy was able to confide in her teacher, Mrs. Wakefield, she told the policeman about her miserable life with Hasan.

"Biddy, I hope you do not feel that I am rushing you, but would you even consider inviting me for a walk with you, and of course Jasmine, in the park, in the next two or three days? We can continue this conversation— nothing else. We'll just have a chat."

"Maybe," Biddy said after a long pause.

"I am off duty the day after tomorrow, around three? It'll be a lovely day."

"How do you know that?"

"I just know it will be. Call it the luck of the Irish."

"So, the Irish have the luck, and also the gift of the gab, and what else?"

"And we can sing too! No, seriously, we in the police force have to monitor the weather, you know, just in case there is an emergency, and the roads are slippery and wet, etcetera."

When David stopped the car outside her door, Biddy held her now sleeping daughter in her arms and turned left toward the front passenger door, thanking David profusely. He placed his fleshy left hand on her right shoulder and stroked it ever so gently as he smiled at her. He then got out of the car to help her with the stroller.

~

Two days later, after lunch, Biddy felt an unusual mixture of excitement and anxiety. She could not make her mind up for the longest time. She knew that it would be wrong for her, a married woman, to encourage David to get close to her. She could see no future in it. On the other hand, her encounter with him, as simple and innocent as it was, did give her enormous pleasure not to mention confidence in herself as a woman, and she did want to savor it again, to reassure herself that David was for real. She got Jasmine and her stroller ready and made herself a cup of tea for the road. She then changed her mind and poured herself some gin and topped it with several slices of lemon. Hasan strongly disapproved of alcohol at home, but he turned a blind eye to the occasional drink. She needed to steady the fine tremor of excitement that began to affect her hands that afternoon. She justified it by telling herself that she needed steady hands to safely maneuver her baby's stroller.

The park was only ten minutes away, despite the stroller. It had a small children's playground with a slide and a sand box where Jasmine had enjoyed herself with other toddlers. Sitting at one end of the green painted bench, only thirty yards away, was David in smart civilian clothes. He walked toward her, smiling at Jasmine all the time.

"Didn't I tell you it was going to be a lovely day?"

"I will have to use you for weather forecasts from now on."

"And it has suddenly become a lot lovelier."

Biddy smiled appreciatively.

"Shall I take you on the slide, Jasmine? And give your mummy a little rest?"

Jasmine shook her head enthusiastically and climbed out of the stroller when the straps were loosened by David. They all walked toward the slide, and the two stood together watching Jasmine.

"By the way, I did not tell you which park I was going to. How did you guess? Or was that also the luck of the Irish?"

"You forget that I am a police sergeant assigned to this precinct. I make it my job to know, and this is by far the closest children's playground from your address. Tell me: how is it going at home?"

"The same, I am afraid."

"Why do you stay with him?"

"What can I do under the circumstances? Jasmine needs her father. I have no income. My university ambitions came to a dead end with the pregnancy."

"I can imagine that dozens of men would want to look after you ... and Jasmine. I, for one. You are so beautiful and warm and ..."

"Stop it, David! You hardly know me. And what about your own wife ... or partner?"

"There is no one, not right now. I had two partners, each for two years, and lost them both."

"So, you're a loser? Is that also an Irish trait?" Biddy teased.

"You could say that, I suppose, but I have matured a lot since. I am ten years older than you, you know. When I first joined the police force, it was in Birmingham. I was so focused on my work; and with all the night shift work and doing overtime to make extra money, I neglected my first partner. She was a wonderful woman, but she could not take being alone in the house for extended periods of time. She left me, and I can't blame her."

"And what is your excuse for the other?"

"I left her. You see when the first one abandoned me, I felt very depressed and worthless. So when I met the second woman, I threw myself at her. She had come off her own relationship and was on antidepressants, and alcohol, and was smoking fairly heavily. I thought that when she found me she would settle down and she would want to start a family, but it never happened. She was my age, just a year younger. In the end, I walked out on her. She owned the property, and I was staying in her small house in Solihull near Birmingham."

"So, with that record, I would have thought you would stay away from relationships."

"I always marvel at those people who say that they are happy and contented living all alone. We humans are not meant to live that way. You know, during my working day, I run into so many people, policemen, clerks at the station, the public, mothers, fathers, children, even criminals. I have no shortage of human contact. But I go home, and then it hits me. It is so deadly quiet. There is no one to chat with, to share news and worries and triumphs and ..."

"And bed? Isn't that what men want to share the most?"

"That too. What would life be without that? But at the same time, I have found that a couple needs to share other sentiments and interests and values if they really want to enjoy each other in bed."

Biddy was listening intently, then looked David in the eyes and nodded her head in agreement, for it was as if he was talking about her.

"Come on Jasmine! We have to go home now. It is time for your dinner."

"Same time, same place, next week?"

Biddy nodded, and started to push the stroller home.

∽

Over the following weeks their meetings became progressively longer, and warmer, and Biddy allowed him to kiss her at the end of their third meeting. They would walk in the park holding hands and pushing the stroller along. Their conversation became a lot more animated and the vibes so much stronger. David was sure he was in love again, but Biddy was not so certain. It was only once that she fell in love, but three years later that passion was virtually gone, as she resigned herself to bring up her little girl with virtually no help except the little support from her mother.

Six weeks after their first meeting at the park, Biddy did not turn up. She also did not phone. David was very disappointed that day and started imagining all sorts of possible scenarios. Eventually, he convinced himself that perhaps Jasmine had a cough or a fever. He would wait until the following week. But Biddy did not make an appearance again. David parked his private car in the street opposite her apartment and watched for a whole afternoon, until around six when he saw a young brown-skinned man who fit the description of Hasan carrying a black leather briefcase. He decided to go check on Biddy the next day, well before six. He listened at the door and heard Jasmine shouting to her mother, but could not make out what she said. He rang the bell, but there was no answer. He rang again, and after a few more seconds, a third time. He saw that the light shining through the peephole disappeared.

"Biddy, it's me, as you can see. Let me in, please." He had to ask again before the door opened.

He could not believe what he saw. "Oh, my God! Did he do that to you?"

Biddy stood there with a big blue bruise on her left cheek and a small linear laceration over her cheekbone just below her eye. Jasmine came to look at the visitor and recognizing him gave a big innocent smile.

"You poor thing! Why didn't you tell me? I would have arrested him. It's not too late. I'll personally wring his neck."

Biddy began to sob quietly as she looked down into her daughter's eyes three feet below her own. David opened his arms and hugged her firmly, and as he felt her sobs through his own chest he stroked her back very gently up and down until she stopped. He stood back to look at her face again, then approached and put his lips on her bruised left cheek and kept kissing and kissing. He was interrupted by Jasmine looking up at them saying, "David love Mummy!"

"Yes, I do, I do, I do," he said, planting a passionate kiss on Biddy's full lips, which she returned with total abandon.

David turned around and dashed out through the apartment door, saying he would be back. He was back within five minutes carrying a camera, which he always kept in the glove compartment of his car just in case he needed to document a traffic accident or other event. He took about ten photos of Biddy's face from every angle. When he accomplished that, his rage seemed to subside.

"Tell me what happened," he said.

"He found out. I was afraid of that."

"How? Did you tell him?"

"No, I knew how he would react."

"How, then?"

Biddy turned to look lovingly at Jasmine and said, "She did."

"Oh, my God. I never even considered it."

"Hasan would ask her from time to time 'What did you do today?'

so she told him about you taking her on the slide. He asked who, and she said David. Then of course he asked her about David. Poor little girl, she even innocently volunteered "David love Mummy." All my denials and protestations were in vain. This is the result. I knew I should not have met you at the park. I will not see you again, David. My daughter's happiness and future come first."

"You can't mean that. I love you, and I want to protect you. This is a monster. Are you going to let him treat you like this? Every time you look at another man, or talk to one, you get beaten to a pulp? This is not Islamistan. Here women have rights, *equal* rights. If he chooses to marry a British woman and live in Britain, and has a British daughter, he has to go by our rules, not his bloody Quran."

"And what choice do I have, David?"

"You should lay charges for assault and battery."

"And then spend months in court? How is that going to affect Jasmine? You talk about my trauma. How about her psychological trauma? And where do we live while the court case proceeds? You know, this is *his* house; that was the deal he got from my dad, who was so ashamed of my pregnancy that he wanted it hushed up with a shotgun marriage, lest his congregation should hear about the scandal."

"Jesus Christ, he holds all the cards, that bastard!"

"Yes, he does. Look, David, let's just forget this happened. Thank you for caring. But don't ask me to see you again. I ... I ... I will miss you so much ..." Biddy could not finish her sentence but went into a long sob, throwing herself against David's big chest and shoulders.

～

Sergeant David Dooley had the photos in his camera developed and printed and wrote the date on them. He then went through the whole database at the police station looking for any information on Hasan Alawi Al-Qirshi. There was hardly any, other than his date of birth, and those of his wife and child, and his address, from an old report where Hasan had reported that someone in the neighborhood shouted racist remarks at him. He also found out that he was a law student and that he carried a British passport, not a Yemeni one. David needed a lot more information, and he set about to find it.

He decided to follow Hasan for a period of one week to see where he went and whom he met, and where he would eat or drink. His lecture and seminar routine was unremarkable. He did not frequent any pubs. On Friday he went to the mosque at noon. But he did also visit a small apartment in East Ealing on Tuesday and Saturday of that week. Hasan had increased his visits to Jill since he found out about David, as if to avenge what he considered to be her infidelity.

David soon identified Jill as the object of Hasan's attention. Once again, he documented their comings and goings with his camera. He knew that he was acting as a private detective, and felt very guilty about it, but his love for Biddy, and the memory of that bruise on her beautiful face, gave him sufficient excuse to carry on. He had asked Biddy if she ever met her parents-in-law but found out that not only had she not meet them, but that they were never told about the wedding. Hasan had convinced her that if they found out, they would disinherit him, which would eventually deprive Jasmine of any estate that might be passed on to her after his death. In the interest of her daughter, Biddy went along with the secrecy deal.

~

Sergeant Dooley followed Hasan to the Bar Resto, a restaurant near the law school, where Hasan often went, and where he had just ordered some vegetarian pizza because he never trusted that the meat used was completely free of pork or lard. The waitress put the food in front of him together with a drink of lemonade. He was eating alone, which for him was the rule rather than the exception. The restaurant was only half full at that point. David took the table immediately next to Hasan's, the latter being right in the corner of the room.

"Not very busy today," David started.

"No."

"My first time here; do you come here regularly?"

"No, not really."

"How's the food here?"

"Okay, I suppose."

"There's nothing like home cooking, if you ask me."

"True."

"Do you have someone that cooks for you, a wife I mean?"

"No."

"I take it you don't like questions?"

"I am usually the one who asks the questions."

"Really, how is that?"

"I am a lawyer."

"Really? That's wonderful! You're so young. But I should have guessed, this restaurant being near the Law Inns and all that. Are you a barrister or a solicitor?"

"Well, actually, I am still a student, a senior student."

"So, you know a lot about the law?"

"Yes. I take my final exams in a couple of months."

"Great. So, what is the punishment, in English law, for assault and battery of a wife?"

Hasan's knife fell out of his right hand, making a loud clang against his plate, and causing some of the restaurant customers to turn their heads toward him.

"Why on earth would you ask me such a question? You have to consult a licensed solicitor."

"I thought you just might know the answer, Hasan."

Hasan looked absolutely ashen with fear when he heard his name, and started sweating profusely. His mouth became so dry he could not swallow the morsel of pizza until he took a big gulp of lemonade. It occurred to him that the man was Biddy's brother Albert, whom he had never met, just back from the United States, and that he was there to beat him up just like a Yemeni brother might do to defend the honor of an abused sister.

"Who are you? Albert?"

"Oh, allow me to introduce myself: Sergeant David Dooley," David said, stretching his big muscular forearm and fleshy hand, which Hasan would not shake.

"Why did you follow me here? I will report you. This will be premeditated assault."

"Sorry, I omitted to say that I am in civilian clothing, and I am not here in that capacity."

"No, but you are in the capacity of a man trying to seduce a married woman."

"Even if it was true, under which section of the penal code of England is that a crime?"

"Back in my country you would be severely beaten, or worse, by her husband and brothers."

"But I am *not* in your country. You are in *mine*. And the punishment for willful assault and battery, if proven, especially against a defenseless woman, is quite severe. Check the code."

"I'm glad you said 'if proven.' I did no such thing. I know the law."

"Well, in that case, you have nothing to worry about."

Hasan motioned to the waitress to give him the bill. As she approached, he stood up, hoping to escape from the restaurant as soon as possible. At that moment, and while the waitress was standing next to Hasan to receive the money, David dropped a five-by-eight color photo of Biddy's bruised and lacerated face. The waitress took a loud audible breath on seeing the picture. Hasan paid her but then sat back in his chair.

"Look, Sergeant, this is a private matter between me and my wife. She did not press charges, and unless she does there's nothing you can do about it. She will tell you that she was sweeping under a table, and when she lifted her head she banged her left cheek against the heavy table top."

"You are right that she did not press charges … so far. But she will definitely change her mind when she sees these photos here." David took three photos of Hasan and Jill walking down the street with their arms round each other's waists.

"My God! How long have you been shadowing me? The law does not permit you to track me unless there is an accusation filed against me. That evidence will not be allowed in court."

"I have not. But a private detective did."

"And who paid him?"

"How do you know it's not a *her*?"

"Well, okay, who paid her?"

"That will come out at the time of the trial, I suppose."

"So, what do you want?"

"Let me put it this way. You are a foreign student, your British passport notwithstanding, here for a defined mission for four years, to get your law degree and then bugger off to South Yemen where you will be *a somebody*—maybe even a judge or minister of justice. You stay with a kind and respectable family; you get their underage daughter pregnant; you then blackmail her father to bribe you with a whole bloody flat, worth his annual salary, in order to marry a most beautiful woman; and within months you start fornicating with Jill, and who knows who else. But when Biddy just talks to me in the presence of Jasmine, you accuse her of infidelity and beat the daylights out of her. And all this time you keep the wedding, and the baby, top secret from your father back home. Are you with me so far? … Good. Well, that alone will make a great story for the *News of the Globe*, and all it will take is an anonymous phone call to their gossip column, and they will do the rest. Can you imagine the headline? 'Arab Barrister Beats Blonde Brit Black and Blue.' I mean from today onward, every time you enter this restaurant, the waitress will probably whisper the story to all the customers."

Hasan paused for a long time before asking, "So, what do you want?"

"Oh, I forgot to mention that someone from Aden will read the *News of the Globe* and will be on the telephone or telegram to your unsuspecting dad there. And who knows what the faculty of law will do about granting an LLB to a wife beater? I wonder which law firm will take you on to do your articling? I guess you might not be called to the bar after all."

"Okay, okay. What do you want?"

"Now we're talking! For starters, this marriage will be dissolved. Custody of the child will be with the mother, not that that would bother you. I understand that you Muslims do not like to have daughters in case they fall victim to some horny man, just like Biddy fell victim to you. The ownership of the flat will be transferred from you to your daughter …"

"You can't be serious. That is mine."

"Really! How did you earn the five thousand pounds to pay for it? It is actually Mr. McCartney's life savings. I am sure he will be delighted to pass it on to his granddaughter rather than to some Arab from Aden. Is that understood?"

Hasan was in a daze, but he managed to nod his head.

"Oh, one more thing: all this will be done ASAP, well before your final exams, otherwise the deal is off. And a personal request from me. Don't come anywhere near Biddy! You can get your sex from Jill. I will not tell Biddy about that part—until after the divorce."

$\sim$

David's instructions were heeded and followed by Hasan to the letter. The day Hasan left the flat in the name of Jasmine, with her mother named as her guardian, he tried to be nice to Jasmine. He was never close to his daughter. Nevertheless, for her he did represent the father figure she was supposed to have. However, he was soon replaced in that role by David, whom Jasmine soon learned to genuinely love, and when he moved in with them, Biddy's life turned to one of true happiness. It was David who wanted an early wedding. He wanted to place a seal on Biddy's previous misery, and he wanted Jasmine to have a father, and to have stability during her crucial formative years.

$\sim$

As expected, Hasan passed his exams without difficulty, and received his bachelor of law degree, after which he embarked on a year of articling with a law firm in Bristol to complete his training. He was subsequently called to the bar.

Back in Aden, he was received at the airport like a hero by his father and most of his relatives, and their friends, as the first truly Adeni lawyer. There were two practicing lawyers at the time, but these were Indian lawyers who came with the British colonial system then decided to make Aden their home after the British left.

It did not take long for him to catapult to fame through his work at his private law office. Despite the socialist system, money began to pour in for Hasan, especially given the lack of competition in his profession, and he got to know and hobnob with many men in the government and establishment. He loved the sense of importance which he acquired in such a short time, and when he compared that with his situation of surrender in front of David only a few months before, he knew that he had arrived, at last.

However, his sexual needs remained virtually unanswered in that very conservative society. Many times he wished he could be back in London just for one week. He did manage to find an outlet on the very few trips he made to Ethiopia and to Egypt, for which he had to pay for his sex. His father urged him a week after his return to allow his mother to find him a wife, but he was too busy to consider that at the time. But a year after his arrival, his mother set out on her traditional task. Like her husband, Fatima was born in Turba in North Yemen. She was a simple and illiterate but kind mother and dedicated and subservient wife. Even before Hasan returned home, she had been dreaming about her grandchildren and scheming to find the right wife for him. She knew a handful of mothers of her own age, and once a month or so would pay a visit for tea to one of them, for she was not allowed to go out on her own at any time. She would have to request permission from her husband, who would drive her there and collect her a couple of hours later.

During the three months before Hasan's anticipated return, she increased the number of such visits and was much more inquisitive about any daughters in those households. She went out of her way to meet them and evaluate them. Her lady friends, for their part, when they heard about the impending arrival of an eligible single lawyer, spared no effort in showing off their daughters in their best finery and clothes and instructed them to be extra polite and welcoming to "Auntie Fatima."

By the end of those numerous visits, Fatima had formed a secret shortlist of eligible brides for Hasan. There were three girls on that list, but her favorite was the daughter of her closest friend among the mothers. Hasan had a few female cousins of marriageable age who naturally assumed that they had first kick at the can, but Fatima, who was never accepted by her in-laws when she herself was a young bride, wanted to have nothing to do with them or the Qirshi family. She wanted a bride who would look up to her and obey her and whose mother liked her. When Hasan eventually agreed to get married, his mother laid out the plan.

Fatima began, "When you make up your mind, I will get photos of the three or four girls I have in mind, from very nice respectable families. You can choose from the photos, but also we will get information about which schools they went to and anything else you need. Then after you select the one, you can come with your father and me to visit their home for tea. You will see her there in the flesh and make up your mind. But she will be with the rest of the family."

"And what if she turns me down after she sees me?"

"She won't. But her father might. It is all up to him."

"How do you know she won't?"

"Because I am a woman; the worst thing that can happen to a girl in this society is to remain on the shelf, as the saying goes. So, she is not going to take that risk. No woman wants to remain a spinster for life. Maybe there in London, they do that; not here."

~

Over the next few weeks, Hasan went through the process of examining the photos and comparing physical attributes, school performance, and most importantly the status of the fathers of the three girls. Hasan's ambition drove him to choose Salma, the daughter of the ex-minister of trade and the sister of his old classmate, Ahmad. Although he had spent several years as his classmate, he never knew that Ahmad had a sister. It was not something Adeni boys talked about. Boys bragged about their fathers, and sometimes about their brothers, but no one ever talked about mothers, much less sisters, or even mentioned their names. If it became absolutely necessary to mention a sister, she would be referred to as *alkareemah* [the honorable one].

Salma was five years his junior. Shortly after meeting, the two were married in the bride's home in the presence of an imam, the ceremony being attended by most of the members of both families. The two mothers were happy to cement their friendship with that marriage, although the fathers hardly knew each other. Ahmad, still in Edinburgh, was unable to attend the wedding but was sent a bundle of wedding photographs by post several weeks later. The couple settled into married life, and Salma had her first baby boy nearly two years later. It was around that time that Hasan was appointed deputy minister of justice by the socialist government which ruled South Yemen.

CHAPTER 11

~

THE CLINICAL YEARS

Four years after his arrival in Edinburgh, Ahmad began the final two years at the faculty of medicine. These were the clinical years when he was allowed to see and assess actual patients. It was an exciting part of his life, and he knew that he was well past the halfway mark; he was confident that he would make it. It was just a matter of time, and another hundred thousand more words to read, and numerous diagrams to learn, and hundreds of patients to assess, and a dozen babies to deliver, and then he would be called Dr. So-and-So. His parents would be so proud of him. But even more importantly, Ann would be. They were still in love and deeply cared for each other. They decided that they would not get married until after his graduation. Ann also preferred her freedom and continued to live in her own home, and sometimes with her parents, although she spent a lot of time with Ahmad.

The clinical subjects he had to study at that stage were the standard ones of medicine, surgery, gynecology, and therapeutics, plus forensic medicine. Ahmad, who had read so many of the stories of Sherlock Holmes, had a special interest in the latter subject and was surprised that most of his fellow students were either not interested in it, or treated it with scorn. Here was the one subject where he did not have to commit thousands of factoids to memory but where he could use his sharp skills of observation and deduction to arrive at a diagnosis.

He went over all the days and weeks and months in his second and third years when he had to commit to memory all those names of arteries and veins and ducts and nerves and muscles. Not only that, but also which one passed behind which and whether the vein was lateral or medial to the artery. *And why did he have to remember the names and relative positions of all ten of those little bones in the wrist?* He pondered all that and came to the conclusion that most of that midnight oil was burned in vain, and in *vein*, as he told himself with a suppressed smile at his own wit. If only his anatomy professor had somehow found one of the many middle-aged, overweight ladies with carpal tunnel syndrome and brought her to the classroom to tell the medical students about her symptoms, he would have learned about all the different branches of the median nerve in a jiffy. And he would never have had to revise that subject for the rest of his career in medicine.

He was doing a four-week attachment in the gastroenterology ward at the Royal Infirmary when, to his surprise, his Sudanese flat mate Sharif was admitted to the emergency room, known there as "the casualty room." Sharif had seemed a little depressed and lethargic, and when they shared a meal in the flat, he would eat very little. He did not complain much and had no fever or vomiting—only some nausea. But, being a heavy drinker, like a lot of the Sudanese students Ahmad knew, he was assumed to be overdoing the alcohol. His girlfriend who might have taken greater care of him, and perhaps observed the changes in his health, was away in the Hebrides in the north of Scotland. As Ahmad was the only medical student in the unit, it was his duty to evaluate the patient and report to the resident, who in turn would report to the registrar, who in turn would present the case to the intensely feared consultant at clinical ward rounds the next day.

Ahmad was stunned by the apparently precipitous deterioration in his friend's health and looks. He appeared very ill and confused. He was dehydrated and almost emaciated. As he examined him, with considerable discomfiture, even he the novice medical student thought he was very ill, but he had no idea why. His history was patchy and not helpful. The only positive physical finding he detected was an enlarged liver, and he congratulated himself on being able to tell the resident that the liver edge was enlarged by three fingerbreadths, which the resident confirmed. Ahmad had read that alcohol could cause cirrhosis of the liver and dismissed the finding as due to alcohol. He set up an intravenous drip of saline with glucose at least to rehydrate the patient.

When the resident came, he listened to Ahmad's presentation while nodding his head. He asked, "What do you think of his eyes?"

"His eyes? There is nothing wrong with his eyes, and he did not complain about his vision."

"Look at them again!"

"Sorry, Doctor, I think they are normal. Obviously they are not, otherwise you would not ask."

"Look how yellow they are. The man has jaundice from some form of hepatitis."

"I am sorry. I missed that completely."

"Don't worry. That's why you are a student and I am a resident. The reason you missed the jaundice is that his skin is very black, but the white of his eye would show it. That is why we always say "inspection before palpation." You look before you touch. Now get all liver-function tests and a full blood count done, and check the urine for color. And do a routine chest X-ray."

"Oh, the chest X-ray was done at casualty, and was unremarkable."

Sharif was later evaluated by the registrar and the consultant, who came to the conclusion that this was the severe type-B hepatitis, for which there was no specific treatment and therefore a poor prognosis. They were indeed correct, and the patient gradually drifted into hepatic coma. He died within four days.

Before he did, and when he was lucid, he would talk about his life in the Sudan, his mother, and the rest of the family; how much he needed them to be with him in his hour of need; and above all how much he wanted to be buried at home in the cemetery where his grandfather and grandmother lay.

For many days after, Ahmad thought about his friend, about life, and especially about death, and how rapidly and unexpectedly it can come. He questioned the presence of god, for why would he allow such a young, healthy, and pleasant man to die? What did Sharif do to deserve it? Yes, he drank alcohol, and he fornicated, and he did not pray or fast, but wasn't that exactly what Ahmad was also doing? And another billion people too?

As he slowly got busy with work and life, he was even more determined than ever to do everything within his power to reduce human suffering. But that was not, by any means, the only death he saw over the remaining months before his graduation as a doctor, except that Sharif was a friend and the loss was personal.

One day the registrar asked him to reassess an elderly man of seventy who had been in the ward for nearly a week, admitted with congestive heart failure, who was responding well to the diuretics and digoxin. The man loved reading *The Scotsman* newspaper every day and did so religiously. But because he had all day to read it, and because of his age, he would read the different segments over the morning and afternoon with long periods of rest in between. He would frequently doze off, and being supine in bed the paper would fall onto his face so that the nurses would pull it away and shake him whenever they brought him food or a cup of tea or had to measure his blood pressure. One morning Ahmad walked up to him, pulled the newspaper off as he had done many a time, and almost jumped out of his skin when he saw him dead with eyes wide open staring at the ceiling, with saliva still drooling from the corner of his mouth. Later on, the head nurse on that ward, called "sister" in Scotland, in trying to console him pointed out that the nurses would go through such scary experiences all the time.

～

The final exams were a huge ordeal for Ahmad. He hated exams, but he detested oral exams even more. He knew that his memory would fail him. It always did. With written exams, he had time to think and drag the facts from the depths of his useless memory, and therefore he never failed any written exams. But with an oral interrogation, there was no time; there was only panic. He wanted to run away or fall sick or get run over by a bus. Then Ann reminded him that he had passed all the exams of the previous five years and that he was on the oral exam list only because he had passed the written one. He felt better, but only transiently.

When the time came and his name was called, he was unable to stand up from his chair for several seconds; his knees felt wobbly when he did eventually stand up.

As he entered what he considered his torture room, he saw seated the professor of surgery and one consultant in medicine.

The surgeon started by asking him about McBurney's point. What great luck that was. It did not require much memory. He proceeded to explain the incisions used for removing an appendix and why they were done in that manner. The professor maintained a poker face, which shook Ahmad's confidence to the core. The professor of medicine had a question about the innervations of muscles and asked about the different branches of the brachial plexus. That required a lot of memory and was Ahmad's dreaded question. For that reason, Ahmad had drawn the plexus several times that week and had a fresh visual memory of it, but he thought that he got most of it wrong even then.

The poker faces continued. Now the physician asked him about the differential diagnosis of jaundice. Ahmad thought about Sharif, and that focused his mind so that he was able to offer a good list of possible causes.

It was time for the next student victim and Ahmad was ushered out, quite sure that he had failed miserably, judging by the poker faces of the two professors. So sure was he that he asked his Somali flat mate, Moosa, to go to the notice board of the medical quadrangle on the Monday after the oral exams to see if his name was on the board. He did not want to go himself, where many of his classmates would be congregating, only to experience the shame and humiliation of not finding his name among those of the successful students.

~

He stayed in his flat all day, depressed and distracted, unable to read or concentrate or even watch television, waiting for word from Moosa. From the bow window of his room on the fourth floor, he looked down at the bus stop on the street below, carefully considering how much suffering he would go through before actually dying, if he were to throw himself out of that window. He could not take that risk of not dying immediately. It would have been a much easier decision to make if only he had a loaded gun.

At four thirty that afternoon, the door opened with a key and in came Moosa asking, "Is Dr. Ahmad Shawqi Saleh here?" then repeating it before Ahmad emerged from his room. The sudden switch from utter despair combined with suicidal ideation to unprecedented elation was indescribable. He had never felt that happy as at that very moment. Although he hated hugging men, a very common custom back home, he rushed forward and embraced Moosa silently, with the beginning of tears of joy welling into his eyes. He was glad Moosa could not see them from that position of embrace. He wanted Ann to be the first to know, but she was out of town, returning by train later that evening. He decided to meet her train at Waverly Station at eight.

~

The graduation ceremony was a grand and glittering affair that was the biggest and most momentous he had ever attended. He was amazed at the pomp and ceremony involved, and the huge number of graduates, not only at the bachelor level but at the master and doctorate levels, in so many specialties. Photographs, on his own, with Ann, and with his classmates were taken by the professional photographer, which he would keep for the rest of his life.

~

After a thoroughly enjoyable month of rest and celebrations, Ahmad was to start his internship at the Heal Hospital, a peripheral hospital which had a good reputation of training competent interns and residents. The hospital provided free accommodation and meals and a meager monthly allowance, just enough to cover pocket expenses. Ahmad therefore gave notice that he would vacate his room in the shared flat. Although his friends there were sad to see him go, they knew it would happen as soon as he graduated and gave him a farewell party.

He moved all his worldly belongings to his bed-sitting room at the hospital, a two-hour journey by bus, and settled in for hard work, being on call on alternate nights, which meant spending many a night without sleep, depending on how sick the patients were. Fortunately for Ahmad, the other intern, who was starting on the surgical unit, happened to be his closest Scottish classmate, Brent Looney. The two got on very well together, and had several common interests. Brent, however, was a tall and handsome young man with a typical Scottish accent. Occasionally, before exams, they would study together, and ask each other test questions to sharpen their memories. Neither did brilliantly in class, but that fact only brought them closer together.

Their internship together at the same hospital—one in medicine and the other in surgery, for six months, then switching places—cemented their friendship. Brent was not committed to any one girlfriend when he started at the Heal Hospital, whereas Ahmad was committed to Ann, although that passion was cooling off toward his final year. It was a rather isolated place, which made travel on off-duty days or nights difficult, but the doctors found ways of keeping themselves socially busy within the big house assigned to them. There they had full dining facilities, a library, a sitting room, and a pool table, a game that Ahmad never played before. However, with abundant practice, he soon became good at it, and fell in love with the game. Brent, on the other hand, found himself very popular with the student nurses because of his good looks and friendly manner. He was nearly always with a woman, which sometimes left Ahmad on his own. However, Ahmad was making nearly monthly trips back to Edinburgh to be with Ann on long weekends. Brent found a pretty nurse, eight years his junior, who mesmerized him and stole him away from all the other nurses chasing him. Shortly afterward, they had a modest wedding and settled in that area, where Brent went into family practice.

Parting with Ann was very difficult for Ahmad, who had failed to persuade her to go with him to Aden. They decided to test their love for each other by going through a period of separation.

CHAPTER 12

~

DR. SHAWQI RETURNS HOME

On that early September morning, after a very long flight from Heathrow, with a stop in Cairo, the Aden Airways flight landed at Khormaksar Airport. It was already hot with a temperature above thirty degrees and a high degree of humidity, which became even worse later in the day. Ahmad's whole family was there, but so much had changed. Everyone looked older after those seven years of absence. The one that changed the most was his little sister Zahra, who now was clearly a mature and pretty woman of sixteen. They had exchanged a few letters and even talked once on the telephone, but the change was so obvious only after he saw her. Had she not been with the family, he may not have recognized her after all those seven years.

Salma was there too, very happy to see him, conveying her husband's apologies for not coming with her. She told Ahmad that Hasan was too busy traveling with the president to the eastern part of the country, in the city of Mukalla, but hoped to see him on his return.

Two weeks later, Ahmad was invited to lunch on a Friday, after the usual Jumaa prayers, where he enjoyed meeting his old classmate, now his brother-in-law, and a very influential member of the government of the day, reaching the level of deputy minister within three years. They reminisced about their times together in London, and Hasan's short visit to Edinburgh. Hasan's house was clearly a very expensive one, and Ahmad could not believe how his brother-in-law managed to pay for it after only three years as a lawyer. Ahmad had noticed a black Mercedes in his garage as he came in, as well as two armed guards and one civilian, presumably the driver. Affluence was everywhere.

After lunch, while Salma was busy in the kitchen, they talked.

"I didn't see you at the Kabeer Mosque," Hasan said.

"Surely, you know me well enough to know that I wouldn't be there."

"Well, I was hoping that Allah would have guided you toward righteousness since then."

"I think I can confidently claim that I am more righteous than most already. I don't need to attend prayers to prove it."

"Of course. It is up to you, but in this country appearances are everything ... if you want to get ahead, that is. People need to see that you have not abandoned Islam and your traditions."

"I'll try to remember that, but the Prophet said, 'A Muslim is one who does no harm to people, with his actions or his words.' I think I fit that description perfectly. In fact, I go one step further because as a doctor with special interest in human rights for all, I try to protect people against disease and trauma, even psychological trauma, and marginalization and poverty and homelessness."

"Have it your way. Anyway, what are your plans?"

"I have only been here two weeks, but next Monday—I mean Saturday—I will report to the ministry of health for all the paperwork. I guess I will be working at the old Queen Elizabeth Hospital."

"It is now the Revolution Hospital."

"Does not surprise me. A rose by any other name ... and all that."

Hasan looked puzzled, as though he had not come across that phrase in all those years in London.

Ahmad continued, "You seem to have done very well, judging by all the wealth I see around you."

"Praise be to Allah."

"I didn't think you would be able to amass that much in three years as a lawyer—and a Mercedes too!"

"No, the Mercedes is a gift from His Excellency, the president; the house is rented for me by the ministry."

"Wow! What have you done for him?"

"It is just appreciation for all the hard work; other hardworking ministers and deputy ministers get them too."

"For hard work or for blind loyalty?"

"Both, I suppose. There is nothing wrong with knowing the right people."

"And the expensive furniture and all the rest?"

"As a lawyer, I act as consultant for certain big companies bidding for contracts, and when they win them, they can be very generous."

"But aren't you deputy minister of justice? Is there perhaps a whiff of conflict of interest here?"

"No, I do not see it that way. I just review their applications and tell them whom to contact to have their applications considered, just like any other applicant, based on my knowledge of the people in charge in the different ministries. I do not try to influence the final decision."

"And this is not considered bribery or corruption?"

Hasan looked upset but said, "This government has very strict laws on bribery. There are laws that allow the death penalty for bribery. One man, who is distantly related to my mother's family, was executed last year."

"Well, I am learning something new every day."

Hasan looked embarrassed but offered his help to Ahmad, if needed, as the latter said good-bye.

∿

At the ministry of health, the processing of Ahmad's joining the medical staff of the main hospital was quite efficient, and smooth. The bureaucracy left by the British was not yet dismantled seven years or so later, perhaps because the government's anti-corruption laws helped to keep it that way.

The next day, Ahmad reported to the medical director of the hospital, who welcomed him warmly. He was his junior at school, and later trained as a male nurse, and eventually was appointed director only one year before Ahmad's return. The medical staff at the hospital was sparse. The Yemeni physicians were the minority, the majority being from India, Pakistan, Egypt, or Eastern Europe, most of them being specialists. Nearly all the Yemeni doctors were trained in Egypt, with a few in Eastern Europe or the Soviet Union. Ahmad was looked upon as British trained and therefore a better doctor.

He rapidly became popular in his town and beyond. He was assigned frequent duties in the casualty room, in arduous eight-hour shifts, where he saw a huge amount of pathology. Apart from the garden-variety infections and traumas, he saw for the first time numerous cases of meningitis, especially in children where actual pus would spurt out of the spinal tap needle, brain abscess in comatose men, severe uterine hemorrhage, loads of trauma and tetanus, and a classic case of rabies after a dog bite. He had read about all these conditions but never seen any such cases in the affluent Scottish population in Edinburgh.

However, one day there was a case that he was not prepared for. He arrived at the casualty department in time to take over from an Egyptian-trained, obese male physician, who was just finishing his eight-hour shift, and had honed his sense of humor during his years in Cairo. There was a lot of commotion in the casualty department. As Ahmad donned his white coat and entered the area, there were two female nurses and one tall, strong local man of around fifty holding a small, young one by the back of his collar and repeatedly accusing him of raping his goat. Just behind him stood a small boy of about ten who was holding a leash tied to the goat's neck. Every time the accused would swear by Allah that he never committed such a crime, the tall man would shake him by the neck. The obese doctor was trying to calm them down with great difficulty because of the loudness of the accuser. Eventually he said, "So, you say that he did, and he says he did not. How can we prove it? I am not a veterinary surgeon."

"By Allah, he did."

"I swear by Allah that I did not," came the answer from the accused.

"So let us ask the goat then!" said the doctor. Only the nurses dared laugh.

"How dare you make fun of my goat, Doctor? What are going to do about this?"

"Look, I am not her father. Don't ask me. Take her to the police station."

The doctor then suddenly became aware of Ahmad entering the room.

"Ah, here is the new doctor who should be able to solve the problem. He has just come from Britain and knows everything. Dr. Ahmad, this man here says that the other man raped his goat. I am sure you have learned about this in Britain."

He waved Ahmad in and bolted out of the room before anyone could stop him. The saying goes that doctors have to think fast on their feet, and if ever there was such a situation, this was it, thought Ahmad. He had no idea about the goat's anatomy but he was playing for time, and he thought he would get help from the owner.

"How much would this goat cost in the market?" he asked the owner.

"Five hundred shillings," replied the owner, deliberately exaggerating.

"So, if that man killed the goat, he would have to pay five hundred, right?"

"Yes."

"But the goat is alive. And when you sell it no one will be able to tell what happened, right?"

"Yes, but I know what happened; the goat is no longer pure."

"So, why don't we get this man to pay you a compensation of one hundred shillings for abusing your goat? Then you can keep the money and sell the goat for the usual price."

"Yes, you must make him pay."

The accused now protested, "If I did rape the goat, that would be fair, but by Allah I did not. Bring me the Quran! I will swear on it."

Dr. Ahmad had to come up with something now that the Quran was involved.

"Since we do not know for sure, let us split the difference and you will pay the owner fifty shillings."

The accused beamed a little smile and shook his head in agreement.

"I am going to examine the goat from below, just like we do with raped women, and will send the material to the laboratory to be examined under the microscope. We will get the answer tomorrow. That way, we will be sure. So if we prove the rape, you will have to pay the full one hundred, otherwise the police will have to deal with you as they see fit."

Dr. Ahmad beckoned the nurse to get him a wooden spatula, and while two nurses held the goat down he inserted it in what he guessed was the right orifice. He scooped out a minute amount of fluid.

The smile on the accused man's face disappeared, and he said, "But the material ... the semen could be from a ram."

"No, no, the sperm of a man look quite different under the microscope," Ahmad explained.

"I want the brother here to be happy, and I want to settle this matter. Look I will pay him the fifty shillings as the good doctor judged appropriate, and will add another twenty-five, an extra gift from me, just to make him happy. And he who is forgiving will receive his reward from Allah."

The surprised owner agreed. He thanked the doctor for his wisdom, pocketed the seventy-five shillings, and ordered his son to lead the goat out of the hospital.

～

Before attending to the long queue of patients that had formed during the goat episode, Ahmad uttered a sigh of relief and wondered whether he should change his name to Dr. Solomon.

At the end of his shift, he put a droplet of that material on a glass slide, placed a cover slip on it, and looked down the casualty microscope, which he had previously used to diagnose bilharzia from the shape of the eggs in the urine. He saw the unmistakable shape of human sperm, none of which were mobile by then. The story of the goat spread like wildfire at the hospital, and everywhere Ahmad went his friends would tease and ask him for an appointment for their goats.

Ahmad reframed the episode to himself as further experience in forensic medicine, the only part of medicine he was really passionate about at university. He concentrated on reading more and more journals and books on drowning, hanging, gunshot wounds, and stabbings. He yearned for the opportunity to go back to Edinburgh, or any other university to do graduate training in forensic medicine, but at that point in his career he just wanted to survive, make a good impression, and accumulate a nest egg for his future.

The socialist government kept tight control on incomes but had difficulty controlling top professionals, especially in the legal and medical fields. Lawyers, including Hasan, and physicians, including Ahmad, were permitted some private practice, mainly because of acute shortage of such qualified professionals. By the time Ahmad went home, Hasan's legal practice was well established. Ahmad, on the other hand, had to start from scratch, but his patient load increased as he gradually became known in the community. He was pleasantly surprised when Hasan sent him an official working for the British communications company Cableco to ask him to commit to being the private general practitioner for its employees, whose health benefits were part of their pay package. The government did not at all mind taking those people off its own responsibility. Ahmad signed a contract with the vice president for human resources and started seeing those patients, which generated him a steady guaranteed monthly stipend, for which he was grateful to his brother-in-law.

Two months later, he ran into his sister Salma at his parents' home, where he would sometimes go for Friday lunch.

"How is your practice going?" Salma asked him.

"Quite well, I think."

"So, no regrets about coming back home?"

"So far none, but who knows what the future holds?"

"I am sure it will be good. Hasan is doing very well indeed, but he had to work very hard to achieve all that."

"Yes, I saw your palace and was most impressed."

"You will do the same, and make lots of money, I am sure ... hmmm, which reminds me to give you a message from Hasan."

"Oh?"

"Well, he said to tell you that he is very happy that you signed the contract with Cableco, whose CEO is a personal friend of his ..."

"Yes, I am most grateful to Hasan. He is a true brother, and not just in-law!"

"But to be fair to him, he thinks you should pay him ten percent of your monthly retainer for making the deal possible. When are you going to start?"

Ahmad looked quite stunned and did not know how to react, but his anger then made him ask, "I can't believe what I am hearing, Salma. Are you asking me to part with ten percent of my hard-earned retainer to your millionaire husband just for connecting me with this company?"

"I am not! But there are such things as finder's fees, you know."

"But you are my sister! Cableco, a British company, was in desperate need for a British-trained doctor, or so I was told. No one told me upfront about the finder's commission. I just assumed that my dear brother-in-law was anxious to help me, and that is why I showered him with thanks. And you are my dear sister. Do you think that would be fair, or even ethical?"

"It is not me. I am just telling you what he said," Salma said, trying to cover her discomfiture.

"But your conveying the message implies that you agree. Did you not think to challenge him?"

"You don't know what he's like when it comes to money."

"Well, you take this message back. Say to him 'Mr. Ten Percent, have you no shame?' That's all. Good bye Salma."

Ahmad rose from his chair, said good-bye to his parents and his sister Zahra, giving her a big warm hug, and then drove back to his small apartment behind the hospital. He poured himself a glass of beer, in anticipation of the arrival of the East German female radiographer, with whom he had finally secured a date.

~

Ahmad's mother was a well-connected woman who knew lots of women in town. Unlike Hasan's mother, she was able to get around on her own without permission from her husband to visit her lady friends. Her husband, a university-educated man and ex-minister, employed a driver to take her and other family members wherever they wanted.

She waited a few weeks before broaching the subject of finding a bride for Ahmad, who had kept in touch with Ann by letter but kept that relationship secret until he would settle down in his new job and surroundings. Then he would send for her, if she would agree to come. His mother started suggesting names to him, especially first cousins and second cousins, but he kept resisting all such discussions, while recognizing that as a young physician he was one of the most eligible bachelors in the country. His medical work did keep him busy, but he was clearly longing for regular intimacy with a woman as he had been accustomed in Edinburgh.

One day his mother had a favor. "Ahmad, my love, I have a special request to ask you. One of my closest lady friends wondered if you would assess her daughter who is not well."

"Why? What's wrong with her?"

"Her pulse is irregular, she says. She has palpitations, which make her feel faint at times."

"Oh, that is common enough. I am sure her doctor can sort it out."

"No, they have seen more than one. They could not help her. Anyway, they heard about you, and they want to see a British-trained doctor."

"I have not established a private clinic yet, Mother, as you know. I am currently working at the casualty department and for that private company."

"I promised her that I would take you to her home to do a house call. Please don't let me down. You know, the girl's father has enormous respect for your father, and her mother is very close to me and has helped me in the past. I owe her."

"Well, if you have given her your word, Mother, I have no choice. But please don't volunteer my services in future."

~

Later that week, in the late afternoon, the driver took Ahmad and his mother to the plush home of that family and waited for them at the gate. The twenty-year-old patient, her two younger sisters, and her mother received them very warmly, since in the culture of the day a male doctor was an exception when it came to the mixing of men and women. There was a feast of pies and jam tarts and all sorts of Turkish delight and dates, together with mango juice, papaya juice, and pots of tea to enjoy. The young lady's father, who was busy at work, was the owner of the best patisserie shop in the country.

The two mothers monopolized the conversation, whereas the young ladies kept strictly silent until spoken to, as tradition commanded. However, Ahmad's mother asked the young woman several questions to demonstrate to her son that not only was she pretty, but she was also well spoken.

Thirty minutes later, it was time for the medical consultation. Ahmad and his patient went to a much smaller family room next door, but were not followed by any chaperone, to Ahmad's surprise. He started his evaluation with the usual history taking, which was quite unremarkable. He then proceeded to feel her pulse, measure her blood pressure, and look at her neck and mouth. It was then time to examine the source of those palpitations, the heart, which required some degree of undressing. She had truly beautiful breasts, and Ahmad had to place the palm of his hand on the left one and just underneath it to feel for the apex of the heart. He had not been with a woman for some time, and he kept reminding himself that he was there on a professional mission and that his mother's attempt to interest him in the girl would not succeed. The heartbeat was very regular but quite rapid, and the obviously excited patient submitted to that with eyes closed. The doctor then placed the bell of his stethoscope on the apex and other areas of the heart and chest, finding nothing wrong. He reassured his patient and left the room to join the others, where he also reassured her rather excited mother.

"But Doctor, why does she have all these palpitations, if everything is fine?"

"I am not sure, but I can tell you that her examination is entirely normal."

"Oh, I am so worried about her, Doctor. Do you think it is psychological? Among her sisters, she is the delicate and sensitive one. She has such strong emotions."

"Well, that is not necessarily a bad thing, especially in a woman."

"But she needs more support and love."

"Well ... hmmm ... She is lucky to have such a supportive family. I think the palpitations should settle down now. If they continue, it would be advisable to do a thyroid test, just in case."

"Oh, thank you, thank you, Doctor. You can do any tests on her; it does not matter how much they cost."

"I hope that will not be necessary. Well, with your permission, we have to leave now."

"Please come again and visit us any time ... I mean not as a doctor, but as a son... consider yourself family. Your mother and I are like sisters, you know."

"Yes, indeed; she speaks very highly of you."

∼

Ahmad's mother was dying to ask her son his opinion about the girl but had to hold back lest the driver should overhear the conversation.

Back in the house she cornered her son. "Did you like her?"

"She was a very pleasant and compliant patient."

"I meant as a bride, you rascal!"

"She is certainly beautiful, and well proportioned!"

"And very intelligent too."

"I could not judge that from this visit; for that I would need to sit with her a whole evening."

"Her mother invited you to go visit them any time."

"But I would need to talk to her one on one, and outside her home."

"Look here, son, this is not Britain. You cannot do that here. There you can take a woman out any time, and for any length of time. I understand that you can even *sample the goods* there!"

"I wasn't thinking of sampling the goods, as you put it, but to have several meetings, just the two of us. I have many questions. I need to feel that I love her before I marry her."

"I have heard all about this love before marriage of Europe. It's not love. It's lust. There they marry the women they love. Here men love the women they marry."

"I like that. I think that's witty and clever. If only it was true! If it was true, why do some men take four wives in this culture?"

"These are men who either have more money than sense or who feel so insecure that they want to prove their virility with a younger wife, the age of their own daughters."

"Look, I am not going to marry someone just because of her looks. I can't."

"If she goes out with you, and then you change your mind, she will be considered damaged goods even if you don't touch her, and no other man will ever ask for her hand."

"Why? Why is this society so obsessed with honor and shame—only for women mind you, not for men—that a conversation with a prospective suitor becomes a scandal?"

"But these are our traditions. Would you allow your sister Zahra to go out with a potential suitor?"

"Of course I would. They have a right to be alone with each other at a restaurant or coffee shop or on the beach. Why do we assume that if they did go out, then they would end up in bed? You have brought up your daughter to be chaste and respectable, didn't you? Even in Europe, couples don't end up in bed the moment they meet."

"My God! You cannot mean that. It seems that Scotland has ruined your values. One day you will have daughters, and you will want to protect them with your own life; you will see."

"Protect, yes, against men who would abuse her or take advantage of her, or make her an addict, or lead her into crime, but not ban any contact with men, as we are doing here."

"No man would ever want such a woman if she has spent any time alone with another man."

"Why?"

"Because he will assume that she has been compromised, because there was no chaperone."

"So, once again, it means that you think that Adeni girls are so horny and so desperate that they will jump into bed the moment they have the opportunity."

"No, we don't, but there is temptation during youth. Remember the saying of the Prophet, peace be upon him: 'Whenever a man and a woman are together, the devil will be the third.'"

"All right, what about the men then? As you already guessed, I have been with more than one Scottish woman. Why should this bride you are trying to find for me not also refuse me because I am not a virgin?"

"Now you are talking nonsense! Virginity is only for women."

"Why?"

"You are testing my patience; women are born virgins, and then ... when they go with a man, they lose their virginity. You are a doctor. You already know that."

"So, you are talking about anatomical virginity; I am talking about loss of innocence."

"It does not matter how you argue this issue scientifically. At the end of the day, what matters is what our society and our culture accepts as the norm, and what is right and what is wrong."

"I do respect your values, but it does not mean that I have to share them, not all of them. We are different generations and have different understandings about right and wrong and *halal* [kosher] and *haram* [forbidden]; and my children will also have different values from me, I fully expect."

"But you cannot thrive in a society if you do not share its values."

"There, you are absolutely right. But what if I tried to slowly change those values?"

"You will be considered a pariah. People will reject you. Your own family will disown you."

"I was afraid of that. Perhaps I should not be here?"

"Where else will you get the respect and appreciation that you will get in your own country? Do you want to go back to Scotland, where you will always be the brown foreigner? Didn't you tell me that some boys in Inverness on bicycles one day shouted at you 'Blackie go home!'? And you're not even black."

"Those were two ignorant teenagers. I can't judge all Scots by that episode, just like we do not want the Scots to judge Arabs or Muslims by what a handful of us might do."

"And what about the man in the bowler hat, the one you told your father about, who walked up to you on King Street in Edinburgh while you were holding hands with your girlfriend and told you to let go of it? I have not forgotten the story that you told us. As a mother, I felt the pain and humiliation you went through."

"Yes, true; that was on Princes Street, not King. I was really taken aback that afternoon. He was an educated man, just from his gray striped suit and bowler hat, a banker or a lawyer, and I was hurt. But Ann told him off so fiercely that he left with his tail between his legs."

"Son, just as there is no perfect bride, there is also no perfect homeland. It's your choice."

"I know. I need time to plan my future. I must go back and take a specialty degree."

"And leave us again for another seven years? Do you not feel that you owe us something in our old age?"

"What old age, Mother? You were seventeen when I was born. You are in your early forties, and Father is in his early fifties and he looks as healthy as a horse. He looks healthier than I am."

"*Alhamdulillah.* May Allah give him long life! But he has high blood pressure now and has to take pills. You never bothered to check his blood pressure."

"I did not know. But in general it is not correct to treat close family members. It is frowned upon."

"Maybe there in Scotland; here it is the exact opposite. He would feel so happy when you put your hand on him, his blood pressure would just drop to normal. He said he was not going to badger you about marriage, but I know that he would be in seventh heaven if you did find a bride."

"Here we go again! In any case, she may not like me or want to marry me, and that would solve the problem."

"Don't worry about that! Where else would she find a young, educated doctor from a very respectable family? And she will do what her father tells her to do."

"That is exactly what I fear."

"All right. Tell me what you don't like about her. You just admitted that she is beautiful. She is fair skinned, just like the British girls you knew there. You know, her father is originally from Iran; they are fair skinned. She is slim; she is always respectful to me. What else do you want?"

"She is not going to live with *you*, Mother. She will live with *me*. Anyway, I am in no rush to marry. "

"As a doctor, you should get married. For one thing, men will not trust you with their wives and daughters if you are not."

"So, they have not heard about the Hippocratic oath that doctors take?"

"All they go by is their gut feelings."

"But if I was bent on taking advantage of a female patient, how would my being married stop me? Lots of married men cheat on their wives; maybe the majority?"

"It will make it less likely. And the unmarried women will know that you are taken."

"So, it is not only because I am not to be trusted, it is also because they do not trust their own horny women?"

"Listen, son! I am getting tired of arguing. I have done my best to find you the ideal bride, but you won't find a perfect one. Frankly, I don't think you want to, at present. Maybe your heart is somewhere else?"

"Thank you, Mother! I really appreciate your efforts. Let's just leave it be for now."

⁓

Ahmad's experience with the goat was a mixed blessing. He was the butt of many jokes, but he began to be consulted about medico-legal issues.

He recognized that he had almost no training in that field, but he also realized that there was no one in the country who did. He therefore tried to gain some experience in the subject and made plans to leave home again to acquire formal training and certification in forensic science. He planned to leave after working in Aden for two years, during which time he would accumulate enough money to help him survive abroad.

The economic situation in the country was rapidly going from bad to worse, with poor productivity in a country with very few natural resources. Foreign aid from the Eastern Block was meager. The politicians running the government had no experience in administering a country and spent a lot of time making alliances, and plotting against each other. Despite poor salaries and obvious poverty, government employees were required to go out on weekly demonstrations in support of the government and demand that their own salaries be slashed in order to help the country's economy. Those who did not were labeled as traitors, and many who dared to oppose the official line were imprisoned. Some were tortured.

One of these was Farook, a well-spoken athletic young man in his thirties who was popular with his coworkers. He was a simple man who enjoyed the fresh air and loved swimming in Seera Bay, beyond Seera Island, where sometimes he would also catch fish for his children's supper. He defiantly refused to go out on those demonstrations, explaining that his salary was already so low that he could hardly support his wife and four children. He would not scream out that it should be reduced further, because that would come only out of fear and it would not be honest. Many of his colleagues at work were equally underpaid, but they did not stand up to authority and preferred to play along.

Farook thought he would set an example and hoped that at least some would follow him. Each government department had a political officer whose job was to educate the staff in their civic and patriotic duties to the government and the nation. One such had more than one chat with Farook, warning him that his disloyalty to the state was a serious crime and threatening him with serious consequences. Farook decided to stop urging his friends to defy the government, but he was determined never to go out on those demonstrations himself.

One Saturday morning, his absence from work was noted by his office coworkers. They waited a couple of days, wondering if he was perhaps sick. Then on Monday, one of his closer friends called at Farook's house on his way back from work. He spoke to his wife across the door, for it would have been improper for her to invite him in without her husband being there. She told him that on Friday afternoon, Farook had left home, as he often did, to go for a swim in Seera Bay, and that was the last she saw of him. She was worried sick and spoke to her mother-in-law, but she had not seen him either. The next day, her father-in-law reported his absence to the local police, who promised to investigate. That Monday evening the police went to see Farook's father to inform him that Farook had drowned and that his body was found floating in the sea, near the rocky beach by some fishermen returning home. The father was to collect Farook's body for burial.

In that small community, the story spread like wildfire. Those who knew Farook, and his swimming skills and prowess, found it very difficult to believe that he drowned, even if the sea was rough at the time, for he would go swimming every weekend no matter how high the waves were. The sad but irate father requested a meeting with the deputy chief of police, someone that he remembered from his childhood, as the son of the *imam* [preacher] of one of the smaller mosques in the town. The deputy chief assured Farook's father that the local police had nothing to do with the death of Farook and that they simply transported his body to the hospital mortuary, as required by their routine procedures. He then took the father to identify his son's body.

The father almost collapsed when the white sheet was pulled away from his son's face, but he did not see any evidence of external injury. He uttered the usual phrase in such situations, namely, "There is no strength except through Allah," as the sheet was pulled back to cover the face. However, he told the deputy chief that he suspected foul play because of the warnings Farook had received from the political officer in his department, which Farook had related to his own father rather than to his wife. He demanded a postmortem examination, which he had heard on the radio could sometimes reveal the truth about the cause of death.

~

In the absence of any police pathologist, Ahmad found himself summoned by the police to determine the cause of death of Farook. He had never done that before. This was serious business, which could have enormous implications, he reminded himself.

"Look, Chief, I am not a qualified pathologist. I am not trained to perform autopsies."

"You are the best we have. You have acquired a good reputation in this country. And in the country of the blind, the one-eyed man is king. That's what they say in the UK, where you trained."

"Why don't you bring in a proper pathologist from abroad?"

"You must know how difficult that would be. Furthermore, the body may deteriorate in the meantime and the evidence lost. And Muslims have to bury their dead as soon as possible, as you very well know."

"But if I make a specific diagnosis, there might well be serious repercussions."

"That is not your responsibility. You will provide the facts only, and the coroner will pronounce the verdict. Look at it this way: if you don't do it, there may be a miscarriage of justice. Would you want that on your conscience?"

"That is intellectual blackmail, Chief!"

"Thank you. I owe you one."

~

After revising all the notes he had on forensic medicine, especially with regard to drowning, Dr. Ahmad began the gruesome task of the carefully recorded forensic examination of Farook's body. He did not find any bullet wounds, stab wounds, or burn marks. The only external findings were mild bruises on the forehead, a cyanosed blue face, and a few lacerations on the elbows and knees, which he attributed possibly to the waves throwing the floating body against the rocks which surrounded Seera Bay. The hands were limp and open, not clutching any seaweed or other objects. The neck showed no laceration or impression of a rope. He estimated from the degree of rigor mortis that death occurred within a few hours and not since Friday, the day that Farook headed for the sea to swim, but he was not sure as he had virtually no experience in that part of the evaluation.

He scratched his head for the next move. He had no choice but to open up the chest. He was not sure what he would find, but this was a case of drowning, and the lungs would have something to do with it. As he looked at the slightly collapsed lungs, with the mortuary assistant looking on, he started imagining himself drowning. *What would happen?* he asked himself. He recalled how he almost drowned when a school friend pushed his head under the water at the Hoqqat swimming pool in Aden to scare him. He recalled how he resisted taking a breath to the last second, and how he did so, only as his face was emerging from the water, and then coughed and coughed while his bully friend was laughing his head off. And then it struck him. He cut through the lungs in four different areas and noted the absence of any water in the bronchi and bronchioles and the air cells in the parenchyma of the lungs. There was normal air in all those spaces. That might also help explain why the body was floating in the water. He then checked the hyoid bone, which is usually broken in the process of hanging. It was not broken.

∼

Ahmad prepared the autopsy report in detail and handed it to the deputy chief of police the next day. The latter wanted this done very quickly to make it possible to bury Farook's remains, as Islamic tradition of dignity of the dead dictated. He in turn would have to hand it up the line of command to his boss.

The chief of police for the city was flabbergasted by the unexpected findings. He summoned Dr. Ahmad to his office at the police headquarters, situated on top of a hill overlooking Seera Bay.

"Thank you for coming over, Dr. Ahmad. We appreciate your help."

"I am not sure if I was of much help. But I did my best with the limited experience I have."

"I know. My deputy told me that he really had to persuade you to do it."

"It is one of those unpleasant but inescapable duties of a doctor."

"I read your report, but could you tell me in plain language what your conclusions are?"

"Well, based on the scientific evidence, Farook did not drown."

"Did not drown? But his body was found floating in the sea, after he went swimming. It seems to me …"

Ahmad interrupted, "Let me tell you the reasoning behind my conclusion. It is in the report, but I will go over it in case you have questions. Yes, we are told that he was a very good swimmer, making drowning very unlikely. But it is still possible. My opinion, and you can seek a second opinion if you like, in fact I wish you would, is that Farook was murdered by suffocation and then his body was dumped in the sea."

The chief looked incredulous.

"Who would want to do that?"

"That is for you to find out. There is a rumor that he was cautioned by the political officer in his ministry because of his refusal to march in demonstrations supporting the government."

"Maybe, but he would not go this far, surely. Why couldn't it be drowning?"

"More than one reason. He went to the beach on Friday, but the time of death is estimated to be between eight and twenty-four hours before the autopsy, not three days."

"But these are only estimates and depend on the ambient temperature and whether the body was immersed in cold water."

"True, but the most important factor is the amount of gas or air in the chest, which would help the body float in water."

"But floating could occur because of postmortem gas formation in the bowels."

"Again, you are right. But if he drowned, despite being a great swimmer, he might have tightly clutched seaweed or other objects in his fist, which he did not …"

The chief interrupted, "Maybe there was no weed or such items around him."

"I was about to give you the most convincing evidence yet, Chief, namely that there was no water in his respiratory system, which makes the theory of drowning impossible."

"So how did he die? Or maybe I should say how was he murdered? You said in the report that he was not shot or stabbed or electrocuted or hanged."

"In my humble opinion, he was suffocated."

The police chief looked alarmed.

"But there were no rope marks on his neck. Did you examine his hyoid bone in the neck?"

"The hyoid bone was not broken."

"Then how can that be?"

"The hyoid would be broken with hanging, or strangulation with a very strong grip round the neck. But if I handcuff you and place a strong plastic bag over your head to block air entry via the nose and mouth, death would occur in just a few minutes, with cyanosis of the face but without hyoid fracture or water in the lungs. I think that is the answer, as I am sure you know from your own training."

"That is amazing. We did not learn these things in my days. Perhaps the young police cadets are taught this science nowadays."

"I myself need to go abroad to learn more forensic science."

"Well, I will have to turn this to the Criminal Investigation Department tomorrow. Thank you, Doctor."

~

Within only two days, the story went through the offices of the chief prosecutor, the ministry of justice, and the national security office, which answered directly to the president and was headed by president's brother-in-law. If this was murder, the implications would be serious, and in a small population like that one, the news would spread in no time.

Ahmad thought that he did a reasonable job in coming to a probable cause of death. Thus when three men arrived at Ahmad's home in a Land Rover just after he had his lunch, he was very surprised indeed, especially since he thought he had explained everything to the chief of police.

Their leader asked him to accompany them to "national security," a term that evoked terror in most people's hearts. He was so taken aback that he did not remember to ask them for identification. He tried to find out what it was about, but was told that he would find out once he was there.

He was ushered into the office of a middle-aged man in plain clothes who identified himself simply as Alwan. He said, "Welcome, Doctor. How are you?"

"*Alhamdulillah*. What is this all about?"

"National Security is very interested in this *miskeen* [poor man] who drowned."

"Really? Why? Is he a spy or something?"

"No, no, he was just a government employee, but we are always concerned when such a young man dies, and there is controversy about the cause of death."

"I am sure you have a copy of the pathology report which I handed over to the police."

"Yes, of course, but I just wanted to hear it directly from you. You know how sometimes things are misunderstood when they are written."

"On the contrary, I find that there is a lot more misunderstanding with verbal communication."

"In any case, Doctor, I wanted to know how sure you were about your findings, because I understand that you are not a qualified pathologist."

"You are absolutely right, and I am going back next year to study forensic science properly. But the police asked me to investigate. I tried to get out of it, but they insisted. I wish you would bring a proper pathologist from India or Egypt to check my findings."

"Yes, I think we should, because your report accuses someone of suffocating this poor man who had no money or power or enemies."

"It sounds as though there is absolutely no motive. And yet there is a murderer, or murderers, somewhere, who have perpetrated this crime. But I am surprised at the interest shown by you. May I ask why?"

"We have our reasons, and we are the ones who ask the questions, Doctor. But until the investigations are completed, we don't want you to mention any of this, or even your visit here, to anyone whatsoever. Not even to your immediate family or your wife … Oh, you don't have one, I just remembered," Alwan said, looking down at the top of his desk covered with paper. "Not even to the pretty East German radiographer you have been seeing!"

Ahmad felt terrified at the final warning. He knew then that he had been under surveillance for some time and that Alwan meant what he said.

~

The rumor that subsequently circulated in the city was that Farook drowned because the sea was particularly rough the day he went swimming, and Ahmad heard nothing more about that episode. However, he became somewhat depressed about the miscarriage of justice of which he was a reluctant and silenced accomplice, and he became constantly anxious, knowing that his every move was being monitored.

As if he needed more trouble, a month later his father had a massive heart attack walking up a long flight of stairs, and although he was rushed to hospital by some people around him at the time, he was pronounced dead on arrival. As the man of the family, Ahmad had to attend the usual prayers performed on such occasions and to receive men's condolences at his father's house, while his mother together with Salma and Zahra also received their women friends and acquaintances.

~

Ahmad was somewhat reassured that his professional standing, as one of the very few Adeni physicians, protected him to a limited extent from the vagaries of the thugs at national security. But he was determined to keep his secret, bide his time until his course in forensic science began at Napier University in Edinburgh, and then speak out the truth that hung heavily on his shoulders.

He was therefore concerned when, nearer the time, he began to make preparations to inform his administrator at the hospital of his plans and to obtain an exit visa. When he had returned to the People's Democratic Republic of Yemen, he was carrying his old British passport and never considered obtaining a local one, at least not until that one expired. But he still had to obtain an exit visa, which was repeatedly denied him, the ostensible excuse being the shortage of medical staff at the hospital. He found himself trapped, and the prospect of missing the beginning of his training course in Scotland depressed him even more. He found himself drinking more heavily than usual. The socialist government of the day relaxed the rules against alcohol, which became his companion most evenings. In his alcohol-induced daydreams, he began planning his secret escape—whatever the cost.

CHAPTER 13

~

PARALYZED IN SLEEP

One of the obvious advantages of being a physician is the vast number of people that one interacts with. On a working day, Ahmad would easily talk, often intimately, with a hundred or more men and women, discussing their symptoms of course but also their work, families, eating habits, sleep pattern, and relationships with their family members. Some conversations might be much longer and more hush-hush than others. All that was normal in the daily routine of a doctor, and it raised no suspicion.

Luck was on Ahmad's side the day he saw a thirty-year-old man called Khaled, who had a bizarre complaint.

"Good morning, Khaled. What is the problem?"

"A morning of jasmine to you, Doctor. By Allah, I have come all the way from Rahidah to find you. I heard from a man in our village that you cured his seizures just with one pill a day. He says that since he started taking that small white pill every morning, the convulsions never came back, even though the pills are very cheap. When he was taking three different very expensive pills prescribed by another doctor, it made no difference and he was sleepy even during the day. He could not do his work properly. Abdo sends you his warmest greetings, and says if you need any service from him, he is at your command."

"Abdo who?"

"Abdo Haifani, from the village of your grandfather's father."

"Oh, yes! I remember now," Ahmad pretended, trying to make Abdo out of the thousands of patients who had passed through his hands.

"Well, sir, I have a different problem. You could say it is the opposite of that of Abdo. Whereas he convulses when he gets his attack, and his arms and legs and the whole body shake repeatedly for a few minutes and he cannot stop it, and even his family cannot stop it with all their strength holding down his body, I cannot move. I cannot move at all. Not even one finger. I am totally paralyzed for what seems like an eternity, but I am sure it is only minutes."

"Can you talk during the attack?"

"No, not a breath. I want to talk. I like talking, but I cannot."

I can believe that! Ahmad said quietly to himself.

"If I could talk, I would call out to my wife lying next to me for help. But I cannot make any noise or utter a single letter. But I can see her, because my eyes are open. There she lies happily sleeping or snoring. *Subhan Allah* [the wonder of Allah], how women are so happy! It is only us men that experience catastrophes!"

"So, you are trying to say that this happens only at night when you are in bed asleep?"

"No, I mean yes. It happens at night when I am asleep, but if I have a long siesta in the afternoon after lunch, or during the month of Ramadan, it can happen too. It is very scary, Doctor. I feel paralyzed and completely helpless. At first I thought I was dead but alert. *Subhan Allah.* But after I had a few of these attacks and I woke up, I knew I would not die. But our fate is in the hands of Allah."

Dr. Ahmad briefly examined the patient with special attention to his muscle tone, power, and deep tendon reflexes, finding them to be completely normal.

"Khaled, I have good news for you. You have a very rare condition called sleep paralysis, and while it is very frightening during the few seconds or minutes it lasts, it is not dangerous. It can be controlled with one daily pill."

"Just like my friend Abdo?"

"Yes, just like him. Here, take these three pills, I happen to have some in the drawer, and come back in three days to tell me what happens. Then I will give you a prescription and you can buy enough pills for the whole year. You may not find these in Rahidah." Ahmad had a few imipramine tablets he was using to control his own depression.

"Thank you, thank you, Doctor. I swear by Allah that if you cure me, I will do anything you ask of me, *anything!*"

~

Three days later Khaled came back, the answer written all over his face. It was the first time in his life that he had three nights in a row without sleep paralysis. He showered the doctor with praise and brought a box of *halawa,* the local version of Turkish delight.

"Now, Doctor, I am at your service, whatever you need."

"Actually what I need is for you to take me across the border to Rahidah, and then I can make my way to my great grandfather's village. I have always wanted to visit his grave. I was told that he was a very pious man who always helped the people in the village. But I don't want anyone to know anything about this. I want it to be a total surprise to the village, because I want to take some medical equipment and pills for their local clinic. Can you do that?"

"Consider it done, even if I had to carry you on my shoulders!"

"Great, thank you. How much would that cost?"

"Nothing!"

"No, I insist that I pay you."

"You have changed my life with one small pill. That is payment enough. In any event, I travel that way almost every month, whenever I come down to Aden to buy things we cannot get up there in our village, including medicines, so you will just ride with me. If we find that we need money, I will let you know. When do you want to go?"

"I will have to organize myself and take a week off work, and then slip out during that week so that I will not be missed at the hospital. This must remain top secret. Is next month all right with you?"

"Do not worry about the secret, Doctor. If the security people find out, I myself will be in big trouble. So, I will come down on the last Thursday of next month, and we can leave on Friday. It is a blessed day, *inshaallah*."

~

That summer witnessed the government executing its nationalization policy. Land, buildings, and property that once belonged to ordinary, law-abiding citizens and private businesses were nationalized and, almost overnight, became government owned. The Marine Port of Aden, once rated one of the best in the world, next to New York and Singapore for bunkering facilities, suffered badly.

With a very heavy heart, Ahmad disclosed his plans to his mother but not to his sisters. He did not worry too much about Salma, who was married and secure with her husband, Hasan. But he very much wanted to hold Zahra in his arms and to promise her that he would come back to look after her, and help with her education, but could not take that risk. His mother could not control her tears as she helplessly embraced him and wished him good luck. They hugged for a moment, and with a quivering voice she whispered, "As soon as you arrive at your destination and feel safe, please let us know somehow, okay?"

Ahmad placed a big wad of banknotes in her hand, enough to keep them going for one year. They had no other source of income, but at least they had their own home, which his father had built when he was minister in the previous government.

"I know what will happen," his mother said.

"What?"

"I can just see it. You will go back to Scotland, you will marry a foreigner, and we will never see you again."

"Mother, marriage to a foreigner, or to a Yemeni woman for that matter, is the last thing on my mind just now."

"I believe you. One starts thinking of a wife only when one is settled, both physically and mentally. Over there, that will happen. Even these modern European girls want to get married in the end. Don't think that they want to remain unmarried forever. They want to have children, and they want stability and love, not just sex. I know; I am a woman."

"I am sure you are right, Mother."

"That's what I fear, because some lucky girl will find you, and when she does, I will lose you; and your sisters will lose you too."

"No, I will always look after Zahra."

"I am happy to hear it. I know deep in my heart that I will never see you again. But, on this Quran, I want you to promise me that you will not abandon Zahra, that you will help her study and develop and that you will be there to give her away when she gets married to a good man."

"With the help of Allah, I shall do that. But I know that I will see you soon, Mother. I am only going for specialization and should be back in two years. You will see."

"May Allah be with you wherever you go, and may He help you in all your endeavors!"

~

A month later, as Ahmad was walking out the front door of their residence, he could not fight the urge to see his mother's face one more time, perhaps for the last time. Both she and Zahra stood on the top of the stairs motionless and looked down at him as he lingered by the front door. They had the look of helplessness, yet the look of hope and good wishes for a loved one. One final wave, and he was out on the street.

He walked two blocks, turned the corner, and saw Khaled sitting in a dilapidated truck on the side of the narrow street, near the stinking rubbish dump where they had agreed to rendezvous. A couple of goats were chewing at some of the garbage that spilled out of the huge metal rubbish bin. Khaled had collected Ahmad's suitcase ahead of time, as Ahmad did not want any of his neighbors to see him carrying a suitcase, for that would spell disaster for him in such a small community.

They drove north for less than an hour. He had never traveled to the northern part of the country before and had mixed emotions filled with a sense of excitement and adventure. Khaled said, "Please forgive me,

Doctor, but I will no longer call you Doctor from now on—only Ahmad. We have to pretend that you are a poor villager acting as my assistant, and I want you to pretend that you are stupid, like me ... and that you cannot read or write. And another thing, Ahmad. I don't like what you are wearing; you need to change. We will hide your nice trousers for when you are across the border. Now you have to wear an old cheap *footah* [sarong] and completely blend with the background."

They stopped at a local flea market, which sold used peasants' clothing and old shoes. Ahmad wondered how he was going to change into his new attire, without attracting attention to his camouflage. However, Khaled led him into a nearby mosque where he changed into a footah, a crumpled long-sleeved shirt, and oversized old shoes without laces, as well as a turban-like head cover.

"From now on, don't say a word to anyone. Let me handle it, you understand?" Khaled warned.

"Why?"

"Your city accent will give you away."

Ahmad nodded quietly, wondering if he could play the part correctly. Khaled took care of the procedures at the checkpoint and then proceeded to the next destination, the village of Al-Howta about twenty-five miles north. They arrived a little after sunset after a very dusty and rough ride.

There they stopped at a very modest local restaurant that served *foul moudammas* [fava beans] dressed with olive oil and cumin accompanied by a slice of lemon. Halfway through that meal, the first one since they left Aden, Khaled suddenly jumped to his feet as he saw a military Land Rover with two soldiers stop about fifty yards away and turn its lights off. He wiped his hands against the side of his *footah* [sarong] and waved to Ahmad to jump back into the truck in case the soldiers decided to eat at the same place, and happened to interrogate them. Ahmad also quickly wiped his greasy hands against the side of his footah and dashed toward the parked truck with his mouth still full of beans.

It was pitch dark on the road except for the beam of the headlights of the moving truck. The smell of dust and manure filled the warm air.

They drove for approximately three hours into the dark, humid night

on unpaved and dangerous winding dirt roads. The low terrain gave way
to a mountainous road where they found themselves ascending a hill. The
higher they went, the cooler it thankfully became.

It was about two in the morning when they finally arrived at a village
off the main road. The village dogs greeted the arrival of the truck with
almost incessant barking which, combined with the noise from the old
truck engine, disturbed the peace of the starless night.

They had barely slept two hours in the truck when around 5:00 a.m.
the village mosque loud speakers called the villagers to dawn prayers. They
rushed over to the mosque but did not pray. Instead, they were glad to
use the washroom facilities. The village was the last one on the southern
side of the border, where Khaled would normally rent the truck. On other
occasions he would drive to the border and then transfer his goods to
another truck on the Yemeni side. This time, however, he had a special
passenger, and he did not want to be caught smuggling him across the
border. He therefore had to park the goods he bought with a shopkeeper
he knew, to be collected later, and they started their long walk toward the
border while it was still dark and cool.

There were hills all around them and Ahmad had no idea where they
were heading, but he felt that he had to place his trust in Khaled. And for
a moment he found himself praying to God, something he had not done
for ages, to allow him to complete his escape.

Because of all the walking and the friction from the heavy old shoes
that did not fit, Ahmad developed painful blisters on his feet. But despite
excruciating pain, he was determined to continue.

At about noon, Khaled suddenly stopped and looked behind to survey
the mountainous area. He seemed to be trying to verify their location
while talking quietly to himself. Hesitantly, he asked if Ahmad could see
a flagpole on top of one of the hills behind them. When Ahmad confirmed
the sighting, Khaled pointed to the flagpole in the distance and said,
"Hey, guess what! That is the Communist territory. You are now on safe
ground!"

Ahmad could not believe his ears. Ecstatic that he had safely arrived in
the neighboring country of Yemen, he hugged Khaled while tears welled

up in his eyes. But he checked his tears and accelerated his pace to the next village, toward freedom, toward a new life.

~

The village of Rahidah was a mere twenty kilometers from the border, with a relatively decent road, traversed by many cars, including some rickety taxis. One such stopped to pick up the two passengers, even though there was only room for one.

"Space is in the heart," the taxi driver said, encouraging the two of them to squeeze into space meant for one passenger. They looked at each other and decided that they wanted to get as far away from the border as possible, just in case they were discovered by the security agents. They would have to be returned to the south, or would have to pay a hefty bribe. Once again Khaled put his forefinger on his lips, telling Ahmad to say nothing.

Minutes later, they arrived in the small village of Rahidah. The outskirt of the village on the eastern side was lined up with stalls selling fruits and vegetables, or halawa, or all these together. The taxi stopped just outside a traditional restaurant, a *mukhbazah*, where Ahmad had his first hearty meal of flatbread, *khubz,* all mashed up with dates, and big helpings of ghee, together with numerous cups of tea stewed with milk and sugar and cardamom. His ordeal over, his mind was so relaxed that it seemed to him like the best meal he had in a very long time.

"Khaled, can you find a way to get me to my grandfather's village, Haifan?"

"No problem, Doctor, even if I have to carry you there myself."

They walked together to the taxi stand in the middle of the small village. It was a noisy, totally disorganized taxi stand. Khaled inquired, but none of the taxis would go to Haifan because the road was far too rough. Suddenly Khaled saw a friend loading many boxes of soap and shampoo and cleaning material, together with a huge number of plastic buckets for holding water, onto the back of a medium-sized truck. There were already many boxes of biscuits and sweets destined for some shops in the area around Rahidah.

"*Assalamu alaikom*, Mahmood!"

"*Wa alaikom assalam*! What a pleasant surprise! What are you doing here, Khaled?"

"I came over to buy a few things from the market for the family, and to accompany the doctor here. He is a dear friend, and the best Yemeni doctor in the world."

"Welcome, Doctor," Mahmood said, extending his hand to shake with both men.

"Are you from Taiz, Doctor?" Mahmood wanted to know.

Khaled butted in. "No, but his village is Haifan, and he wants to visit his grandfather's grave there. Could you take him there? It should be on your way."

"But that is my father's village. What a coincidence. No problem, but I have to make a few stops to deliver these goods. I will be going to Taiz after that. There is a lot of choice of goods over there."

"That's even better. It will be like a sightseeing trip for the doctor. And I am sure he can see your father for you. You told me he had a stroke three weeks ago, right?"

"That would be wonderful. I would be very grateful. We hardly see any real doctors here. The ones in this area are useless."

"With pleasure," Ahmad reassured the man.

～

The road to the village of Haifan was rough. The lurching of the truck was so bad that Ahmad felt nauseated after only a few minutes. The road, such as it was, was wide enough for only one car, except for the occasional passing places. Fortunately, there were hardly any other vehicles, and the driver was able to park his truck where it stood to give Ahmad a chance to get out and stretch his legs, and get rid of his nausea.

The air was so fresh up there, and considerably cooler than what Ahmad was accustomed to in Aden. Fortunately, it was not a long haul, and the trip took under one hour. Mahmood dropped some household goods at a very small general store as he entered the village. Ahmad stayed near the truck but could see money passing from the hands of the shopkeeper into Mahmood's. The next stop was Mahmood's father's little house, which was built of stone. Ahmad was very warmly welcomed by Mahmood's father, Ali, as if he was an old friend. Even Mahmood's mother came into the little front room to greet him, without covering her face, that custom being less strictly observed in those small villages than in the bigger towns of Yemen. Tall glasses of grape juice, almost overflowing, were brought in by the mother.

"So, Mahmood tells me that your grandfather is buried here in our village. What is his name?"

"It is actually my great grandfather. My grandfather was buried in Aden. His name is Abdo; and his father was Saleh."

"Oh, Saleh must be the son of Ghanem who had a small farm and a house just up the street from ours. I still remember the family. And Saleh had three sons and one daughter. The daughter married a man from Taiz. Two of the sons emigrated, one to Eritrea where he married a woman from there, and the other one became a sailor and traveled on the big ships sailing between Britain and India. He used to stop in Aden from time to time and would come up here to the village, which he always loved. Then, he married a Christian woman in Cardiff and had six children by her; but they all stayed in Britain and lost touch with the village. But your grandfather, Abdo, was smart. He left for Aden, where he had the advantage of living in comfort because of the British system, and yet he would come up to the village almost every year at the time the *Eid* [annual religious holiday]. He would bring so many nice presents for his nieces and his sister before she moved to Taiz. I still remember him. He was a handsome man, very nicely dressed, with a gray beard. And he was smart because he knew how to read and write."

"You seem to know the whole history of my family, Uncle Ali."

Ali was very pleased that Ahmad, a highly educated, Western-trained doctor, would address him as uncle, as tradition would dictate. He felt gratified that his education did not make him forget his roots and manners.

"In a small village like this one, everyone knew everything about everyone else. And the people here are very nosey. They like to find out things about their neighbors," he said with a chuckle. "So, your full name is Ahmad Shawqi Abdo Saleh Ghanem. *Mashaallah!* [How wonderful!] This afternoon, after the afternoon prayers, I will show you where Saleh Ghanem is buried; it is just behind the little mosque where we will pray." The change in Ahmad's face must have been quite apparent to Ali, who continued, "You do pray, I take it? Or have you abandoned the pillars of Islam while you were in the West?"

"Um, um, well, not regularly. Life is so busy, especially when you are a doctor."

"Life should never be too busy to remember Allah."

"No, of course not! We all have to do what we can. The Quran itself says that Allah does not demand of man more than man can deliver."

"True, true," Ali said, nodding his head in agreement.

To Ahmad's relief, Mahmood changed the subject by asking him about the weakness of his father's face. Ahmad had already noted the facial asymmetry and the sagging left cheek.

"This happened to him a month ago," Mahmood volunteered.

"How did it happen? Did he hit his face on some object?"

"No, no, Doctor. I just woke up with it one morning," Ali replied.

"Was there any pain, Uncle Ali?"

"No."

"Is your hearing okay?"

"Funny you should ask. Actually, when it happened at first, I could hear better with that ear, the left one, I mean. Sound seemed louder than before."

"Are you taking any medication for anything else?"

"No."

"I told him not to bulge his cheek with so much qat," Mahmood interrupted. "He is not as young as he used to be. But he does not listen to me. Maybe he will listen to you, Doctor."

"So, Mahmood, you think that the big lump of qat stretched his face on the left side?"

"Perhaps?" Mahmood replied.

Ahmad asked the patient to blow his cheeks up with air and noted that air leaked from the left angle of his mouth. Then he told him to close his eyes tight and to stop him from forcefully opening them. On the left side, Ahmad was able to open the father's eye just a few millimeters. He then verified that his four limbs were working normally.

"I have good news for you," he said.

Mahmood and his parents beamed big smiles.

"This is a facial palsy, which will recover completely, inshallah, within one month from now."

"And what is the treatment?" Mahmood asked.

"No need for any pills."

"Or an injection? We will pay, Doctor, don't worry."

"No injection either. It is not required. It will return to normal. I think it is already improving."

"Yes, it is true," Ali agreed. "It is less severe than last month."

"Tell him not to chew so much qat, Doctor. It stretches the cheek," Mahmood insisted.

Ahmad smiled and looked at the father, who smiled back asymmetrically.

~

After visiting his great grandfather's grave, Ahmad felt a surprising closeness to the village, which he got to know for a couple of hours only. He knew his origins, and there was something good and reassuring about that. He felt some pride that he was a highly educated doctor who came from such humble beginnings only three generations before. He knew then why some people would go out of their way to trace their roots to the direct descendants of Prophet Muhammad; until then, he did not understand why it was so important to them. He promised himself that if he had money he would come back and build a clinic or a library for the villagers of Haifan. But Ahmad's preoccupation, at that point, was to make his way back to Britain, where he would find Ann and plan the rest of his training in forensic medicine, a subject that he had become obsessed with, recognizing how little he knew of that important science. He reckoned that he would have little difficulty because very few physicians chose that career.

~

Mahmood and Ahmad shared the small extra room in the house, but there were no beds, only very thin homemade mattresses and pillows, and each man had a moldy blanket, which Mahmood's mother managed to fish out of a big wooden chest in the corner of the same room. Before Ahmad lay on the mattress, he had not realized how much the floor of the room sloped from one wall to the opposite one. He wished he had a water level just to measure the degree of the slope. He was glad he had been assigned the mattress closest to the lower end of the room. Mahmood was at the higher end. Unlike most Yemenis, Mahmood was moderately overweight with a big belly, a thick neck, and a double chin. Ahmad attributed it to the fact that his job consisted of sitting in the driver's seat of his truck day in and day out. As he blew out the flame of the kerosene lamp, he said good-night and turned away from Ahmad and toward his own wall.

Ahmad was exhausted and ordinarily would have gone out like a light. However, that night in those unfamiliar surroundings, lying on a thin mattress on the hard cement floor, and with all the events of his escape flashing in his visual memory, he had some difficulty falling asleep for at least ten minutes, although he could not check his watch in that total darkness. Just as he began to doze off, Mahmood's snoring started, at first low but soon building into a loud, regular auditory crescendo interrupted only by irregular snorting and stoppage of respiration, which Ahmad recognized as the classic pattern of sleep apnea. He decided that he would take the initiative in the morning to tell him to start losing weight as soon as possible. The pressure for sleep built so much that, loud snoring notwithstanding, he eventually fell into a deep slumber, with only brief interruptions.

At dawn, he was awakened by the call to prayer from the minaret of the local mosque and the chorus of the village roosters. At that moment of awakening, when human beings just realize that they have been asleep and dead to the world for hours, he became aware of Mahmood's big torso pressing against his right shoulder. And during those few seconds when he was still half asleep, he was alarmed by the fat body next to his and did not know what to make of it. He pushed Mahmood's trunk away from his own shoulder, which caused him to open his eyes momentarily.

"Oh," Mahmood said, "I am very sorry, Doctor. I must have rolled over all the way from the other end of the room. How can I apologize, especially when you are our guest? Please forgive me."

Ahmad started giggling.

"Don't worry about it. What do you expect when the floor is sloping that much? If I had slept where you did, I would have rolled all the way down too."

The two looked at each other and laughed together.

"I am glad I did not imagine you to be a woman during the night, Doctor!"

"I sure am glad too!" Ahmad countered, laughing even louder.

After thanking Mahmood's father and mother for their hospitality, Ahmad traveled back to Rahidah in Mahmood's truck, and after a brief stop for some sweet boiled tea, they headed for Taiz, which was forty kilometers away. The closer they got to Taiz, the prettier the landscape would become. Only the tiny village of Dimnah was in their path, but they did not stop. However, some of the villagers stared as they drove through, and a few little boys waved to them, big smiles beaming from faces with big, dark eyes. The little girls just stared; they were not allowed to wave to male strangers.

~

Taiz is a beautiful and ancient city with a long history, culture, and civilization, often used by the Imam of Yemen as his summer capital. It is the second largest city after Sanaa. In the twelfth century, it was made capital of Yemen by the Ayyubid Dynasty, of which the most famous leader was Salahuddin. At a height of one thousand and four hundred meters above sea level, it is relatively cool, especially for those arriving from Mokha on the Red Sea to the west or from Aden in the south. The city lies in a large area like a wide crater, surrounded by mountains, the highest and most famous being Saber, itself three thousand meters above sea level. Homes dot the lower reaches of these hills and mountains and are reachable by steep, serpentine, and difficult roads. Some of the prettiest mosques nestle in the city.

Ahmad fell in love with the city at first sight. He had planned to reach the capital, Sanaa, as soon as possible, but once in Taiz he decided to stay for a few days. In that small and close-knit society, his arrival did not go unnoticed, especially since the alarm was raised in Aden about his escape. Somehow the news reached an old schoolmate of his, who was practicing medicine in the city. Being a very well-connected doctor, he soon tracked Ahmad down to the Wadi Hotel where he was staying.

After the obligatory hugs and kisses, Ahmad told Nageeb his story and heard about his too.

"So, you have decided to leave your country?"

"Frankly, it is my country that left me. It is not possible for someone like me to live there. Not now, after this change of government. I really felt that I was in danger there."

"You have always been one of those people who like to say it like it is, even at school."

"And so were you, as I remember it. I think that's why we became friends."

"Look at us now. We have not seen each other for ten years or more."

"I too am surprised to see you here—in Taiz, I mean in North Yemen. You were born in Aden, were you not?"

"Yes, that is how I went through the British school system with you. But, my links with Taiz are very strong, because unlike your father, who was born in Aden and lost his Hugari roots, mine was born here but then got married in Aden, and I was born there. "

"Actually, my father, may he rest in peace, did not really lose his roots. I still remember how he could speak the typical accent of Hugariyyah. It is a lovely accent; I love it."

"It is this constant search for one's roots that seems to occupy everyone I know. People are always asking me, 'Are you from the south or from the north?' as if we are so different. Look at us for example. We are both Adeni, but I am more Hugari because of the accident of my father's birth and my coming over here where I still have several uncles and aunts, and of course dozens of cousins. All these borders were drawn by kings and emirs and sheikhs, not to mention colonial powers; it's just like with Syria and Lebanon, or North Korea and South Korea."

"And all these people living across barbed-wire fences," Ahmad lamented. "In some countries, families are split up and are never allowed to meet. How cruel! At least here we can come and go across the border, and before the Communists took over in the south people movement was quite free. We always had laborers and servants doing a lot of work in the south. Then we heard nasty things said about how the Adenis mistreated them. I am sure some employers were nasty, but the majority was not; just like in any country that imports labor, like Saudi Arabia."

"So, you want to go back to the UK? Have you not had enough?" Nageeb changed the subject.

"It is an island of peace and tranquility compared with here. But I need to specialize; I don't want to be a general practitioner all my life."

"And what's wrong with being a general practitioner like me?" Nageeb said, feigning anger.

"I just have this desire to go into forensic medicine, which I loved at medical school, but we only scratched the surface of the subject then."

"How can you earn a living doing that?"

"I would have to work at a medical school, or a major hospital, or as consultant to the prosecutor general, or a law firm."

"Are you sure that's the reason? Is it not some woman that is beckoning you back there?"

"No, not really."

"No wonder you did not get married in Aden. Did your mother not find you someone?"

"Oh, she tried; very hard in fact."

"No problem. It's not too late. We will find you a beautiful girl here.

Did you know that the girls who live on the mountain of Saber are the most beautiful in the whole of Yemen, north and south? And it is rumored that they are just as horny as those British girls that you got used to!"

"Nageeb, stop that nonsense! I am not staying here. First of all I am not a citizen here ..."

"No problem. We will get you a Yemeni identity card and passport. I have so many friends here, and if I did not, a wad of riyals will do it."

"Thank you, my dear friend. I will always remember your kind offer with gratitude, but no."

"Well, I have another offer for you. I am sure you will be much more comfortable staying with me in my house for a few days while you plan your next move."

"No, I cannot ..."

"Look, we are not in Scotland here. This is your country, and I am your close friend, and Ahlam will be very happy to feed you and look after you."

"Your wife? I did not think I would be allowed to meet her."

"This is Taiz, my friend, not Sanaa. We are modern people; she has a university degree in psychology; things are rapidly changing. In any event, you will have your own private quarters just above my *mafraj* [qat reception room] and you can walk across to eat with us. So tomorrow, Friday, I will collect you from the hotel after breakfast. You, being so British, probably eat early. Yes?"

Ahmad nodded his head, as Nageeb turned and left.

⁓

Nageeb came over in his big four-wheel Toyota, but there was very little luggage because Ahmad had left Aden with very little in order not to raise suspicion. Ahmad had a great tour of Taiz on his way to a grand and beautiful house, built of gray stones, on the lower slopes of one of the many hills encircling the city.

As they entered the house into the living room, Ahmad noted the obvious affluence of the place. He sat in a big armchair, upholstered in brown leather, and turned his head round in a circle, surveying the lovely furnishings. There was a porcelain vase with fresh pink oleander flowers, their sweet fragrance permeating the room, and an expensive-looking Persian carpet hanging from the wall.

His survey was interrupted by the arrival of Nageeb, who had left Ahmad unnoticed, now back, hand in hand with a very beautiful woman of about twenty. She wore a yellow and blue dress down to her knees, below which Ahmad noted a pair of shapely and smooth legs in low-heeled blue shoes. Her straight, shiny, black hair was down to her mid back. But most stunning were her dark eyes with long black eye lashes. Her warm personality was radiating through that pair of eyes as the couple came forward, and she firmly shook hands with Ahmad. Ahmad knew that local custom would not permit him to compliment her on her beauty, lest it be considered flirting, and so he complimented her on the beauty of her house instead. It was Nageeb, however, who said, "As you can see, Ahlam comes from the mountain of Saber."

~

Friday after lunch is the ritual of chewing qat all over Yemen, and for Nageeb that was a great opportunity to introduce Ahmad to a large number of people. And what could be a better captive audience than a bunch of Yemenis chewing that famous green leaf? Deep in his heart, he was hoping that getting Ahmad to know several people, some perhaps from his childhood years, might persuade him to stay in Taiz and join his practice. Although none knew Ahmad personally, several had heard about his father who had been a government minister in Aden, and even more men either knew or had heard of his grandfather, who left Haifan for Aden many years before. Ahmad was quite pleased to know that, for this sense of belonging was still nagging at him, especially as he was trying to settle in one permanent place which he could call home one day. The conversation was quite animated that afternoon, because of the new guest.

"Dr. Ahmad, I hope you don't mind, but this is a rare opportunity for me to ask you a medical question," one obese qat chewer facing Ahmad began. "Every week when I sit down to chew qat, my left thigh becomes so numb that I cannot feel it anymore. What do you think that is?"

Ahmad thought, *There we go again. I cannot go anywhere without giving free medical advice to some unabashed customer.* But then he was on the spot, and he knew that he had to prove to the people in Taiz, just like he had in Aden, that he was a good doctor."How long has that been going on?"

"One year I think, but it does not happen when I am standing or lying down."

"Did anything happen a year ago?"

"Nothing to my leg. Oh, I did have a disc operation, disc number five, I was told."

"This is amazing, the same thing happens to me, only on the outer aspect of my right thigh, and I never had a disc operation," another big man volunteered on overhearing the discussion.

"Are you left-handed?" Ahmad asked the second man.

"Yes. But how did you know?" the man replied in amazement.

"Now I can answer your questions."

"You mean without doing an X-ray or any other tests?"

"X-rays would not help here. You see, the first brother is right-handed, so he leans on the two cushions with his left elbow in order to pluck the qat leaves with his dominant right hand. And his left thigh is tightly flexed at the hip, under his body on the floor. This puts extra compression on a very thin nerve in the groin, for the length of the qat-chewing session; let us say three or four hours. Thus, the area of the skin supplied by that thin nerve cannot feel anything, so you feel pins and needles or burning there. And when you stand up, the leg is no longer bent so the nerve is no longer stretched and sensation returns very slowly. The second brother, I noticed, is leaning on his right elbow because he is left-handed."

"This is amazing, Doctor!"

"Not really. You just need to know all the facts to make a correct diagnosis."

Now the first man shouted to all the twenty people in the qat room, "Listen people! This doctor is a genius. Don't let him leave Taiz; we have to keep him here, where we need him."

"That's right," said the second fat man. "We will not issue him an exit visa from Taiz!"

Loud laughter broke out among the whole group.

~

After the qat-chewing session, during which Ahmad did not chew despite the numerous offers of small bunches of carefully plucked tender leaves, the two doctors headed home for dinner. Ahlam had prepared a delicious dish of oven-roasted fish, delivered to the Taiz fish market fresh from the Red Sea coast every day. She had made some typical loaves of round flatbread, for which the Hugariyyah region of Yemen is famous. But she also had a whole roast chicken, as custom would dictate; no Yemeni table would have just one main item. That would be considered mean.

"Oh, I forgot the main course," Nageeb said, getting up from his chair and walking toward the kitchen.

Ahmad looked admiringly into Ahlam's stunning eyes, and she could see his longing. She blushed through her olive skin; neither said anything. Then Ahmad heard that familiar popping of the cork, followed seconds later by Nageeb's reentry into the dining room.

"I hope you don't mind?" Nageeb asked.

"Mind? I have been without for far too long. I am delighted I moved from the hotel."

"I only have red. We Yemenis are not sophisticated enough to drink white with fish and red with meat; we drink whatever we can get our hands on."

"But red is the choice of real drinkers. Only where do you buy this? Is it readily available?"

"Anything and everything is available for the right number of riyals, my friend."

"But who sells it? It must be a dangerous pastime—I mean selling it."

"Not when the seller-in-chief is Ali."

"Ali? Ali who?"

"The commander of an army brigade from the north, which is occupying Hugariyyah."

"Are you serious?"

"Don't talk like that, Nageeb!" Ahlam chided. "Your tongue will get you into trouble."

"You are right, my darling. Hand me your wine glass. Let me fill it."

Ahmad could not believe his eyes. Not only was wine available, but it was sold by some very high-ranking military officer, and everyone knew about it. On top of it, some women drank in Taiz, at least Ahlam did. He chuckled, raising his glass to his host and then to his hostess, looking longingly into her eyes.

~

That night, Ahmad lay in his strange but very comfortable bed with fresh smelling sheets. Ordinarily, after three glasses of wine, he would fall asleep within a couple of minutes. Not that night though. His mind was buzzing with so many thoughts: his escape, his great grandfather's grave, the little village of Haifan, the little boys waving and little girls just looking at him in the truck, and the beautiful mountains of Taiz, especially Saber. And when he began to imagine that imposing mountain of Saber, he saw Ahlam's stunning eyes and imagined them looking deep into his soul, and then his thoughts turned to Ann, the soul companion he left thousands of miles behind. It was then that he decided that he would return to Britain and marry Ann, if she would still have him, and he would embark on his specialization studies, and then who knew? Whatever the future held would surely be better than his situation at that moment in time.

~

Sanaa was another beautiful city where he had never been. It had unique architecture that would bring in thousands of European tourists, and being the capital was the most populous and most prosperous city in the country. In the midst of that unique beauty, there was an interminable state of chaos that he had to get used to. He found it annoying, in fact maddening. The chaos of the traffic was phenomenal, and it was not because of a large number of cars; it was just that there were no rules. In the *suq*, it seemed to Ahmad that everyone in the street was shouting all at once, and no one was listening. So many men, and there were only men on the streets, were jostling for a path on the road or the footpath whenever there was one. So many were walking, apparently aimlessly, and just as many would simply stand and stare or would crouch in a shady spot and keep staring at the mass of humanity before them.

And yet the city had its charm and unique architecture, and above all it was cool, a lot cooler than Aden, being almost four thousand meters above sea level. He did not have time to get to know the city but promised himself he would return one day for a much longer visit. He needed a few days to book his flight to London, connecting to Edinburgh, and to buy a decent suitcase and some clothes. With his British passport, he had little or no difficulty getting the obligatory exit visa, so common in many dictatorial regimes in the area. The airport was totally chaotic, but as the Yemenia airplane took off, he uttered a sigh of relief and started to fantasize about Ann's embrace.

CHAPTER 14

~

BACK IN ADEN

Τhe news of the escape of one of the few highly qualified doctors in the country spread like wildfire. The national security officials could not understand how he managed to slip between the fingers of their tight grip. The chief of security sent two of his juniors to interrogate Ahmad's mother, and even his younger sister, Zahra, but they got no information from them. They also had a meeting with the East German radiographer who met regularly, albeit infrequently, with Ahmad. However, she could not give them any information since Ahmad had been careful not to take her into his confidence, knowing the risk of doing so. They did not interrogate Salma, since she was the wife of the deputy minister of justice; however the chief did have a word with Hasan, who reassured him that he was as surprised as he was.

That day, back home from work at one thirty in the afternoon, Hasan asked his wife about it. "So, your brother has abandoned ship without telling anyone! Or maybe you knew about it?"

"Of course not; I would have told you if I had known."

"Would you? You would tell on your own brother?"

"Only to my husband."

"So blood is not thicker than water, in this case?"

"But you are not water! You are much thicker than blood, as far as I am concerned."

"It just tells me that he does not trust you, his own sister."

"I think because he has seen my loyalty to you all these years."

"I am sure he told your mother, don't you think?"

"I don't know. I suppose so. But he might have just given her the impression he was going away for a week's holiday to Ethiopia or somewhere near, where so many single men seem to travel."

"I guess we will never know, but this is going to embarrass me in front of the president. You know, he likes me and trusts me a lot; he might never believe that I did not know. I will have to talk to him and assure him of that."

"Yes, I think it would be wise. You are the best judge of that; I always trust your judgment. You are so clever and wise."

"Who knows? Perhaps the president is thinking of making me minister of justice. That would be so wonderful for me ... I mean for us, and for our son, who should be here in a couple of months."

"Yes, I hope so for you, but you have not done too badly since you came back home only three years ago."

"Alhamdulillah [praise be to god], but as minister I will make a lot more money."

"Why? Is there that much difference between the salaries of the minister and his deputy?"

"You are so naïve, my dear; it is not the salary that matters. It is all the extras that come with being at the top of the pyramid, with no one above you watching what you are doing. They will all come to me with their projects for approval and advice and signatures. That's when they write the blank checks."

"But don't you have to be careful and act within the law? Of course you know the law."

"I know the law, and as minister I will *be* the law!" Hasan said with a big smile, almost licking his lips.

~

Two months later, Salma gave birth to a healthy baby boy after a rather long labor, that being her first delivery. All the relatives in town, from both sides of the family, came over to congratulate her and admire her first male birth. She felt fulfilled. Hasan was very proud that he now had a son, rather than another daughter, although no one in Aden knew, including Salma, that he already had a daughter in England. Hasan announced to everyone that he would call him Antar, after the president of the country. In Arabic history, Antar bin Shaddad was a legendary brave fighter who was very skilful with the sword. The president just happened to be given that name by his own father, but during the independence struggle he proved his daring and ruthlessness as a guerrilla fighter against the British. That was his passport to the highest office in the land. He was otherwise a poorly educated man, with elementary education, who hated reading and could only speak Arabic. He therefore relied on a few trusted friends to coach him on how to respond to all the official diplomatic messages which were sent, mostly in English, by international bodies, such as the United Nations, UNESCO, UNDP, and so many other organizations and governments.

One of these trusted assistants was Hasan, who had good command of English and was very familiar with legal documents. His boss, the minister of justice, likewise was another ruthless fighter for the Liberation Front, who had no qualifications either. But he had to be rewarded with a ministry, even though the president did not trust him to be loyal and thought of him as a potential rival. Needless to say, no one expressed any objection to the choice of the baby's name, not even Salma, who was not consulted. She knew it would be futile, even if she did have a more suitable name.

Over the next few days, nearly all the employees at the ministry of justice took turn to visit Hasan's office to congratulate him, and the senior assistants arrived bearing expensive gifts for the baby. When he met with the president over some legal consultation several days later, he made sure the president knew why he called his son Antar. The president feigned great pleasure and told him that he was honored to have his name chosen out of all the other possible ones. A couple of days later, he sent an expensive baby cot to the house.

Hasan's dreams came true three months later when the president reshuffled his cabinet. He got rid of three ministers, including the minister of justice, who never gave him his undivided loyalty, and appointed Hasan in his place.

That night Hasan could not sleep until near dawn. Even though he only achieved one hour of sleep, he started his day early, knowing that he would move his office to the much grander one of the minister who was told not to report to work that day.

Just as he had predicted to his loyal wife, on that day Hasan became the law, and the number of VIP callers at his office suddenly more than doubled. Although he thought he knew lots of important people, he now was in demand by all sorts of lawyers and judges, foreign company directors, contractors, bank managers, and community leaders. By then the government had started relaxing the rules limiting private enterprise and Hasan found himself having to approve numerous legal agreements and documents, and above all contracts. He more or less had a carte blanche from his trusting president who put him in that enviable position of enormous power.

It did not take Hasan long to amass a huge fortune made up of deposits in foreign banks scattered all over Europe, the United States, and the Cayman Islands. However, he knew deep in his heart that his luck could not continue forever, and that his wealth and fate were closely dependent on the survival of President Antar. He knew he could live the rest of his life very lavishly on the foreign deposits he had amassed, and he began preparing himself for that eventuality. However, he needed a legitimate reason to leave the country with his possessions intact.

～

One day his mind strayed to his long-ago classmate, Ahmad, and then it struck him. Yes, he too would go for graduate studies in law, and then from the safety of Europe he would decide where to end up. He had kept his

British passport a deep secret and told everyone that it had expired, even though United Kingdom passports were issued for ten years. The PDRY was offered all sorts of scholarships by international organizations, such as UNESCO, but also directly from different countries in Europe and North America. Several of those came to him for approval of PDRY students. Thus he awaited a suitable one for himself, and started making his plans.

He did not have long to wait, for there was such a graduate training course in international law, which he had studied as part of his law degree, but this was going to be a whole course of two years on this very subject, and it would also qualify him for the post of ambassador one day. Soon he got organized, after asking for the blessing of President Antar who gave it reluctantly. He had very few assets in the country, especially since the grand house that he occupied belonged to the government and the Mercedes car was a gift from the president, which he did not dare sell in order not to arouse suspicion of his planned one-way trip. But he instructed Salma to quietly sell everything that was worth selling, and he told her that she could buy gold for herself with all her earnings from those sales, which he knew would enhance her enthusiasm for selling those items. She was to tell people that because they were leaving for an unknown period of time, she did not want the appliances and other items to rust in the humid heat of Aden, or to go out of date.

~

Hasan's graduate study of international law was to take place over two years at the Center for International and Comparative Law at the University of Michigan in Ann Arbor, but it could be shortened to eighteen months if everything worked out. He was to receive a monthly stipend adequate for a man of his position, and his salary from the government of the People's Democratic Republic of Yemen was to continue and to be paid in dollars in Michigan. He was to have an apartment for his family of three but no car. He did not really need one since his assigned apartment was within the university campus. He arranged to travel ahead on his own and thus give Salma time to quietly sell their belongings, and then she could catch up, with the baby. Although she did not like to be lumbered with that responsibility, she knew that she had to do as she was told.

~

The day of departure came more quickly that they had imagined. Hasan was replaced by his deputy minister, to reassure him that his position would be kept for him upon his return. The president wanted it that way. Hasan said good-bye to his wife at home and did not want her to go to the airport, emphasizing that she should not leave her son, only months old, unattended. In any event, Hasan, like all important people in government, or in the private sector, had his own fixer, a young man called Qassem Qirshi. These fixers were usually young, aggressive, and hands-on men who might have worked for national security or the police or the armed forces and tended to know people, and thus they got things done through connections or, when necessary, intimidation.

Qassem would run secret errands as instructed by his paymaster. He was therefore busy all day performing last-minute chores Hasan assigned to him. He had the luggage packed in the Mercedes and proceeded to drive the minister to the airport. Hasan was issued a diplomatic passport since he was still minister. It was of great advantage in his previous travels and made the risk of his luggage being searched at entry points virtually zero, which enabled him to smuggle lots of cash and precious metal abroad. He was very happy with such treatment, but since he was not planning on returning to PDRY, he also needed to carry his British passport, which was still valid for a few more years. However, he did not want to run the slightest risk of being searched by airport security, even though the risk was very small. He therefore arranged for Qassem to carry it for him, and to hand it over once he was in the departure lounge. The plan worked out very smoothly.

~

Word came back to Salma that her husband settled nicely into his new environment and that his studies began, and so the doting Salma was reassured. She herself felt rather depressed at being somewhat isolated. As the wife of an important minister, she kept her distance from people, including her former girlfriends, because she did not want to be inundated with requests for jobs and recommendations, and donations. She was under strict instructions from Hasan not to do so, or to ask him for favors for her friends, although he felt free to do such favors for his own friends. But those were reciprocal, he told her, and he needed those friends to climb the ladder.

~

Between Salma and Qassem, all arrangements were made to sell the appliances, cutlery, crockery, and furniture. There was surprisingly little difficulty in disposing of all those things, because of the high quality of the goods offered for sale and the near absence of such items in the shops. In fact, some were bought by the wives of the many diplomats in the city and others by the more affluent members of society within the city. Transactions were conducted in cash, and as most purchases were made by diplomats, Salma managed to get paid in American dollars, which she carried to Ann Arbor three months after the departure of Hasan.

It was a warm and passionate reunion for the couple. Hasan was amazed at the major changes he noted in his son, not only in his size but his ability to smile, to roll over from his stomach to his back, and to make all sorts of happy but unintelligible noises as he stared at his own hands. He felt so proud of him. That night the couple made passionate love.

~

Three months later, Salma announced to her husband that she was pregnant again.

"That is wonderful, darling. I am very happy," Hasan said.

"I am happy too, if you are."

"This is good news for more than one reason. You see our second son will be an American citizen. What could be better than that?"

"How do you know that? They may say you are only a visitor, and your son, or daughter, is a Yemeni."

"Have you forgotten that I am a lawyer? I read the law several months ago. In fact, this is why I chose to do this course here in the United States rather than in England, where I did my undergraduate training."

"Oh? Would it not be better if the two children had the same nationality?"

"No, no, no. We are not going back to that miserable country; all that socialist stuff where you are not allowed to make money or get rich! They look at you like you are a criminal if you have wealth. So, we can go to England, because of my passport, or to another country; maybe to North Yemen. I have a few friends in Sanaa, mostly Adenis who moved there because they were disillusioned with the south."

"And what about my mother? I cannot leave her there in her old age, especially now that she is a widow, and also my little sister Zahra."

"That is not a problem. Once I decide where we will settle, I will send for them. The regime there will not worry about losing one old woman and one little girl."

"So now you call it a regime? You were their minister!"

"I have learned to survive, my dear. I made use of them, and they made use of me; we are quits."

"Somehow I thought you were an admirer of the president. Is there no loyalty?"

"Loyalty? To scum like that? They are all professional liars and thieves. It would not surprise me if they started assassinating each other soon. They are there to plunder the country and then jump ship to settle in a rich and affluent country, somewhere: Saudi Arabia, Dubai, Egypt. So, if they are going to plunder, I might as well get my share."

"Anyway, it is all in the hands of Allah. He will determine the good path for us."

"Yes, my dear. Inshaallah!"

~

That weekend Hasan decided to take his wife and son to the town center for a change of scenery and to show his wife how nice and organized the town was, and then to do some window-shopping. They had bought a pushchair for their infant, who had just had taken his first few hesitant steps across the room. Salma made sure he had enough blankets to keep him warm, and a bottle of milk tucked next to the baby's thigh.

The couple enjoyed their stroll past shop windows and in the small park in the center of the town, and Salma had her first hamburger; she seemed to like it, to Hasan's surprise. He had become so used to it during the few weeks which he had spent on his own. There was a hamburger joint near the university, which catered to the thousands of students who poured out of their classes at lunchtime. Hasan would go there most days, although for his evening meal he would go to a proper restaurant or a pizza place for a change. But he got used to the hamburger joint and also fancied one of the young women who worked there. She was quite pretty and always met him with a broad welcoming smile, which he misinterpreted as personal interest in him. Encouraged by the smiles, he probed to see whether she would go out with him but soon found out that he was not as desirable as he had imagined, despite being such an important minister back home.

~

At the end of the family visit to the downtown area, as the couple started walking back toward their home, with Salma behind the pushchair and walking next to Hasan, he could see three white, tall, young men. They were walking straight toward him, eyes fixated on his own, with obvious disdainful smirks, talking to each other, although he could not make out what they were saying. He could sense danger even though they were about thirty paces away but approaching rapidly, not taking their gaze off him. He knew he had two or three seconds to act. He quickly gripped the handlebar of the pushchair to stop it, took a couple of rapid steps in front of the pushchair, spun round on his heel so that he was facing the baby, and crouched on the ground in front of him while fumbling for the milk bottle next to the baby's thigh. He pulled it out and stuck it between his welcoming lips. His back was now toward the menacing threesome who did not know what to do, and after slowing down and looking at each other for a second decided to walk past the couple and their baby. Salma, who was oblivious of the three men, waited for her husband to get up, now that the baby was happily sucking his milk, but Hasan did not.

"Hasan, what are you doing crouching on the dirty ground in your nice pants? Why don't you get up?"

He looked up at her and said, "I can't! I can't just now; give me a minute."

"I don't understand. Why? Did you injure yourself?"

"No, my legs won't carry me. Now I know what is meant by rubber legs!"

She held her arm toward him and asked, "Do you want me to help you up?"

"No ... I think it is okay now; my legs are okay now," Hasan said as he stood up in slow motion.

"And why did you suddenly have to feed the baby? He was not crying for milk."

"You mean you did not see what those three men were planning to do to me?"

"I am sorry. I must have been looking away from them."

"They decided to swarm me and beat me up, probably very severely, and if I had not crouched in front of the baby that is exactly what they would have done."

"So why did they not kick you while you were down, if that was their intention?"

"Two reasons. One was because I was in the act of feeding a little baby. The other was precisely because I was already on the ground. There is something about combat, some unwritten law, that if your enemy is already on the ground, you cannot beat him. That is why in a boxing match, you have to wait until the other guy stands up before trying to knock him down again. Even thugs like those three follow those unwritten rules. That's what saved me. I never imagined this sort of thing would happen to me, just like that without the slightest provocation. Maybe it is because we are not white? I don't know, and I am not going to find out either."

~

For the next few days, Hasan went into a phase of depression and paranoia; paranoia not only because he just missed being set upon by three strangers, who could have caused him severe injury, but also the paranoia that Salma may have thought him a coward whose legs turned into rubber in the face of a fight. He did not want to talk about his feelings with her. After all, he was a man who was supposed to have courage and who was tasked with defending his family, and yet he could not even stand up physically, let alone stand up to those three thugs. He skipped many of his classes at university and avoided being out after dark, and even in the daylight he would look very carefully at all young men in his vicinity to prepare himself for attack. When he went through the school of law in London, he did study litigation after physical injury but did not actually handle such clients. But now he realized the psychological damage caused by the mere threat of physical injury, let alone actual physical trauma. His sleep became shallow and fragmented, he experienced nightmares, his appetite for Salma's food diminished, and even his usually strong libido was virtually nonexistent.

CHAPTER 15

︿

RETURN TO EDINBURGH

A nn was at the airport, where she had driven her Morris Minor car. Ahmad's flight from Heathrow Airport touched down with a slight lurch at three in the afternoon, and Ahmad's hearing was back to normal, as he took another yawn and heard his eardrums pop. He felt on top of the world, with that indescribable relief that all his anxieties were behind him and Ann would be there. She had not abandoned him for another man all this time, and he wondered why. After all, he was neither tall nor muscular and neither handsome nor rich. What did she see in him? She was highly educated, intelligent, and sociable. She was not a stunning beauty, but she was so good in bed. And now he imagined how he would run the tips of his fingers over her warm, smooth, white skin and draw circles around her nipples, and how she would close her eyes and wait for him to suck them before she would put her hand behind his head and pull it toward her breasts.

He was interrupted by the stewardess making an announcement about connecting flights and woke up from his reverie.

He picked up his single suitcase from the luggage carousel and walked out to the reception area where dozens of people awaited the arrival of family and friends. He spotted Ann immediately. She had not changed much in all the time he was away, but she looked more beautiful. She wore a red blouse and beige skirt, and her hair, it seemed, was very recently done. She walked slowly toward him, while he wheeled his suitcase toward her with a big smile on his face. He became self-conscious as he asked himself whether to kiss her on the lips, as he wanted to, and imagined that everyone in the airport reception lounge was looking at him and watching to see what he would do.

At that moment, the two came face-to-face. Ann did not allow him time to make up his mind, for her lips were against his as he let go of the suitcase and put his right arm round her waist. They stepped back after five seconds or so and looked deep into each other's eyes.

"This way," Ann said, pointing to where her car was parked.

In the car, they turned toward each other and smiled. Ahmad stretched his right arm, put his hand behind Ann's neck, and pulled her head toward his own for a much longer kiss.

Ann had her own apartment in the Marchmont area of Edinburgh, quite familiar to Ahmad from his student days. It had one bedroom, a smallish living room, and a kitchen large enough to also accommodate a square dining table. There was also a tiny storeroom, which was almost completely occupied by a sofa bed, above which there was a long shelf full of books. Ahmad dropped his suitcase in the hall just past the front door. The apartment was warm, and had a large window facing south toward the big park. As he surveyed the different parts of the apartment, standing in front of the sofa, he pulled Ann to him, very slowly, until their chests were pressing against each other, and then their lips and their groins. Soon his raging erection signaled his desire to Ann. She was more than ready for what took place over the subsequent half hour.

~

As they lay naked under the large blanket of her queen-sized bed, he rolled over on his left side to face her. He looked at her profile, with that cute, slightly upturned, delicate nose, and said, "I cannot tell you how much I was dreaming about today."

"You mean about the sex?" Ann said teasingly.

"I mean about seeing you, and touching you, and breathing you. It has been a long time."

"I know, but you are here now."

"And I will never leave you again."

"Are you sure? Didn't you tell me that you wanted to do forensic science so you could use it back in Yemen?"

"I want to do that because I fell in love with that science, but I don't need to go back home, if I can get the right job here."

"And if you don't?"

"Then I'll take you with me."

"What if I don't want to go to a third-world country with all its problems?"

"Then I'll just stay here, and you can earn the money, and I'll cook. I like cooking, you know."

"And what about the cleaning, the laundry, and the ironing? Men always remember the cooking, I think because they are always thinking about their own stomachs—correction, about their penises—first, *then* about their stomachs; the rest they shut out."

"You mean you didn't realize that the average man thinks of sex on average every thirty minutes?" Ahmad said with a big smile.

"Yes, I can believe that. So when you were in Aden, what did you do every thirty minutes when those thoughts overwhelmed you?"

"Well, fortunately for me, it wasn't every thirty minutes."

"Okay then, every thirty hours. How did you manage?"

"Oh, I just thought about you, my love."

"You mean that put you off sex?"

"Don't be silly! You know what I am trying to say."

"Trying, but not very successfully. Anyway, have you been faithful to me all this time, or did all the nurses throw themselves at your feet?"

"No, no, that is a very conservative society. Women are very carefully watched. It just does not happen. Anyway, most of the nurses in that place are men."

"So what do all the horny single males do there?"

"I am not sure. I suppose there are prostitutes, if you know where to find them. But it must be very risky, with all sorts of infections …"

"Does that mean that there is a lot of homosexuality?"

"I don't know that either; it would not surprise me though."

"I hate to be personal here, but what did you do, and I know how horny you are, remember?"

"Well, men have a friend called the hand, and if they can get some erotic material, it helps."

"If it is such a puritanical society, why would it allow pornography?"

"That's a good question. Even though it is available, it is all done in a hush-hush manner, as you can imagine, just like it used to be here, until it was allowed in Holland and Scandinavia, and only years later did the British catch up. And now you can find it everywhere, quite cheap too. I read somewhere that the pornography industry generates worldwide revenue of ten billion—billion, not million—dollars. I don't know what all the fuss is about, do you? I mean if you, an adult, want to watch it in private, what harm can it possibly do? And you might even learn one or two techniques."

"That's typical of a man's attitude. Have you thought of the abuse of the female performers in those films? Do you think they are keen to show themselves in those acts, especially in what they call a gangbang or doing anal sex? But these are unfortunate poor girls, who are paid large fees which they would never dream of in the open market as sales assistants or cooks."

"Good point. But why do you only talk about the female actresses? It is the same with the male porno stars. How is it you don't feel sorry for them?"

"You know, I never thought about that. Somehow, because men are the … you know … the aggressors … the ones who are always trying to have sex, I did not feel sorry for them. They seem to enjoy their roles in these films; I mean, they actually come."

"Well, in the few, I mean very few, films I have seen, the women seem to be having orgasms galore. Do you suppose they are only faking it?"

"I don't know."

"Anyway, were you faking it when we did it just now?"

"What do you think?"

"I think it was genuine, and the proof is that you want to do it again just now, right?"

Ann smiled and brought her pubic area closer, pressing it tightly against Ahmad's rising stiffness.

～

Ahmad soon registered for the course in forensic sciences at Napier University. He was surprised how keen he was to be a student again, for he had feared that he might not be happy doing that after being away from academic medicine for some time. But it was all coming back. He was so grateful that Ann invited him to live with her. *What luck*, he thought. How many students would just walk into that situation, and for free? He wondered how different his situation would have been if Ann had found a man while he was back in Aden. Was that because of her deep love for him, or was it just luck?

As he settled down, he found part-time work as a demonstrator in the department of anatomy at the faculty of medicine. The cadaver dissection hall was still in the same old building, still smelling of formaldehyde. Even the amphitheater was the same. He looked at the long, curved benches of yellowish brown hard wood and remembered where he had sat in the second to last row, with his Scottish classmate. From that height, he could see the rest of the class and would study the female medical students who sat in the front two rows. There were only seventy students in his class, and only twenty were girls. When he started doing anatomy in his second year, he feasted his eyes on the tall blonde Fiona, but he knew he did not stand a chance with her, with all the competition around, so he did not even try. He dreaded the humiliation of being turned down, or even laughed at, by Fiona. Suddenly, his thoughts were interrupted by one of the second-year students.

"Excuse me, sir, last week I was trying to dissect the saphenous nerve in the thigh of our cadaver, but I could not locate it. Could you show me where I should look when we have our class at eleven o'clock this morning?"

"With pleasure! It is a very thin nerve, so it is not surprising that you could not find it."

"Thank you, sir."

Ahmad would spend four days doing his own studying and one day as anatomy demonstrator, thus earning his pocket money. He was glad he did not smoke, otherwise his modest earnings would have gone up in smoke, literally that is.

On the second week at the Napier University, he was having a cup of tea and a piece of shortbread in the cafeteria when a young man of about thirty had to share a table with him, as the other seats were, more or less, taken. He could immediately tell that the man was an Arab, and judging by his thick black beard and rather dark skin, he was a Muslim from the Gulf area. After a few exchanges, he confirmed that he was from Saudi Arabia and was taking the same course in forensic science.

Ahmad was curious that he had not seen him in the class, although the course had started a few days before. He asked, "But Ibrahim, I did not see you last week when we had our introductory week of lectures."

"That's right. Last week was the final three days of Ramadan, and then the Eid festival, so I skipped it, but I did get the lecture notes. How was it?"

"I thought it was interesting. Of course it was also basic, given that it was an introduction."

"Anyway, *Eid Mubarak* [happy new year] to you. How did you cope with the fasting when sunset is so late here?" Ibrahim asked.

"I … I … I don't fast, actually."

"Really! Is the brother … a … a Muslim?"

"You can assume that virtually any Arab from Yemen is a Muslim. I just don't fast. Never did. I did try it when I was a teenager, many years ago; I got such headache and dizziness that I stopped."

"I never get that. In fact, I feel much better after fasting Ramadan."

"In what way much better?"

"Well, there is a feeling of inner peace, and that you are close to Allah."

"You mean spiritually? That, I can understand. But I was asking physically. I mean, you are a doctor after all, aren't you?"

"The peace of the soul is more important than that of the body."

"I suppose so, but I have peace of mind without having to fast, or pray."

"You don't even pray?"

"No, I don't."

"Okay. I can understand that the headache and dizziness made it impossible for you to fast, but how does prayer cause any problem?"

"It is not only a question of side effects. I am sure the ritual of prayer five times a day is very beneficial for those who believe in it. But, by the same token, it is not for me. Can you not see that?"

"If nothing else, it is a form of useful physical exercise."

"Now that's stretching it. If I want to exercise, I would do weights, or run, or do twenty-sit ups. That would be useful exercise, not bending down five times a day and touching my head to the floor."

"Well, I can see that you are a nonbeliever. I was going to ask you to sign this petition by the Edinburgh Muslim Students Association, but now I won't."

"I didn't expect to hear that there was such a group. There can't be many Muslims here. Anyway, just out of curiosity, what was it about."

"The petition asks the government here to recognize Islam as an official religion in this country."

Ahmad was not prepared for that, and asked, "Why would this European country do that for Islam or Hinduism or Judaism or any other religion?"

"Because the number of Muslims is increasing in Britain and the whole of Europe, and to make Muslims feel equal to other citizens."

"But Muslims are already equal."

"You can't mean that!"

"Yes, of course, there is some discrimination, which I absolutely resent and condemn, but it is mainly based on color against West Indians and East Indians and others. Islam has nothing to do with it. I experienced it myself twice, but the idiots who expressed it did not know I was a Muslim and had no way of knowing. And if it's because of increasing numbers, then the numbers of Hindu laborers in Kuwait and in your own country is in the millions. Did you demand of the Saudi government to recognize Hinduism as another official religion there, where there are thousands of Indians? What we should do is ban states from calling themselves The Islamic Republic or the Islamic Kingdom of such or such, and equally the Catholic state of Spain or Italy or whatever.'"

"I told you I wanted to change the subject, but you insisted."

"Yes, didn't the Quran say 'You have your religion, and I have mine'? Are you here as a foreign student for this degree, or did you immigrate to Britain?"

"No, I am here just for the length of my scholarship, and I have a job waiting for me at home," Ibrahim said with obvious pride.

"I wish I could say the same," Ahmad lamented. "I have to earn my living by doing part-time work as anatomy demonstrator. Did you bring your wife with you?"

"The family is here, yes."

"Oh, you have kids? How many?"

"No, I don't have any children. Just the family, the wife."

Ahmad reminded himself that some Muslim men do not utter the word *wife,* preferring to call her *family* instead, and occasionally *mother-of-the-children.*

"That's great. So you are all socially organized."

"But I found out that there is a club for Arab students here in Edinburgh. I have been, once already. It was a good experience, very pleasant. It was a lecture on the oil industry in the Middle East, followed by dinner. I should take you with me next time."

"Sure. How did your wife find it?"

"Oh, no, the family don't go to such things. They are busy enough at home."

"Were there any non-Arabs at the dinner?"

"Not many. I think only two white women, probably girlfriends. But there were Arabs from many different countries, especially Iraq, Libya, Egypt, Lebanon, Kuwait, but I did not meet anyone from Yemen."

"I am not surprised; I think I must be the only person from that area in Edinburgh."

"And I must be the only Saudi."

"It just struck me, as you said 'Saudi,' that yours is the only country in the world in which a whole nation of—I don't know, seven million maybe?—are labeled after one family! I mean what if instead of Kuwait we call it the Emirate of Sabahi Arabia, or we call Kuwaitis Sabahis instead. Or we call Oman the Sultanate of Qaboosi Arabia, and the Omanis Qaboosis instead?"

Ibrahim suddenly looked left then right, and lowering his voice said, "Well, it is only a name. As long as they look after us, who cares?"

"What do you mean by 'look after us'? They are sending you here to study using your own money. They are not doing you any favors. How is it you cannot see that."

"Listen, my friend, I never talk politics. I just concentrate on my studies and my duties to Allah, and … sometimes to the family … at night," Ibrahim said with a mischievous smile. Ahmad was not amused.

"Well, let me know when you next go to the Arab Students Club. I think I should try it, at least once."

"Inshaallah!"

Over the next few weeks, the two Arab physicians got to know each other a little better, notwithstanding their major religious and political differences. Six weeks later, the club was holding its year-end meeting, and this time it was going to be a talk about the origins and development of Arabic music in the twentieth century. The speaker happened to be a good lute player, and the audience was to be entertained over dinner. Ahmad took Ann along, but Ibrahim went without his wife, as was fully anticipated by Ahmad.

All three had a great time, and Ahmad really enjoyed listening to the lute, *oud* in Arabic, something that he had enjoyed ever since his early childhood. Ahmad also enjoyed meeting so many friendly and sometimes loud Arab students. He was pleased to see that there were no restrictions against the sale and consumption of alcohol at the party. He struck a quick friendship with a Sudanese student, in his final year at the faculty of forestry, who was the social coordinator of the club. Soon he was being asked to join the management committee of the club, which he reluctantly accepted, justifying it as a welcome light distraction from medicine. Most of the members of the committee represented the different associations, such as the Libyan Students Association. However, Ahmad was accepted as an individual member, since he was probably the only Yemeni at the university.

~

Back at Ann's apartment, Ahmad asked Ann, "You seemed to enjoy the Arab musical evening?"

"Yes, I did, as a matter of fact. I didn't think I would, but felt I should come to give you company. But I needn't have worried about you; you got on famously there. You made contact with so many people; I was watching you. Quite the socialite, I would say!"

"I really appreciated you coming with me. It wouldn't have been so much fun without you, my darling."

"Well, I have to admit the Arabs are very friendly people, also very loud people. Oh, the noise! Why do they have to talk so loud, and all at the same time? Does anyone listen? But the music really got to me; I loved it."

"You know, if you marry me and go back there with me, you will hear nonstop music."

"That's what I am worried about—nonstop. I don't mind it at all in small doses. Anyway, I am not going to live like a Muslim woman in some primitive male-dominated country with my face covered, period!"

"But society changes, my love. I mean here in Scotland women were accepted as equals only this century."

"When it does, then I'll think about it; we'll probably be dead and buried by then!"

"The sad thing is I agree with you; it will take a hundred years."

"If you really love me and want to be with me, you will stay here. You can work here and travel and vote and drink your favorite wine and no one will ever stand in your way."

"Again, the sad thing is that I agree with you, but I need a challenge, a real challenge. And, please don't laugh, but I really want to give back to that society."

~

Christmas and the New Year seemed to whiz by for Ann and Ahmad. They were invited to several parties in town, and they spent Christmas Eve, Christmas Day, and Boxing Day at the home of Ann's parents in the small village of Kirkudbright, where her parents retired several years before. Ahmad remembered with a grin the day Ann told him about where her parents had retired on the southwest coast of Scotland. She had told him it was "Kirkoobree." At least that was what he heard. Being obsessed with maps, he grabbed an atlas and surveyed the whole of the coastline, never to find a village by that name. After several frustrating minutes he asked Ann to show him the place on the map.

"But that says Kir-kud-bright," said Ahmad. Ann laughed.

"Yes, love, but here in Scotland we pronounce it *Kirkoobree!* I should have told you. My mistake, but I thought that having lived in Scotland all these years, you would know."

It was already getting dark when Ann pulled up in front of her parents' house. Her mother was soon at the door to welcome them, for although they were only a hundred miles away, they hardly ever came down to visit. Besides, she was very curious about the dark Arab that her daughter teamed up with, in preference to the many native Scots that she could have chosen from.

Her parents chose the village because it was so picturesque, but above all it was quiet and peaceful. Her mother was a reasonably good painter, and the scenes around the village provided her with ample material for her oil paintings, which seemed to cover most of the walls in her house. She had a huge painting of the ruins of McLellan's Castle that remained standing, and another of Broughton House, still well preserved through its three centuries of existence.

The couple was assigned the comfortable guest bedroom, on the top floor, at the other end from the parents' own bedroom, but they had to share the bathroom with them. It was a very comfortable bed, much more than the one in Ann's apartment in Edinburgh, as even Ann would admit.

It was already getting dark, and Ann left the sightseeing to the following day, after Christmas dinner. Ahmad was very pleasantly surprised by the warm hospitality shown to him by the parents. In fact, it was Ann's mother who seemed to be in total command, and it soon became obvious to Ahmad, especially as a physician, that Ann's father had a significant degree of dementia, together with a rhythmic tremor of his hands, even as they rested in his lap or on his knees. He remembered that he had somewhere read about the dementia-Parkinsonism complex. Conversation with him was rather difficult, and Ahmad found himself having to repeat his phrases in the hope that he would be understood. Ann's father mostly exhibited a vacant, fatuous stare punctuated from time to time by brief spells of frustration. Ahmad wondered how it would be for himself if one day he was in that situation; but then he was grateful that he was many years away from such possible fate.

$$\sim$$

That night, Ahmad lay in the comfortable bed in deep thought. Ann seemed happy because she received the approval of her mother of the man she brought home. She looked radiant and desirable to Ahmad, but he was somewhat anxious. He did want her that night but could not get rid of the idea that he would be having sex with a woman, not yet married to him, under the roof of her own parents, who might even overhear their loud lovemaking, and it put him off. He could not explain that to Ann, because he knew that she would not think twice about making love to him within earshot of her parents. For her, it was normal. She was an adult, and made her own choices. Ahmad, on the other hand, thought he should be respectful of the couple who opened their home to him, and he could wait until he went back to Edinburgh. He contrasted that with his own life and family values back home. He recalled that even when he smoked in Aden, he would not do so in front on his parents, out of respect, even though he was a fully qualified doctor. They never told him not to smoke in their presence, but he knew it was expected of him.

The next day, Christmas, the family went through the routine of opening presents, chatting in front of the coal fire, and eating huge amounts of turkey and stuffing washed down by ample sips of white wine. But the climax came when the plum pudding was carried into the dining room, the brandy lit and large chunks placed on the dessert plates. Even Ann's father seemed happy at that point. Nothing beat sitting around a coal fire on a cold day late in December, with sparks occasional flying off the lumps of coal, sometimes landing perilously close to the carpet in front of the fireplace. The smell of burning coal being in the air, and with a mixture of turkey and plum pudding, and a little brandy in one's stomach, life seemed to be happiness itself.

Ahmad looked at Ann's mother, still a handsome woman at her age, and imagined his life thirty years later with an older Ann looking just like the mother he was beginning to love and trust. As if she read his thoughts, Ann's mother returned his warm smile, and her eyes beamed her full approval. Then they both turned to look at Ann, as she placed her palm on the knuckles of her father's right hand, and rubbed it very gently.

Late in the afternoon on Boxing Day, the couple drove back to Edinburgh. There was a mild but continuous drizzle nearly all the way. Ann drove in silence, as Ahmad stroked the back of her neck with his right hand. If only time would just freeze there!

In the New Year, hard work resumed. The course was harder than he imagined, yet Ahmad did keep up with it. At the same time, his work as a demonstrator in anatomy was something he enjoyed; it kept him in touch with young medical students, in their early twenties, and reminded him of his own youth and innocence. Their unquenchable thirst for more and more knowledge was remarkable, and Ahmad convinced himself that he was fulfilling an important role in society.

~

As a people person, he decided to help with the functions and meetings of the Arab Students Club. The undergraduates in the club appreciated that and hoped that this somewhat older graduate student would show them how to run their club effectively. So, when Ahmad suggested that the group hold a big dinner aimed at non-Arabs, they were enthusiastic about it and chose him to organize the dinner, and selected a couple of volunteers, a male and a female, to help him.

Ahmad was determined to do a good job. He had not done anything like that for some time, although when he was an undergraduate medical student he was quite active in the students union, where the regular Saturday dances were held. The elected president, Gaby, was a Christian Lebanese man, while the vice president was an Iraqi woman called Khadeeja. The treasurer was Susan, an Egyptian woman, and the secretary, Muna, was Kuwaiti. There were also three male members-at-large on the board: Misbah, representing the Syrian Group, Fadi, another Lebanese, and Mufeed, a Palestinian.

As they were all busy with studying and some with exams, they were more than happy to let Ahmad do the work, which he took quite seriously, all the while keeping the president and vice president in the picture. Since he had been an undergraduate in the same city only a few years before, he was very familiar with the hotels and catering services and soon found a musical trio for the dinner. In consultation with the board, he started looking for an after-dinner speaker who could say something of interest to a big group of young Arab students and their non-Arab friends. He called a journalist who reported for the *Scotsman* newspaper from the Middle East, but he declined the invitation mainly because of his busy travel schedule.

One day, as Ahmad was casually turning the pages of the same paper, the title of an article made him stop. It read, "Semites for Each Other." The author was David Rubin, a name he had never heard before. He lived in London, according to the newspaper. Ahmad continued reading, coming to a paragraph which captivated his attention. It said, in part, "We are Semites who grew up in the same cradle, sons and daughters of Isaac and Ishmael, descendents of Abraham. My family shares food, song, and culture with the Muslim Arab world. Let us share the land, just as we share so much else. Let there be no more conflict among cousins."

When he looked him up, Ahmad, not so versed in politics, was amazed at all the writings of the Jewish man who was born in Iraq. He had not previously been exposed to such talk of brotherhood between the two Semitic groups from either side. It took a lot of time and effort to track down Mr. Rubin's address and telephone number from the *Scotsman* newspaper. Eventually he managed to have a conversation with him, and asked him if he would be the guest speaker of the Arab Students Club. David Rubin sounded surprised to get such an invitation. The two men exchanged a few words in Arabic at first, and Ahmad recognized that distinctive Iraqi accent which he had heard many times before. Although David Rubin was used to public speaking, it was the first time that he received such an invitation from an Arab group. At first, he was reluctant to travel all the way from London to Edinburgh, as he was not sure what kind of reception he would receive at the Arab dinner. However, Ahmad reminded him of his words in that *Scotsman* article and how his personal appearance was likely to be reported by the *Scotsman*. Ahmad asked, "Would it not be a lost opportunity for peace if you did not come?" That seemed to work.

~

The next day, Ahmad called Gaby about his success in finding such a guest speaker. Gaby, who was in political science and had read some of David Rubin's writings, was most impressed that Ahmad managed to persuade him to come. Ahmad put the phone down momentarily then dialed Khadeeja, the vice president. He had established good rapport with her.

"Hey, Khadeeja, guess what?"

"Hello, how are you? What's happening?"

"Just wanted to tell you that I found a prominent Iraqi man to be our speaker at the dinner next month, and I want to ask you to introduce him, seeing you belong to the same country back home."

"Really, who? I don't know any prominent Iraqis here."

"No, he is not in Edinburgh, but he is willing to travel from London."

"All right, who? Stop teasing me."

"It is the historian David Rubin."

"Oh, yes. Daoud Roobeen, that's what we used to call him in Iraq. So, he lives in London now?"

"Yes, he moved here years ago, but he still speaks Arabic, with an Iraqi accent."

"Of course, what else? It is the best accent. He was born there. I am impressed that you found such a great speaker. I read some of his work on the history of the Middle East."

"So, are you going to take him under your wing and introduce him and seat him at your table?"

"Of course, with pleasure," Khadeeja said.

~

Having secured the blessings of both the president and the vice president, Ahmad lost no time in booking a banquet hall at a local church, sufficient for the anticipated one hundred participants, and paid a nonrefundable deposit of seventy-five pounds of his own funds. He contacted David again and told him that he had reserved a room for him at the Glen Hotel. Members of the club were informed about the date and location of the dinner dance, and Ahmad managed to sell several tickets within the next four weeks.

The president called a meeting of the board ten days before the event, so that Ahmad could explain the agenda and assign roles. Ahmad detailed the arrangements and then proudly announced that the club was going to blaze a trail by having as its guest speaker David Rubin, a Jewish historian, as already enthusiastically approved by the president and the vice president.

As soon as Ahmad finished his sentence, there was a scream from the other end of the table emanating from Misbah, who declared aloud that he would never agree to that, and that Ahmad had to change the guest speaker.

"The man has already been invited," Ahmad said.

"Uninvite him!" came the loud response from Misbah.

"The dinner is in ten days and all arrangements have been made, and I paid a nonrefundable deposit of seventy-five pounds for the meeting hall. That's my monthly allowance. And I booked his flight and reserved a room at the hotel for him."

"Why did you not consult me?"

"I did not know that I had to consult every member of the board. I consulted the president and the vice president, and they enthusiastically agreed and congratulated me on finding such a prominent speaker. And the vice president said she would be delighted to introduce him, since they are both from Iraq. I assumed that they would have in turn consulted the board, or at a minimum informed them."

"I don't care who agreed. I will never agree, and I hereby veto this decision."

Now Khadeeja intervened. "What is the problem? Why don't you want him?"

"Because he is a Jew!" Misbah replied at the top of his voice, banging the table very hard with his fist.

"You mean because he is a Zionist?" asked Gaby, the club president.

"No, because he is a Jew!" reiterated Misbah, again at the top of his voice.

Now Susan, the Egyptian treasurer, joined the heated discussion. "And what if he is a Jew if he says the right things and talks about peace and reconciliation?"

"I cannot allow it. I represent a whole association, and the by-laws of our association stipulate that no Jew should ever be allowed near a microphone."

"Why?" Susan asked.

"Because they might have a hidden agenda," Misbah screamed out.

The anger in that last statement seemed to stun everyone around the table. The secretary was busy writing minutes, and recorded the conversation verbatim, as later confirmed by Ahmad. The other Lebanese and Palestinian men maintained their utter silence, as they had done throughout the meeting.

"This is unbelievable!" Ahmad said. "Are you telling me that a student association, approved by the university in Scotland, could possibly have such a racist article in its by-laws?"

"Yes, it does. My hands are tied, even if I personally agreed," Misbah insisted.

"Are you going to allow this, Gaby?" Ahmad asked the president.

"My hands are tied too, because according to our own by-laws Misbah is entitled to veto the choice of the speaker."

"Even if his veto is based on racism, ten days before the event?" Ahmad asked angrily with a tremulous voice.

"He does not have to give a reason for the veto according to the by-laws."

"That maybe true, but he *did* give a reason, and it was a very racist reason."

"But he is also right that he was not consulted."

"Why should I consult every single member of the board? I consulted you, the president, and you were very impressed that I managed to find such a prominent speaker, that quickly. And I consulted the VP asking her to introduce him, which she gladly agreed to do. Why did you two give me the go-ahead? Why did *you* not consult your board? I did not even have to consult the two of you, because you had agreed to give me what we called 'a free hand,' which is what your Egyptian member, Abeer, had insisted on. And when she later withdrew from organizing the dinner, that same free hand reverted to me, and you and I discussed that free hand issue, in writing. Can you deny that?"

"Look, I am at breaking point here. I am an inch away from resigning, myself. But we have no choice but to postpone this dinner," Gaby said.

At that point, the recording secretary Muna, a young woman from Kuwait, added, "Yes, according to our by-laws, the dinner will need to be postponed if it is vetoed by any member representing an association."

"Postponed? You must be joking! This dinner is finished forever. And this racist so-called club is finished too," responded Ahmad.

Ahmad was so shocked by that turn of events, that he felt nauseated and sweaty, and left the meeting, never to return. He later learned that the club broke up after that and that Misbah's association never had such article in its by-laws. His statements were blatant bluffs. However, by then it was far too late to do anything about it. To his utter dismay, Ahmad heard from a mutual professor of human rights that both the V.P. Khadeeja, and the treasurer Susan denied that any such statements were made by Misbah.

CHAPTER 16

∼

HASAN MOVES TO SANAA

Hasan managed to finish his graduate training in the shortest possible time and obtained a master's degree in international law. Throughout his time there, he was weighing his options about the next move. Things were clearly deteriorating in Aden, mainly due to bitter rivalries among the original leaders of the revolution who started plotting against each other, and finally assassinating each other. On the other side of the border, in North Yemen, there was an absolute military dictatorship, but it was stable after the assassination of the first two military rulers. The one that had just taken over started off as a sergeant and somehow rapidly rose to the rank of colonel before driving his armored column from the city of Taiz to Sanaa and declaring himself president. Rumor had it that he invited the top brass of the armed forces, some very senior to him, to a large room, placed his revolver on the table in front of him, and declared, "There is a vacancy for the position of president. I plan to fill it. Who is with me?"

But there was palpable economic progress, at least for the upper and middle class, to which Hasan believed he belonged. He learned that several people he knew back in Aden had crossed the border into Yemen to seek a better and safer life.

Despite the distance, he managed to communicate with a couple of his closer friends who encouraged him to put up his shingle in Sanaa, where there was a very acute shortage of lawyers and total absence of Western-trained ones. As he mulled the idea, Hasan reminded himself that he was fully entitled to live and seek his fortune in Yemen, where he was born, as his father had reminded him on his way to the airport some eight years earlier. Besides, he still had his British passport, and one of his sons was American born and could, in his old age, sponsor him to live in the United States. That was the hope, which he conveyed to his devoted Salma, and the couple began to plan accordingly.

However, before they left, Hasan made sure he purchased a piece of fallow land in the outskirts of Ypsilanti, in the state of Michigan. It was very cheap because it was in the middle of nowhere, but Hasan had worked out that as long as couples produced children, land would become a progressively rarer commodity, and that investment would double or triple in value in a relatively small number of years. He was quite willing to take that gamble, and it paid off extremely well, later.

～

The American Airlines flight from Detroit to Frankfurt was fairly crowded, and the restlessness of the two little boys in that cramped space added to the anxiety of the couple during the seven hours of the flight. The German ground crew was especially kind and fussed over the two little boys, while the family was in transit awaiting the Lufthansa flight to Sanaa. As luck would have it, at the passenger waiting lounge Hasan came across an old school friend from Aden also traveling to Sanaa, where he had established a modest travel agency, which was going to rely heavily on Lufthansa. As usually occurs between Yemenis, there were warm greetings and cheek-to-cheek kisses repeated three times between the two men, but only a nod between Salma and the school friend. After a long and somewhat loud conversation, Hasan knew that he made the right move by returning not to Aden but to Sanaa.

~

It did not take much effort to establish a home and a law office in Sanaa once Hasan told everyone that he was born in Turbah, in North Yemen, and after he formed a circle of friends and acquaintances who were keen to receive free legal consultations from the new and important lawyer. There was no process of licensing new lawyers in effect, and for any difficult tasks closed doors readily opened to suitable bribes; thus in no time Hasan was busy practicing law.

He became known as the lawyer from London, and from America too, and his rapid fame ensured a steady and later exponentially rising income. The lack of competition from qualified lawyers greatly accelerated his fame and wealth. Soon he was involved in the successful aborting of the prosecution of some prominent and very influential local citizens, one of which was a case of rape and murder of young university students for their body organs, and the other of embezzlement of a large fortune from a well-known company run jointly by Yemeni and foreign owners.

Life was becoming sweet and beautiful for Hasan. He began to accumulate friends in high places and took up the local custom of chewing qat, that green leaf which proliferates in Yemen and the horn of Africa and is used as a mild stimulant, usually chewed all afternoon after a big lunch. Hasan would thus take his turn to hold court, so to speak, on a Friday, after prayers and lunch, to which he would selectively invite those important and influential men to join him for qat. As host, he would provide all the soft drinks and the *sheesha* [hubble-bubbles], which needed a whole team of employees to keep the embers burning for the whole afternoon. His guests would come, as tradition dictated, with their individual bunches of qat twigs, tightly wrapped in plastic sheets, tucked under their arms. They would be seated by Hasan around the four walls of the dedicated qat-chewing room in a specific order, with the richest and most influential guests being assigned the cushions nearest to him. On the following Friday, he would be a guest at one of their chewing sessions, and so on. Thus, the qat cliques would develop over time into small groups of twenty or so members, with fairly similar political orientations and social strata. Over the next two years, Hasan found his niche, and life was very sweet and fulfilling.

One of these very wealthy friends was Tawfiq, an assistant deputy minister at national security.

"Hey, Hasan, guess what?" Tawfiq said.

"What?"

"I heard some very important news."

"You mean another unsubstantiated rumor?"

"Call it what you like, but you will like this one."

"Okay, okay. So, tell me."

"Only if you promise me a huge present for the big news."

"Okay, I promise. What did you hear?"

"I hear you are going to be minster of justice in the new cabinet."

"That's not good news! That's terrible news. I don't want it," Hasan pretended.

"It's not up to you. If this president invites you to be a minister or any other government official, you cannot refuse, unless you want your life to become intolerable."

"Why? There must be hundreds who want to become minister of justice. They would sell their own grandmothers for the title. In any case I tried that job back in Aden, and I am not sure that I want to do it here too."

"Maybe, but the president is the one who decides, and he chooses the person."

∽

The next morning, Hasan heard confirmation of his appointment on the Voice of Yemen, the official radio channel of the ministry of information. Within minutes, he received a call from the prime minister, whom he had met three months previously through a mutual friend and then again when the prime minister invited him to a qat-chewing session only a few days before the announcement. They had talked there about a few general subjects, but it never crossed Hasan's mind that the visit was part of the job interview!

⁓

Over the next two or three days, dozens of people called to congratulate him, some totally unknown to him, but these were people who wanted him to at least be aware of their names just in case, as they would say. The closer friends sent all sorts of presents to Hasan's home, including huge baskets of fruit, large boxes of baklava, a watch, and several pen sets, and some even dared to send expensive jewelry for the minister's wife. It was only for a brief moment that Hasan's Western training in law reminded him that such gifts to a minister of the state might be inappropriate, if not downright illegal. He did consult his wife for a change, but Salma, as usual, deferred to his judgment, while deep down in her heart she was quite thrilled with the gold bracelets and necklaces. In the end, Hasan informed Salma that he would find it very difficult to return the presents, especially the ones from the president and prime minister, but he assured her that he would keep a list of all the donors and he would pay them back with gifts of similar value "in order to satisfy his conscience," as he put it.

⁓

The new minister of justice set out to examine the state of the courts in the country, starting with the capital, Sanaa. Having practiced law for several months, he was already aware how deficient the system was, but he now had access to a lot more information, especially the budget, revenue, and spending in the ministry. He was struck by the wasteful system used in the ministry and the incompetence of the staff, which adequately explained the inertia of the system. He discovered that the number of employees on the payroll was about double that of the ones who actually came to work. So many people were delegating family members to collect their salaries, and subsequently send the money to the villages where those nominal employees of the ministry were farming or trading, or simply staying at home. Salaries were also being paid and collected in the name of employees who had been dead for many years. He was soon to discover that such a situation was by no means peculiar to his ministry. He therefore decided to appoint a hierarchy of command and had to select a deputy minister and his assistant.

There was no shortage of candidates, but none of them was impressive, or even qualified. Those who were there got their appointments through nepotism and graft. He also had to make sure that his deputy posed no threat to him as a possible replacement. After all, in Aden, he had gone through that scenario when he displaced his minister of justice through servility, or loyalty as he would prefer to call it, to president Antar of the PDRY. But he soon found his man, whose main qualifications were blind loyalty to him and willingness to spy and report on the other members of the staff. After testing his loyalty for a few weeks, he recommended him to the prime minister and got him appointed.

∼

A few months after the appointment of Hasan, a rebellion started in the Saada area in the north, where people felt ignored and alienated. In that area which stretched toward the Saudi border, the carrying of guns was the norm; indeed it was virtually synonymous with manliness and importance. Rebellion there was an intermittent phenomenon, which was ever present but manageable by the central government, which would send platoons of soldiers to keep the peace and frequently arrest, and sometimes kill, rebels. The government considered those rebels terrorists, even though they never attacked innocent civilians but concentrated on ambushing army units approaching or operating in their area of Saada. Frequently enough, Hasan would have to deal with those captured rebels and put them through the court system, or what there was of it, and most would be jailed under sometimes horrendous conditions in filthy, dark, damp, and miserable jails, often shackled to the wall or floor. Hasan avoided visiting those jails, possibly deliberately so that he could not be accused of condoning the inhumane conditions under which the prisoners were held.

~

A year after Hasan and his family arrived in Sanaa, they learned from Aden that a suitor was asking for the hand of Zahra, who was almost seventeen at that time. Salma was very excited for her little sister, although she realized how young she was and that she would not be able to finish her education. Their mother expected Salma and Ahmad to be there in Aden to marry her off to an airline pilot from Jedda in Saudi Arabia. In his favor was that he was of Yemeni origin but born in Jedda, which is close to Yemen, and from which there were almost daily flights to Sanaa, and Aden.

Because of the distance, Ahmad could not be expected to return to perform the duty of the only remaining male in the family since the death of his father. Besides, he had illegally absconded from PDRY, and he would almost certainly be jailed for that. The bride's elder sister, Salma, was the wife of another university graduate who escaped from Aden in order to settle in the north, and she would run the risk of being detained and held for a ransom in Aden if she was to go there for the wedding. Therefore Salma suggested that the wedding be held at her house in Sanaa, and she offered her mother a room in her house where she could live the rest of her life. Thus Ahmad's mother made her plans to leave Aden for Sanaa with the young bride, and she found a cousin to move into her house to prevent it from being taken over by squatters or being broken into and burgled or ransacked. That was not difficult at all, since the average family was quite short of space in its home.

~

The wedding ceremony was rather modest, partly because Zahra's friends were left behind in Aden. Some man had to give the bride away at the small Islamic ceremony where the marriage contract was sealed. As Zahra's elder brother Ahmad was far away in Scotland, Hasan stood in for him, which according to the imam performing the ceremony was still by the rules. However, the wedding night was postponed by three days to occur when the groom was to take his bride back to Jedda, where he had a lovely and well-furnished home.

Young Zahra spent an hour with the *mukaddiyah*, a woman whose job is to explain to a virgin bride, literally untouched by a male hand, all that she might expect on the wedding night. This included the importance of that pink stain that needed to be seen on the white bed sheets the following morning by the groom's family as proof of virginity. She was naturally anxious, even more so because she knew that she would not have her mother in Jedda to support her during those anxious hours of her life. Her mother had to tell her a little white lie the day she left Sanaa. She promised her to join her the following month, knowing that once the marriage was consummated Zahra's anxiety would have rapidly evaporated. In fact, she knew deep in her heart that Zahra would rather be alone with her husband, Zuhair, during their honeymoon. After all, that was how she felt when it was her turn some thirty years before.

Zuhair was a tall, light-skinned, almost handsome man sporting a small goatee. But even more importantly for Zahra and her mother was that he treated them with enormous respect and courtesy. He was highly trained, being a qualified airline pilot who had won his wings in that industry. He would have been a very eligible suitor in Jedda except that Saudi women were hardly ever permitted to marry foreigners, least of all Yemenis who were considered beneath them in social class.

~

Over the next several months, Hasan prospered, and his contacts with the president became a lot more frequent, partly because his advice on international law was sought as Yemen developed bilateral trade and political relationships with an increasing number of countries. Besides, the common language in most of those negotiations was English, at which Hasan was excellent, having studied both in Britain and the United States. Furthermore, the president was especially pleased with his ability to neutralize the opposition through persuasion or prosecution, and sometimes intimidation. To the president, the method did not matter, as long as the job was done. Thus, whenever there were visiting dignitaries, including foreign ministers or presidents, he would have Hasan by his side, rather than his own foreign minister whom he had appointed in that portfolio in order to appease a large and important tribe in the north of the country. At cabinet reshuffles, which were decided entirely by the president, albeit announced by the prime minister, Hasan never lost his post.

~

The president actively encouraged corruption within his cabinet, knowing that corrupt ministers would never dare challenge his authority for fear of being prosecuted for all the millions of riyals they had embezzled. He also showered Hasan with special favors and gifts. One of these was a nice big house just outside Sanaa, supplied with a guard and a gardener who sometimes doubled as the cleaner and driver. It was situated in a large open area of sand and rock but was surrounded by palm trees and other tall trees, somewhat sheltering it from the view of trucks and cars passing by in the distance. It had its own power generator and was well equipped with a pump to draw well water.

Hasan would occasionally invite his very select friends to chew qat there, and although they had to travel an extra thirty minutes, the seclusion and solitude were worth the extra effort and expense. Alcohol was not allowed by Hasan, who did not drink at all. However, Hasan realized that the main advantage of the place was its isolation from the city and therefore from prying eyes, and he soon started inviting certain willing young women to spend time with him there. These were foreign women who worked at the ministry of justice, transient visitors, or sometimes maids from the Horn of Africa or the Far East. Hasan's sexual appetite, which had lain dormant for several months due to his hectic pace of life, the few duties he performed toward his two sons, and the lack of variety, suddenly received a boost. He therefore found himself going to the villa every two weeks, and later every week. His explanation to Salma, whenever he bothered to give her one, was that he was meeting important foreign dignitaries, or prominent Yemenis, in confidence, on behalf of the president, and that they did not want to be seen in his company in public. He knew that once he mentioned the name of the president, any further questions would cease.

CHAPTER 17

~

THE SEPARATION

Over breakfast one day in March, Ann hesitantly approached the subject. The previous night she had returned home late from a long weekend in London.

"I need to talk to you, Ahmad."

"Sure, I hope it is good news. Are you pregnant?"

"Oh, no! I am certainly not pregnant."

"Okay, tell me then."

"Look, dear ... I ... I ... I don't want to hurt you, I mean hurt your feelings."

Now Ahmad literally sat up in his chair as an ominous feeling of nausea came over him.

"Why? Did anything happen in London?"

"Well, it ... It is to do with my visit to London ... It involves my old high school friend, Diana."

"Oh?"

"Well, we were very close at school you know, best of friends."

"I am glad you were able to reconnect with her. We all need close friends; sometimes I wish I had such a friend, I mean a male friend, here in Edinburgh, as opposed to a woman that I love physically like you."

"But that's the point, Ahmad. I love Diana … as a friend … yes, but also physically. Look! We were lovers when we were at high school. It did not start like that. She was just a tender and warm person. But she was molested by a group of boys at school, and I was the one who came to her aid and supported her."

"Were those boys put in jail?" Ahmad asked.

"No, there was no actual rape, but it was sexual assault, with not a single witness except for that gang of boys who denied everything, of course."

"What a shame. That really pisses me off. And the thing is that it happens a lot more frequently than we think, because it is grossly underreported. In Yemen and the whole Middle East too, I imagine, except that it tends to occur against the more vulnerable poorer girls and maids, not within affluent families. Sometimes I feel, despite being a doctor, that such animals should be castrated."

"Well, that's putting it strongly! In any case, my dear, I spent a wonderful weekend with Diana. We talked and laughed and ate and drank and walked for miles and miles. And we made love all night! I need to tell you Ahmad, I'm in love again."

"You can't be serious? You are in love with me! You told me that so many times."

"Yes, I did, and you did too whenever you were on top of me, or I was on top of you. It's part of the act, which takes you to that indescribable climax. I said it to Diana too as we glued our bodies together. I am in love again, but with a woman. I don't expect you to understand that. Women do that more readily, at least I think they do. With men, it's all about penetration, and it does not matter which of the three orifices as long as it is penetration."

"You didn't seem to mind penetration, as I recall."

"Of course not, with a man. I am a woman after all, with all the right equipment. What I am saying is that lovemaking with a woman is not *only* about penetration. It's not even about physical contact, necessarily."

"She must be very beautiful, this … Diana?"

"She has a beautiful soul, but she is not beautiful to look at. That would be how a man would typically judge beauty in a woman. We're from Venus, remember?"

"But why does it have to be the one or the other. I love you, Ann, and I am willing to share you with the woman you love, at least in the hope that after the novelty is over you will come back to me fully. I certainly would not share you with a man; but with Diana, it's … it's okay … I suppose."

"That's really interesting; you won't share me with another man, but in the same way that you would not share me with another man, she does not want to share me with a man either. We actually talked about this over the weekend. I plan to invite her up here to live with me, forever."

Ahmad looked devastated as he realized that Ann was dead serious, and he was losing her, forever.

"So, how soon do you want me to move out? This week?"

"Oh, no. She won't come up here until May. She'll have to give in her notice and find a job here. But we will visit more frequently."

"What kind of work does she do?"

"She's a social worker."

That evening, in glum silence, Ann prepared a separate bed for Ahmad in the tiny room which was used as a storage area. She thought that a clean break would be best for the two of them, and she wanted Ahmad to know that she was serious about Diana and had no intention of changing her mind during a few climactic moments of passion.

～

Ahmad had a very sleepless night. He was depressed and felt rejected, but his main preoccupation that night was the fact that he was so isolated and lonely. He had not developed any new close Scottish friends. His Arab group fractured in all sorts of directions after the disastrous cancellation of the Arab dinner event. He had no family to talk to; his relationship with Salma was ruined by her blind loyalty to her devious and domineering husband. He ruminated over the idea that he never attended his father's funeral or Zahra's wedding and had virtually no contact with Salma or his mother. And the one person whom he loved, for whom he returned to

Edinburgh and for whom he lived, or so he thought, was abandoning him for a woman lover. At least she was not doing so for a man, and that made him feel less inadequate, for the last thing he wanted to imagine was that he was not man enough for Ann.

~

That June, he was going to finish his course and all his exams, and hopefully receive another diploma, something to show for all his work and perseverance. He had hoped to get a job with some police department, but when he inquired, there was none. At the medical school, the opportunity to continue as an anatomy demonstrator was still available, but it was part-time work and there were no long-term prospects of promotion there.

It was at that very moment that he thought of the Arabic word for *travel,* and as soon as he did that he heard from his remote childhood memory the famous song of that Egyptian crooner, Farid Al-Atrash: "Travel, travel, travel in peace; and come back home, safely." That was it, that's what he was going to do, as soon as possible. It was as if he wanted to prove to himself that he did belong somewhere, anywhere, and he was going to prove it to himself and the world, and even to Ann. He knew that he would one day return to the Edinburgh that he loved, and he wished he could buy the smallest apartment, which he could call his own pad and which would be waiting for his return. He could also rent it out to some medical or other student while back in Yemen. However, he was virtually penniless, which made his departure an even more urgent matter.

CHAPTER 18

~

AHMAD GOES TO SANAA

The Lufthansa airplane was spotless, and the service, even in the tourist class cabin, was excellent. There was the inevitable brief stop at Frankfurt Airport only two hours after take-off. The rest of the trip was smooth and uneventful, apart from the snoring of the obese German man sitting in the aisle seat next to Ahmad, who had the widow seat. The German had started drinking beer as soon as the bar opened and downed three mugs in less than two hours. Over dinner, he also managed to drink a mini bottle of red wine, about one third of the standard one. Even before the air stewardess collected his tray, he started breathing heavily, not quite asleep, moving restlessly to left and right, until he found just the right position to allow him to sleep. As he drifted to sleep he would gradually stop breathing, utter a loud snort, and then momentarily open his eyes and look vacantly in front of him before returning to sleep. The whole cycle would repeat itself every minute or two. Ahmad found it difficult to concentrate enough to read, for he was all the time trying to anticipate when the next snort would occur. He had read about Japanese torture, where a prisoner would spend the whole sleepless night trying to anticipate the dripping drops of water landing on him. He thought that the two were very similar, at least for him at that moment.

~

Touchdown at Sanaa Airport was perfect. The sun was shining brightly, and the air was warm that afternoon in June. His passage through customs and immigration was surprisingly smooth, but he had obtained and paid for a visa from the Yemeni consulate office in London. The uniformed official did take a long time to examine his documents but eventually let him through. All he had to do was to say that he came to Yemen to visit his family there, something that the immigration officer must have heard so many times from the thousands of Yemenis in the ever expanding diasporas.

The chaotic scene at the luggage retrieval point did not surprise Ahmad, but the loud voices and other noises did. He had been away in quiet and sedate Edinburgh for many months, and that was a real contrast.

For her brother, Salma had organized transportation with one of her many drivers and helpers, at the request of her mother who was so excited to see Ahmad that she came to the airport with the driver. However, she stood a fair distance behind the area where the men were jostling for suitcases and cardboard boxes, completely covered in black *hijab* and *niqab*. She never wore the niqab over her face in Aden, but this was Sanaa. Her two eyes appeared congested, and tears of happiness could be detected by anyone standing close enough.

The driver had to point her out to Ahmad, who would not have recognized her. As he handed his luggage to the driver, Ahmad walked up to his mother and bent his neck down to plant a kiss over the black scarf wrapped round her head. Her hair, even through the scarf, smelled sweaty, with a lingering whiff of that heavy scent commonly worn by Yemeni women. She held him through all the layers and folds of the black robe covering her and sobbed quietly for a few moments, then turned toward the car where the driver had arrived ahead with both suitcases.

Ahmad sat in the front passenger seat next to the driver, as the driver sped toward the city of Sanaa. He had been in Sanaa briefly after escaping from Aden, and before returning to Edinburgh for graduate studies. Despite that, he could not help but notice how chaotic the traffic was and how ugly the buildings lining the route were. They were nearly all the same two-story cuboids with residential apartments on the upper floor and stores on the ground floor, with huge metal doors, nearly all painted blue with the occasional green one. The store signs, in Arabic and occasionally in English, were a motley collection of size, shape, and color. Only a few stores were open, and there were hardly any customers buying things, but many goats were chewing whatever they could find in front of the stores. They were sometimes chased away by a stray dog.

"Nothing has changed since I was here, Mother?"

"And nothing will."

"Really! Why do you say that?"

"You will see for yourself. This is a stagnant country. Nothing seems to get done."

"It is a poor country."

"It is, but whatever little it has or generates is wasted."

"What do you mean?"

"The main reason is corruption. Everyone is on the take, from the little clerk to the minister."

"Really! Does that include Hasan? He's a minister."

"No, he is a good man. He is the exception, the only exception."

"You're not biased for your son-in-law? I don't suppose."

"Only Allah knows, but according to Salma he is honesty itself."

"Ah well, if Salma says so, then it must be right," Ahmad said with obvious sarcasm. "I remember one conversation when she told me that he was as holy as a prophet!"

"He has become a very important man, but he is always kind to me; he has opened his home to me."

"But it is also your daughter's home; it was she who opened her home to you. Why wouldn't she? Didn't you make all sorts of sacrifices for her, and for me, and for Zahra, to help us get education and to be where we are now?"

"She would not be able to invite me to live there, if he did not agree. This is his home; she does not own any of it. In our Islamic laws, she would be entitled to one eighth of it, only if he were to die. But until then, it is his and his alone."

"What a terrible system we have in this Islamic law. Everything is the property of the husband, including the wife herself, sold to the highest bidder at the age of fifteen or even younger, by the father or brother, the very two people who are supposed to protect her. And if she challenges her owner, she gets divorced without a single riyal to her name. Or he can take another wife, while she stews in her own juice."

"Look, son, don't exaggerate! These are our customs and have been for hundreds of years, since the days of Prophet Muhammad, peace be upon him, and nothing will change them. You have just come from modern Europe, but you cannot compare the two societies. They have their system, and we have ours. The Quran says 'To you your religion, and to me mine.' Or have you forgotten?"

"I still remember that verse. It is used, I mean abused, all the time to explain irrational laws and rules; but that verse simply said to non-Muslims that they did not have to become Muslims and could worship whatever or whomever they wanted."

"Ahmad! We had all these arguments already when we were in our own country, Aden, and you left, and now you are back. I am so happy, but if you want to prosper in this country, you will need to follow its rules now that you are here, not those of Scotland. You are a highly qualified doctor, and you can do very well here. You have been away for half your life, and I cannot believe that I am, at last, seeing you again today. Please don't rock the boat, and try to be flexible."

"This is not my country either, but I shall try to be *flexible*, as you put it."

"Good. We have arrived."

"After you get off, I will ask the driver to take me to the Queen Arwa Hotel."

"No, your sister invited you to stay with them, at least for a few days, until you get organized."

"No, thank you. I will get off the car to greet her and Hasan, but then I will go to the hotel. I need my independence."

"She will be disappointed, you know."

"Not for very long, I am sure."

~

It did not take Ahmad long to find a small number of his schoolmates in Sanaa. In that small community, news of the arrival of a new doctor, especially a Western-trained specialist, traveled fast. One of those was a surgeon who had studied in Birmingham, and the other was a childhood friend who worked as a translator for the French Embassy and was fluent in four languages; he seemed to know everyone, especially in the expatriate community.

Soon people were asking him where his private surgery was and when he would see them about a myriad of complaints and symptoms. The task of getting registered as a physician would have been very daunting, what with the translation of all his medical degrees and documents from English, and even of his MD degree from the University of Edinburgh, written in ornate Latin, but for the luck of treating the middle-aged, overweight wife of the assistant to the deputy minister of health. She had severe pain and numbness in her right index finger and thumb, especially while cooking during the day and in bed at night. Ahmad did not need to have an examination room, only a cursory examination of the lady, which confirmed his diagnosis of carpal tunnel syndrome. He gave her simple advice, which controlled her symptoms within one week. The grateful lady insisted on inviting him to lunch with her husband at home, and although she was not supposed to join an all-male lunch, she made an exception out of respect for him. She thought that she would have him at her beck and call for any future ailments that she might have, and even introduce him to some of her carefully chosen lady friends.

The assistant deputy minister gave the necessary orders to expedite the licensing of Dr. Ahmad, who soon was in business with a steadily increasing number of patients. In the meantime, he was putting out feelers for a more academic or salaried position which might meet his interest in forensic science, knowing that the system in Sanaa allowed him to do both at the same time. The assistant deputy minister, who heard no more complaints from his wife, especially in bed at night, was also helpful there, for he knew a relatively senior police officer and arranged for Ahmad to see him over a meal. Once the two men got to know each other, Ahmad was offered the job of part-time consultant to the police department, after the approval of the commissioner of police. He was to be paid on a fee-for-service basis, but Ahmad had the feeling that once he proved his skills to them, he would have a permanent job, not that he was desperate for income, for he was earning good money from his private practice.

However, in order to hold such a job with a government department, Ahmad had to obtain an identity card, which would be useful to have as a citizen of Yemeni origin, albeit from the south. He mentioned this to Salma on one of his rare visits to his mother who resided with her.

"When you get your ID card, make sure that you do not write 'Aden' as your place of birth."

"Why?" Ahmad asked, looking puzzled. "What else can I write except Aden, where I was born?"

"I wouldn't do that if I were you. Southerners are under great suspicion here. There are so many of them held in interrogation centers; you might not even get a job."

"I already have a job; I am a doctor, just like your husband is a lawyer. They need us here, otherwise we wouldn't be here. What did Hasan write as his place of birth?"

"Oh, he's different."

"In what way?"

"Well … he wrote Turbah, but that is where he was actually born."

"What? He was born in Turbah? This is the first time I hear it. So why was he an Adeni all these years? Like going to government schools as an Adeni and getting a scholarship to the University of London, as an Adeni, paid for by the British government? What is happening here?"

"Well, it is a long story."

"I have plenty of time!" snapped Ahmad.

"He actually *was* born in Turbah and is very proud to say that here, but his older brother, who was born in Aden, died as an infant, so his parents called him the same name as his dead brother and used the already existent birth certificate of the Colony of Aden. They meant well; they just wanted their son to have the advantages which we Adenis had. I don't see anything wrong with that."

"I don't suppose you would, when it is your husband. But what if every child born in Turbah did that? Then what?"

"But every child did not."

"So, he might have taken the seat of some deserving Adeni at school."

"Never! He was always top of the class," Salma replied with enormous pride. "He was either first or second all his life."

"I am very aware of it; he often beat me in grades. But that has nothing to do with depriving a real Adeni boy of, let us say, secondary education."

"How do you know he has?"

"Okay, let me explain this in simple language. As you know, at Aden College, and at your own Girl's College, the first grade which we entered after passing the intermediate school exams, around the age of thirteen, had limited seats, about forty, as I recall. So the top forty pupils were admitted. Are you with me so far? Good! Pupil number forty-one had either to go the Technical College in the town of Maalla or to go to a private school, such as St. Anthony's, and his father would have to pay. So, if your darling Hasan had not occupied that seat, under false pretenses, this pupil number forty-one would have been accepted at Aden College and Hasan would have rightfully gone to St Anthony's and paid for it, like many other northern Yemenis who were educated in Aden. As you might know, so many of them became prominent ministers and professors in the north because of that education. Do you get it now?"

"He did not do it; it was his father. Anyway, he went and served Aden faithfully, and everyone admired him."

"I just cannot believe that you approve of depriving an innocent Adeni pupil of his right to education."

"That is all in the past, and even I have my place of birth as Turbah."

"Really? I did not know that our mother delivered in, or ever visited, Turbah! And what is your place of birth on your British passport?"

"Aden, of course."

"So, are you not worried that this discrepancy might be noticed when you cross borders, which I understand you do fairly frequently?"

"No one is ever going to notice, because they would never see both passports at the same time, and in any case we travel with diplomatic passports."

"And all this does not bother your conscience?"

"I am not going to continue this ridiculous conversation. You can do what you like. I gave you sound advice to help you avoid being harassed by the secret service. This is the gratitude I get. I don't know why you harbor such a grudge against an angel like Hasan. You are full of envy and venom because he achieved so much while you did not. What he achieved was with hard work alone, and everyone knows him and respects him. You can declare that you were born in Haifan, where our grandfather came from, or Aden, or Timbuktu, for all I care!"

"Wow, isn't all that falsification of the evidence interesting, especially for a minister of justice!"

Salma looked down toward the floor, reflected for a moment, then looked up at Ahmad with contempt. She left her own living room, a clear signal for Ahmad to leave her house.

Ahmad's mother sat quietly in the easy chair listening to that long conversation but never interfered. She saw sense in both arguments. She had refused to write anything else but "Aden" on her own documents, but as an unemployed old woman it would not affect her status in any significant way. In her heart, despite her strict scruples, she found an excuse for Salma, and yet she knew that Ahmad was right. She secretly admired his honesty and pride.

As Ahmad said good-bye to her, she knew that two of her own flesh and blood would be apart forever, and it tore her heart. But as an old widow sheltering in her son-in-law's house, she knew she would have to keep her pain within her bosom and take it to her grave. She wished that Ahmad had a Yemeni wife with whom she could share her concerns, and with whom she could take refuge when she wanted a change from Salma's company and the occasional humiliations she experienced there. She had desperately tried to find him a wife in Aden without success, but now in Sanaa it would be even harder. Whereas she knew so many families in Aden, she hardly knew any in Sanaa, where local families would not readily marry their girls to southerners unless they were very wealthy or extremely influential.

CHAPTER 19

~

FORENSIC CONSULTATION

A few weeks later, the story broke in Sanaa that a wealthy man with a beautiful home had shot dead a would-be burglar late the previous night. The owner belonged to the well-known Taleb tribe, who originated from an area a little to the north of the city. The burglar was a tall, muscular, black-skinned man with clear African facial features. He was found dead, facedown, with a sharp knife with an eight-inch blade about ten yards behind his body. He was lying in a pool of blood by the time the police arrived to investigate. The loud single bullet sound had caused the wealthy man's male neighbors to come out of their homes to see what happened. Some found him standing in front of his house, pistol in hand, with the gate still wide open, four cars parked in front of the house, and his driver standing near one of the cars. The driver had called the police on instructions from the owner to come and pick up the body.

~

Two policemen arrived surprisingly quickly, which the driver attributed to the importance of the wealthy man. They came over to him, greeted him with great respect, and congratulated him on his safety before walking to the burglar and ascertaining that he was dead. Then they walked back to the wealthy man and started asking questions, one of them attempting to write notes in the dim light coming from the lamppost on the street.

"What happened, Uncle Muhammad?"

"This was a dangerous armed burglar. He must have decided to burgle my house, and when I surprised him as he was coming in stealthily through the gate, he tried to kill me with a big knife. So I decided to shoot him before he could kill me."

"Do you know him, or have you ever seen him before?"

"No, no. Why would I know someone like that, a *khadem* [street sweeper]? He must have come up from Tihama on the Red Sea. That's where these sweepers come from to burgle our homes."

"Oh, there are too many of them here. And they are increasing in number," agreed one of the policemen.

"He is dead, you know," said the other policemen.

"Well, it was either him or me."

"So, how close was he to you?"

"Close enough to slash my throat. So I had no choice but to shoot him before he could kill me."

"Thanks be to Allah that he did not. So he must have been close?"

"Very close. I just told you, if I did not shoot he would have slashed my throat."

"Never mind, Uncle Muhammad. Go inside the house now and have something to drink, and then sleep. But, if you don't mind, please come down to the police station, near the vegetable market, to make a statement."

"What for? I just gave you my statement, didn't I?"

"This is just routine, Uncle Muhammad. We have to submit our report to the captain tomorrow and he will need you to sign the documents to close the case. May Allah save us from these black burglars! Good night."

The body was placed in the back of the police van and taken to the morgue as was the routine.

~

Late the next morning, Muhammad Bin Taleb was driven down to the police station. The captain greeted him with great respect, if not awe.

"Brother Muhammad, I read the police report, but I am puzzled about something."

"What?"

"You said that you shot him only once, right?"

"Yes, once. I did not want to kill him, but he was lurching at me with his sharp knife, that … that big knife, more like a sword. Did you see how big it was? I had to shoot to save my life."

"But how do you explain that he has four bullet holes in his body?"

"I swear to you on the Quran that I only shot once."

"Maybe the other two holes are from some other injury, or caused by his own knife?"

"Maybe; Allah knows best. So where do you want me to sign?"

Muhammad signed the documents after a very quick glance at them.

~

One of the policemen at that station recognized the burglar's face and went to the shack at the bottom of a rocky hill where his wife and daughter lived. His wife was very ill, with breast cancer that had spread. She was emaciated and could hardly stand up. However, her sixteen-year-old daughter, who eked a living as a prostitute, was a healthy, articulate, and attractive dark-skinned girl with big hips, thick lips, and penetrating eyes. She screamed in horror when the policeman conveyed the bad news. Her mother sobbed quietly, and then said, "I told him to stop these burglaries many times. Even last week, I reminded him. But he never listened to me all the time we have been together. He insisted on eking out some income to pay for our food … and now he is gone. There is no strength except through Allah. Never mind, I shall soon join you, father of my children. And then who is going to look after Haleemah? Poor Haleemah, she had to sell her body to buy medicines for me. Even dogs have a better life than we. Haleemah, go bury your father. Talk to some of the men in these shacks. He has one or two friends left, but I cannot remember their names anymore. My body is ruined, and my mind too."

⁓

Haleemah went down to the morgue, in the police car, with one of her father's male friends. She was not prepared for the horror of seeing her father's body with four bullet holes, and major bruising of his face and severe lacerations of his nose. She could not take it and started screaming at the top of her voice that someone shot him four times, and kept saying, "Why four times? Why four times" even after she left the morgue. The policeman tried to calm her down, telling her that it was only one bullet and that the wounds in the right leg were probably from the knife he was carrying. However, Haleemah was inconsolable and decided that she would not have the body buried until she had an answer. The policeman threatened her that if she did not, then the body would be taken to the shack and left there to rot or eaten by the dogs. That was enough to set her off screaming even louder.

Eventually, the police captain agreed to see her in the hope of persuading her to change her mind. When he could not, he undertook to get the new forensic consultant to look at the case with an open mind.

The captain said, "But you have to promise that once you hear his opinion, you will accept it and bury your father. You know, in Islam, we say that the dignity of the dead body necessitates its burial as soon as possible."

"Yes, I will accept it," she replied. "I do know that saying, Captain. I did go to *madrasah* [elementary school] but had to quit to support my mother and to buy all the medicines she was put on by the doctor, although they made no difference in the end."

⁓

Dr. Ahmad had the gruesome task of examining the body as soon as he got there. Once placed on a trolley under a bright neon light, he looked at it in the nude in the supine, then in the prone, and kept all clothing in case he needed to reexamine it. The face was disfigured with bruises and lacerations especially to the prominent parts, such as the nose, forehead, and cheekbone areas. There was a small bullet entry hole in the lower back, just below the lowest rib, to the right of the spine, and a large gaping exit wound in the top part of the belly just below the lowest rib. There was congealed blood in that area, and a soft mashed material which the doctor recognized as liver. There was also another bullet entry wound in the anterior right thigh, four inches above the right knee, and a larger exit wound on the posterior aspect of the same thigh, where muscle was severely lacerated.

The skin over the right calf muscle showed a long but superficial horizontal laceration. The kneecaps were also severely bruised. The patient's dark skin made it difficult to delineate the exact extent of the hematomas and bruises, but Ahmad thought he had the evidence he needed. Corresponding holes were noted in the burglar's shirt, one at the mid back and to the right, and a second one at the front, also to the right, where much blood staining was noted. The right leg on his shorts also had two holes corresponding with the bullet holes in the right thigh. He also looked at the burglar's knife for evidence of blood but found none.

He went over the police report, including the policeman's and Muhammad's statements, and noted that the knife was found ten yards behind the body and five yards from where Muhammad had stood in front of his gate. The report also said that only one bullet casing was found on the ground near Muhammad's gate.

At the end of that gruesome process, Ahmad told the morgue assistant to take the body back to the refrigerator and proceeded to write his detailed report. He had some difficulty writing it in Arabic, which he had never done before, since all the technical terms he knew were in English or Latin.

One hour later, it was on the captain's desk. The police captain was quite alarmed as he finished reading it. He asked the doctor to return to his office as soon as he could.

"Dr. Ahmad, this is serious what you wrote here."

"Of course it is. Death is usually quite serious!"

"You are saying that the account given by Muhammad is false?"

"It would appear to be."

"He said that the burglar came at him with a long knife and was close enough to slash his throat, and therefore he shot him because he feared for his life. And you are saying that the burglar was, at the very moment of the shot, at least five yards away from him and running away from him, not toward him. You were not there. How can you possibly know all that from your brief examination of a dead body?"

"That is why I spent two years at the department of forensic science in Edinburgh—so that I can make such statements based on scientific evidence."

"Okay, fine. Just take me through the scene. I did not study forensic medicine."

"I cannot tell whether the burglar confronted Muhammad, and at what distance. What I do know for sure—from the evidence—is that there was only one bullet that killed him, probably by causing massive internal bleeding from his liver, which as you know sits in the upper right abdomen. At the moment the man was shot, he was not facing Muhammad but was running away at great speed, and the bullet hit him while he was at the very spot where you found his knife. When he was hit, the knife fell out of his hand, but the momentum of his running, plus the momentum of the bullet itself, propelled him another ten yards away from Muhammad, before he fell face forward, which bruised and lacerated much of his face, especially the nose which probably scraped the rocky ground underneath him."

"But there were four bullet holes, according to your report, not two?"

"Yes, that is the most interesting part. You see, the bullet came in through his back, through the liver, out of the abdominal wall in the front, carrying with it parts of the shattered liver and heavily staining the front of his shirt. Because the victim was so close to the gun, the bullet had a lot of momentum, so it went farther forward, penetrated the front of his thigh, finally exiting through the back of his thigh."

The captain looked puzzled and interrupted. "How can the bullet come out of the *back* of his thigh? It is impossible for it to do a loop."

"You say this because you are still assuming that the burglar was standing still. He wasn't. He was running very fast. If you watch the hundred yard races at the Olympics, look carefully at how the runner would bend his knees, one at a time, and lift them way up almost to the height of his chest. So this man's right knee was exactly in that position when the bullet went through. And that is also why the skin over his right calf was grazed with that horizontal line on it as the bullet exited."

"But this is serious, if it is true. It implies that Muhammad was in no danger from the man. In fact, the man was trying to get away from him."

"Precisely! This looks like murder to me. Maybe he was trying to teach him a lesson by shooting at his legs or something, but the shot was higher than that, much higher in fact."

"Oh, my Allah! This is a very influential and rich man. What are we going to do?"

"We? I have nothing to do with this. This is *your* responsibility. I am only the scientific consultant; I collect and deduce and record facts as I see them."

"You had better speak to the major in charge of this section; this is too big for me."

"I don't need to speak to him; it's all in my report."

∼

As Ahmad left the police station, Haleemah was standing outside. She rushed toward him, and, guessing from his smart civilian attire that he was the doctor in question, she confronted him.

"Doctor, Doctor, what did you find?"

Ahmad was taken by surprise. He looked at the distraught black, almost pretty, teenager, but all he could say was that his conclusions were all in his report.

"But why would you not tell me to my face?"

"I don't think I am allowed at present."

"Why? My father is already dead."

"Yes, but there may be investigations or legal actions taken by the police, so I cannot talk about it until we know the next steps."

"Legal actions by the police? You mean that the rich man did something illegal?"

"I did not say that. I only said *may be*."

"You are a doctor. You are supposed to be like an angel … or like a father. Just because I am young and poor, and black, and a prostitute, I am still a human being and a grieving daughter."

"You are absolutely right, and I did not even know that you are a prostitute, as you say, but that makes no difference to me. I am not hiding things from you because I think you are less important than Muhammad but because of the legalities involved."

"In this country, the poor don't have a chance. I know they will hide the evidence from me, and no one will care. I had some hope in your integrity."

"Look, sister, one thing I can promise you, that is telling the truth, no matter where it takes me."

"You called me sister! You actually called me sister! No one ever does when they know what I do to earn a few riyals. They think I am dirt. That was kind of you to call me that."

"We are all brothers and sisters on this earth, and when we go, just like your poor father, we are all equal heaps of bones—nothing more, nothing less."

"May Allah be with you, Doctor!"

～

Dr. Ahmad dreaded his arranged meeting with Major Aqlan the next morning. He had written a meticulous report so there was no need to go over it anymore, and nothing more to discuss. But he was wrong about that. The colonel offered him tea and asked him lots of questions about his past, which Ahmad answered fully, guessing that the colonel must have had a thick dossier on him since his birth, especially since he was a southerner and especially after what Salma told him about all the southerners under interrogation.

"So, Doctor, what do you think happened?"

"But you must have read my report?"

"Yes, but it does not make sense."

"Well, the decision is yours. I have done my duty."

"But, is it possible that you are wrong?"

"We all can make mistakes. But if my conclusions are wrong, then what is your theory?"

"No, no, my dear Doctor, not wrong, not from a highly qualified man like you, from Edinburgh, no less. But I am only asking if perhaps there are some inaccuracies. I mean we cannot accuse an influential man from an important tribe of killing this ... this ... knife-wielding black burglar unless we are one hundred and one percent sure."

"I would suggest that you seek a second opinion, with my full blessing."

"Who from? You are the only specialist in Yemen, in fact in the Arabian Peninsula perhaps. No, I am afraid you are it."

"You can find someone in Egypt or India, I am sure."

"We don't want to spread our dirty linen in front of foreigners. But I have a question. You say that the burglar was running away from Muhammad, and that is how one bullet created all four holes. Why can we not say the same if he was running toward Muhammad, and was hit where the knife was retrieved?"

"First, if he was hit where the knife was dropped while running toward Muhammad, his body could not possibly travel ten yards backwards ..."

"But if he was shot where he fell, he might have just thrown the knife at Muhammad as a final effort to harm him, but it did not reach Muhammad," the major interrupted.

"In that case, Muhammad had no need to shoot him, because he was so far away that Muhammad was not in any imminent danger."

"You have an answer to everything, Doctor."

"Not really. I have learned, in the practice of medicine, to keep an open mind and be prepared to be wrong and to revise my opinion. So, if you have any better answers, do tell, please."

"No, no, you are the expert."

"But there is an even more compelling reason. If the burglar was facing Muhammad, the bullet would have had to start in the back of the thigh, and he would have to be running hundred yards style toward his victim, which is not possible. Then it would have had to exit through the front of the thigh, enter the abdominal wall through a neat hole, then burst out of the back with a lot of tissue damage there, taking some liver tissue with it through the back, near the spine. The liver bits were on the front."

The major was in deep thought. He knew the difficulties ahead.

"Perhaps we should ask Muhammad to offer compensation to Haleemah and her mother without telling them that he was guilty, but just out of the kindness of his heart. Maybe you can convince him. He will listen to a doctor and a professor."

"Major, what you do from this point on is your business. It would be inappropriate for me to talk to him or even to meet him."

"Why? He is a very nice man, and he is very *generous*," replied the major.

Ahmad got the message, smiled, but decided to say nothing.

"You did speak to Haleemah. So it would only be fair to speak to Muhammad."

"No, it's not the same. He is accused of murder. Haleemah is a child, and the bereaved daughter of a murdered man."

"But you show your bias already. You called him a murderer. He may be totally innocent."

"No, I did not call him a murderer; I said he is *accused* of murder. The court will decide if he is a murderer, not me."

"What if he came to see you at home? You know, he is a man of great influence and power, and would never condescend to visit anyone at their home. People dream of being invited to his palace. But I think he will make an exception and come to you. And ... and ... he is likely to be laden with gifts, I mean real gifts. This is our custom here, and especially the custom of his tribe."

Ahmad was getting very uncomfortable under the major's relentless pressure to somehow modify his evidence.

"Well, Major, I must go. I hope I have done my duty to my profession, and to Allah, and to my conscience. Obviously, if this comes to trial, you will need me to testify."

~

Ahmad left the police station with a very heavy heart and troubled mind, which prevented him from sleeping that Thursday night.

He slept in on Friday morning, which is the weekend in that part of the world. But he was particularly looking forward to that day, because he was going to cook lunch for a friend in his own little kitchen above the clinic. They chose to do that because Adel, who worked for the French Embassy, was going to bring him a bottle of Bordeaux, a rare treat for him, and they were going to enjoy it together with some beef around midday. So Ahmad started cooking the only dish he knew how to cook, namely the beef stew which he had cooked dozens of times during his student days in Edinburgh with his Somali friend Moosa and his Sudanese friend, the late Sharif. He had already bought the most crucial ingredient, onions, and had shopped for okra and a decent piece of stewing beef, rarely cooked in Yemen where people nearly always preferred lamb. Having sautéed the onions, he added the beef, sprinkled some salt, and added a generous helping of ground cumin and lots of water, then let the whole thing simmer before adding the final component of okra.

He sat back, reading a book of poetry by one of the many famous poets of Yemen, and marveled at its beauty and its complexity compared to the other two languages he could read. When he eventually looked up at the clock, he was alarmed at the passage of time. It was already thirty minutes past midday; Adel was supposed to be there at noon, because, like him, Adel did not attend mosque on Fridays. Ahmad began to worry. Was it possible that even this French-educated Yemeni, who worked for the French Embassy, was just another Yemeni who could never be on time? Was it really genetic this lateness of Yemenis?

He checked the pot of stew, added some water, and stirred it as the stew began to stick to the bottom. Another half hour went by, but Adel never came. Frustrated and disappointed, Ahmad spooned out some of his overcooked stew and dug his fork into it, washing it down intermittently with water instead of the long awaited Bordeaux.

However, only two minutes later the bell rang, and he opened the door to Adel.

"I am extremely sorry, Ahmad."

"Don't say a word! You're just another Yemeni. You know the saying, 'You can take the Yemeni out of Yemen, but you can't take Yemen out of the Yemeni!'?"

"Listen! Here is a nice bottle for you. Just open it first, take a sip, and let me tell you what happened. The food smells good. It must be that lovely spice."

Ahmad struggled with the corkscrew, mainly because he was out of practice. But it was worth the effort when he swirled that deep red liquid and put his nose just above the glass. He took a sip.

"Okay, that's better!" he exclaimed. "Tell me what happened. It had better be good."

"Believe it or not, I was out on the street by twelve, and I hailed this *dabbab* [local taxi] thinking I'd be with you in ten to fifteen minutes. The driver was in a rush to get to the mosque, but your place was on his way there and he could not resist the extra qat money he was going to make. So, he agreed to take me. But he was speeding and hit a cyclist who was meandering all over the road and who was mildly injured but wanted to make a fuss and get something out of it. So while the two were arguing, a police car came by."

"I think I know what happened next."

"No, you don't. The policeman released the cyclist but took the driver *and the passenger* to the police station and put us both in a cell, and locked the door!"

"You too?"

"Exactly, I told him I was invited to lunch and all that stuff and that I was only a passenger, but he insisted that since I was an eyewitness I had to give my report."

"So, why didn't you give your report and come here?"

"Oh, no, that would be too logical for Yemen. I was told that I had to be interrogated by the station sergeant, who was praying at the mosque, and had to wait until he came back after his prayers."

"You're kidding?"

"That's exactly what happened. The sergeant came and asked me a couple of questions. He didn't even record my testimony; then he let me go. So, I then had to find another dabbab to get here. There you have it. You know, I don't think anyone in France who hears this story would even believe it."

Ahmad did not know whether to laugh or scream. Suddenly, the two friends went into a long fit of laughter together, and enjoyed the stew and the rest of the bottle.

~

Over the next week, Ahmad attended his private clinic, according to the usual schedule. He had rented a small building, where he made the upper floor his home and the lower floor his clinic. He had hired one retired male nurse, since there were no female nurses to be found in Sanaa. The clinic was always busy, and he saw a lot of gross pathology. However, he was distracted by the murder case he had to deal with and felt very tense all the time. He had a feeling that his involvement in the case would bring him trouble, but he did not know what kind.

By the end of the clinic around seven in the evening, he felt utterly exhausted. He was looking forward to climbing the stairs to his living quarters, eating something light, and then sleeping. The male nurse, who normally would tidy up after the doctor and close shop, came in to ask permission to leave one half hour ahead of time and promised to come in an hour earlier for the next clinic to ready it for the patients.

"How many patients are still waiting?" Ahmad asked.

"There're all gone, except for one teenage girl who wouldn't go away. I tried to get rid of her, and offered her the first appointment in the next clinic, but she says she has a bad pain in her chest and cannot breathe."

"I am really wiped out, but I'll see her in case it is serious. Is she wheezing?"

"No, but she is holding her left chest all the time. She is too young to have a heart attack, I think."

"Okay, you can leave. I'll lock up after she leaves."

~

Ahmad went to the wash-hand basin and scrubbed his hands with a soapy brush, having done a rectal examination on the last patient. He then wetted a face towel and washed his face. He felt so much better. He then walked across to the patients' waiting room.

He could not believe his eyes. "Haleemah, what on earth are you doing here?"

"Can't you see that I have pain in my chest? I had it all afternoon; I am worried."

"You are not making this up in order to see me about what happened?"

"Of course not, and here is my hundred riyals. I will pay; don't worry."

"That's not what I worry about. It just might complicate things, my seeing you. All right, come in to the examination room and lie down on the examination couch while you tell me about your pain. Undo your bra when you get there."

Having taken the history in detail, Ahmad proceeded to do the usual medical examination which in Edinburgh they taught him consisted of inspection, palpation, percussion, and finally auscultation with the stethoscope. After feeling her pulse, he looked in her mouth first, and then at a pair of stunning breasts, full, heaving, with large purple nipples and areolas on a background of dark skin. He then placed the palm of his right hand on her left breast, trying to feel for what doctors call a thrill, this being the slight vibration that occurs when there is something wrong with the heart valves. It was a sensual feeling, even as he kept telling himself that he was a doctor and should not feel that way. He kept reminding himself that the last time he was intimate with a woman was one day before Ann started sleeping in her own bed, and that was nine months ago—the duration of a whole pregnancy!

There was no thrill on either side of the chest. He tapped his right middle finger over the left one as he moved the latter across the chest and down to the area of the liver. Finally, he pulled his stethoscope, asked the girl to slightly lean over to her left side, and placed the bell of the instrument over the apex of the heart, just below that shapely and firm left breast. He closed his eyes. He always found that helpful in detecting mild soft murmurs, since it tended to shut out any other distracting visual stimuli.

As he leaned over, eyes closed, he felt Haleemah's right hand probing his crotch and finding, to his utter shame, an erection which he could not control. He broke loose immediately and bolted back to his desk, trying to camouflage his erection by sitting down in his chair behind his large desk. He kept staring down at the top of his desk, feeling utterly humiliated. Haleemah sat up, got dressed, and walked up to the chair next to Ahmad, where patients would sit to relate the history of their complaints.

"I am sorry; I seem to have embarrassed you a lot. Please forgive me."

"Yes, you have. Why did you come here? There is nothing wrong with you."

"I know you won't believe this, but I came because I had *kadhmah* [suffocation] in my chest. I did not know what it was. My father was just murdered, my mother is riddled with cancer which has spread to her lungs, and she keeps feeling this kadhmah, and I was worried. I am glad you found nothing wrong. Perhaps it is all psychological?"

"In the absence of any signs, I think it must be psychological. But how did you find my clinic? You did not even know my name."

"In Sanaa, that is easy. I just asked people, several people, for the clinic of the new specialist from Britain. How many other doctors would answer to that description? But I did want to see you rather than any other of these useless doctors who only want to write prescriptions. And you treated me with respect outside the police headquarters. Trust has a lot to do with how patients feel. I am sure you know that, Doctor."

"Well, you should be fine. You can go now."

"You know, Doctor, you have a psychological problem yourself."

"Really, what is that?"

"You are starved—sex starved."

"I am not going to discuss sex with a patient. My relationship with you can only be as a patient."

"In that case, why was it … you know … so erect?"

"I am ashamed of that; I should not have allowed it."

"But could you have prevented it? Me, I don't think so. In this city, unless you are married, or homosexual, you have to come to a girl like me for relief. I have hundreds of men every year, and the numbers are increasing all the time; men of all ages and shapes and professions. I recognize some of them from their photos in the newspapers, where they love to appear, and sometimes from what they are saying on the phone while they are with me. Of course they give me false names, but I know they are false. They are so excited to do it to a teenager, and the older they are the younger they want the girl to be. So I tell them I am thirteen or fourteen and that I have just been 'opened'. They just love that. Some would be the age of my grandfather, if he was alive today. They are nearly all married. I can nearly always tell. The married ones are very secretive about themselves, where they come from, although I can tell from the accent, and they are in a hurry to get it over with. And they like the kinky stuff, the stuff their wives would not indulge in, like putting it in the rear, sucking, and other variations. It helps them to get it up. The older ones are content with the oral stuff, because they are embarrassed by the softness of their tools. So they get off that way. They all share one thing though: contempt for me, the whore, who can be bought with less than they spend on qat [leaf chewed in Yemen and the Horn of Africa] on the weekend."

Ahmad seemed mesmerized during that long explanation.

"But where do you meet your clients? I mean, if I were to come to your shack, everyone would notice, wouldn't they?"

"Of course! The only ones who come to my half of the shack, and I try to plan it when my parents are out, are the poor single men from the area. They belong there, so no one pays any attention to them. No, those upper classes have what you might call their safe houses. They tend to be in secluded parts of the city or homes in large compounds with high walls. I go there by taxi. The driver does not know who I am. The *hijab* [scarf over the head] and *niqab* [veil] are very useful. There is no way you can tell if I am a whore or the man's sister or wife. And when it is over, these important people all have drivers and fixers, so they drop me off in town and I find my way home easily. There is one minister who orders my services at a grand house out of town. He seems to be very rich. He likes to be cruel during sex. That's how he gets his kicks."

"How do you know he is a minister?"

"Just from the one and only time when his driver took me back into Sanaa and got a call on the car phone, obviously from the minister because the driver said, 'Yes, Your Excellency.' He said it quietly, but loud enough for me to hear it. I am glad he did not think I heard, otherwise I might have ended up in a ditch on the side of the road. These people are ruthless, and while they cannot live without whores, they despise us, and to beat or even kill us is nothing to them. Do you despise me?"

"Me? No, not at all. The way I see it, human beings are all equal; only they have different opportunities during the sixty or seventy years of life they live on this earth. I had all the luck; the right educated father, the supportive family, the opportunity to go to school then university, and a lucrative job to settle into. You had none of these, not even one of them, because even your primary schooling was interrupted. You had to, not only survive, but you had to support your parents. You made the sacrifice. You are a heroine, at least to your family!"

"Now, now, don't go overboard! People here will think you are stark raving mad if they hear you saying that a whore is a heroine. But thank you, Doctor."

"I must say you have interesting things to say, much more interesting than what doctors would talk about," he said with a smile. "Do you hate yourself for doing this sometimes?"

"Sure, but I have to pretend that I am enjoying it and make lots of noises as if I am coming. That way they think, they are real men who can bring a teenage girl to orgasm. The worst thing I hate is the kissing part. Imagine being kissed by an ugly old brute with a dirty moustache and smelly beard, and moldy brown teeth. Yuk! But even worse than that is the man who chews qat all afternoon, then gets congestion in his prostate from the qat and wants to do it. There is no breath worse than that, believe me."

"I wouldn't know. No qat-chewing brute has ever kissed me!" Ahmad said with a smile.

Haleemah giggled back, stood up, walked up to Ahmad who was still sitting in his chair, and pushed her chest into his face, gently massaging his scalp, something Ahmad simply could not resist. He told himself to break free but succumbed to that indescribable feeling that he fantasized about for nine months, whenever he masturbated. He lifted his arms and placed his palms on each firm, round buttock, and pulled Haleemah closer. After a few moments, she knelt down in front of him.

"I want to do this for you, Ahmad. I know that as a doctor you are worried about picking up some infection from doing the real thing, and you probably don't have a condom here, but let me give you the relief you have been waiting for for months. Just tell yourself that you are a man called Ahmad, not that famous doctor!"

As she said that, she pulled open his zipper, gently coaxed his stiff rod out, and proceeded to give him the greatest blowjob he had ever had, or so he thought after nearly a year of sexual starvation.

~

Ahmad heard no more from the police. However, a month later he ran into the minister of justice, Hasan Alawi Al-Qirshi, at a qat session held at the home a mutual friend, a prominent surgeon who owned a private hospital and who had referred a handful of patients to Ahmad, which ended up with accurate diagnoses and some with good outcomes. Ahmad never developed the habit of chewing, but the oppressive loneliness of bachelor life in that exclusively male society that was Sanaa forced him to indulge in such pastimes out of sheer boredom.

His surgical colleague, Dr. Harb, was very welcoming. He placed him against the same wall as himself but three placements away. He had a visiting Egyptian poet immediately to his right. The spot between Ahmad and the poet remained vacant for some time. On his left, Dr. Harb had his own father to demonstrate the obligatory respect that runs naturally in Yemeni families, and the spot next to his father he assigned to a brigadier in the army.

The room filled slowly, and all four walls of his large qat mafraj [chewing room] were soon lined up with sixty men, each with his own bundle of qat wrapped in transparent plastic covers. Harb's three helpers were busy setting up the hubble-bubbles and carrying dozens of plastic bottles of water or cola. As tradition would dictate, Harb offered Ahmad a few twigs of qat, even knowing that Ahmad did not chew, which Ahmad politely declined. He was not planning to stay long in any case, because unless one chewed the leaf, it was rather boring, just like going to a pub where everyone had three beers that evening but one in the group only had a coffee. At least at a pub Ahmad would have ogled the women to wile the time away.

~

Ahmad knew that his chewing neighbor to his left was going to be an important man from the proximity of his spot to the host; little did he know, however, that it was going to be his own brother-in-law.

Hasan arrived late, claiming that he had to deal with important and urgent matters, dropping a few big names in the process, before he could relax with some twigs of qat. He greeted the host with the usual three-cheek kisses, then the host's father, and the brigadier. Then he moved to the right side where he was introduced to the Egyptian visitor and finally shook hands warmly with Ahmad, who knew that the excessively warm handshake was for the audience, and he decided to reciprocate. In a big room like that one, private conversation was not easy, even with the person immediately next door. However, a little later, having dispensed with the usual pleasantries, Hasan asked Ahmad what he thought about the murdered burglar case.

"That was a sad story, the one about the burglar who attacked Sheikh Muhammad bin Taleb," Hasan began.

"It certainly was a disaster for the burglar and his family."

"Yes, of course, for them too. I hate dealing with such cases."

"Why would *you* deal with that? I thought it was something for the police and the chief prosecutor and eventually the judges. You are only the minister of justice."

"Maybe in Britain, but here in Yemen everything goes to the minister, not just in the ministry of justice but also those of national security, finance, even health."

"No wonder there is so much inefficiency."

"I wish I did not have to deal with these things, but every scandal that happens reflects on His Excellency, the president, and we can't have that."

"Why not? When good things happen, he takes the credit. So, when scandals occur he should take the blame. Isn't that fair?"

"That's only in a European democracy," said Hasan, lowering his voice.

"So, you are a lawyer, and I now understand that you know the case. What did you think of it? And what did you think of my forensic report? You know that was my first case since I came here."

"Your report seemed very meticulous."

"Thank you, I thought it was fairly obvious."

"Not really; I mean there were some unanswered questions. It is not an open-and-shut case."

"Isn't that where the courts and learned judges come in? Let them do their job."

"But, I think we can settle out of court. I think Sheikh Muhammad would be prepared to give a generous compensation to the burglar's family. I told him he should consider it *zakat* [alms] seeing that the month of Ramadan is upon us soon."

"Is that legal in Islam? I thought *zakat* was given without any strings attached, simply from the rich to the poor and not as blood money."

"It *will* be from the rich to the poor. It is *not* blood money, because guilt has not been established."

"Obviously, it will not be established if the chief prosecutor does not lay charges and the case does not go to court."

"The important thing is that both sides will be happy."

"I am sure his wife and daughter will not be happy about losing him, soon to be followed by the wife due to cancer, leaving a young orphan to fend for herself."

"Oh, the daughter is only a whore."

"A whore?"

"Oh, yes, she is a prostitute, didn't you know that? She's good for a one-night fling," Hasan added with a contemptuous smile.

"As a matter of fact, I did know. We met outside the police HQ. She is a human being, who found herself selling her body in order to buy medicines for her dying mother's cancer," Ahmad replied, raising his voice involuntarily.

"Shhhh. Don't let people hear you defending a whore, especially against someone like Sheikh Muhammad bin Taleb, a friend of His Excellency, the president. He gave one of his daughters in marriage to one of the president's nephews. I think she is his third wife. Some say she is his favorite. So, Muhammad is the president's nephew's father-in-law."

"What is happening here, Mr. Minister of Justice? Are we back to the days of Henry the Eighth?"

"Look, my friend! I was concerned about you when you first arrived. Now I am really worried. This is not Britain where we both studied. It is not even Lebanon or Syria. This is Yemen. If you cannot live within its laws ..."

"Don't you mean its lawlessness?"

"No, I mean with the local laws, based on our *sharia* [Islamic jurisprudence], and all our values, then you should not be here. Why can't you adapt to the system around you and improve it slowly from within? Why does it always have to be your self-righteous way or the highway? And the problem is that what you do will reflect on your sister and me ... and your mother too."

"Ah, ha! Now you're speaking the truth. It is all about *you*, isn't it? And your relentless climb to power and fame, and endless wealth. Let me tell you something, Hasan. You have always been a selfish bastard all those years when we were students in Britain. You have brainwashed a gentle and honest but gullible woman and molded her into an accomplice. I know how powerful you are and that you have the ears of those whose asses you lick, but this is also my country, in a manner of speaking, and I will stay here, and I will even thrive here. While I don't have your millions, I enjoy the wealth of respect of ordinary people, yes including burglars and whores, and I will go to my grave, prematurely if I have to, with that knowledge."

Ahmad stood up, walked over to doctor Harb to thank him for his hospitality, and left without looking in the direction of Hasan.

CHAPTER 20

∿

A VISIT TO ZAHRA

Ahmad became somewhat depressed after his row with Hasan. How power and greed can change people, he reflected. Here was a friend he grew up with, who seemed so intelligent and refined and honest, now casting his principles to the wind in return for power and money. Perhaps Hasan was right when he said that Ahmad did not belong in Yemen either. They both had to leave Aden for similar reasons, yet one was thriving so well while the other was just managing. But maybe it was because he was so lonely and isolated. Sanaa was no place for a bachelor, at least not a Yemeni bachelor. There was something to be said for the Yemeni tradition of early marriage, after all. Perhaps his mother had a point when she kept badgering him to take a wife. But at that time he was in love with Ann, who let him down and left him for a woman. He also knew that his career as a forensic expert was finished in that society which was totally controlled by the rich and famous, and where the rule of law and human rights took a back seat.

∿

That week his mother told him that she would leave for Jedda soon to be with Zahra who was expecting her first baby in a month. She invited him to come along for a change of scenery from Sanaa. She knew how much he loved Zahra and guessed that he would not be able to resist. She was right again. From her point of view, he would also provide the male *muhram* [male escort] required to accompany, and be legally in charge of, any woman traveling to the Kingdom of Saudi Arabia, being a male who would not be allowed by sharia law to marry the woman, such as a father or brother or son. Getting a visa was a most complicated affair, made slightly easier for him by his British passport. He therefore uttered a sigh of relief when, eventually, visas were stamped on their two passports.

∽

The flight on Yemenia Airlines to Jedda Airport was a short two hours. He wished he could order a beer or wine, as with some other Gulf airlines, but he resigned himself to a long abstention while on that trip. At least in Sanaa he had a supply of wine from here and there, albeit intermittent and very secretive.

His young brother-in-law, Zuhair, met them at the airport, facilitated their entry process, and drove them to his lovely home in his brand-new Mercedes. Jedda was much bigger than he had imagined and very well developed and manicured, at least compared to Sanaa, but it did not have Sanaa's natural beauty. Tall, new, modern buildings dominated the commercial center, as with so many emerging cities in the Arab Gulf countries. The road eventually took them along the beautiful seafront and beach, and then deep into a smart residential area with walled homes surrounded by wide metal gates guarded by smartly dressed men from the Indian subcontinent.

∽

As Ahmad's mother entered the house through the heavy, ornate, wooden door, Zahra already heavy with child rose to her feet, as respect dictated, and walked slowly toward her mother, listing from side to side. There was a long embrace, then the obligatory kiss on the forehead of the mother, then another long embrace. Tears started flowing down the mother's cheeks, who attempted to wipe them with the end of her black headscarf, which she then used to also wipe the tears trickling out of her nostrils. No words were exchanged, and the two women broke free, for it was Ahmad's turn. He had not seen his favorite sister for a few years, and he hugged her warmly, placing his cheek on hers and telling her how much he missed her. He then stepped back to look at her big belly, which had pushed against his own during the embrace.

"Looks like twins, I would say."

"No, it is not, but it will be a big boy, inshaallah," Zuhair said.

"How do you know it's a boy?"

"Just hoping; it's fine if it's a girl too."

"So you must have a boy's name ready?"

"No, not really; we will wait."

"You should call him Zaki, and if it is a girl Zainab. Then you can be Zuhair, Zahra, and Zainab or Zaki!"

"Oh, you've always liked these silly alliterations, even when you were at school," Ahmad's mother interjected.

"I hope you are hungry? There is a big lunch awaiting you in the dining room," Zuhair declared.

"I can smell the *biryani* all the way here. There must be lots of saffron in the rice. Do you call it *biryani* or *zurbian* here?" Ahmad asked.

"Mostly *biryani,* because there is a big Indian and Pakistani population here."

⁓

That week, Zahra's home was suddenly much busier with female visitors who came to see her mother and pay their respects as tradition would dictate. The vast majority were from Aden and had known her or members of her family back there, where they had grown up together or gone to the same school. They too were still feeling very Adeni, despite making Jedda their home. Some, just like Zahra, were married to Saudis or Yemenis who emigrated to Saudi Arabia and made their home there. One of these was a second cousin to Ahmad and Zahra, about five years younger than Ahmad. Her father had moved to Jedda with his wife and five daughters when he was no longer able to stand life in Aden under Communist rule. He was a British-educated bank manager, and the regime in Aden had no use for bank managers, it would seem. Thus, he sent his eldest daughter to university in Beirut and placed the younger ones in private schools in Jedda. However, she never finished her university education because her parents found her a husband. That marriage did not last, Ahmad found out later.

~

Ahmad's mother did not miss the opportunity to point out Meethaq to him as a possible bride, and went out of her way during that stay in Jedda to give the two of them the opportunity to evaluate each other. She resorted to the old and tried method of telling Ahmad that her cousin, Meethaq's mother, wanted to consult him about her back pain and that she would consider it a great favor if he did that for her. Ahmad recognized the ploy, which she had previously used in Aden, and pointed out that he was not licensed to practice medicine there. However, partly because of some curiosity of his own, Ahmad made the trip to Meethaq's home. Her mother had prepared a sumptuous lunch for him, claiming that it was nearly all prepared by Meethaq. After lunch, a short medical consultation took place, at which time Ahmad could find no cause for concern and politely advised Meethaq's mother to try to lose some of the excessive weight she was obviously carrying and to do regular exercises, which she solemnly promised to do. She claimed that his was the best advice she had ever received from doctors, who were more interested in ordering X-rays and CAT scans rather than listening to and analyzing her symptoms.

~

Both Meethaq and Ahmad knew what was in store after lunch. Her mother excused herself in order to have her customary siesta. Her sisters all had schoolwork or other chores to perform.

Meethaq broke the silence in the empty living room. "So, their plot has worked!"

"Yes, indeed. Would you agree with me that Yemeni women are the most scheming on earth?" Ahmad replied.

"Although I don't know mothers from other nations, it would not surprise me."

"Look! Don't feel that you have to stay here to talk to me; I can just leave."

"No, no, I am in my own house. You are the one that should feel trapped having been lured here under false pretenses, to treat back pain!" Meethaq said with a sarcastic smile.

"I am pleased to talk to you. People should talk to each other a lot more. You know, I have been in Sanaa now for quite a while. People don't really talk to each other, because whenever two people meet they are never alone. Like at these qat sessions, there are always a few dozen people in the room so the conversation is never private but rather monitored and artificial and very shallow. Even when the subject is serious, it is still shallow because people are guarded about what they can or should say in front of strangers who, they fear, may be police informers."

"Here too! There is no qat chewing here; it is forbidden, but still the conversation is very basic and shallow, at least among the women, because we are not allowed to talk to men, other than to our muhrams, or to give orders to our Pakistani drivers and servants."

"What a waste of talent and time! You are a very intelligent woman."

"Thank you. I am not used to people saying that to me. The best I get is, 'You are a good cook' and 'Your sewing is really pretty.' That is how society assesses our worth."

"Tell me about your teen years. Were you in Aden?"

"Yes, we lived in Crater, just like you, although you first lived in Tawahi, right?"

"Yes absolutely! In those days we used to think that a trip from one town to the other was a long journey of adventure. It was only five miles, the length of your sea front road her in Jedda!"

"As the eldest of my sisters I had the opportunity to go to beautiful Beirut to study."

"I've never been to Beirut, but I used to hear father speak so fondly of it."

"I think people speak fondly of the place where they fall in love or achieve their dreams," Meethaq agreed.

"And which one applies to you?"

"It was not achieving a university degree."

"Can I take it that you fell in love there?"

Meethaq blushed. "Yes, very much so; but Muslim girls are not supposed to fall in love. They are not born with emotions or a heart, didn't you know?"

"Was it a Lebanese boy?"

"No."

"Then who?"

"Why do you want to know? To embarrass me or to despise me?"

"Far from it, Meethaq. I applaud you for being honest with yourself."

"I was very young, only nineteen, and away from the spying eyes of Mother and Father, living at a girls' hostel near the university. I was like a prisoner who was just released from a long jail term and wanted to go here and there and everywhere, not to mention that I was awash in hormones. So I fell in love with this tall but gentle boy in my French class."

"Where did he come from? Was he Arab?"

"Oh, no! An Arab boy is programmed to think that I am a loose woman, if I go out with him, and certainly his family would think that even if he didn't. He would be very happy to take me to bed, but then I would be considered damaged goods for marriage, even for him. So, there would be no future in such a relationship. Girls do think about the long term, you know, unlike you boys just looking for easy prey." Meethaq smiled provocatively.

"You are keeping me in suspense."

"Well, he was Greek, if you must know. Not Arab, not Muslim, therefore not acceptable. But tell me, do you believe in love, Doctor?"

"I am not sure anymore. There is love of course, but true love is that unselfish love of a mother for her child or a father for his daughter or son. It is when the parent would give her or his life to save the child but not in return for anything material or physical, or even spiritual. It is what a lioness does for her cub. The other love between the genders is really mostly lust."

"Lust? You mean you did not love any of the numerous women you knew?"

"How do you know I had numerous women?"

"Of course you did. In fact, if you are a typical man, which I have to assume, you probably tried to seduce every woman in sight, within reason, and probably recorded the number in your pocket diary. Tell me that I am wrong!"

"There is some exaggeration in what you say. But those days of counting the score are gone."

"I like your honesty. But now tell me, also honestly, what if I had the same number of partners – whatever it was, thirty, fifty, whatever – as you; would you say that I was loose, or a whore, or at least promiscuous?"

Ahmad paused to think, then said, "Well, I did have around fifty partners. I have to admit that, at one point in my life, I would have called you very loose. Not any more. The double standard will never completely leave us, I fear."

"But you are avoiding my question about love and lust."

"I hope that I am honest enough to admit that it was mostly lust, because it did not last—lust does not last! Yes, I like that pun!"

"What a cynic you are! What about Romeo and Juliet? Was Shakespeare wrong?"

"One could argue that the lust they had for each other became such a famous love story only because it was forbidden lust. And if they had fallen in love, and gotten married, and enjoyed each other's bodies, like all the other billions of couples, that story would not have been written. They would have woken up a couple of months later, when the novelty was over and the lust satisfied, and would have said, 'Hey, what's for breakfast today?'"

"I have never heard anyone say that before. Frankly, I am disillusioned. I was hoping you might have just a little romantic streak in you."

"We all have every right to live in a fantasy, if we choose, but you asked me a question, and I answered it truthfully."

"Okay, do you love God?"

"We are getting into deep waters here. First you have to define God. Your god is quite different from Juliet's god. And my god is different from Gandhi's. Let's not go there. Anyway, your attempt to distract me won't work. What happened to your love then?"

"Even in modern, cosmopolitan Beirut, secrets leaked. My parents went into high gear and found me an Adeni husband whose father was a close friend of my own father, and I had to discontinue my studies. He was studying in the United States and was planning on marrying an American girl, ironically, of Greek origin. So we were both saved from marrying Greek infidels. And, applying some of your wit, Doctor, after a few years it was his infidelity that broke up our marriage!"

"I imagine that it did not last because it was arranged. Did you meet him before the wedding?"

"Surprisingly, that is not true. No, we did not see each other until our wedding day, which was organized in Cairo. But he saw me in a photo and apparently approved. I was given his photo, and I found him stunningly handsome. I loved *my Greek,* but with *his* support I agreed to marry Nizar, my Adeni, instead. He was very understanding and told me it was like that in Greece too. There, many disapprove of mixed marriage. They are a close-knit community, and a small population, and so they do not want to dilute their identity. They are a very proud nation, just like the Arabs, and when you think of their history and Alexander the Great and all that, you can understand why."

"May I ask why it came to an end?"

"He did not love me at first. He was still thinking about his Greek-American girl. But with the passage of time, and after we had our daughter—somehow daughters seem to predominate in our family—he appreciated me and I think he loved me. But then he started fooling around with other women. Never trust a good-looking man. They are so vain and feel they have a divine right to multiple affairs."

"What about beautiful women? Could we not say the same about them?"

"Maybe in the West; not here. Our Muslim culture would not allow it. But that was not the only factor. He began to drink heavily and became violent when he was drunk. The bizarre thing was that even though it was he who was playing around, he started accusing *me* of infidelity and reminding me of my affair with my Greek boyfriend in Beirut. He became suspicious and jealous of my telephone calls and my visits to my friends. Of course, as you know as a doctor, alcohol affected his own sexual performance, which exacerbated his jealousy."

"You are describing a classic medical syndrome; it is called the jealous husband syndrome, which occurs in some alcoholics."

"Well, there you are. I did try to make him stop drinking, or at least cut it down."

"It must have cost him a lot of money, because alcohol is supposedly banned in Yemen, and whatever is banned, usually costs a lot more in the black market."

"Of course, but we all know it is available. Not only that; but the people behind the smuggling rings were the people in power."

"So how did it end?"

"I asked him for a divorce, but he kept refusing."

"Why didn't you initiate divorce proceedings?"

"As a woman, I can't. It is a man's prerogative! Unless, of course, on the wedding day the bride's father insists on having a specific clause inserted in the marriage contract that says the bride has that option, which is called *ismah*. But my father never did. He and my husband's father were close friends, and there was a lot of trust between them. Anyway, about three years after I asked for divorce, he sent me my divorce notification. I had to leave his house with my little daughter. I was left with nothing; that's what happens to a divorcee in this society. That's why wives just have to bite the bullet and obey."

Suddenly, the doorknob turned, with a low metallic squeak, and the door opened. Meethaq's youngest sister entered. "Mother asked me to check to see if you wanted something to drink."

"Would you, Doctor?" Meethaq asked.

"No, thank you. That was a big lunch."

The little girl smiled and left.

"That was Mother's way of checking to see whether we are behaving ourselves!"

Ahmad smiled broadly and said, "I hope she was reassured that I was not molesting you. I suppose I should go now?"

"No, please stay a little longer. I have not had a conversation of this kind with a man, or even a woman for that matter. It was like a catharsis for me. I hope you will not send me your medical bill!" Meethaq said with a mischievous smile.

"I have to say that I too never had that kind of conversation with a Yemeni woman. Of course, I did do so with British and European women many times. That would be quite normal there. In fact, I would have been flirting by now."

"So why didn't you flirt with me? Am I not worth flirting with?"

"I ... I ... don't ... didn't think ... I thought you might be offended."

"You forget that I have been around, as they say. I have seen it all: love, marriage, sex, pregnancy, motherhood, divorce, happiness, loneliness, the lot."

"You are a very interesting woman. You would make someone a great wife. Could we continue this conversation elsewhere, another day?"

"Can I bring my mother along?" Meethaq said impishly.

Ahmad burst into laughter and stood up. He put his hand toward Meethaq, who eagerly placed hers in his, and kept it there for several seconds while their eyes peered into each other's. Their breaths almost mingled with each other's.

CHAPTER 21

~

AN OLD FRIEND

One of Ahmad's closest classmates, who had moved to Jedda from Aden, even before Ahmad escaped the clutches of the Communist regime, heard of Ahmad's arrival through the usual bush telegraph of the Yemeni community in that city. He had heard about his sister Zahra marrying a Yemeni airline pilot living in Jedda. He would from time to time send her greetings through the female members of his family whenever he learned that they were about to visit her or see her at a wedding or other function.

Waleed was a very gentle and sweet boy at school. Some of the cruel boys in the class would poke fun at him and occasionally bully him. They would call him "Waleedah," the female equivalent of Waleed, a definite insult. Ahmad never shared their opinion of Waleed and maintained his close friendship with him, to the extent that he was accused of having a homosexual relationship with Waleed at their all-boys' school, where homosexual crushes and liaisons were apparently common. Ahmad always remembered how, when he was at Aden College during morning assembly in front of the British principal, all the boys would stand to attention in six long rows, and when they were told to stand at ease, three senior boys would often, with their hands behind their backs, openly fondle the crotches of the boys behind. Ahmad thought it was disgusting behavior but never had the courage to do anything about it. And yet, Waleed was not one of them.

~

Waleed came over in his blue Lincoln to pick Ahmad up from his sister's house. He gave him a detailed tour of the city while they caught up with the news of each other, and then he took his friend to a very good Lebanese restaurant where the meal was absolutely delicious and the atmosphere so pleasant and happy. They discovered that neither was married.

"So, you never got married either, ha? We must be the only two in our class that remained single," Ahmad said.

"Well, yes, we are bachelors, by choice. I think marriage is overrated. When I hear about all the fights and infidelities and ugly divorces, I think I made the right decision."

"But how do you manage in this puritanical society? It can't be easy."

"I manage the same as you manage in Sanaa."

"But I've only recently moved to Sanaa. I spent most of my life, I mean my *adult* life, in Britain and in Aden, where it wasn't as closed as here."

"So, who was your latest victim?" Waleed asked with a mischievous smile.

"I hear that Sanaa is rife with sex for those who know where to find it, but yours truly here has been starved. Well, I had a woman in Edinburgh, until just before I left for Sanaa," Ahmad replied.

"Scottish? Why didn't you marry her, or at least bring her to Sanaa with you?"

"I am not exactly proud of the fact, but she did not want *me*."

"Really! A charming, educated, wealthy doctor like you?"

"She did not share your opinion, it would seem."

"Was she seduced away from you by another man?"

"By another woman."

"Really! You mean she is a lesbian? She must be bi."

"Apparently! I never detected that until the end; there were no signs whatsoever."

"Why do you say to that? Do you think there are signs? You think you can look at a woman and diagnose homosexuality?"

"Obviously not! What I mean is that we were very open with each other, but she never hinted at her fantasies or preferences. I am told that with some lesbians, they behave in a masculine butch manner."

"And can you tell with males?"

"I think it might be easier with men."

"In what way?"

"Well, people say that they tend to repeatedly flex their wrists as they talk."

"And what do you think of them, I mean homosexual men? Do you despise them?"

"No, not at all! I think there is a bit of the homosexual in all of us, but in most people it is a brief transient phase while in the minority it is how they have been wired, probably from birth. I don't think they can help it. Doctors always like to say that disease is multifactorial. I think sexual orientation is like that too. One day, science will discover more about the causes. But the fascinating thing is that you do not see it in animals; at least I have never read that it exists there. It is a huge stigma in this part of the world, but that too will change. I mean, if the statistics are true that up to ten percent of people are homosexual, then it will become very common when they decide to come out."

"Ten percent is probably unlikely, but even if it was just one percent, I mean one percent of five billion is the population of Britain. But, do you remember how at Aden College those horrible boys used to accuse us of being homosexual partners? Well, they were partially right."

"What do you mean?" Ahmad asked, looking puzzled.

"You know that *you* are not. So, that leaves me," Waleed said, carefully studying Ahmad's facial reaction. He was relieved to see a smile on his face instead of the expected disgust.

"To be honest with you, I did not suspect it. But thank you for trusting me with that."

"And thank you for your wonderful friendship all these years. I hope that you will come to Jedda again, and perhaps Mecca next time. Have you performed your pilgrimage yet?"

"No, have you?"

"Yes, I did. I mean it is so close."

"You know, you are the only homosexual *hajj* [pilgrim] that I know, or should I say the only homosexual musician-hajj!"

"That reminds me I must drive you back now. I have a lot of musical preparation to do for tomorrow's party. But let us talk the day after. We'll go for a nice meal this time."

"Fine. It will be on me."

"No, no, you are a guest in *my* country now."

Waleed knew he was running late. Although he loved to perform on his beautiful and expensive Syrian lute to all sorts of audiences, and to be the center of attention, he was somewhat anxious about his performance that evening. He had to do something extra special, judging by the fat fee he had received in advance. Ordinarily he would get three thousand riyals for an evening of music. But ten thousand was something special, which he had never attained before. He knew that Hajar bin Sultan was an important junior minister in the Ministry of Internal Affairs and that he had something to do with the local police department. Waleed was, therefore, determined to please him and earn that huge fee. After all, if he could secure a few invitations a month, he would not have to work on other days. And that would give him more time to do all the other things he loved to do, especially teaching music.

His partner, Omar, had some potential as a musician but was lazy. He did not realize how much practice he had to put in every day if he had the slightest hope of becoming as accomplished a musician as Waleed. He was the passive partner in that relationship, but he knew that Waleed, twice his age, was in love with him, and he was quite an expert at manipulating his older friend. Ordinarily, he would accompany Waleed to all his performances and would accompany him on his tambourine or the *darbooga* [drum]. Whenever they performed together, not only did their instruments play in great harmony, but as they would look into each other's eyes they would feel their souls flying together in unison into loftier and loftier heights. And it showed in their rousing music, to the wild applause of their many audiences.

But that night Waleed was to go by himself, on instructions from Hajjar. He had his expensive lute carefully stored in a specially shaped box, strings tightened to just the right notes. He put the lute in the trunk of his Mercedes-Benz and drove rapidly along the seafront toward Ameer Road, then down a narrow unnamed road until he saw the huge villa surrounded by that high white wall and the wrought-iron gate freshly painted black. He was glad he had time to quickly swallow a glass of cabernet, before leaving home, because by the time he reached the gate the wine had started to do its work. Waleed felt a lot calmer.

The Sri Lankan guard opened the gate to the Mercedes, and having ascertained the guest's name let him drive up to the grand house that looked a lot more like a palace with a stunning, carefully manicured lawn around which stood beautiful tall palm trees. It was already after sunset and the tastefully arranged outside lights bathed the palatial walls in their beams. Waleed carried the box of the lute by its special leather handle and headed for the door, which to his surprise opened almost before he had time to ring the bell, but it was none other than Hajjar who stood behind the door.

"Good evening *tal umrak* [may you live long]. That was quick; I did not even ring the bell. How did you get here so fast?" Waleed said.

"There are dozens of cameras monitoring everything that moves around this house. We do not like uninvited guests!" Hajjar responded with a chuckle.

"There must be half a dozen guests already judging by the number of cars outside."

"Oh, those cars are all mine. The guests are parked in the inner yard, so that the ladies do not have far to walk. *Ahlan wasahlan.* [Welcome.] This is your first time here?"

"Yes, tal umrak, and I consider it a great honor."

"And I hope it will be the first of many, but that would depend on your performance tonight. I have heard a lot about your musical talent and I'm looking forward to a very enjoyable evening of music … and *other* things!" Hajjar said.

"Leave that to me, sir. You will only see what pleases you."

By this time the two men reached a large bedroom assigned for the evening to Waleed. It was a very expensively furnished and decorated room with its own bathroom, a huge flat TV screen, and a king-sized bed with a sitting area next to the bed.

"When you are ready, go through that beige door, with the golden handle, where you will find the rest of the party."

Hajjar left by the door through which they had entered the room.

~

Waleed took his lute out of its box and laid it face down on the very soft bed cover. He went into the bathroom briefly, and as he left he looked at himself in the mirror and brushed his rather thick black hair. He looked at his face and wondered why he was not born handsome like his partner Omar. His face was rather course and round with a broad nose and thick, greasy skin. His lips were thick, perched above a goatee. But he had put on his best white silk shirt, without any tie, and his well-pressed blue pants held up by a black leather belt, just below a moderate middle-age bulge, which he could never get rid of. He then stopped blaming his luck and reminded himself that he was just a hired hand there to entertain some millionaires and that his looks did not really matter.

As he pushed the very heavy door, he was able to hear several loud male voices intermingled with lower feminine voices and a lot of giggling. But before he could see any human figures, he became fully aware of a strong and pleasant aroma of wine blended with wonderful fragrances emanating, no doubt, from the women in the room, and that unmistakable aroma of the sheesha with that honey-like smell of burning tobacco called *mu'assal*.

He became aware of the opulence in the room, as his feet almost floated on the expensive and thick wall-to-wall carpet. A large glass-topped table in the middle of the room was surrounded by eight very comfortable loveseats with blue and gold upholstery. A so-called mini bar in one corner was well stocked, and not that mini. On the central glass-topped table, there were three half-empty bottles of expensive red wine and two bottles of white wine in ice buckets. A huge bouquet of imported pink roses sat in the center of the table.

There were five middle-aged men in *dishdashas* [long white robes], all sporting neatly trimmed black beards. Two were sitting together in one loveseat, drinking beer. Next to them, in a loveseat was the fourth man, sipping red wine. Yet another relatively younger one sat on his own, looking somewhat overwhelmed by his surroundings. The host, Hajjar, was in the next loveseat with a beautiful blonde Russian woman of about thirty. Facing them were four women in their own love seats and holding glasses of white wine, nicely chilled, judging by the layer of condensation on the glass. One was beautiful and black in a tight red dress, big breasts virtually hanging out of the top. She was from Ethiopia, he found out later. She seemed to be the life and soul of the party at that point. Two looked Middle Eastern. Waleed found out later, from their accents, that one was Moroccan and the other was Iraqi. The fifth was Hungarian but seemed to understand some Arabic. Waleed was introduced to the group as a great and famous musician, but he was not told the names of the guests. He did hear some names used as the group addressed each other, like Fifi, and Zizi, and Mona.

In one corner, Hajjar placed a comfortable but armless chair for Waleed, such that he could comfortably hold his lute across his chest, and there Waleed got himself organized. Hajjar, always the perfect host, asked him what he wanted to drink and poured him a glass of the Shiraz he desired.

Sweet tunes began to emanate from the strings of the lute, and, to Waleed's surprise, the guests almost stopped talking as they listened to those melodic tunes of Fareed Al-Atrash, that most famous Egyptian crooner. As the group got into the mood, what with wine on their lips and music in their ears, Hajjar decided to dim the lights and make the ambience "more romantic," as he put it.

As the minutes rolled by, Waleed's performance became exquisite, and the reactions of the guests were on their faces. As Waleed started singing the lyrics, and the beat became faster, the black woman, Maria, spontaneously stood up from her seat and started a sensuous gyration of her ample hips to the raucous approval of the half-drunk men and the rhythmic clapping of the women. She slowly made her way to Waleed's seat and started rhythmically gyrating her rear across his face, where he was sitting.

"Come on Zizi, get up and help her!" Hajjar beckoned the Moroccan woman, the prettiest in the group. She did not need to be asked twice. Wine glass in hand, she stood up and, acting drunker than she actually was, stood next to the Ethiopian dancer and moved her own shapely hips to the rhythm. The clapping suddenly intensified and the howls of approval from the men grew louder and wilder. Waleed's tunes on the lute seemed to rise to the occasion and now sounded even sweeter and louder.

"Zizi," said one of the men, "I think her dress is too tight. Help her out of it."

Zizi looked at him with a broad, mischievous smile, put her wine glass on the coffee table, and started undoing the Ethiopian's zipper on the back of her red silk dress to more howls of approval from the men. As the zipper reached the small of her back, Maria pulled her arms out of the dress without once stopping her dance. The dress began to reluctantly fall to her feet, exposing very sexy red bra and thongs, leaving very little to the imagination. Now the howls from the men peaked to even greater heights. One of them stood up in his dishdasha and stepped toward Maria. Taking a wad of banknotes from his pocket, he placed them very slowly between her breasts to the loud approval of the audience.

Zizi slowly made her way back to the loveseat, but before she could get to it another man grabbed her hand and pulled her to his own loveseat where she pretended to fall against her will. He tried to kiss her, but she moved her face away. He tried again, but she would not let him, pointing out that the others were looking. He now produced a one thousand riyal note, saying, "Just for one kiss!"

"Just one!" said Zizi, seductively.

"Just one," he agreed, making it a very long one. But then she broke away.

~

Hajjar gave the signal to the party to begin in earnest by turning to the Russian woman sharing his loveseat. He started fondling her left breast after undoing a couple of buttons in her blouse. She had been his guest before and knew what was coming.

The Iraqi woman got up to do a belly dance as the song of Fareed Al-Atrash took a faster tempo, while the Ethiopian, Maria, kept doing her own version of the dance. One of the men stood up and placed his hands on her big African hips, as if to claim them, and then pushed her by the hips toward one the six doors which surrounded the music and fun room; the two disappeared behind the door while the men cheered loudly.

That seemed to signal the pairing off the others. The Hungarian woman was still in her chair when one of the men walked up to her and pulled her up gently by her slim hand and decided to dance a slow shuffle with her, ignoring the faster belly dance music. Waleed found the effigy of the shapely woman dancing with a man in his dishdasha rather comical, but he waved his eyebrows up and down to them as they smiled back at him.

The fourth middle-aged man stood up and extended both arms toward the Iraqi woman in her seat. She extended her arms towards him, and he pulled her up to standing, then walked behind her to another bedroom door.

Now there was only one man left sitting down. He was the youngest in the group. The Moroccan woman beckoned him to her with her index finger, took a big gulp of wine from her glass, and led him by the hand to another of the six bedrooms.

Hajjar was the perfect host; he and his Russian woman were the last to leave, to the fifth bedroom. But two minutes later he returned to Waleed and invited him to that bedroom.

The blonde Russian was already totally naked on the bed.

"Go ahead, Waleed, have her."

"No, no, thank you."

"It's all right. Enjoy it. It's part of your fee."

"No, really, tal umrak, I am not in the mood."

"Not in the mood? You have put us all in the mood with your music, and you are not in the mood?"

"I just don't feel like making love to a woman just now."

"Oh, I understand now; you want to do it in her rear. Okay, she'll let you."

"No, really, another time," Waleed said. Then looking down at the blonde pubic hair of the supine nude woman he said, "You are really beautiful," and bolted out of the room.

~

The next evening, Waleed drove over to Zuhair's house to pick up his old schoolmate Ahmad and took him to a nice Chinese restaurant for something different. The smartly attired pretty young oriental woman at the door received the two men with radiant smiles and a bow, and then led them to a nice rosewood table adorned with a fresh bouquet of flowers. There were very few diners at that relatively early hour of eight. The male waiter arrived with a jug of water, and after a brief bow poured some in their two glasses and handed over two huge menus with another smaller bow, then he left them to ponder their selection. It took a long time to read through the menu, during which Ahmad wished he could have amused himself with a few sips of white wine, but he knew ahead of time that such would not be available. Eventually, the waiter returned and the two men gave their orders.

"So, how was it, your musical evening?"

"Oh, very interesting; it was a brand-new experience for me." Waleed then proceeded to relate the story to the fascinated Ahmad.

"Wow! I suspected that such things were going on, simply because I know what human nature is like, but this was really a graphic description of debauchery. Where do they find all the alcohol you talked about? Here I am dying for just one glass of wine to go with my spicy Chinese chow, and I cannot get it."

"Listen, my friend, everything is available for that class of people. You need to be in that group to enjoy life the way you want to, or you need to know the right people and hang around them and get some of the crumbs off their tables."

"But who can reach them? I mean everyone would want to do that."

"Very few can, and it comes at a huge price."

"Like what?"

"They will only admit you after you have proved your complete, unquestioning loyalty, and for many years, before they would trust you. After all, they cannot afford to have anyone spill the beans on them."

"So, what have *you* done to deserve their trust?"

"In my case, it's not trust. It is just that I have this gift of music, and they just love the lute. All Arabs love the lute, even those who are familiar with Bach and Mozart and who enjoy Sinatra and Tom Jones. They still can't get away from the lute of Fareed and Abdul-Wahhab [famous Egyptian musicians]."

"But there must be other musicians. Why you?"

"Well, I don't want to sound conceited, but I am told that I am the best here; maybe I am the best of a bad lot!" Waleed said with a chuckle.

"I must hear you play some, if we have time."

"Sure, I was planning to take you back to my house after dinner for a nice cup of tea with cardamom, or *grape soup* if you prefer." Waleed winked.

"Is that what you call it? Is it red soup or white soup?"

"Either! We also serve barley soup for those who prefer it."

"Well, well. I have suddenly developed a great appetite for soup."

"I was going to take you there in any case to meet my friend Omar."

"I would be pleased to meet him. How come you did not invite him to join us this evening?"

"Frankly, I didn't know how you would react. I can see that you are a broad-minded person, just like you were at school. In any case, I just wanted to catch up with your news first."

~

The food arrived in numerous dishes of different sizes, placed neatly on that big table by not one but two waiters who made sure the two diners had everything they needed.

"I am curious though, and I hope you don't mind me asking intimate questions. One day I hope I will write a novel about our culture, and I really want to hear the facts from the horse's mouth. When in your life did you realize that you were homosexual and not interested in women?"

"You know, it is very difficult to answer that. I know that I did not wake up one day only to discover that I have a homosexual orientation. I think I was probably born like that. As boys at school, we all had affinities and even crushes for other boys, especially those good-looking ones. Such feelings were of course suppressed by society. You couldn't possibly admit it to your parents, much less outsiders. Did you not go through that phase?"

"Not that I remember, but I had the usual curiosity of looking at the *thing* of another boy in the shower or at the swimming pool just to see how I compared. I even remember being challenged by a cousin to draw my sword so to speak, to compare with his; and of course I did, otherwise he could claim victory in that contest! As it happens, I need not have bothered, because he won hands down—I mean pants down!"

Waleed went into howls of laughter, which caused the Chinese waiters to stare.

"You are a doctor; what do you think is the cause?"

"I really don't know. There is indirect evidence that lesbian women do not have the same degree of sound discrimination as heterosexual women, but that's all I know. The fascinating thing is how homosexuality was fully accepted during the days of the Greek Empire, then it became demonized, then was apparently accepted in the days of Napoleon, then again became taboo, and now at the end of the twentieth century it is gaining rapid acceptance. It just proves that it is a matter of societal attitude. I think Arab and Muslim society is really hypocritical about this. It claims that it does not harbor homosexuals, and yet we all know that it does, and big time too."

"But you are not allowed to say that here."

"So, what else is new? Arab countries, without exception, denied that they had patients with AIDS. Do you remember? You are not allowed to say anything controversial here. The curse of Arab society is the absence of freedom of expression."

"Why is that, do you reckon, my dear Doctor?"

"I have my theories; I think our Islamic upbringing hammers into us, from day one, that we have to obey and obey and obey. It tells us 'Oh, believers, obey Allah, obey his messenger, and obey those who are in charge of you!' So, we are not encouraged to think for ourselves or to challenge the teacher or the parent or the uncle or the imam or the ruler. That is why we have dictators who rule for thirty years or more, or until they die. It is in their interest to promote those teachings, but not the other great teachings of Islam, such as seeking knowledge even if in China, and the concept of *shura* [consultation]. Have you ever heard an imam, at Friday prayers, promoting the concept of *shura*? I hope this restaurant is not bugged," Ahmad said as he looked under the table. "I want to be able to go home, not to a torture chamber here."

By the time Waleed paid the bill, the restaurant was almost full, and a few expatriate women had joined the diners. The big room looked far more attractive with their presence.

Omar was a good-looking, charming, and refined man, several years younger than Waleed. He poured out the drinks, some red wine for Ahmad, which he justified by calling it his nightcap, and he made some spiced tea for himself and his partner. Thirty minutes later, Waleed drove Ahmad to his sister's house.

~

As he parked the car in front of the gate, he turned to face Ahmad and teased him by saying, "It was a real pleasure to see you again after so many years, Ahmad. I hope I will see again in the not too distant future. You don't know how sensual it is to kiss another man on the lips, so would you like to try?"

Ahmad was not alarmed, for he understood the joke and said, "You mean you want me to vomit all that nice Chinese food?"

They both laughed heartily as they shook hands.

Zahra delivered a baby boy soon after Ahmad left Jedda. Her husband was overjoyed and invited his mother-in-law to stay with them for as long as she wanted to help Zahra with her baby, even though he could have easily hired a Filipino maid for the job. Ahmad never got to see the baby, but Zahra called him a month later for a consultation. Her baby started vomiting around the age of three weeks but had absolutely no other symptoms. His vomiting was mild initially but increased steadily, and instead of running out of the sides of the mouth and down the chin it was projectile and would shoot forward with a force that might hit objects a foot away. Zahra had waited a whole week, and her experienced mother had advised her to give it time to settle down, but she only trusted her brother, even though he did not train in pediatrics. Just as she expected, Ahmad was sympathetic and interested. He asked her to ask her own mother-in-law if Zuhair had anything similar when he was one month old. Zahra found the question very odd, but she really loved and trusted her brother and did exactly what he asked. Both she and her mother-in-law were amazed at the astuteness of that question, for Ahmad's guess was absolutely correct.

"Okay, your baby has a rare condition called congenital pyloric stenosis ..."

"Ahmad! Stop speaking Latin to me. Tell me in layman terms."

"This is an inherited condition, usually in boys, where the exit of the stomach is narrowed by a tight muscle. So the milk accumulates in the stomach and the stomach has to empty it, so it goes upward to the mouth instead of downwards into the intestines."

"So, will he be all right?"

"Sure. His father had the same thing, but the narrowing has to be corrected with a small surgical operation."

"You are my hero. You always have been. By the way, Salma is here this week."

"Oh? What is she doing there?"

"Hasan is in Jedda to attend the Arab League meeting of ministers of justice, and she came for the ride. It is so much easier because they enter on a diplomatic passport; no searching of any kind."

"You mean the Arab ministers of injustice?"

"Shush! You will get me and my husband into trouble. We may be monitored. They don't trust Yemenis, especially Adenis, here."

"Poor Adenis, they are mistrusted in Jedda and persecuted in Sanaa!"

Suddenly Ahmad overheard Salma shouting, "Zahra, let's go before Barclay's closes. Your driver did not come back and I have to do this transaction at the bank today because we are flying back to Sanaa this evening. Shall I call a taxi instead?"

Then he clearly heard Zahra, still on the phone, say, "No, no, you can't do that in a taxi. With that huge amount of money and gold, we need our own driver to drive us right up to the door of the bank. What if someone somehow got to know about it and ambushed us on the way to the bank? Are you crazy enough to take such a risk? Let me just finish talking to Ahmad. It is important. It is about the health of my baby. Ahmad, please excuse me, I have to rush, but thank you, *habeebi* [darling], for your advice. May Allah give you health."

"Bye, take care, little darling, but take the baby to Dr. Ammari at the Shifa Hospital in Jedda. He is a very well-trained professor of surgery. He was five years behind me at Aden College. Please tell him who you are, and give him my warmest regards."

"Thank you. I will. May Allah give you health! Good bye."

CHAPTER 22

~

LETTER FROM ANN

When he returned from Jedda, Ahmad found a letter from Ann in his mailbox. He was very excited. So many thoughts came to his mind. He wondered if she had broken up with her lesbian partner and was asking him to go back to her. Then he dismissed the idea, thinking that even if she did, she would just find another lover. After all, there was plenty more where that came from. Then he wondered if perhaps the two women decided to get married officially and wanted him to be there. He would be so happy to be there, just for Ann. But then he asked himself why they would even bother, when they could just be together. Perhaps it was to warn him that she was on her way to Sanaa or to Dubai and she wanted to meet him there.

By the time he got the letter opener, his hands were trembling. He was not prepared for what he read.

My Dear Ahmad:

You must be wondering why I am writing after all these months. I'll explain.

But first let me tell you that I often think about you, your warmth, kindness, humor, and love for me, and I try to imagine your caresses, and kisses and how you filled me—yes, literally too!—with pleasure and love.

But I am very happy with my wife Diana, and she is content with our lives. She sends her love by the way, even though she never met you!

Diana was telling me something which might be of interest to you. If it is true then it would be an amazing one in a million coincidence.

You know already that she was living in London before moving here. Well on one of her visits back to London to bring some personal belongings here, she stayed with her sister, who took her to a party at the home of one of her friends, called Biddy, who is married to this Irish policeman. Apparently, Biddy had a twelve-year-old daughter, called Jasmine, who was proudly showing off her school report to the visitors, with all the stars etc., when Brenda noticed that her name was recorded as Jasmine Alawi, not Dooley. So she asked Biddy. It seems that Biddy was married to a law student from Aden called Alawi, before she married David Dooley, and that Jasmine was his daughter. Diana did say that the girl did not look a 100% white, more like Spanish. But the little girl thinks of David as her father, of course, because she was only three when David married Biddy. When she told me that, I remembered that you mentioned that you came over to London from Aden with a classmate who took law, but I don't remember that you mentioned his name. Or maybe you did and I forgot it. Anyway, I thought you might still be in touch with this lawyer, and could tell him about her school performance. I am sure he will be proud.

Take care, my dear, and if you ever come back to Auld Reekie, you know you have a bed (a separate bed!) here.

Love,

Ann

Ahmad reread the letter three times before he was sure it was not a dream, and he reflected on all the little crimes and indiscretions of his brother-in-law. At first he was determined to tell Salma about it; then he convinced himself that even if he did, she would still back her husband. Her devotion was one hundred percent, not ninety-nine, so he decided to leave it be.

Ann's letter also signaled to Ahmad that the faint hope he still clung to, namely that Ann would one day miss him, or break up with Diana like any other couple, was gone. He knew that he could not continue his lonely existence for much longer. He began to seriously think about Meethaq in Jedda. After all, he did enjoy their conversation, her openness, and her evident intelligence. He was even more impressed with her rebellious nature that questioned the traditions on which she was brought up. He prided himself on being a maverick, despite the difficulties of being one among his people, and accorded her the same degree of admiration.

He decided that he would return to Jedda in a couple of months, that he would somehow spend two hours with her alone, no matter what, and then he would either propose to her or leave and never think of her again.

～

The next morning, he found time to head for the Saudi embassy to get another visa valid for three months. As he approached the embassy, the teenaged, armed guard ordered him to stop, pointing his Kalashnikov at his chest and yelling *"Tasreeh!"* [Permit to visit embassy!]

Ahmad was alarmed at the danger from a trigger-happy teenager trying to assert his authority. He said, "Brother, I don't need one."

"Of course you do. Everyone needs one."

"No, only Yemenis do."

"You are a Yemeni, and a southerner too!"

"None of us can control where we were born, like Aden in my case and Hajja in your case."

"How did you know I am from Hajja?"

"The same as you knew I was born in Aden. But I am British, and here is my passport."

"Oh, I see." The soldier opened it upside down and pretended to examine it. "It seems to be in order. How did you get this? Where can I get one?"

"Try the British Embassy, but I doubt that you can. I have it because Aden was British when I was born. So, this is the benefit."

"The only benefit, I am sure. Alhamdulillah [thanks be to god], it no longer is! Now we are free."

Under his breath Ahmad muttered, "Are we indeed?"

"Go ahead!"

~

The following month, Ahmad had another visit from Haleemah. She just came to his private clinic like any patient, and the receptionist let her in like any other patient. Ahmad was taken aback, however, for he knew that she had important news for him.

"Do you still remember me, Doctor?"

"You know that I do, and often think about you and your predicament."

"I don't have any chest pain this time; I am here to warn you. I am worried about you."

"Oh? Why? Listen, I have patients waiting, so I hope you will be quick."

"Yes, I saw six people outside, but some of them must be family members of the patients. But I want to tell you about a recent visit I had from one of the assistants of that sheikh, Muhammad bin Taleb. He found my little shack, somehow, and brought me what he called a gift from his boss, which he called sadaqa [alms], on the occasion of the Eid celebrations. It was fifty thousand riyals! He told me that his boss wanted to help me because I had lost my father."

"I see. That's about a thousand dollars. Did he take responsibility for the death of your father in anyway?"

"Not at al! In fact, the messenger added, 'Don't think that this means that the sheikh is guilty. He is not. But he is a very kind man and gives alms to many people at this time of the year. He is very religious. But he also told me to tell you never again to talk about what happened; otherwise harm might come to you.'"

"And what did you say?"

"I told him to take his money back to Muhammad and that he cannot buy my silence. I told him that the courts will decide who killed my poor father, and even if the courts fail me then Allah will be our final judge."

"He must have been surprised at that?"

"Surprised is not the word; he was enraged. He then reminded me that I am only a prostitute, and the daughter of a black sweeper from Tihamah, who found shelter from his original home in Africa here in Yemen. He then told me that the police already decided that it was a case of self-defense, after examining all the evidence. That is when I dragged your name into this … I am sorry, Doctor, really sorry, but I had to show him that I knew that what he was saying was not the whole story."

Ahmad was alarmed. "What did he say then?"

"I remember his exact words. He said, 'Don't believe what that useless doctor says. He was not there when it happened, whereas Sheikh Muhammad was. The courts always insist on eyewitnesses, even for adultery, not some fancy medical evidence taught in some university in the land of the infidels. Here, praise be to Allah, we follow our own sharia laws that come from the Quran. Do you not believe the word of Allah? Besides, this doctor is not even a Yemeni, he is from the south, and he is not a Muslim, not really. We have a detailed dossier on him. He will get what he deserves, soon, very soon.'"

"That sound very serious."

"That is why, Dr. Ahmad, I came to see you as soon as I could. I am sure if they know that I came here, I will be in deep trouble. However, I came here wearing the niqab. But I felt that I owed you something for your kindness. You are the only person who has treated me like a normal human being."

"Look, Haleemah, go back home now. This is potentially serious. Don't come here again in case they have someone following you. You can use the telephone next time you need to get in touch. We have so many powerful people against us simply for insisting on justice, from the corrupt police to the rich elite, and even the minister of justice, my own brother-in-law."

"So the man who sends for me once a month to that grand, secluded house outside Sanaa is your brother-in-law?"

"I have never been to that house myself, but I think you must be right. Tell me, when you are with him, what do you call him?"

"Oh, they all give false names, but his driver used the term Excellency once in the car. He has an Adeni accent, I think. But he himself told me his name was Alaa. So I call him Alaa. I think he is beginning to like my company ... I mean not just the sex, although he also likes the kinky stuff which he cannot get at home."

"How do you know that?"

"He tells me, but I know it's true because most men do so."

"Are you serious? You mean men tell you about their own wives' sexual secrets?"

"Of course! Why does that surprise you?"

"Well, because it is a private and intimate matter between a man and his wife."

"It is obvious that you are not married," Haleemah said with a smile.

"But when I was in Britain, I lived with a woman for years. I never told anyone about her likes and dislikes."

"But this is how men justify fornicating with a prostitute. You know, 'My wife does not like to suck my ...' or 'She doesn't take it in the rear end' or whatever. The implication being, if only she would, I would never look at another woman."

"Wow! I am learning so much every day. I must write a book about all this one day; a novel perhaps."

"I hope you write it in Arabic; I don't know any English."

"So, what else do you do with this sex maniac?"

"He invites me to eat with him sometimes, when there is no one else in that huge house. He says that he hates eating alone. I must say, he is one of the few who do not drink, but he loves our strong Yemeni *qeshr* [coffee made from the husk of the coffee bean] and gets me to make it for him, with cinnamon, the stronger the better. He has to have one last big cup before he goes to sleep. I don't know how he manages to sleep after that. I usually get his driver to take me home after I make him that special drink of qeshr. He sleeps early, like nine, because he insists on waking up at the dawn call to prayers; very strict about prayers. He even prays in between ... you know ... doing it, if it is prayer time."

"What do you talk about?"

"He's always talking about himself, and how he is misunderstood. But he is very secretive when I try to ask him questions. He just says he does not pay me to ask him questions."

"Alaa? Alaa? I think he must be the man. His father's name is Alawi. That would make sense. All right, go home right now, and keep a low profile. We are both in real danger, and if that thug comes to see you again the safest thing for you to do is to accept Muhammad's money. And you must pretend that you are very grateful. You must say that the gift is so huge, that you are overwhelmed with gratitude. Hopefully, they will leave you alone, but you must sound genuine. Then leave Sanaa, and go back to your village of Hais. Do you have any relatives there?"

"Only an uncle, a terrible drunkard. I would never stay with him."

"Is that the one who sexually abused you?"

Haleemah's eyes momentarily appeared to double in size, as she asked Ahmad, "How on earth did you know that? I never told you, or even mentioned that I had an uncle."

"You did not have to. It is so common, this abuse and incest, especially in your condition of poverty and overcrowding. Sexual abuse by an older cousin or an uncle is the usual story. Even I went through it, would you believe?"

"I find that difficult to believe, in an affluent family like yours."

"True, but it happens when the circumstances are right. I think I was only seven at the time. Father had a very small car, called Baby Ford. He was going to drive mother and myself, together with a friend of his own age, together with the man's wife and teenage daughter, on an outing on the beach. The females always sat in the back, and just fit in that space. The two men were in the front. I tried to fit in between them, but the hand brake was sticking up in that area. So my so-called uncle lifted me and put me on his lap, obviously with the acquiescence of my naïve father who was driving.

"It is vague in my mind now, but soon I became aware of something firm but blunt digging into my backside. I had no idea what it was then, at the age of seven, but it continued throughout the trip, and the man kept bouncing me on it and telling me not to fidget, when in fact I was not fidgeting at all. But now I think it was to fool my stupid father, who was busy concentrating on watching the road, and thus he camouflaged his bouncing me on his erection. Now, decades later, I still feel betrayed, abused, taken advantage of, and all that within inches from my unsuspecting father. So, whenever I read about all the little boys that have been abused by the Catholic clergy, for example, I can relate to their anger. You know, when it comes to sex, even the most honorable of men can sometimes become wicked fiends."

"Now you can imagine what it is like for a girl, even worse after she matures."

"So, was it your uncle who took your virginity?"

Haleemah nodded as tears welled in her dark, pretty eyes.

"That's what some men do when they are trusted to protect vulnerable girls," he said, "and sometimes even boys. Not just here, in the West too. I will always recall the story I heard in Aden when I was only twelve or so. There was this blind woman who went begging door to door along the street. She took her twelve-year-old daughter, same age as me, at the time as her guide; I think that's what makes me remember. Anyway, the daughter would knock on the door at the bottom of the long stairs that would lead to the apartment where a family would live. In Aden, the ground floor was always a store or a restaurant, etc. Usually the mother in the apartment would say 'Allah is generous,' meaning 'Go away' or 'I have nothing to give,' but occasionally they would invite the girl up the stairs to collect leftover food or old clothing. But one day, the girl was invited upstairs by a twenty-year-old man living alone. I suppose you can guess what happened. But the sad thing is that after he finished with her, she continued to scream, so he had to silence her by strangling her. And even sadder was that he got away with it. My mother told me that the boy's father paid the blind woman a handful of shillings—that was the currency in Aden then—and the scandal was simply hushed up."

"Yes, Dr. Ahmad, my own uncle raped me and threatened me with worse if I told my parents. Here in this country, if a girl is not a virgin, any chance of marriage is ruined, even among our so-called sweeper people—that's what they call us for keeping their streets clean. It is all very sad. And now this! Sometimes I wish I was dead. You know, I cannot sleep anymore. I spend so much time awake in bed, and then wake up so anxious and depressed, and with a massive headache. Could I ask you one last favor? Some sleeping pills, real strong ones?"

Ahmad wrote her a prescription for one dozen pills of Somnital, saying "Here! I don't usually encourage the use of sleeping pills, but in your case I see some justification. These are strong; don't take more than two. If you took more by mistake, you might never wake up. And as soon as you manage to sleep for two or three nights in a row, stop using them. I gave you a dozen because I will probably not see you again, not for a long time anyway. I wish you well from the bottom of my heart. I will always think about you."

"And what are *you* going to do? Will you be safe? I wish I could help you. I would give my eyes and my life for you."

"That is so sweet of you. Don't ever think that again! Do you hear? They will find it very difficult to neutralize me, but they could harm you very easily."

Haleemah took a tentative step toward Ahmad and said, "Ahmad, I hope you will not be upset if I, a mere prostitute, tell you that I love you—very much in fact. Even prostitutes have emotions, you know. Will you kiss me good-bye just this once, before I leave?"

Ahmad appeared flustered momentarily but regained his composure, and as he stepped forward said, "It would be my pleasure to kiss such a beautiful girl!"

～

Ahmad knew that he was in danger, but did not realize that the threat by Muhammad's thug to Haleemah would come as early as that week. He later learned from the relatively sympathetic assistant deputy minister of health that earlier that week, the minister of justice was the honored guest of Sheikh Muhammad bin Taleb, an event so rare that when it did occur, word would spread throughout the city like wildfire.

A police Land Rover with three uniformed policemen pulled up at the clinic door in the very middle of the clinic hours, to send a negative message to the doctor's patients and for them to see him humiliated, being arrested, and being taken, handcuffed, to the police station. One patient stood up to show support to his trusted family doctor, asking politely what the problem might be. He was forcefully pushed back onto his chair and told to mind his own business. Ahmad's receptionist took the hint and froze in his chair.

~

At the police station, Ahmad had his handcuffs released before Colonel Taha of the Criminal Investigation Department entered the room. He had a poker face as he sat down, without the usual Muslim greeting.

"Dr. Ahmad, I'll be honest with you. I have spent several weeks studying your case, and I can tell you that you are in deep trouble. So, I hope you will make it easy on yourself and tell the truth, and just get back to your medical work. I understand that you have lots of patients, and that you are very popular. Unfortunately, you dabbled in things that are beyond you, things that we in CID specialize in. As you know, these days one has to specialize, because no one person can cope with everything."

"I'll be honest with you too, Colonel. I did not ask to be consulted. Some captain or major involved me, probably because he thought it the right thing to do. I did what my training—and my conscience—told me to do. I submitted a report based on all the evidence put together. The rest was up to you. Now you tell me, where did I go wrong?"

"The crime, correction, the *allegation* which the CID is investigating is falsification of evidence. As you know, that can lead to miscarriage of justice."

"Falsification, by whom?"

"By you of course!"

"I see! So, that's what I am being framed with? All the evidence in my report was supplied by the police department, except for the autopsy of course, where I was the expert, but even there I pleaded with the officer to call in a pathologist from Egypt or India, but he wouldn't."

"We do have your autopsy report, signed by you. But it is your conclusions that are in dispute."

"Look, Colonel! I have been over this many times. What else is there?"

"You wrote that the black sweeper, I mean the assailant, was shot in the back while he was running away and that he was more than ten yards away from the president's brother-in-law. But it is equally possible that he was two yards away wielding his long sharp knife, and the Sheikh raised his gun to save himself and pulled the trigger as the sweeper turned to run away. And as the bullet struck him, he dropped the knife and staggered and fell right there."

"But the body was found ten yards away from where the knife was dropped. That was recorded by one of the two investigating policemen who were first on the scene of the crime."

"No, it was not."

"Yes, it was. I read it myself."

"How could you have done so? I have the ledger right here. It states exactly what I said. Here! Take a look, if you wish."

Ahmad took a careful look at the document consisting of three pages. He recognized his own handwriting on the final page. He then looked at page one, which had the report of the two policemen who were first on the scene. But this time the report said that the burglar's body was found where the knife was, which placed it only five yards in front of where Muhammad was standing. As that was Ahmad's first forensic case in Sanaa, he clearly remembered the original report written by one of the two policemen, and his heart sank as he realized that he was being framed by the very people who were supposed to protect the citizen and apply the law equally to everyone.

"Colonel, that report has been altered. You know it and I know it. I think the phrase you people use is 'tampering with the evidence.' But even if he was only five yards away, he was still shot in the back, while running away from the gun." Ahmad was now kicking himself for not retaining a photocopy.

"So, Doctor, if you want to change your statement to five yards, then if the sweeper was only five yards away, one can understand the sense of fear experienced by the Sheikh, who will, I am sure, hire the greatest forensic scientists in America to explain the trajectory of the bullet, on which you have placed so much weight. If I were you, I would be very careful what you say, Doctor! That is a very serious accusation."

"Not as serious as taking the life of an innocent man. Where is that policeman? I would like to talk to him."

"You are not allowed to talk to him or to try to influence his evidence. That in itself is a crime. But your lawyer will have a chance to question him in court, when your case comes up next month, or the following month. In the meantime, I will release you on bail, but you are not to leave the country, or even Sanaa. Is that understood?"

~

That night, Ahmad had to take a Somnital capsule. He had spent the whole evening going over the events of the previous few weeks. As he reviewed his meeting with the colonel, Haleemah's encounter with Sheikh Muhammad's thug, and the rumor of Hasan Alawi being invited to lunch, he came to the conclusion that Hasan and Sheikh Muhammad struck a pact to get rid of him, each for his own reason. For a moment, he wished he had not been so rude to Hasan at the qat session. He also wished that he never had been asked to solve the murder puzzle and that he had learned from his previous experience in Aden, which forced him to leave his own country. Most of all he wished that he had stayed in his wonderful city of Edinburgh, with or without Ann. He even blamed it all on that horny man who raped the goat in Aden.

He looked at the lineup of formidable enemies he created with his honesty. Then he tried to conjure up a group of friends and came up with almost none. His first thought was of his mother, always a reliable friend, but her relationship with Salma would sabotage any action plan he might envisage. Salma, he did not even consider. She would act against him, without a moment of hesitation, if the choice was between him and her husband. His loving sister Zahra was out of the country. Haleemah, his only true friend at that moment, was leaving town soon, he hoped to safety. He did call the assistant deputy minister of trade, who had helped him with his registration as a physician at first, but that man never returned his call, and Ahmad got the message. His friend Adel was out of town, possibly in France. He thought that if the case came to court, he would simply convince the judge by stating the facts, but what if that judge was beholden to the minister of justice? Then he also wondered if they might eliminate him by having him run over by a speeding motorist, as had apparently happened to the editor of a newspaper who had openly criticized national security. He wondered if Hasan would stoop that low, in his case, and concluded that he probably would, with relish.

$$\sim$$

Two weeks after his meeting with Colonel Taha, Ahmad heard on the radio about fierce skirmishes across the borders with the PDRY army. By the next day, many pronouncements were issued by the president, and threats uttered by the minister of defense and foreign minister. The country was getting into a state of war readiness against the Communist threat, was the message repeated dozens of times a day on the government-controlled radio and television and in the state-run newspapers. Ahmad learned that southerners in general, and Adenis in particular, were being carefully watched.

One week later, war broke out, and the country descended into even greater chaos. The function of civil society seemed to come to a halt while all attention was focused on the war. Consequently, Ahmad was commanded to attend hospital to look after the many wounded. Those who were seriously wounded were admitted to the Taiz General Hospital and the Revolution Hospital in Sanaa, where Ahmad found himself dealing with severe injuries he had never dealt with before. There were only two surgeons: one trained in Egypt and the other in Moscow. It did not help the process that the two were deadly enemies who could not stand each other, especially since they had to do alternate night call for surgical emergencies. Ahmad, no surgeon, soon distinguished himself as the doctor who cared. He would take his time to ask patients not just about their wounds and pain but also about their sleep and worries, and their family and social support.

One such soldier was Hameed, a twenty-year-old from a prominent family in Saada, the major town in North Yemen close to the Saudi border. He sustained a blunt neck injury after a South Yemen shell hit the mound of sand behind which he was sheltering and shooting intermittently. It threw him up in the air, and he landed on his flexed neck. He was quadriplegic, with paralysis of all four limbs, and complete lack of control of his bowels and bladder. He was in a state of acute and deep reactive depression, for there he was a healthy, strong, young man one moment and a living corpse the next. He could talk and swallow, and move his neck and eyes, but nothing else.

There were several other men with similar injuries and total paralysis, and they were placed in hospital beds next to each other, partly to facilitate their management by the same medical-surgical team and partly to demonstrate to each one that he was not alone in his predicament. The surgeons were not much involved, since they had nothing to operate on, but they had plenty of other patients who needed their operating room surgical skills.

Ahmad developed a warm relationship with those paralyzed men, and he would examine them almost daily, always looking for any recovery, however slight, in their ability to move their fingers or wiggle their toes and their ability to feel touch or pain or vibration. The lack of bowel and bladder control was a source of enormous distress to all of them. Ahmad knew that such contusions of the spinal cord took many days to show even rudimentary signs of recovery, and he went out of his way to encourage the patients to give it time. One of the older patients was noted by a to have an erection, which progressively became more continuous and even painful. Even in their misery, the paralyzed men began to joke about it with their usual Yemeni sense of humor, quoting the Yemeni proverb, "A dead donkey with a stiff dong." The affected man started bragging about it and predicting that it was a sign of impending recovery.

It was only natural that Hameed, only twenty, would ask the doctor why he did not show the same hopeful sign.

"To tell you the truth, Hameed, I think you are going to be the one who makes the most recovery out of all the men."

"Are you sure, Doctor? Even though my ... you know ... did not stand up?"

"Actually, that is a bad sign, but do not say so to that man. It happens when the cord is completely severed, but if it is only bruised, it usually does not occur."

"Alhamdulillah! I was just thinking that it is better to be dead than be like this."

"No, don't think that way. There is another reason for optimism in your case, and that is your young age. So, cheer up and spend your time doing useful things. I will bring you some novels to read while you are here."

∼

Ahmad's predictions were surprisingly accurate, and Hameed began to feel vague sensations in his legs. Within days he could move his fingers and then his toes. As soon as that happened, Ahmad managed to find an Indian physiotherapist to take over Hameed's exercise program. Although still slightly unsteady on his feet, Hameed was to be discharged the following week to make room for more severely injured patients.

As he was discussing his plans to return to Saada for convalescence, he asked Ahmad what he could possibly do to pay him back for his kindness.

"The only thing I need is something big, which I don't think you can help me with."

"Doctor, I have a big family back home, and if I cannot personally help, I am sure they can. They are prominent in our town. In fact, the person who will drive down from Saada to pick me up is my Uncle Khalaf who is a captain with the border guard, and in the past he was involved in border skirmishes against the Saudis. I was supposed to join his section, but because of the trouble with the south I was transferred down here. So, just tell me what I can do for you. I want to serve you, *even with my eyes!*"

"What I have done for you is just part of my job as a doctor. But I am desperate for help to leave for Jedda, and I cannot leave the normal way because of the war and other reasons, which I cannot divulge just now ..."

"Doctor, you don't have to explain anything. Your word is good enough for me; if I cannot trust a man like you, who can I possibly trust?"

"Well, my mother is in Jedda and so is my sister, who is married to a pilot with Saudi Airlines, and I have my fiancée there and we want to get married as soon as possible ..."

Hameed's face lit up and he interrupted. "Getting married? How wonderful! I assumed that you were already married to the most beautiful woman in Yemen. Or are you taking a second wife, Doctor?"

"No, no, Hameed, I am not married ... not yet. That's why I have to go there, but I cannot get there in view of all the fighting."

"Let me speak to my uncle, and you get yourself ready to leave next Friday, just after dawn prayers. Is that clear? Where shall we pick you up?"

Ahmad gave him the address.

Ahmad did not share the information with anyone else, nor did he call his mother in case his telephone line was under surveillance. But he did withdraw most of his money from the bank, telling the assistant manager that he found a bargain of a secondhand Volvo and was determined to buy it immediately.

CHAPTER 23

~

HALEEMAHS REVENGE

After her long chat with Ahmad, Haleemah decided to take his advice and go back to the small town of Hais, where she had grown up. She still knew a couple of girls of her age whom she could call friends, and who might put her up for a few days. It would be difficult to trace her there, and in any event no one would bother as long as she did not rock the boat. She thought that she should leave after her next monthly visit to Hasan's bed, so that she would not be missed for a whole month. She estimated that it would take about one week before he sent for her. As just another john who wanted a night of sex with her, she had no strong feelings about him one way or the other. She did not enjoy her visits. He was not generous with her, and he bored her by talking about himself. But after she found out about his mistreatment of her hero, Ahmad, the man she was in love with—or so she thought—she had nothing but contempt and hate for him, on top of the hate she would have for his part in aborting the investigation of her father's murder. And yet she could not refuse his invitation lest he became suspicious.

~

During that week, she gradually disposed of many items in her little shack, easily managing to sell furniture, kitchen utensils, and clothing. She threw out many smaller items. She did not dare put up her shack for sale, for fear of raising suspicion. Her anxiety about the unknown in her future was at a peak, and she was very grateful for the sleeping capsules she got from Ahmad. She took one that first night and was amazed at the very deep and long sleep she had. It took her ages to become alert after nine hours of sleep. And the next evening she took one capsule and slept very well. She did not need the medication on the third night.

Her usual clients from near her area continued to demand her services, and despite everything she had to continue servicing them in order not to raise suspicion. She had her big suitcase ready for a sudden departure, and she made inquiries about the location of the taxi stand for Hudeidah, Yemen's main port on the Red Sea, and the cost of a seat.

She had just given up on getting any compensation from Sheikh Muhammad, when his familiar thug came up to her shack again, with the money.

"Sheikh Muhammad told me to bring you this money again," the man said, "to give you a second chance, but there will be no third one. Here it is!"

Haleemah, remembering the words of her doctor friend, gave the man a big smile, took the wad of riyals, and thanked him. "Please say thank-you to the Sheikh for this huge gift; may Allah bestow more wealth on him and give him long life."

The messenger appeared surprised at the turnabout. "What made you change your mind?"

"The first time you came, I was still in mourning and very sad and angry. But since then, I have reflected, and I have prayed for guidance. And what is the use of being angry? It will not bring back my father. Besides, a young, defenseless girl like me needs money, and this is such a big amount. I will have to work for years to make this much."

"Well, I am glad that you appreciate the generosity of the sheikh. I will tell him. But what about showing appreciation to me, for coming to see you twice?"

Haleemah was not prepared for that demand, but she played along. "You men are all the same. All right, let's get on with it."

~

Almost one week to the day, Hasan sent for her. The state of war against the south did not seem to change his routine, but Hasan appeared more preoccupied than usual when Haleemah got there. He spoke about his worries as was typical, but this time he kept repeating how ungrateful the southerners were, despite the fact that the northern government was trying to rid them of communism and improve their standards of living. He told her how he himself helped them, years before. He looked a little haggard, and the usual sparkle in his eyes had somewhat faded.

He got Haleemah to make him an omelet around seven that evening, which she made in the usual kitchen next to his bedroom on the upper floor. That came with a cup of tea. Hasan remarked that the taste of the omelet was not as good as usual, adding that it was perhaps because he was suffering the flu.

~

The evening call to prayer was heard at seven thirty, and Hasan went into the bathroom to do his ablutions before performing his prayers, which took a little longer than usual. With all that out of the way, he got Haleemah to do her undressing routine, and they embarked on their routine of intercourse, which she noted was not as vigorous as usual. Hasan seemed exhausted. In fact, he asked her to get up on top, while he lay on his back, and tried to meet her thrusts with some of his own, but it was a rather feeble attempt. He felt warm, as though he had a fever. He then asked her for an extra large cup of qeshr, "extra strong," as he put it. She crawled out of bed, put a towel around her waist, and went into the kitchen to make him his favorite drink.

As the water was boiling, she was suddenly overwhelmed with the thought of revenge against the man who covered up the murder of her poor father and who was at that moment planning to prosecute and jail the only man she ever had fallen in love with. That was her chance to help her hero.

Out of her handbag, with tremulous hands, she took the small plastic bottle with the remaining ten capsules of Somnital. The qeshr of the coffee bean was starting to turn the clear boiling water into a deepening brown color. She added some more coffee husk to make it stronger, as Hasan wanted, then emptied the white powder inside six capsules into the boiling water. The powder had no smell, and did not change the color of the qeshr. Just in case six capsules were not enough, she added the remaining four.

Cinnamon sticks were in a little jar next to the stove. She crushed two and added them. There were no sounds from the bed; Hasan had dozed off. She poured the liquid into a half-liter cup. She took the smallest sip to ensure that the taste was that of normal qeshr. It was, and so was the smell.

As she picked up the cup, she began to have second thoughts. Then she heard stirrings in the bedroom and heard Hasan shout, "Hey, my black whore, what's taking you so long? I need my qeshr, and I need a massage to my shoulders."

She carried the big cup into his room and placed it by the bedside table. Hasan sat up and took a couple of sips. The qeshr was not too hot so he drank half the cup.

"Oh, that is so good," he said. "It is so soothing to the throat. I am glad you made it extra strong tonight. Your money is by the door. You deserve it, sometimes."

He lay down on his stomach. "My muscles are aching. Give me a deep massage, especially over the shoulders."

Haleemah did as she was instructed.

Hasan twisted his trunk and reached for the cup. Half reclining, he drank the rest of it. "That is so good. I think I have to sleep for a long, long time."

Haleemah was in a panic at that point. There was no turning back, for the entire dose was in his stomach. *What if she is caught red handed?* She wondered. She got dressed quickly. Hasan was not moving, but his breathing was audible. She picked up the cup and rinsed it thoroughly under the tap. Coming back into the bedroom, she called him. There was no response. She shook him, and again there was no response. His breathing seemed much shallower than only minutes before. She pinched him hard on the skin of his neck. There was a brief snort. She had to leave, because she did not want to be there when he finally stopped breathing. She convinced herself that if Allah wanted him to die, he would die, and if that happened then it must mean that he deserved it.

She got dressed, got her handbag, and looked at her watch. It was a quarter to nine, not different from any other night. The driver should not be suspicious. She left the room, but before locking it behind her, as she usually did, she remembered her fee and picked it up.

Downstairs, the driver asked, "Ready to go home? He seems to like to sleep around nine, doesn't he?"

"Yes, it is time to go home."

"Until next month, I imagine?"

"I suppose."

"How was he tonight? To me, he appeared unwell today, and he was coughing. I was surprised he sent for you when he was so ill."

"So was I. He asked me for a massage."

"One day, all this sex will kill him," said the driver, laughing heartily.

Haleemah picked up her ride to Hudeidah at six the next morning, Friday, while most people were still asleep.

CHAPTER 24

~

ESCAPE TO JAIZAN

O n Friday at dawn, Captain Khalaf pulled up in front of Ahmad's private clinic and apartment in his big four-wheel-drive Toyota van. His nephew Hameed was in the back seat with two crutches leaning against the seat next door as well as a small suitcase, bottles of water and juice, and the daily newspaper. Even before Captain Khalaf tapped on the door, it opened and Ahmad popped his head out, shook hands with Khalaf, then walked out with a large suitcase.

It was still almost dark, and the street was deserted except for two stray dogs. Ahmad was relieved that there was no one in the street to note his early departure. He locked the door and carried his suitcase to the trunk of the car, just opened by Khalaf. He also placed a large cardboard box next to the suitcase, as Khalaf helped him carry it from the bottom of the stairs. There was another very warm handshake between the two men who never before had set eyes on each other; to Khalaf, the man who looked after his young nephew so well was already much more than a casual friend.

Once in the front passenger seat, Ahmad did the traditional cheek-to-cheek kiss with his patient, who leaned over from the back seat while flashing a big smile. With a *bismillah* [in the name of Allah], Khalaf put the gear shift into drive and proceeded down the main road, heading north toward Saada.

The city was only a short distance away but on a winding and difficult road. At the edge of the city, he slowed down at the checkpoint, but the corporal waved him on when he noted the captain's uniform.

~

"So, Hameed tells me that you are getting married soon," Captain Khalaf said to Ahmad. "Congratulations! Is this your first one?"

"Yes, I am still a bachelor."

"How come? You must be near forty now; an important doctor would have been married to the best and prettiest woman by now."

"I suppose it is my luck. What can I do?"

"You will soon find that there is nothing better than to have a wife. Women are both a blessing and a curse."

Ahmad did not dare laugh, but Khalaf continued.

"In the end, a woman is really a vessel where you place your seed and hope that things begin to grow. You see, I already have eight children, and I am giving my fifteen-year-old girl to Hameed once he gets better."

"Fifteen?" Ahmad protested before he could stop himself.

"Yes, fifteen, going on sixteen, but mashaallah [as Allah wishes], she is a fully developed woman."

Ahmad turned his neck round toward Hameed, who beamed a big smile of acknowledgment from the back seat. "Congratulations to Hameed, and to you! These days, fifteen would be considered too young, and most girls would still be finishing their schooling."

"She can read and write, and she is very intelligent. But any more education than that is unnecessary for girls; for boys, yes, but not for girls. In any case Prophet Muhammad, peace be upon him, married Aisha when she was even younger—only nine. And what's good enough for the messenger of Allah is good enough for us."

"Some girls do very well in higher education, some better than boys.

And as you know, things are changing. I think that, in the future, higher education for Muslim girls will be routine." Ahmad said.

"When that time comes, we shall see. But now if we do not get our girls married this early, they just start having strange and foreign ideas, and some bring shame on their families. All this modernity is not good. And how old is the bride you are going to marry? She cannot be much older than mine."

"Oh, she is four years younger than I am."

"Four years younger than *you*? But you are already over forty! Here we would consider that too old. She may not be able to bear children for you. And how come she never got married until now?"

"She did! But she is divorced." Ahmad explained.

"Divorced by her husband? Then she cannot make a good wife. I am getting worried about you, Doctor."

"No, it was the other way round, actually. She divorced *him*."

"It sounds as if this woman is too independent. She must be one of those educated ones who try to be like Western women. I hope you will not be offended, but why do you not marry a virgin, who … who has not known any men? Then you can train her to do all the things you enjoy, in bed and in the house." Khalaf implored.

"Well, I happen to like her, and we think alike on many issues. Isn't it true that one of the wives of the Prophet was a widow? And his first wife Khadeeja was much older than he was?"

"Peace be upon him; no one can question his wisdom."

They were already halfway to Saada. The road became rougher and more mountainous, and the air was somewhat cooler. Hameed remained silent throughout that conversation out of deference for his uncle, who was soon to become his father-in-law as well.

At the southern approach to the city, there was another checkpoint. Here, Khalaf was immediately recognized and saluted by the two corporals manning it. They also shook hands with him. He asked them about members of their families that he happened to know. Three small glass cups brimming with steaming, red, sweet tea soon appeared from the tent by the roadside, and the three men enjoyed it immensely after driving over some dusty patches of road.

As they prepared to continue the journey, there were the obligatory good-bye handshakes between the two corporals and the three travelers.

~

They arrived at Khalaf's big house after going through that long road that encircled Saada. There, Ahmad received a big welcome from all of Khalaf's sons, but the daughters were not invited. Ahmad did want to see Hameed's bride, out of curiosity, but never had the opportunity to do so. The boys filed past to shake his hand as their father called out their names. Ahmad had difficulty remembering all the names, but it did not really make any difference.

Khalaf pointed out that the second eldest son wanted to be a doctor. "He is the most intelligent of the boys, so he wants to become a doctor, inshaallah [if God wishes]."

"You don't have to be the most intelligent to be a doctor. Any of them can be, if they have the aptitude and if they are prepared to read and read and read!"

"You are being modest, Doctor. You must be one of the brightest people in Yemen."

"I doubt it. In fact, I know it's not true. But I did have to work hard and remember thousands upon thousands of facts and names and chemical formulas and drug side effects and all that. So, the one among your sons who has the sharpest memory should be the one who goes into medicine. The brightest should go into physics or engineering. And the most honest should go into politics. Perhaps he might be able to change things for this unfortunate nation. At least that is my opinion."

Khalaf laughed and then looked at his eldest son. Khalaf said, "Go tell *alwalidah* [the mother] to have breakfast ready. *Yallah!* [Quickly!]"

The boy disappeared in seconds.

Khalaf continued. "You are right. All our politicians are crooks. They do not care about us, only about themselves, and their families and their tribes."

"I don't belong to any tribe, so I would be among the most neglected and marginalized, because we don't have tribes in Aden."

"You are not alone. Even we, here in Saada who do have tribes and the people of the Taiz area, all are oppressed. It is all in the hands of the president's tribe; not even, it is all in the hands of his family. *La hawla wal quwwata illa billah.* [There is no strength except through Allah.]"

~

Breakfast was an elaborate meal, possibly for the benefit of the guest. Bread was served in several forms, from the usual baguette to the local Yemeni flatbread or *khobz* dripping with ghee, and a huge omelet was served, together with boiled eggs, minced lamb, yoghurt, and honey. The men washed these down with an endless supply of *chai* tea already boiled with milk, sugar, and cardamom.

As they were getting ready to depart, Ahmad discovered that, despite the large size of the house, the toilet was simply a hole in the ground, but he was grateful to have the opportunity to wash his hands and face.

Hameed stayed behind, but once again thanked the doctor for looking after him so well. There were the usual cheek-to-cheek kisses, and then all the boys came over to shake hands with Ahmad.

Just before they set off, Ahmad pointed out that the large cardboard box in the back of the car was the latest-model television set, which Ahmad had bought only three months previously and that he wanted to leave in Saada for Khalaf's children. A long discussion ensued, during which Khalaf swore repeatedly that he would not take it, and that his help was not in return for any payment but was merely inadequate gratitude for the special care given by the doctor to his nephew and future son-in-law. Ahmad then addressed the boys and asked them to lift the television set out of the trunk of the car and take it into the house. Not one child moved, as they all looked at their father for approval. It was perhaps the looks in their eyes that made Khalaf relent, and in no time the box was gone.

Soon, the two men were driving in the direction of Khamis Mushait, in Jaizan, a triangular region at the very south of Saudi Arabia, right on the Red Sea. It dipped right into the body of Yemen, well south of Saada itself. At one point, it was part of Yemen, until the military government ceded it away to Saudi Arabia.

~

Ahmad made his way to Jedda by road and booked a hotel room. He did not want his mother or Zahra to know about his plans yet, because even up to that point he was not sure whether he was doing the right thing. He did not know for sure if Meethaq was still in Jedda. He had never been so confused before, and he had great difficulty falling asleep, but perhaps that was because he had forgotten his Somnital in Sanaa.

When he woke up the next morning, the sun was already shining bright. He ate a hearty breakfast at the hotel restaurant, where many European guests were having breakfast. The affluence of the place compared to Sanaa struck him. A long line of taxis waited outside the hotel. He jumped into the first one and gave the driver the address. It was ten o'clock by the time he reached the house, a modest bungalow with a small courtyard. The property was ringed by a mud wall and painted white.

He rang the bell with his tremulous index finger. Seconds later, he heard the shrill voice of a young girl who asked, "Who is it?"

He spoke into the intercom, "Ahmad … Ahmad Shawqi."

He overheard the little girl excitedly scream, "Meethaq! Meethaq! Meethaq! Come quickly, quickly; it's the doctor, your doctor."

There was utter silence for many seconds, which seemed like an eternity. Then there was the screeching metallic sound of the heavy, rusty door handle on the inside of the metal gate and a loud clang as the handle hit the gate on its way down at some speed. The metal door within the larger gate opened, and there was Meethaq. She looked anxious, astonished, and regal all at the same time.

"I have come back for you," he said, "if you will still have me!"

Meethaq burst into a muffled but uncontrollable sob as she put her head on Ahmad's right shoulder. Her little sister, several paces behind, just stood there, completely bewildered.

CAST

Moosa and Sheila	Somali student and Scottish girlfriend	Edinburgh
Adel	Ahmad's lunch guest, French Embassy employee	Sanaa
Ali	Mahmood's father	Haifan
Alwan, Colonel	PDRY National Security	Aden
Ann	Biochemistry student, later Ahmad's girlfriend	Edinburgh
Antar	President, People's Democratic Republic of Yemen	Aden
Aqlan, Major	Police officer	Sanaa
Diana	Ann's lesbian partner	Edinburgh
David Rubin	Iraqi Jewish writer	London
Fadi	Lebanese Muslim male student	Edinburgh
Family Al-Qirshi: Alawi and Fatima	Children: Hasan	Aden
Family McCartney: James and Betty	Children: Albert, Biddy, and Stephen	London
Family Saleh: Shawqi and wife	Children: Ahmad, Salma, and Zahra	Aden
Farook	Drowned man	Aden
Gabi	Lebanese Christian male student	Edinburgh
Grimond, Mrs.	Owner of bed-and-breakfast	London
Hajjar	Wealthy government official	Jedda

Haleemah	Burglar's daughter, teenage prostitute	Sanaa
Hameed	Quadriplegic at Revolution Hospital	Saada
Harb, Dr.	Surgeon	Sanaa
Humaid	Adeni student at Moray College	Edinburgh
Ibrahim	Saudi graduate student In forensic sciences	Edinburgh
Isobel	British Council representative	London
Jill and Margaret	Biddy's schoolmates	London
Khadeeja	Iraqi female student	Edinburgh
Khalaf, Captain	Hameed's uncle	Saada
Khaled	Yemeni patient with sleep paralysis	Aden
Linda	Humaid's Scottish girlfriend	Edinburgh
Mahmood Ali	Driver and trader	Haifan
Meethaq	Divorced woman from Aden	Jedda
Misbah	Syrian male student	Edinburgh
Mufeed	Palestinian male student	Edinburgh
Muhammad bin Taleb	Wealthy shooter of burglar	Sanaa
Muna	Kuwaiti female student	Edinburgh
Nageeb, Dr. and Ahlam	Physician in Taiz and his wife	Taiz
Nizar	Meethaq's husband (divorced)	Aden
Omar	Waleed's homosexual partner	Jedda
Qassem Al-Qirshi	Hasan's fixer	Aden
Family Robertson: Donald and Mary	Ahmad's initial landlord and landlady	Edinburgh
Sharif	Sudanese student	Edinburgh
Taha, Colonel	Criminal Investigation Department	Sanaa
Tawfiq	Bearer of promotion news	Sanaa
Wakefield, Mrs.	Biddy's teacher	London
Waleed	Musician	Jedda
Zuhair	Zahra's husband	Jedda